Arm of the Sphinx

By Josiah Bancroft

THE BOOKS OF BABEL

Senlin Ascends
Arm of the Sphinx
The Hod King

**Senlin saw the hole in the balloon and experienced
a moment of terror so intense it felt like euphoria.**

They were going to drop from the sky like a shot bird.

But even as he watched, the gash sealed itself as some second skin, some internal membrane, pressed against the tear.

A moment later, they were out of range of the lead soldiers, and the barrage abruptly stopped.

They rose upon a gentle vent of air. The ship felt almost motionless. The sky was serene. They stood up and patted themselves for signs of blood or protruding bones, but discovered neither.

"Well, that was lucky," Senlin said, straightening his cuffs with shaking hands. "Balloons don't usually patch themselves, do they?"

"No," Edith said, kneeling to examine the ragged divot that had been blown into the ship's starboard edge. "Voleta, Iren, get these ridiculous sheets off our ship."

Senlin inspected the drab-colored balloon overhead with a fresh eye. "A self-sealing envelope. It seems a remarkable fixture for a barge like this."

"One of the Sphinx's inventions. Billy Lee traded for it." Edith stood and kicked a portion of the broken deck into the abyss.

"Traded what?"

"An arm," she said.

Praise for
The Books of Babel

"*Senlin Ascends* is one of the best reads I've had in ages...I was dragged in and didn't escape until I'd finished two or three days later."
—Mark Lawrence, author of *Prince of Thorns*

"*Senlin Ascends* crosses the everyday strangeness and lyrical prose of Borges and Gogol with all the action and adventure of high fantasy. I loved it, and grabbed the next one as soon as I turned the last page."
—Django Wexler, author of *The Thousand Names*

"Bancroft succeeds amazingly in creating a baffling world that offers little tenderness or hope, but in which the pursuit of instinct and love, dedication and shared sacrifice can overcome barriers...the reader will find much to applaud."
—*Publishers Weekly* (starred review) on *Senlin Ascends*

"*Senlin Ascends* starts off with a bang, and it never slows down. With its breathtaking pace, this book will appeal to a wide variety of readers."
—*San Francisco Book Review*

"A great fantasy!"
—*Portland Book Review* on *Senlin Ascends*

"This is an exceedingly rich book. A depth of imagination married with a poetic turn of phrase and an engaging cast of characters conspire to deliver an epic story soaring high above the clouds."
—*Fantasy Faction* on *Senlin Ascends*

The Books of Babel
Book II:
Arm of the Sphinx

JOSIAH BANCROFT

www.orbitbooks.net

Copyright © 2015 by Josiah Bancroft
Excerpt from *The Hod King* copyright © 2018 by Josiah Bancroft
Excerpt from *Wake of Vultures* copyright © 2015 by D. S. Dawson

Author photograph by Kim Bricker
Cover art by Ian Leino
Cover copyright © 2018 by Hachette Book Group, Inc.

Maps by Josiah Bancroft

Orbit
Hachette Book Group
1290 Avenue of the Americas
New York, NY 10104
orbitbooks.net

Originally self-published in 2015
First Orbit Digital Original Edition: August 2017
First Trade Paperback Edition: April 2018

Orbit is an imprint of Hachette Book Group.
The Orbit name and logo are trademarks of Little, Brown Book Group Limited.

The publisher is not responsible for websites (or their content) that are not owned by the publisher.

The Hachette Speakers Bureau provides a wide range of authors for speaking events. To find out more, go to www.hachettespeakersbureau.com or call (866) 376-6591.

Library of Congress Cataloging-in-Publication Data:

Names: Bancroft, Josiah, author.
Title: Arm of the Sphinx / Josiah Bancroft.
Description: First trade paperback edition. | New York : Orbit, April 2018. | Series: The books of Babel ; Book two
Identifiers: LCCN 2017046498| ISBN 9780316517959 (paperback) | ISBN 9780316517973 (ebook) | ISBN 9781549168208 (audio book (downloadable))
Subjects: LCSH: Pirates—Fiction. | Fantasy fiction. | BISAC: FICTION / Fantasy / Epic. | FICTION / Fantasy / Historical.
Classification: LCC PS3602.A63518 A89 2018 | DDC 813/.6—dc23
LC record available at https://lccn.loc.gov/2017046498

ISBNs: 978-0-316-51795-9 (trade paperback), 978-0-316-51797-3 (ebook)

Printed in the United States of America

LSC-C

10 9 8 7 6 5 4 3 2 1

For Ian, with whom the adventure began.

SILK GARDENS

PELPHIA

NEW BABEL

THE BATHS

THE PARLOR

THE MARKET

THE BASEMENT

THE SKIRTS

THE TOWER of BABEL
a Map of the Lower Ringdoms

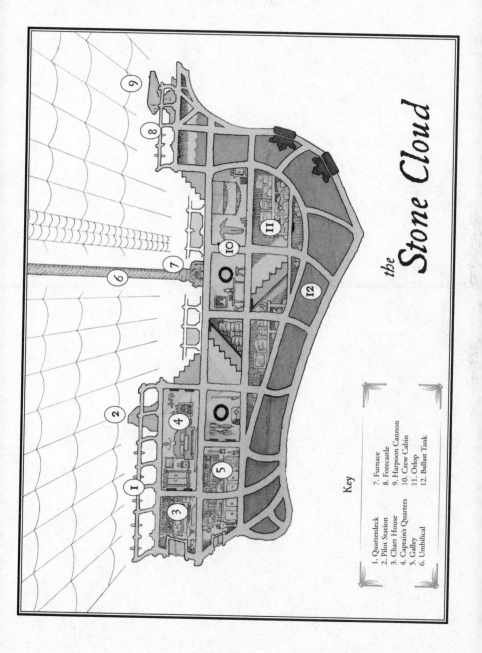

the *Stone Cloud*

Key

1. Quarterdeck
2. Pilot Station
3. Chart House
4. Captain's Quarters
5. Galley
6. Umbilical

7. Furnace
8. Forecastle
9. Harpoon Cannon
10. Crew Cabin
11. Orlop
12. Ballast Tank

Civilization is like sunshine. Spread it about, and the world blooms with culture, innovation, and fraternity. But focus it all upon one spot, and mankind scorches the earth like a ray from a magnifying glass.

—From the *Stone Cloud*'s logbook,
in the hand of Captain Tom Mudd

Part I
The *Stone Cloud*

Chapter One

The difficulty with a disguise is that it must be worn for some time before it hangs credibly upon the shoulders. But if worn for too long, a costume becomes comfortable, natural. A man always in disguise must take care lest he become the disguise.

—The *Stone Cloud*'s Logbook, Captain Tom Mudd

The airship cruised from the hoary mountain pass on a current as cold as an avalanche. Its hull was like a longship's, long and narrow, lacking only oars, with a carved hound's head curling up from the bow. To a jaundiced eye, the ship recollected a rough coffin carried on the back of a laughing dog.

To the crew, it was but a frozen raft.

Swaddled in furs, they stamped about the deck like disgruntled bears. Wind strummed the rigging. The men said nothing. Forty barrels of rum sloshed in the main hold beneath their feet, seeping and sweetening the air with sugar cane and new oak.

The *Cairo Hound* was bound for the Baths, where rum fetched ten times the price it did in the capitals of Ur. In a few short hours, each of them would have half a year's wages in their pockets and all the Baths to fritter it upon. But despite the coming payday and liberty, the crew was anxious. They were afraid to speak because, once begun, idle talk turned easily into nervous rambling, and then terror was sure to follow.

Pirates prowled these skies. Violent wind shears were not uncommon. Then there were the whims of the Tower ports to fret over. A safe harbor one voyage might be a shooting gallery the next. Only a few months earlier, cannonballs and fire had demolished one of New Babel's more reliable ports. A crew could never be sure what sort of welcome the Tower would offer them.

And where was their captain during all of this worry? Drunk again, still drunk, always exquisitely drunk.

No, it was better not to talk. Better to stay stoic.

Far below, rough slopes gave way to a suburb of tents and then a shantytown of canvas and tar-paper roofs. Trains cut through the dense Market on tracks that ran from the Tower like the rays of a compass rose. The Tower did not look like it had been built, brick by brick, by human hands. Rather, it looked like something the world had begun to birth—a new crescent moon, perhaps—before surrendering the effort. The Tower loomed over the encircling mountain range. An imperturbable fog enshrouded its peak. Some romantics called this haze the "Collar of Heaven," believing it marked the point where the Tower passed from blue sky into bleak, black space.

The captain always woke up mean.

He stayed mean, too, but there was an excess of meanness in his waking. Drunk or not, mean or not, the captain would still have to sign the manifest and dicker with the port master over the price of rum. He still had a job to do. They would have to draw straws for who would wake him. The boatswain trimmed straws from a broom and measured them on his palm.

Then the girl appeared.

She seemed to just materialize in the air near the grumbling furnace and the biscuit barrels. One of her arms snaked about the rope that held her; one toe of her boot touched the deck ever so lightly, like a bather testing a bath. She was beautiful—but not garish like those harlots in the pub who sat on your lap if you bought them a drink. Nor was she voluptuous like the sketches in the gentlemen's books, nor handsome like the marble statues with robes no thicker than spilled milk.

She was beautiful like a doe in a glen: lithe, alert, and distant. Her hair was wild, her face small, her eyes bright. Her yellow frock had been hacked off at the waist, and her overlarge gloves looked like something a blacksmith might wear.

They did not all see her in the same instant. She mesmerized them one by one.

The bear-skinned crew of the *Cairo Hound* began to close on her with the slow, deliberate steps of men in a trance. With each step they took, she inched her way back up the rope and toward the gas envelope above. She did not seem nervous at all. The men found her poise captivating. They found it maddening.

When they could stand it no longer, they lunged after her.

She darted into the high netting, quick as a flash, and they crashed together beneath her, toppling the barrels and knocking one another against the singeing furnace as they grappled for the rope. As soon as one man began to climb, the others pulled him down. She tugged at her ears and stuck out her tongue. One crewman threw the water ladle at her. She nimbly caught it and threw it back at him.

They began to quarrel about who had seen her first, and who should go wake the captain, because now he definitely had to be awakened, and somebody had to do it, and where were the straws?

Their lively debate was interrupted by the tattoo of unfamiliar boots behind them.

The crew of the *Cairo Hound* turned to discover they had been boarded.

Captain Padraic DeFord had crawled into a barrel of rum on the first day of the voyage and stayed there. A fleshy man with the mottled complexion of a newborn infant, he was at the point in his career where all other men were fools, the business was foolish, and the pay fit only for imbeciles. His men thought him tyrannical, but in truth he spoiled them. When he was a cabin boy, if he'd once made the sort of blunder his crew did on a daily basis, he would have been whipped till he bled. He wasn't a tyrant; he was a parent stuck with a brood of dunces. And rather than improve, rather than rise to the challenge of his leadership, his men grew sullen and resentful. They slouched toward mutiny.

How the world had changed.

In the face of this, would any man of character blame him for indulging in a drink? He found that if he drank enough, he slept deeply and dreamed little. He could fall into bed the same as into his grave. Every morning was a resurrection; every evening was a death. It was such a pretty thing to come and go into the dark as one pleased.

This morning, he was rudely roused from his grave by something like an anchor chain wrapping about his neck and wrenching him from his cot and out of the wonderful dark.

Having long ago trained himself to nap with a pistol in hand, DeFord was quick to sight the figure behind the chain. He had just put his finger to the trigger when a thick arm knocked the barrel up, and the gun discharged into the cabin ceiling with an earsplitting bang. Wood dust and smoke stung his eyes. Sun beamed through the bullet hole, brightening the dark and giving DeFord his first glimpse of the man behind the iron noose.

But it was not a man. It was a gargantuan woman with short silver hair lying close to a square, stony face. He felt like he was looking up at an ox that was standing on its hind legs.

Captain DeFord gave the amazon a speculative kick, and in return, she picked him up by his arms and thumped him twice against the ceiling. The blows made the chain clang about his ears. When the pounding stopped, his spine felt a little shorter. Docile now with pain and shock, DeFord didn't fight as he was dragged above deck, wearing nothing but his breeches and a tangled white bedsheet.

He was disappointed but not surprised to see his useless crew standing under raised hands. A girl in a ripped dress and a woman with brass plumbing for an arm held them at gunpoint, and confidently so. The realization caused DeFord physical pain: A trio of women had taken his ship. What further proof could one ask for? His men were conspiring against him. They hadn't even put up a fight.

There was one other stranger: a lanky man in a long black coat. He

6

looked as sturdy as a scarecrow. Yet, there was a coolness and a gravity to his expression.

"Ah, there you are," said the scarecrow. "Captain DeFord, is it?" The man offered his hand. DeFord numbly shook it. "I'm Captain Tom Mudd. This is my crew. We have, as you've probably gathered, boarded your ship for the purpose of lightening it."

"Don't talk like you've come for tea," DeFord said, his speech thick with sleep and the lingering vapor of rum. "Give me a sword, and we can settle this like men." They were bold words for a man whose neck was in a chain.

"We're not that sort of pirate," Captain Mudd said. He leaned on his polished aerorod as if it were a cane and not a sacred tool of navigation. This lack of respect for the instruments of the profession told DeFord all he needed to know about this invader. He was not a seasoned airman. His crew of women suggested his last career had been as a pimp or a wifemonger. He was probably the sort of man who never worked very hard, never strove. He was lazy, cowardly, and smug. In short, this Mudd represented everything that was wrong with a generation.

"Oh, don't pretend that you're some sort of rare genius," DeFord said. "A herd of cows wearing bells could've snuck past this lot." DeFord scowled at his crew. They scowled right back at him. He knew it was dangerous to humiliate them in this moment of vulnerability, but he didn't care. They were such a disappointment. "You got no one to blame but yourselves for this gutting!" DeFord told them.

"Come now, there's really no reason to shout," Captain Mudd said. "I'm sure your men are very hardy. In fact, in a fair fight, I have no doubt they would've given us quite a run of it. And we're not going to bleed you dry. We just need a little of your...of your..." The scarecrow trailed off, his brow wrinkling and his gaze glassing over. He seemed entirely distracted, like a man listening to a distant strain of music. DeFord wondered just what sort of lunatic had gotten aboard his ship.

"Rum, sir," the woman with the clockwork arm said. "They're carrying rum." The filigree that decorated the gleaming brass shell of her limb was fine enough for a woman's locket, though the machinery that showed between plates resembled nothing so much as the black workings of a locomotive.

"Yes. We just need a little of your rum," Mudd said, his attention recovered. "We'll also take whatever food you have. Then you can be on your way. By this evening, you'll be in port, paid and drunk, and this whole unfortunate business will be a dimming memory."

"Don't any of you think you're going to be paid! I don't care what this mudbug says—" DeFord stopped, squinting as a thought occurred to him. "Mudd. I've heard that name before. Aye. Aye, I met one of your victims once. I bought him a drink because his story about you was so entertaining. He had the whole pub in stitches. Mudd the half-a-pirate. Mudd the clown. He said you came in under a cloud of gulls and fish guts, and then you, reeking like a chum bucket in July and covered in feathers, demanded a tenth of his cargo. A tenth! What sort of parsimonious pirate are you?"

The woman with the brass arm snorted.

"Thank you, Mister Winters," Captain Mudd said. "Now, we'll take two barrels of your rum, your pantry, and any black powder you have."

"You didn't say anything about powder before," DeFord said.

"That was before you complained about my generosity," Mudd said.

A harpoon crashed into the deck behind them. At the aft, an airship descended past the curvature of the *Cairo Hound*'s balloon. The emerging ship was encrusted with the warts of battle, age, and repair.

A pulley zipped down the harpoon's cable and clunked against the deck. Captain Mudd turned to the crew of the *Cairo Hound* and said, "Gentlemen, the sooner you load my ship, the sooner I'll be off of yours."

The bear-skinned crew looked to their captain with black expressions.

The amazon pulled her chain from DeFord's neck, and he gathered the white sheet about his shoulders and raised himself to as dignified a pose as he could muster, though the wind made him shiver, and he was still drunk. He addressed his men. "You wanted to humiliate me?

Well, you've done it. But I am not humiliated because I stand here in a sheet on a ship given to a mudbug and his harem. No, I am humiliated to stand alongside of you. You will be a laughingstock if you indulge this man, if you give him one single drop of rum, of *my rum!*" DeFord beat his half-bare chest. "If there be one atom of self-respect or loyalty left in you, you will not aid this man. You will stand by me, your captain. You will refuse this injustice, or you will look for other work."

Captain Mudd said nothing in his defense. He smiled at the berated crewmen, awaiting their decision. He hadn't long to wait.

Pirates were as common as pigeons in the airstreams that circled the Tower. Many an honorable captain had been forced by a grim turn of fortune to stoop to piracy at one time or another. Some recovered their scruples as soon as their accounts were leveled. Of course, others who dabbled developed either a taste for the life or an inability to escape it. And then there were those shameless entrepreneurs who chose the bloody work willingly. They considered themselves a sort of ecological necessity: They were the wolves that thinned out the weak and old to the benefit of the herd.

Regardless of the cause, the life of a pirate was dangerous. The wealthy and powerful ringdoms regularly sent gunships to patrol the desert air. Infamy made the work of a pirate captain easier to undertake but more difficult to maintain. A wolfish reputation might soften a target, but it also attracted unwanted attention from military men eager to improve their own name. As often as not, as soon as a captain became the subject of a song or a limerick, he was welcomed to immortality with a mortal wound. One could try to maintain an innocuous or sympathetic profile, as Captain Mudd did, but subtlety was often lost on the sort of men who made their living at the end of a rope, lashed to a sack of combustible gas.

Truth be told, Captain Mudd and his motley crew were, for the most part, a toothless wolf. Their ship, the *Stone Cloud*, was a relic. What firearms they had were unreliable on their best days and decorative on their worst. The ship had one harpoon cannon on the bow that was incapable of launching a ball. If another ship decided to engage them, the *Stone Cloud*'s only reasonable recourse was to run. And run they had on more than one occasion.

According to Mister Winters, the ship's first mate and the only seasoned aeronaut among them, the *Stone Cloud*'s previous captain conducted his piracy purely by boarding party. Captain Billy Lee's crew of a dozen cutthroats would surprise a plump merchant ship, skewer her with a harpoon, draw her in, and overwhelm her while the startled crew was still tugging on their boots. It was a dicey business, and Captain Lee had lost and replaced many airmen during his command.

Under Mudd, the *Stone Cloud* boasted a crew of only five, including the captain. They were too few to swarm a deck, so they had adapted to survive. What they lacked in brute force, they made up for with ingenuity.

Captain Mudd had a talent for devising unorthodox ways to raid a ship. His crew, to their credit, followed his outlandish direction with hardly a squint.

On one occasion, they had snuck onto a merchant ship under the cover of fog and opened a barrel of cooking oil on the deck. The natural sway of the ship distributed the slick evenly, and the next morning they invaded on spiked cleats while the unsuspecting crew skated helplessly about, trying very hard not to impale themselves on their own swords. On another occasion, Mudd's crew had dropped several pounds of rotting fish onto a ship's envelope and then boarded amid a horde of frenzied seagulls. They had once resorted to posing as a wounded vessel full of collapsed damsels. Their would-be princes, who rode in on a barge of cured tobacco, helpfully lashed the two ships together and came aboard armed with decanters of brandy to revive the ladies from their swoon. The rescuers rushed to the sides of the fallen women only to be greeted by gun barrels drawn from under skirts.

"The rules of engagement," Captain Tom Mudd explained to the irate captain who'd been duped by this ruse, "were invented by men who would benefit most from them."

This philosophical pronouncement might've commanded more respect had it not been delivered by a man wearing a frilly bonnet.

The taking of the *Cairo Hound* had been simple in comparison. They had shadowed the ship since dawn. Once convinced their approach had gone undetected, they crossed to the *Hound*'s balloon by a rope ladder and used the netting to climb down to the gondola. Voleta distracted the crew while the captain and the others got into a favorable position. The rest was just talking, which the captain was quite good at.

With their supplies moved from the *Cairo Hound*, the mated ships decoupled and drifted apart.

Edith called to Adam at the helm on the quarterdeck, "Hard burn, please. Let's see if we can't find that southwestward current we came by." Adam repeated the order and plied the lever that opened the flue to the heating element in the ship's envelope. It didn't seem likely that the *Cairo Hound* would follow them, but if they did, Edith wanted them to be the ones squinting into the sun.

Voleta watched the retreating ship for any change in course. Though she had recently baited and eluded a mob, she showed no sign that anything very remarkable had occurred. She balanced atop a rail and leaned over the vast drop, casually gripping a tether in a manner that made her brother Adam quite nervous. A grackle flew into view, and she marked the subtle turn of its wings. "The current's shifted due west now," Voleta said.

"It'll do," Edith said. She turned to Captain Mudd. He stood, straight as a stovepipe, staring at the Tower that dominated the sky. "Captain," she called to him twice, the second time more sharply, but neither disrupted the intensity of his trance.

"Tom," she said with a little softness. Concern had turned her dark eyebrows into a single, severe line. Thomas Senlin refocused on her face and smiled. "Where to, Captain?"

He was still uncomfortable with the formalities that Edith insisted upon. She would only call him *Tom* in private and asked that he call her *Mister Winters* in front of the crew. *Mister* was the title that first mates were due and was only reasonable, but *Winters* was the name of her estranged husband who had edged her out of managing her family's farm and then refused to give her a divorce when she asked for one. Senlin couldn't imagine why she would want to be constantly reminded of such a man.

In quiet moments, Senlin recalled the hours they'd once shared in a cage that was bolted to the face of the Tower. They had been frightened by the unexpected cruelty of the Parlor and confused by the abrupt camaraderie the ordeal inspired. But they had also been only *Tom* and *Edith* to each other.

It seemed a long time ago. That was before she had lost her arm and joined a pirate crew, before he had missed a reunion with his wife by a matter of hours and stolen first a painting and then a ship.

Standing before Edith now, Senlin couldn't help but marvel at how, despite it all, their friendship had survived.

"I think we shall make for the Windsock, Mister Winters," he said. "We have some rum to sell." Really, they had little choice of where to go. The Windsock was the only cove that hadn't turned them away.

"Aye, sir." She nearly turned to spread the order but stopped short. She drew in close to keep her voice from carrying in the serene silence. Unlike the sea, with its crashes, howls, and tattooing waves, the air seemed quite a tranquil medium. "You were doing it again, Tom. You were staring off at the distance." When his only response was a pinched frown, she went on: "If I can see that you're distracted, the crew can see it, too. That worries me. Are you sure you're all right?" Her clockwork arm, beautifully doused in sun, illuminated her face with a golden light.

"Yes, yes, of course." He put a hand on her shoulder. "I was only—"

"Man overboard!" Voleta called from the balustrade. They turned in time to see a flailing figure in a white sheet plummet from the *Cairo Hound*. They were too distant to hear a cry if one was uttered, but the silence of the spectacle only made it grimmer.

No one doubted who it was.

Iren broke the moment of quiet reflection. "He was a bad captain."

"But a worse bird," Voleta said.

Chapter Two

With his ship, I have also taken possession of the late Captain Billy Lee's log. Reading his diary has provided me with two insights. First, penmanship is not a priority in the elementary institutions of the Tower. And second, I have signed us on for a rough life.

—The *Stone Cloud*'s Logbook, Captain Tom Mudd

The Tower of Babel frayed and turned the wind in elaborate ways. Currents broke and rolled upon its rough expanse like waves upon a sandbar. Some ports could only be approached during certain hours and with cooperative weather. Others had been desolated by a subtle shift in an airstream that rendered them inaccessible. Navigating the air about the Tower required the endless revision of charts, a close watch of the telltales, and boundless courage.

Most essentially, though, surviving the gusts of the Tower required a happy crew, and to be happy, a crew needed a few planks in a row to call their own. Without it, they would feel restless and trapped. They would bicker; they would grumble. So, the crew of the *Stone Cloud* each claimed a corner of the ship and retreated there when circumstances allowed.

Adam bunked in the main cargo hold, though he spent little time there. It was dark and low-ceilinged and gave him the feeling that he'd been swallowed by a whale. He preferred the dazzling view from the elevated quarterdeck, preferred being near the helm. A born engineer,

Adam dreamed of one day dismantling and rebuilding the ship and its controls in superior form. As it was, they had to rely on the wind to do most of the steering. He could only move the ship up and down by throttling the heating element and releasing the ballast in the forward tank, though this was a last resort because the tank was tedious to refill and also served as the crew's bath.

Iren and Voleta claimed the main cabin. Having lately been the barracks for a dozen crewmen, the room had reeked of boots and feet before they moved in. They tore down most of the hammocks, aired the room, and scrubbed every inch of planking with sweet-smelling pine soap. They stuffed the old clothes out a porthole, though Voleta kept (and mercilessly boiled) a few small articles that could be tailored to fit her. She'd come to the ship with nothing but a shawl and her blue leotard, the costume she'd worn during her captivity in the Steam Pipe. She pinned the leotard to the cabin wall, where it hung like a headless shadow: a reminder of the life that lay behind her.

Edith's bedroom, technically the chart house, was little more than a drafty closet. Old signal flags of faded bunting and roach-chewed maps decorated the walls. She had assumed the quarters while under Billy Lee's command because it was the only room on the ship that could be reliably locked. In her early days aboard the *Stone Cloud*, she had been feverish and weak from the infection that eventually consumed her arm. She refused to elaborate on the ordeal, and Senlin learned not to press the point. All that mattered was that the chart house had kept her safe when she was most vulnerable, and she had grown quite attached to it.

The fact that Edith's room could only be accessed through the great cabin, which was the captain's quarters, had been inconvenient but manageable during Billy Lee's command. In their private environments, Edith had been all but invisible to Lee. Lee was attracted to a different sort of woman: a waifish, insensible sort. He considered her too "brawny," and besides she was positively ancient at thirty-five. This liberated him, at least to his satisfaction, from the usual expectations of decorum. His casual modesty and crude habits were bothersome, but it was better than being the focus of his ardor.

Senlin found the arrangement much more concerning. For the sake of privacy and propriety, he offered to take a hammock in the hold alongside Adam, but Edith insisted that the captain slept in the great cabin. A crew, she explained, needed unsupervised hours to complain, cavort, and plot their mutinies. It was good for morale.

This justification had amused Senlin, but he understood her earnest point: A crew could never be at rest if their captain was always about.

So, agreeing to share the space, they worked out a system of knocks. Two raps meant, *Coming through*, as in: *I'm only using your room as a corridor. There's no need to look up from what you're doing, but it would be convenient if you were dressed.* Three quick knocks meant, *I'm paying you a visit*, and a single rap signaled, *I am going to sleep. Good night.*

To be more accurate, *they* had not created this percussive vocabulary. Senlin had, much to Edith's consternation. Not only was the knocking an unnecessarily elaborate solution to a simple problem (they could just speak through the doors, after all), it was also irritatingly genteel. It harkened back to the moment, at least in Edith's mind, when they were fleeing through the Parlor and Senlin refused to help loosen her gown. His sensibilities had nearly gotten her killed.

But he could not be reasoned with, and it was a small request. Edith conceded, and they had been counting knocks ever since.

The evening after they poached a few kegs of rum from the *Cairo Hound*, Senlin was sitting at the table in his cabin, poring over a chart of the Tower's lower levels, when three knocks sounded on the outer door. Edith came in, shooed by the wind, with a tin pitcher in one hand.

"The little owl is on watch," she said, meaning Voleta. Voleta's penchant for climbing all about the ship's rigging, though nerve-racking, made her an effective lookout. "I gave Adam and Iren a ration of rum."

"I suppose there'll be no lessons again tonight," Senlin said with a cluck of his tongue. After escaping the port, he and Iren had been free to resume her tutelage, and they had done so at first. But as the days piled discouragements and distractions upon them, the lessons had grown infrequent. He suspected it wouldn't be long before they were entirely abandoned.

She pulled two pewter goblets from a rack. "Well, look at it from her point of view. Before she met us, she had steady pay, reliable meals, and her morning, noon, and night scheduled for her. We haven't seen the same day twice since we shoved off from Goll. We're scrabbling to survive, to keep ourselves fed. And she's got to go along with your bizarre plots. Can you blame her for not having the patience for books right now?"

"You make a point," Senlin said. "I suppose improvisation is its own lesson."

"You wouldn't think a headmaster would be so devious."

"On the contrary. I credit any aptitude for conniving to my old profession," he said.

"Come again?"

"As headmaster, it was my job to teach children how to think like adults. It was their job, apparently, to teach me to think like a child, to expect the disruption, to anticipate the thumbtack on the chair or the lizard in the drawer."

"They played pranks on you?" She poured the rum and settled in, smiling at the thought of Senlin yipping after sitting on a tack.

"Oh, more than pranks. Some of them were dastardly clever. There was one student early in my tenure who gave me such fits—" He couldn't help but smile at the memory.

"One bitterly cold winter morning," he began, "I arrived at the schoolhouse early, as I always did, to stoke the banked fire in the stove. But someone had stirred the coals around, and they'd gone out. I suspected a prank, but thought it rather tame. I laid down some fresh kindling, but when I looked to the matchbox, I found only bare sticks. All the match heads were missing. 'Ah,' I thought, 'there's the real trick! Someone's snapped all my matches.' I went to the closet for a fresh box, and when I stepped into the dark room, I found myself skating on a patch of ice. I nearly took all the shelving down with me as I fell."

Edith covered her mouth when she laughed.

"At this point, I am impressed," Senlin continued. "This is a grand prank, and I am trying to decide which of my students is intelligent and devious enough to dream up such a cascade of tricks even as I take my bruised knees and fresh box of matches back to the stove. When I put a match to it, the stove erupts with a flame that singes my eyebrows. It startles me so badly I overturn a row of desks when I jump back."

"They put the match heads under the ashes?" Edith said.

"She did, indeed."

"You know who did it?"

"Oh, cleverness cannot hide delight. When they all sat at their desks that morning, I only had to look for who had the twinkling eyes." He neglected to mention that the pretty culprit would one day become his wife.

"I'm glad you learned something useful from your bad seed," Edith said, lifting her cup. "To the pranksters."

"To the pranksters," Senlin toasted.

Through a nearby porthole, they watched the dark shape of the Tower glimmer with the lights of skyports, observatories, and the fortresses of wealthy ringdoms. They shone like stars in the firmament of ancient stone.

"It's strange," Senlin said, his mood shifting. "I thought that once I had a ship, everything would fall into place. I certainly didn't think I was giving up bookkeeping to take up piracy. I just pictured this straight line of events. I thought we'd fly to Pelphia, find my wife, carry us all home, and that would be the end of it."

"I could've told you, there's no such thing as a straight path on an airship."

"For the life of me, I can't figure out how to get us through the door." He tapped the cross section of the aerorod labeled "Pelphia."

Pelphia was sandwiched between two inhospitable ringdoms. Beneath Pelphia was New Babel, which they'd just escaped and had no intention of ever returning to. Above Pelphia was the Silk Reef, which had once been a great park shared by the Pells below and the Algezians above. Then a century ago, Pelphia and Algez had fallen into a cycle of hot and cold wars, and the internal entrances to the Silk Reef were sealed up by both ringdoms.

So, the only way into Pelphia now was through its skyports. Senlin had learned all of this from Lee's limited collection of aeronautic histories. "At first I felt as if we had escaped a prison. Now, I feel like we've been locked out of our house," Senlin said, raking his hair in frustration.

"The Tower was built to keep our type out of it, Tom. We're a couple of foxes circling a coop, trying to get at a hen," she said. Senlin gave her an uncertain look, and she laughed. "I'm not suggesting your wife is a hen, Tom. It's just the farmer in me peeking through."

"Well, I'm glad we haven't entirely beaten the farm out of you." He rocked back in his chair and hung his hands behind his neck. "This morning I was daydreaming about my old cottage. I wonder if it's horribly overgrown. I imagine the shutters are hanging off, and the chimney is full of birds. Or maybe the town has sold it. Maybe they gave it to the new headmaster they hired to replace me." The front legs of his chair came down with a concluding thump, and the dreaminess of his expression hardened.

"It's strange to think of your old life carrying on without you," Edith said.

"It is, indeed," he agreed, topping off their cups. "I worry that I wasted my one chance to get back to that life. I regret running after her so rashly and so early on. It was not one of my better plans."

He needn't elaborate. They both recalled their disastrous attempt to enter Pelphia through a public skyport.

In retrospect, it was the day their life as pirates began.

Chapter Three

Compared to how ably Adam and Voleta adapted to
our new life, my own acclimation was painfully slow.
If mankind ever attempts to colonize the islands of
the stars, we should crew the ships with children and
put the youngest at the wheel.

—The *Stone Cloud*'s Logbook, Captain Tom Mudd

After their escape from the Port of Goll, the crew had been
almost delirious with optimism. They had slipped out from
under the thumbs of Finn Goll, Rodion, and Billy Lee. They
had reclaimed their liberty. They had escaped the Tower. And so anything seemed possible, even finding a single soul who'd been lost in
the Tower for the better part of a year.

Senlin had a few clues to direct his search. He knew that Marya
had been sold by a wifemonger to a nobleman from Pelphia named
W. H. Pell. Pell was the surname of the ruling family of Pelphia, and so,
presumably W. H. was a man of influence. He was also associated with
some sort of club called the Coterie of Talents. Pelphia was notoriously
difficult to get into. One had to be wealthy, gentry, or a trader in luxu-
ries. Muddy tourists and common merchants were rebuffed without
ceremony.

The matter of how to approach Pelphia was further complicated by
the fact that Senlin was a wanted man. He'd stolen a painting from
the commissioner of the Baths, a pugnacious man named Emmanuel

Pound, who collected taxes under the authority of the Pells. It was Pelphia's black-and-gold banner that flew over Pound's warship, the *Ararat*.

To prevent immediate arrest upon landing in Pelphia, Senlin adopted a pseudonym, Tom Mudd, and concocted a plan for getting past the port guards. He would play a wifemonger. Voleta would play his charge, his wife-for-sale.

In a move that would later haunt him when they were famished and sick of eating squab, Senlin spent every last penny they had on a dress for Voleta. He bought it from a man who claimed he was a merchant but looked every inch a pirate. Senlin tried not to think about the fate of the gown's previous owner.

The skirt was plump with petticoats, the neck was low slung, and the whole was colored a pale yellow, which made Voleta's lavender eyes all the more spectacular.

She absolutely loathed it.

But she was willing to play the part if it would help her captain, whom she liked.

In an attempt to disguise the rough appearance of their ship, they draped Billy Lee's collection of bed linens all about the railing. Lee, a shameless philanderer, had preferred loud colors and bold patterns. After a little lashing and pinning, their drab craft was transformed into a piebald eyesore.

Port Virtue, Pelphia's northern skyport, was both opulent and immaculately kept: The bollards were gold plated; the cranes were whitewashed; the guardhouses were shingled with pristine slate; and a half dozen palm trees stood in great pots, lining the way to the yawning tunnel that carried on to the city of the Pells.

Stationed at the end of each berth were eight-foot-tall iron turrets, which Edith called "lead soldiers." The lead soldiers looked like standing sarcophagi, and one could see a human face peering through the circular porthole in the bell-shaped head. Instead of arms, the lead soldiers raised a pair of twenty-pound guns.

Senlin began to have second thoughts the moment the smartly uniformed stevedores caught the tethers of his sheet-wrapped ship. A pistol wagged at the hip of each dockworker, and they moved with the practiced poise of an infantry. Port Virtue was not so much a port as a fortress. If their little charade failed to impress, they'd be captured in a second. But it was too late to bolt now. They had to forge ahead with the gambit.

No gangplank was offered to them, and none of the port workers responded to Senlin's lighthearted hellos. He had begun to feel stranded on his own ship when he spied a man in a lieutenant's uniform emerging from a guardhouse.

The lieutenant surveyed the day, seated a white cap upon his head, straightened the gold braid on his breast, and began an unhurried approach. He made a great show of inspecting a hundred details along the way: the unfinished coil of a line, the half-tucked shirt of a porter, a wayward palm frond. By the time the official arrived beneath their rail, Senlin had nearly ground his teeth to meal.

"What's your business here?" The lieutenant's eyebrows and mustache were pared to sharp points, lending his face a thorny quality.

"I'm Captain Tom Mudd. I've come to improve a nobleman with the addition of a wife," Senlin said, and to bolster his claim, he swept an arm toward Voleta standing at his hip, sullen in her yellow frock.

"Which nobleman?"

"The one with the sincerest interest, of course."

"No, no, that won't do," the officer replied with a laugh so dry it sounded like a cough. "Have you a letter of introduction or an invitation?"

"No." Senlin broke into a cavalier smile. "The wind introduces me and fortune invites me."

"That is *un*fortunate," the lieutenant said, and the word seemed some sort of code because the stevedores dropped the *Stone Cloud*'s lines and began an eerily ordered retreat. They didn't stop until they were behind the line of hulking lead soldiers.

Senlin took this as a bad sign. The lieutenant made a show of inspecting the ship's decoration. "Coming from a parade, are we?" The barbs of his brow lifted in amusement.

"Just making an impression," Senlin said.

The lieutenant's examination now strayed up Voleta's broad skirts, over her pinched waist, and her bare golden shoulders. "Of course, if you wish to commit your charge to my care, I'm sure we can make a favorable impression on your behalf."

Senlin sniffed. "I don't know what sort of custom you're used to in this rustic ringdom, but where I come from, businessmen aren't expected to make a gift of their wares. I go where my charge goes."

"Where are you from? It must be a very imaginative country. The ring beyond the Collar of Heaven, perhaps? A lunar colony?" All trace of amusement fled from the officer's face. "Leave the girl, and I'll let you keep your ship."

Before Senlin could form a retort, Voleta leapt onto the balustrade, hiked up her skirts, and began to dance. She balanced on one foot and swung her other leg at the knee. Her petticoats, thick and pale as cut cabbage, flapped wildly. "Kiss my foot, you pocky twit!" she crowed.

The lieutenant looked as if he'd been slapped.

Edith, who'd been watching the situation devolve from the periphery, marked the lead soldiers as they swiveled their guns toward the *Stone Cloud*. She gave Adam a discreet throat-cutting signal, and casually as she could, took a fistful of Voleta's wagging skirts.

At the helm, Adam straight-armed the throttles. The ballast tank burst open, releasing a torrent of water that swamped the port and nearly swept the lieutenant over the edge. The furnace whooped as the coil valve opened, and the ship bucked like a startled horse. Voleta would have been thrown overboard if Edith hadn't yanked her back, ripping her skirt in the doing.

Senlin was driven to his knees by the surge. The ship breached a new current that shoved them to one side. The rigging squealed. Iren, who'd been on the forecastle stair, tumbled against the starboard rail, which cracked but miraculously didn't fail. The sound of gunfire reverberated off the Tower a scant second before a cannonball burst through a corner of the deck, rattling their teeth and pecking their skin with splinters. The silk envelope began to deform at the base, a sure sign they were bleeding gas.

Senlin saw the hole in the balloon and experienced a moment of terror so intense it felt like euphoria. They were going to drop from the sky like a shot bird.

But even as he watched, the gash sealed itself as some second skin, some internal membrane, pressed against the tear.

A moment later, they were out of range of Port Virtue's lead soldiers, and the barrage abruptly stopped.

They rose upon a gentle vent of air. The ship felt almost motionless. The sky was serene. They stood up and patted themselves for signs of blood or protruding bones, but discovered neither.

"Well, that was lucky," Senlin said, straightening his cuffs with shaking hands. "Balloons don't usually patch themselves, do they?"

"No," Edith said, kneeling to examine the ragged divot that had been blown into the ship's starboard edge. "Voleta, Iren, get these ridiculous sheets off our ship."

Senlin inspected the drab-colored balloon overhead with a fresh eye. "A self-sealing envelope. It seems a remarkable fixture for a barge like this."

"One of the Sphinx's inventions. Billy Lee traded for it." Edith stood and kicked a portion of the broken deck into the abyss.

"Traded what?"

"An arm," she said.

They'd had little choice after that. There was no honest work for a small crew on such a lowly vessel. Every port they approached shooed them off like a fly from a table. They turned to piracy to keep from starving.

Senlin sipped his rum and squinted at the memory. "We have gotten quite good at running away," he said.

"We've gotten very good at *having* to," Edith corrected. "You know, we could take a new ship, one with real guns and maybe a thicker hull," she said, turning the cup in her hand. "If we weren't such conscientious pirates, we could—"

"Edith, I don't want to argue about this again. We can't ruin some innocent aeronaut just to solve our problems. If we were equipped to take on one of the Pell's warships or another pirate ship, I might do it.

But we aren't equipped, and we won't make victims of honest men. That's not who we are."

"It's exactly who we are. Like it or not, we are pirates. Saying please and thank you doesn't change that. There are no devils by degree, no gentlemen thieves. There's just strong and weak, the willing and the dead. You heard that boozer captain. Word's out about us, Tom! How long before some honest man decides that we're not so clever or dreadful as we seem? How long before they push back?"

"I am not taking the higher ground to be smug, Edith. These are decisions that change one's nature. Irrevocably. Look at Voleta. We don't talk about it, but I'm sure you've noticed. She's hardening. She's becoming ruthless and reckless."

"She's young."

"A man is thrown to his death, and she makes a joke about him being a bad bird."

"I'll talk to her."

"We can tut-tut all we want, but the fact is I have applied the friction that has raised the callus. I accept the responsibility. I am captain, which is why I refuse to take an iron file to what remains of her conscience by signing us on for murder! If by some fabulous miracle I find my wife, I still hold out hope that she will not receive me as a stranger." A passionate quaver had crept into his speech, and he clipped it now by clearing his throat. "I am sorry. That was a little overwrought."

Edith, who had begun to lean away, settled her elbows again on the table. "At least you're not brooding," she said. "Arguing I can stand; it's the staring off I hate."

She felt along the side of her mechanical arm, tracing the engraved arabesque patterns in search of a discreet release latch. This she caught with her fingernail, and a little drawer slid open, ejecting a glass vial into her hand. Her arm wheezed steam and slumped heavily onto the table. She brought the vial to her face and saw that it was still half-full of the glowing red serum. Satisfied, she refitted the battery.

Senlin had observed this evening ritual many times but knew better than to comment upon it. Any reference to her arm, its fuel, or the mysterious Sphinx who made it was always met with a bristling silence.

She drained her rum and gave Senlin a frank smile. "Tom, don't you wonder if we're even knocking on the right door? Are we sure your wife is in Pelphia?"

"I'm not sure at all," he said. "I'm chasing after hearsay and conjecture, but it's all I have."

"Of course," she said. "I'm with you. The crew is with you. You stood by us, and so we'll stand by you." She stood up and knocked once on the table. "I'm going to bed. Good night, Captain."

"Good night, Mister Winters," Senlin said with a thin smile.

When the door to the chart house clicked shut, he turned finally to the woman in a white nightgown who'd been sitting on his bed for the past hour. She made a childish face at him, like a guppy in a bowl, then raised a brush to her auburn hair. She hummed as she worked out the tangles.

Senlin clenched his eyes shut.

He had set a trap for the commissioner as part of his plan for escaping the Port of Goll. He had packed a crate with White Chrom, expecting Pound and his men to be thrown into fits when they opened it. But Senlin had been caught up in the springing of his own trap. He had inhaled a monstrous dose of the drug, and when he did, she had appeared.

The vision of Marya wasn't dreamy. Her figure was not transparent like a reflection in a mirror that might be dispelled with the dousing of a lamp. Neither did she shine or shimmer or speak in a cavernous voice, nor any other flamboyant habit supposed of ghosts. She looked entirely real, which of course only made the vision worse.

He had expected her to fade once the drug had run its course. He did not tell Edith or his crew about the dosing or the haunting because he didn't want to worry them, and he hoped his suffering wouldn't be long. But it had been months now, and she hadn't tired of tormenting him. She was like a child who could only be consoled by attention, attention he refused to give her because he feared it encouraged her. She sang and flounced and carried on, and he ignored it all as best he could, though it was impossible to be entirely immune to the distraction. Sometimes she disappeared for a few hours or an afternoon, if he was lucky, but just when he began to think he was cured of her, she would reappear and the haunting would resume.

The worst was when she talked to him. He hated it when she spoke because in this respect the vision was nothing like the woman he'd loved and married. The ghost was mean, suspicious, petty, and so quick with the most discouraging advice. He felt wedded to his own shadow of doubt.

Gripping his empty cup of rum, he opened his eyes. The vision was still there, watching him from his bed.

She set her brush aside and placed her hands on her covered knees like she was preparing to address a child. She said, "Oh, Tom. Dear, dear Tom. You don't know what you're doing. You haven't the foggiest notion."

Ignoring the vision, Senlin lay upon the bed and took out the painted study of Marya. In the image, she sat surrounded by orchids on Ogier's terrace studio. The firefly light of the Baths dappled her bare skin. Her expression seemed gentle and bold all at once. Senlin wished he could sink into the painting, could be drawn into that scene. He brought the icon to his lips and kissed the wrinkles and peaks the artist's brush had made.

The vision of Marya smirked at him from the foot of the bed. She said, "You're as lost as I am. And when your darling little crew finds out, they're going to see how good a bird you are."

Chapter Four

Trust is a muscle that works best in reflex.
—The *Stone Cloud*'s Logbook, Captain Tom Mudd

The Windsock was nothing like a traditional port. It wasn't associated with a ringdom; it wasn't attached to an entrance; it didn't lead anywhere. It clung to the Tower face like a moth's cocoon clings to the trunk of a tree, and much like the moth's dressing room, the Windsock was not a pretty sight.

Jumet, the roving poet of the Tower, described the Windsock in the third volume of his *Homage* as resembling "a broken country squeezebox / hung upon a field post / left for years to rot."

The long, rambling structure encompassed several floors and had enough rooms to fill a city tenement. It was a cobble of salvage and wreckage, a product of a thousand hands and half a dozen generations. It hadn't a plumb joist or matching beam anywhere in its anatomy. Instead of a solid facade, the Windsock was sleeved in a single, continuous tapestry. This wool wrapper, stretched over the wooden frame, made the whole assemblage appear emaciated and frail.

The pattern of the Windsock's tapestry was as elaborate as it was disorderly: pictograms, symbols, and hatch marks lay in close proximity and at every angle. It reminded Senlin of an old tattooed sailor.

He had whiled away a few hours on previous visits studying the strange code that filled the tapestry but had never had much insight into its meaning.

The quaint wrapper sometimes fooled newcomers into thinking the Windsock was a civil place. Nothing could be further from the truth. It was a desperate port full of black marketeers, aging harlots, and mercenaries looking for wicked work. It had practical merits, of course: A man could sell his plunder, fill his larder, get drunk, and find a willing companion, all within a short walk. But the fact remained that with each transaction there was a fair chance one would be swindled or shot.

The cove was too rickety to hold an anchor, so visitors had to moor along a great crack in the cliff face of the Tower, traverse the gap between ship and shelf, and make the perilous hike to port on foot. The drop was considerable. A tumble from the crack would allow souls a full seven seconds to reflect upon their lives, even as they plunged to the end of them.

Iren had a knack for finding receptive patches of sandstone that would catch and hold a harpoon. Today, the spur bit on the first shot, and the ship did not pull it free when Adam dropped ballast to tighten the line. Satisfied it would hold, Iren slid across the gulf on a pulley and hanger. Voleta followed but without a trolley, dangling instead by her gloved hands. Adam couldn't bear to watch her, convinced the cable would burn through the leather at any moment. But Voleta was light, and she managed her speed by pinching the cable with the heels of her boots. When they were both safely established in the crack, Adam harnessed the two kegs of rum to a pulley and sent the load down after them.

"And you're going to see if your man has any idea about how to get into Pelphia on the sly?" Edith asked Senlin.

"He's hardly my man, but yes. I hinted after it last time, but he didn't volunteer much. Maybe I can needle him with a little money."

"I wouldn't take anything less than twenty shekels for the rum. It's not rotgut," Edith said. "It may be the best the cove has seen all year."

"Agreed," Senlin said.

"I volunteer to stay with the ship," Adam said in a blurt that suggested he'd been working up to speaking for some time. Senlin and Edith were caught off guard by the announcement, and so Adam forged ahead with his reasoning. "If I had just one day on my own, I could break down the console and figure out what's behind those dead levers." He opened the grate on the furnace to stir the coals. It didn't need to be done, but he was uncomfortable looking Senlin in the eye.

Edith pursed her lips and watched Senlin for an answer.

Adam's request was reasonable enough, and Senlin was about to say yes.

But then the figment of Marya swung around the doorway of the great cabin and chased the thought straight from his head. She wore the red sun helmet that had become so famous in his memory. Her riding boots and white blouse looked ridiculously refined against the pocked deck of the ship.

"Don't be silly, Tom," Marya said, tucking her auburn hair into the helmet as she marched to him. "You're not going to waste your faith on that boy again."

Edith cleared her throat.

Senlin realized that he was glaring at apparently nothing. He pinched the bridge of his nose, shielding his eyes. He tried to recover his original train of thought. His concentration was so easily dispersed now; he was always chasing the tail of an idea.

The trouble was, on this occasion Marya had a point. Adam had betrayed him twice already, and though Adam had done so to protect his sister, the fact remained he was unreliable. Left alone, what prevented Adam from calling Voleta back, casting off with her, and stranding the rest of them? If Senlin's faith in the young man was betrayed a third time, it would not be Adam who deserved the blame.

But was it a fair suspicion? There was no immediate threat to Voleta. Couldn't the boy be trusted in fair weather at least? It was a sensible risk, really, and it might help reanimate Adam's old confidence. He'd become so timid in the weeks since their escape.

Senlin opened his eyes to deliver his verdict, only to find Marya with her nose pressed to his own. Her eyes were dark with shadow.

He grimaced and flinched before he could stop himself. She vanished in that instant. Edith and Adam stared at him with obvious concern.

"I thought I might sneeze," he said lamely.

Edith scowled and turned to Adam. "It's not the pilot's place to stay with the ship. That's a joy for the first mate."

"It doesn't have to be," Adam said, desperation lifting his voice.

"That's a funny way of saying 'aye, sir,' airman," Edith said.

"Aye, sir," Adam said glumly. He lifted a rubber-rimmed monocle from where it hung about his neck and seated it over his good eye. The cycloptic goggle, his own invention, made him appear a little deranged in combination with his eye patch, but he was proud of it, so it had a restorative effect on his dignity.

As soon as Adam stepped off the ship, Senlin turned to Edith and said, "I'm sorry. I was just considering the question thoroughly."

"Can you pick up oil for my arm?" She spoke over him.

"I was going to say yes."

"But you didn't say anything. That's the problem. What am I supposed to do if you turn into a gargoyle during some actual calamity? Wait for you to thaw out, wait for you to *thoroughly consider*?" Her frustration began to color her cheeks. "We're all standing by, Captain. But you can't keep us waiting."

Senlin began to speak, but she cut him off. "Please don't forget my oil."

The seam that led to the Windsock was a crooked, ranging thing. Some parts were as narrow as a ledge, others as wide as a country road. In places, the edge was freshly chipped, hinting at some recent misfortune. The main of the path was scalloped smooth from generations of use, though this fact did not make it feel any safer.

The ground seemed to swing and pitch beneath the crew of the *Stone Cloud* as they struggled to regain their land legs. They had to fight the urge to drop to their knees and crawl along on all fours.

Except Voleta. She bounded ahead, nervy as a mountain goat.

From the crag, the rooftop market looked tame enough. Sunbleached awnings crowded right to the edge of the deck. A barrel organist played a jaunty tune while a woman accompanied in a hoarse falsetto. A funnel of terns circled and swooped, diving after scraps. There was a warm aroma of tobacco and meat that had been so heavily spiced it could pass for incense.

It was a welcome sight. The Windsock was as close to a home port as they had.

They climbed down to the floor of the market and were caught up in a blizzard of feathers being thrown by an old woman who sat efficiently plucking a dove. A pitiful collection of undressed fowl hung in the stall behind her.

Every essential thing was present in the market, though never in very good condition. Whether a rivet or a kettle or a set of tongs, the blacksmith's iron was always rusted. The clothier had plenty of shirts and pants for sale in a variety of inhuman sizes. A blue-skinned doctor sold a powerful tonic, which he promised would cure everything from gout to gunshots without a single side effect other than a slight (and attractive!) bluing of the complexion. Everything was bent, corroded, patched, and mismatched. Yet to a man without a country, the market was a garden of delights.

No sooner had they begun to press through the pickpockets and hawkers than Voleta darted off without a word of warning or explanation. She ducked under a tray of reclaimed hinges and nails, startling the vendor. He swatted at her, but she squeezed under the rear curtain of the booth and was gone.

No one was surprised to see her fly off, least of all Adam. Still, he felt compelled to grumble about her recklessness. These complaints had become part of the docking ritual: They'd come to port, Voleta would vanish, and Adam would swear that next time he would put a rope between them just like the hopeless tourists of the Market. Everyone knew perfectly well he'd have better luck putting a leash on an eel.

Selling the rum was easily done. Alcohol was always in short supply, so a fair price required only a little tasting and haggling. Senlin sold both kegs to a one-legged man and then huddled with his crew. He gave Iren and Adam ten shekels to buy food for the ship and three shekels more to spend at the pub when the shopping was done. One of the shekels was for Voleta, should she decide to reappear. They agreed to reconvene on the *Stone Cloud* in a few hours' time.

Senlin was happy to leave the noisome scents and cries of the market behind. He tramped down the public ramp to the lower floors where the port's wool wrapper dyed the sunlight a pretty shade of ochre. The ramp curved along the tapestry, occasionally branching into chambers where rough men drank and threw dice and sang songs that were childish in tune and profane in lyric. The rooms were divided by hanging rugs of thick felt. Solid walls and doors were unheard of here. If he had a mind to do it, he could nose and worm his way into any room in the cove.

Women with rouged cheeks and charcoaled eyes loitered by the open flaps of cells that appeared no deeper than a wardrobe. They wore great volumes of dirty crinoline, torn netting, and frayed lace. These gowns, which were meant to evoke some better society, some higher virtue, only made them seem more pitiable, like dead flowers laid upon a fresh grave.

They watched Senlin for any sign of interest. He turned up his collar and pressed on.

The tapestry did little to discourage the wind. It flowed and drafted, making the passage throb like a heart. The vision of Marya led him down. She looked back at him over her shoulder, smiling when she saw he was still there, as if he were the one following and not the other way around. He tried not to associate this vision with either the poor wretches in the alleys or the sweet memory of his wife, because if he ever let this phantom pose as a link between his memories and his fears, he had no doubt it would drive him to despair.

The one person in the Windsock that Senlin had any affinity for was Arjuna Bhata. Arjuna had skin the color of strong tea, a candle-bright smile, and an incorrigible joking manner. Though prematurely bald, Arjuna had held on to more of his boyish energy and optimism than Senlin had. These personality traits, which would've driven the headmaster from a room a year ago, held an undeniable appeal now.

Arjuna Bhata's shop occupied the entire bottom floor of the Windsock. The expanse was overstuffed with bibelots, curios, and esoteric furniture drawn from every ringdom of the Tower. Amid all these curiosities sat spools of yarn, balls of yarn, little nests of yarn lying underfoot, under chairs, and in every nook. Senlin had often wondered at this abundance of yarn, and yet it was only one quirk among many, the floor was full of such an incongruous jumble. At a single glance, Senlin saw a throne made of antlers, a rusted gong, an armless statue of a young man with a mawkish grin, and a tragic doll with half a head of corn-silk hair and no eyes.

Marya, *who was not really there*, touched the cheek of the malformed doll and said, "Isn't it gruesome? If we ever had a child, I imagine we'd have something just like this, something unlovable to haunt the rest of our lives."

Senlin shuddered and was still cringing when Arjuna rounded a tower of ottomans and clapped his hands in greeting.

"Tom Mudd! How are you? Are you cold? How can you be? It's like a tagine in here! Do you know the tagine? It's crockery, shaped like this," he said, drawing a figure in the air. "The plainsmen use it to turn their food into pudding. You could put a rock in a tagine and it would come out jelly. Are you sick?"

"Just a passing shiver," Senlin said, shaking Arjuna's hand.

"I have developed, over many years, a theory as to what causes shivers in a warm room." Arjuna's expression narrowed, and for a heart-fluttering moment, Senlin felt as if the merchant had somehow discovered the real cause of his shuddering. "Impure thoughts. Hmm? Yes, yes, it's no good to deny it, Mudd. It is only natural when one comes upon a beauty like this"—he stroked the armless statue's round cheek—"to feel the stirring of passion." Arjuna laid his hand on his chest and affected the beating of a heart. "Pum-pum! Pum-pum! All the blood rushes to the breast, and the extremities freeze, and that is why you shiver. No? Not in the mood for jokes? I'm sorry; I can't help it. I am drunk with loneliness. What can I do for you, my friend?"

"Oil," Senlin said, trying to reflect some of Arjuna's levity in his expression even as Marya flittered about the edge of his vision. "Something for fine gears."

"I have just the thing." Arjuna bent far over an island counter, his sandals nearly falling from his feet as he reached, and came back with a little glass pot. "For you, four pence."

"Two pence for anyone else, I suppose," Senlin said with a brittle smile.

"If you came to rob me, you should've worn a mask!" Arjuna threw up his hands. "All right. Three pence."

Senlin paid for and pocketed the oil, but then made no move to leave. He stood there, seeming for all the world like just another piece of awkward furniture.

"I am happy, of course, that you came to see me, Mudd," Arjuna said, a little tentatively. "But this is a trifle you could've bought anywhere. So, I wonder, forgive me, if you came for something more?"

"Yes, I suppose. I need... direction. I mentioned Pelphia before."

"I remember," Arjuna said. "It is a place you'd like to visit?"

"Yes. But the ports aren't exactly—rushing to embrace me," Senlin said with difficulty. He was uncomfortable sharing so much, even with a man who'd never been anything but pleasant to him. There was always a risk in talking about one's business here, especially when one almost certainly had a bounty on one's head. But he had come to an impasse that he hadn't the influence, wealth, or knowledge to overcome. He had no choice. "Do you know where I might procure a letter of introduction, an invitation, or... a convincing falsification?"

Arjuna laughed but stopped when he saw he was laughing alone. He cleared his throat. "I'm sorry. It's quite a leap from a pot of oil to a forgery, don't you think? I have nothing like that. And be careful who you ask about it. I know of twenty men who'd sell you a bad fake that would get you shot."

"I appreciate your honesty," Senlin said.

"Pelphia is an unfriendly place, Mudd. Worse than this, I think. I'm sorry it is such a trouble to you, but I don't know how I can help. My knowledge of the world is"—he picked up an ivory helmet that had been carved to resemble a curly head of hair; he put the ridiculous thing on and smiled—"mostly useless. My mother says that happiness is a symptom of ignorance." He shrugged, removing the ivory wig. "I am very happy."

"Do you know anyone who is unhappy?"

"Oh, my mother. She is miserable." Arjuna beamed.

Senlin smiled back. "Perhaps she could help me. Where is she?"

"She is here. She is never anywhere else. She is always too busy to leave."

"She is here? Where?"

"Men come to talk to her, men like you. She keeps a record of many things." Arjuna sucked in his lower lip thoughtfully. "But she is a difficult person. Not the sort of mother you introduce friends to."

Senlin was so charmed by Arjuna's concern that he was almost able to ignore Marya as she hopped up on the counter between the merchant and the tapered skull of a giant anteater. "Beware the men who call you friend," she said in a singsong voice.

Taking a breath, Senlin fixed Arjuna with a steady, imploring gaze. "If she will see me, I'd very much like to talk to your mother," he said.

Arjuna searched Senlin's eyes for some waver of doubt, but finding only resolve, his expression clouded, and the candle of his smile went out. "All right. But I warned you, Mudd."

Arjuna waved Senlin around his counter and showed him the trapdoor in the floor.

"You keep your mother in the basement?" Senlin said, sorry to have driven the humor entirely out of the merchant.

A smirk pinched Arjuna's cheek. "You have it backward. She keeps me in the attic," he said, and hauled the door open with both hands. Senlin peered in. He saw only air and the distant ground some thousand feet below. He looked up in alarm as Marya's caution rang again in his ears: *Beware the men who call you friend.*

But Arjuna was not poised to shove him into the trap. He looked only concerned and a little sad. The wind whipped up at them, stirring Arjuna's white kurta and fluttering Senlin's dark coat. It was only then that Senlin saw the ladder, and below, a few crossing planks that formed a stingy landing.

"My mother is very astute and has no sense of humor. I've always found her terrifying. Whatever you do, don't lie to her."

"I will—I mean, I won't," Senlin said, and sitting on the lip of the opening, he reached with the toe of his boot for the first rung. He felt as if he were climbing into an abyss.

"That's very wise of you," Arjuna said. "But very unhappy."

Chapter Five

One can't turn around in a pirate's cove without being accosted by some charlatan selling the promise of treasure. Though I suppose it is comforting to think that there is a reliable wage to be made drawing and selling treasure maps. The same could be said of writing travel guides.

—The *Stone Cloud*'s Logbook, Captain Tom Mudd

Adamos Boreas had never been in a restaurant, or a quaint country tavern, or a city café before. Such institutions, in addition to serving unclouded beer and hot food, had storied and evocative names, names like the Prancing Minerva, or Lord Wimbley's Gilded Spigot, or some similarly noble jumble. The pubs that would serve him had crude, descriptive names or only pictures drawn upon a shingle that were easily identified by the illiterate masses.

And so, though it was dim, rank, and furnished with uneven benches, Adam felt at home in the Ugly Rug. The eponymous rug lay under his feet, collecting tobacco burns and beer stains. A constant draft bled through the tapestry walls, endlessly stirring a layer of red dust that had been blown up from the valley and now clung to everything.

Whenever a new patron entered the pub, the publican barked the house rules with mechanical emphasis: "*Black* scotch for killing; *black* scotch for bailing on yer bill." If the crowd was feeling lively, they'd join in the chorus: "*Black* scotch for killing! *Black* scotch for bailing on yer bill!" Anyone who was black-scotched could expect to be mobbed and strung up by the neck if they were ever foolhardy enough to visit the Windsock again. The black scotch was the only law, and even the hardened criminals respected it.

The shopping hadn't taken long. Their money went quick, and the port hadn't much to offer. The groceries sat in two crates on the table. Lentils, potatoes, onions, carrots, and apples lay in one, and in the other a can of cooking oil and paper sacks of sugar, salt, and rice. In a moment of indulgence, Iren had bought a little sachet of dried chilies, and Adam had purchased a tin of cinnamon sticks. It was a modest pantry, but it seemed a great treasure to them after many days of eating desert birds and a gelatinous blue-gray buckwheat porridge, which they all hated and which Voleta had dubbed Stone Pudding.

"Captain doesn't trust me," Adam said to Iren.

The big woman peered at him over the rim of her wooden tankard but did not stop drinking. The two of them had been at odds while employed by Finn Goll. Back then, Adam had thought of Iren as Goll's dim-witted guard dog, and Iren had thought of him as a sulky hustler. But since their escape, the old animosity had been softened by the forced intimacy that life on a ship brought. They were not friends exactly, but they had come to respect each other.

"He thinks I'm a thief," the young man continued. "The only time he leaves me alone on his ship is if there's a boarding party and he's standing between me and my sister." Adam slid four pence to the edge of their table, and the publican came around to refill their tanks from his pitcher. "He thinks I'm biding time until I can figure out a way to steal his ship and run off with Voleta."

Iren, who had never been one for wasting words, shrugged at this and then tapped the table insistently when the publican stopped filling her tankard too soon.

"But I can be trusted," Adam said. "I deserve a second chance."

"You had one," Iren said. A link in the chain girded about her middle wasn't sitting right, and she made a jangling adjustment to relieve the pinch.

"Mmm, maybe. But he doesn't understand the position I was in.

Rodion possessed power, men, influence. He had my sister!" Adam jabbed at the air between them. Iren was distracted by a fly that had taken up orbit about her head. "A deal with Rodion was worth something. At least, I thought it was. All the captain could offer then was a dream. It was a betrayal, yes, but a reasonable one. And only one. The robbery in the Basement doesn't count. I was under orders, and if I hadn't—"

"I don't trust you either," Iren said. "I'll tell you why. You're still making excuses. You won't own what you did, which means either you're a coward, and I don't trust cowards, or you don't think you did anything wrong. So you'll do it again." Iren made a darting grab at the fly, closed her fist, then opened it for inspection. It was empty. The fly resumed its orbit around her scowling head.

Adam turned his cup against the table like a man working a drill. "I just didn't believe he could do it! It's the first lesson of the Tower: There is no escape. You can plunge deeper in, or you can cling to your little piece of the rock, but there's no getting out. And yet"—he stamped the cup fervently—"here we are."

"Here we are."

"I don't want to be the leper on the boat, Iren. I want to be part of the crew. I want to be trusted." He had been gritting his teeth but stopped as he suffered a moment of clarity amid the thickening swamp of drink. "You're right. Of course you're right. I can't expect him to trust me a third time when he has never gotten anything for it. I am in his debt. I have to repay him." Adam clutched Iren's wrist where it lay on the table; she made a sour face. "I must buy his trust back. I must *give* him something. What does he need?"

"Money," Iren said, and picked up her wrist so that he had to let it go.

Adam blanched. "I was hoping you'd say a new hat or a book or something small I could steal." Iren snorted at the irony of this. "Well, how else is a pauper supposed to repay his debts? But, you're right. It wouldn't be enough. It won't ever be enough. He wants to find his wife, but he can't even begin because we're so poor, and the ship is so wretched, and we all look like we've come crawling out of the desert.

We need clothes, shoes, proper arms, a new envelope, a new furnace, a new helm, a new everything." The young man brooded on this, tapping the lens of the goggle that stood on his forehead. He came to a conclusion: "We need a fortune. Where does one get a fortune?"

Adam's voice had been rising with his frustration, so he was readily overheard. An aeronaut with gray hair and a red mustache, a swaying and volatile sort of man, leaned in from an adjoining bench and said in a stage whisper, "A fortune? Once you have it in your head, you're done for. It's riches or rags for you, now."

"Rags I already have. What do you know about fortune?" Adam said.

"Not me. Not me specially. Everyone. Everyone knows where fortune waits. It's in the clouds!"

"Oh. Thank you, wise sir," Adam said with a patronizing dip of his head.

"I'm not a half-wit!" the old airman said, lips snarling over a comb of brown teeth. "It's not in my head. It's in the clouds! In the Collar of Heaven. You know what's up there? Trees of silver and rivers of gold. There are jewels as big as apples. All you have to do is run up, stick out your arm, and pull treasure in by the handful." His pantomime nearly threw him from his bench.

"Then why haven't you done it?" Adam said.

"Because it's somebody else's treasure. There are things up there not like us. Beings so far beyond us mudbugs, their daily doings look like magic. Every once in a while, a sky-boy like you takes a peek up there. It never goes well. You end up with your insides spread across the Skirts, feeding the vultures."

Adam gave Iren a surmising look, trying to tell whether she was convinced by any part of the man's yarn. She jabbed a finger in her ear, worked it around, and then examined the result.

"Now, why don't you thank an old man for sharing his wisdom," the mustached airman concluded, upturning and shaking his empty tankard.

Understanding the game and wishing to preserve the peace, Adam grudgingly set a pence on the man's table edge.

"*Black* scotch for killing! *Black* scotch for bailing on yer bill!" the publican called.

Voleta appeared at the end of their table, and Iren made room for her on the bench. Iren's preference for Voleta was plain only to those who knew the subtleties of the amazon's expressions. Where others saw irresponsibility and caprice in the young woman, Iren saw a reflection of herself: Voleta's rebelliousness, her preference for solitude, her daring, all recalled a youth Iren had packed away long ago. She'd grown quite fond of Voleta.

"Why are you always wandering off?" Adam said.

"Why are you always sitting still?" Voleta replied, pulling off her gloves by the fingers. She snaked around the fort of Iren's propped arms, grabbed her beer, and took a gulp. Iren, uncharacteristically, allowed the invasion to occur.

When Voleta set the cup down, a gray flash erupted from her sleeve, coiled once around her arm, and formed a crouching lump on her shoulder. It took a little blinking of Adam's eye to decide it was a rat.

"Why is there a rat on your shoulder?" Adam asked.

"She's not a rat. She's a squirrel. A flying squirrel," Voleta said, reaching up to pet the animal, which fleetly retreated around her neck to her other shoulder. When Voleta reached for her there, the squirrel scurried back to her original perch. "Her name is Squit." Squit burrowed through Voleta's dark tangles and then climbed to the peak of her head.

"But where did you get it?"

"I adopted her."

"You can't adopt a squirrel."

"Of course I can. Some horrible man was selling her for six shekels. Can you imagine trying to sell such a wonderful creature at any price, but for six shekels? It was an outrage."

"*Black* scotch for killing! *Black* scotch for bailing on yer bill!" the publican called.

"You stole her," Adam said.

"You can't steal a living soul. I liberated her," Voleta said.

"Out of the mouths of babes!" a voice from behind them said. They were all so absorbed by the antics of the squirrel and the argument that none of them had seen the man approach. But they saw him now. He was stout and dressed in leather with dark cancers on his face like the spots of a leopard. He nimbly snatched the squirrel from Voleta's head before she could react. "I suppose if you'd stolen a ham, you'd say it had a soul, too. It's quite a convenient defense," he said, and adopting an ironic tone, he continued: " 'Oh, no, your honor, I'm not a thief! I'm a redeemer of souls!' "

"Give her back," Voleta said blackly, coming to her feet. "Don't squeeze her so."

Iren and Adam did not sit dumbly by. Adam discreetly extricated his pistol, unreliable though it was, and held it at the ready under the table. But Iren intuitively found the barrel and turned it to the floor. Her gaze reassured him that she would not let anything happen to the girl. Adam glared hotly back at her but did not raise the gun a second time.

"Oh, doxy," the leopard said. "I'll squeeze whatever I like." He raised the squirrel in his fist, its little gray head craning to and fro in alarm. "You owe me six shekels and one more for having to chase you. You can pay with your purse or, if you'd rather, with your skirts." When he leered at her, his gums were thick and black as a dog's. "I can tell you which I'd prefer."

Iren stood to face the cancer-spotted man and said, "I'll pay for the squirrel."

He leered back. "If it's coming from you, I prefer the purse."

"Two shekels."

"I said it'd be seven. Seven, or no squirrel," he said, raising the clenched animal above his head. When Iren neither flinched nor revised her offer, the leopard gave an apathetic shrug. "All right. No squirrel."

He threw the pitiful creature to the floor with such violence that it bounced upon the yellow rug. The squirrel lay dazed or dead on its back even as the villain raised his boot over it.

Despite these antics, the leopard was not a reckless man. In fact, he was quite calculating. Unlike most of the denizens of the Windsock, he was not a fool for numbers, not a counter of fingers, or a simple tallyman. He was artful with an abacus. He could perform elaborate computations with ease, which allowed him to access the mysterious forces that turned men's pockets in and out, made fortunes and fallow fields, the force that lesser minds called *luck*.

The leopard was a devotee of the odds.

He could've just reported the little tart when he saw her snatch the squirrel from its cage, but there was no profit in a black scotch. So, he followed her, squeezed her for money in front of her friends, proposed a lurid alternative to invigorate the haggling, which he expected would resolve at four shekels, two pence. He'd rejected the hulking woman's first bid and tweaked the urgency of the negotiation by dazing the rat and threatening it with his boot. He had no intention of stamping his own enterprise to death.

Unfortunately for the leopard, Iren was not a follower of odds.

He was unprepared for what happened to him next: He began to levitate. A force at his belt tipped him back, and another force at his collar kept him in the air. He was floating. Something touched the top of his head. It was not unpleasant at first, but then the pressure spread down to his ears, his neck, his shoulders. It felt as if a too-small hat was being forced onto his head. Then the resistance gave way to a ripping sound and a bright, unfiltered light. For one remarkable moment, he felt naked and weightless like a babe in arms.

Then he began to fall.

The publican watched the big woman pick the spotted merchant up by his shirt and britches and hike him straight through the tapestry. The man seemed to just disappear into a beam of light.

The amazon looked at the publican with a speculative expression, as if she wondered whether he'd seen her throw a man through the wall.

But of course he had. Everyone had.

The publican sighed and said, "Black scotch for killing..."

Chapter Six

Omissions become lies, etc.

—The *Stone Cloud*'s Logbook, Captain Tom Mudd

Senlin found more air than floor at the foot of the ladder.

What few planks there were raised a disconcerting chorus of creaks and pops when he shifted between them. He took his bearings. On one side, six long coats and six grand hats hung from pegs on a board. Some of the coats had been scoured of their color by the elements; others were as dark as the closets they'd come from. One handsome tricorne looked fit for an admiral. Senlin wondered what sort of noble company he had stumbled upon.

But it only took a little glancing about to realize that whoever owned these coats had left them behind. There was not a soul around, nor a stick of furniture for that matter, and no flooring to speak of. There were only bare studs and joists and the air between. Not even the tapestry wrapped this far.

With nothing to slow it, the wind coursed all about him. A sudden surge sent him groping for the ladder again. Clinging to the rungs, he had to fight the competing urge to return to firmer ground and the morbid impulse to look down.

The same gust that teased him also parted the barrier of coats. Senlin glimpsed a vivid starburst of color behind them. Curious, he gathered his courage and pressed through the curtain of sleeves and tails.

He was greeted by a vision so thrilling and unexpected it was like pushing through a bland hedge into a secret garden in full bloom.

He stood at the edge of a web of yarn.

Thousands of strands of every color flowed from the rafters, gathered into bands, and funneled down to a central point. In a flash of insight, he realized this was the reason for the sprawling collection of yarn in Arjuna's shop; those spools ran through holes in the floor and emerged here as the rays of a web.

At the heart of the web sat a bald woman wrapped in a shawl. She cradled a loom in her lap, and the loom absorbed all of her attention. Nothing else stood beneath her but long tendrils of yarn and a great volume of sky.

This could only be Arjuna's mother.

He looked for some path by which to approach her but found none. There were no planks, no beams, and no rafters in reach. There were only the strands of the web sloping downward with crossing rungs, and irregular gaps, and a woman waiting at the bottom.

A gust caught his coat and nearly blew him from his ledge. Now he knew the reason for the coat pegs; a loose coat could turn a man into a kite. Still, it wasn't until he hung his own coat alongside the others that he fully grasped the implication. The coats belonged to men who had come to this point, ventured onto the web, and never returned.

Six empty coats: six lost souls.

"This is a fine place to turn back," Marya said, stepping around his elbow and peering down. "Let's be honest, Tom; this is a little desperate, even for you. Think about what you're doing: risking your life to get advice from some arachnid in the root cellar of a pirate cove. Such a reliable source! What could she possibly say that would make any difference? Even if she knew what you wanted to know, knew how to get into Pelphia by some funny subterfuge, what then? Will you wander the streets calling my name?"

She parted the strands of the web and tried to pull herself through. "I'm not even there! I escaped a long time ago. I went home. I'm already accepting gentlemen callers. I'm dusting off my piano bench as we speak!" She squirmed a little way forward and then tipped into a gap in the thread. For a moment, she hung before him, upside down. She looked just as she had the day she climbed a tree to retrieve the kite he'd made for her. Then her weight shifted, and she lost her grip. She plummeted away without another word.

Senlin stared dumbly after her with his heart in his throat. It was only a vision, and still he had to suppress a wail of shock and frustration.

Perhaps he should turn back. Perhaps this was reckless. But then, what was there to return to? Confusion? Ignorance? The inevitable slide into a life of violence? Surely, it was better to go forward into ruin than backward into rot.

He took the vibrant strands in his trembling hand and climbed into the weaver's web.

Edith sat in her bath observing a lonesome cloud sail over the valley. Idly, she wondered what body of water it had risen from, what lands it had laid its shadow to, what crops it had watered. The thought carried her back to her family's farmland. She missed the life of seasons and harvests. She even missed the floods that ruined one crop only to improve the next. Now, that entire period of her life seemed as distant and unrecoverable as her arm. As she watched, the lonesome cloud thinned and burned away.

The ballast tank, which could be accessed by pulling up the planks of the forecastle, served as the crew's tub. The water wasn't really potable but was fine for bathing if one didn't mind the cold. She found it a great luxury, shivers and all. She was momentarily free of responsibility.

She sat with her arms resting on the deck: The left was subtly muscled and fawn colored, the shoulder spattered with the dark freckles she had begun collecting as a girl. The other was a bulky assemblage of plates, bolts, valves, and a host of mechanical parts she could not name. But she knew how to care for it well enough: She had to refill the water reservoir daily, oil the joints weekly, and replace the liquid battery, of which she had a limited supply, about once a month. Strange as it was to say, the engine was a part of her. She couldn't imagine life without it.

There were some jobs for which the clockwork arm was ideally suited: The prying open of crates, the carrying of freight, and the dashing of teeth were all more ably done by the engine on her shoulder. But other tasks, often simple ones, were made onerous. Dressing and undressing took twice as long as it used to. Tying a knot raised a sheen on her brow. Even washing her hair, which had once been such a meditative process, was now tedious, sometimes painful work.

For a moment, she considered forgoing that particular labor. Then she smelled her hair, and her resolve to wash it returned.

An hour later, she stood dressed at the helm, her skin glowing, her dark locks drying in the breeze. She took readings from the wind vane, barometer, and anemometer, calculated their altitude, marked the placement of the sun, and then decided that she would go to the great cabin to record the measurements in the ship's log.

While Billy Lee was captain, Edith had grown accustomed to maintaining the log since Lee was so often distracted by one conquest or another. Back then, she had just begun to learn to write with her left hand, and so her additions were short and inelegant. Her script had improved, but slowly. Since becoming captain, Senlin had taken over the record. He had expectations of penmanship, spelling, and punctuation that verged on the fanatical. Edith left Senlin to fuss with his serifs and tittles because for some inconceivable reason, it made him happy. She hadn't cracked the log in months.

But today she was annoyed with him. His vacant glaring, which had only worsened in recent weeks and which made him seem simultaneously aloof and a little mad, was wearing thin. His lapses in focus worried her because it was his obsession, after all, that occupied them. If his determination was flagging, what hope did they have?

So, she decided to update the log in her clumsy, inadequate cursive just to remind him that he was not alone in this adventure.

She opened the great leather-bound book by the ribbon bookmark and scanned for the last entry. She was surprised to see how much Senlin had embellished the daily log. Lee had written in fragments, making the occasional observation, and she had been briefer still, but Senlin had apparently decided to narrate their comings and goings in elaborate detail. She felt doubly embarrassed. First, on his account because using a ship's log as a diary was like confessing to one's grocer. Second, she was embarrassed on her own account because, unexpectedly, she found that she was snooping. She no longer felt like she was standing in the great cabin. She suddenly felt she was in someone's bedroom.

Forgetting her original prank, she swatted the logbook closed.

But she had not been quick enough. A flourished *M* leapt from the closing page, and she absorbed a phrase from the narrative without meaning to.

She stood frozen over the closed book, reviewing the words like a startled sleeper reviews an unexpected noise in the middle of the night. Had she imagined it? Did it seem sinister only because she had taken it out of context? She pondered the phrase with growing anxiety until she realized she was holding her breath.

She forced herself to exhale.

The ship was empty. Her hair was still damp from her bath, but she felt the weight of her responsibilities, heavy as a yoke, return all at once.

She opened the log and found the line that had arrested her: "I see Marya all hours of the day. I fear that I am going mad."

She pulled out the chair, sat down, and read on.

Chapter Seven

I find myself in the unenviable position of having to rely upon another man's impression of my wife to correct my recollection of her. I don't know what I would do without Ogier's portrait of Marya to clear my muddled head.

—The *Stone Cloud*'s Logbook, Captain Tom Mudd

He felt like a marionette tangled in its string. It was difficult to move without getting a boot heel caught or snagging a button. The yarn was at once constricting and entirely insufficient; he was just as afraid of getting stuck as he was of tearing a hole in the fragile net. Looking down was an absurdity. The ground seemed as far off as the moon.

Every few feet he stopped his descent and hailed the weaver at the bottom of the web. But either the wind swallowed his salutations or she ignored them, because they were not returned. Since he could not be sure which it was, he had no choice but to struggle on, sliding and grappling his way deeper into the many-colored web.

Soon, he was close enough to see that she was a striking woman, though not in any fashionable way. Her features were shapely but strong to an almost masculine degree. She hardly seemed old enough to be a man's mother. Her bald head reminded him of a perfect hazelnut. She made no attempt to hide or adorn it. What might have proved a fatal blemish on another woman only made her more handsome.

She tamped the weft with a bone beater, adjusted the batten, and began weaving the next color, pulling yarn from an indistinguishable tangle that surrounded her. She gave no indication that she had noticed his approach or heard his hellos until he was nearly at the bottom of her prismatic funnel. Then, without looking up from her work, she said, "What is your name?" Her voice was light but impersonal, like a nurse in a busy hospital.

Senlin lay in an awkward sprawl before her, trying to project a modicum of dignity. "I am Captain Tom Mudd."

Her expression never shed its composure even as she set down her shuttle, reached into her robes, and extracted a pair of gleaming blade shears. She snipped a braid of thread at her feet.

Senlin plunged only a few inches before the web caught him again, but in that fraction of a second, his blood had time enough to turn from a fluid into a thrumming, electric current. Every part of him buzzed with panic.

"Be still, young man," she said. "Don't bounce around."

Senlin wanted to say that he wasn't bouncing, he was spasming, but his terror had fused his jaw for the moment, and all he could do was grunt in reply.

She looked at him for the first time, and whatever she saw seemed to confirm her initial impression. "Let me show you what the truth sounds like. My name is Madame Fulmala Bhata. Do you hear it? How it rings in the ear? Do you feel how the truth quivers through the thread, to your fingers and into your bones? You can feel the honesty of my pulse. The truth is as guileless as a child."

A bead the size of a walnut slid down a strand from a pipe in the ceiling above. She caught and opened the bead, removed a little scroll of paper, and uncurled the scrap with her thumbnails. "You sold two kegs of good rum to John Hamm not an hour ago," she said. "How did you come by the rum?"

"Piracy," Senlin said, his jaw finally loosening.

"An honest answer at last." She slipped the little note into her robes and resumed her weaving. "Now, we can talk. What is your name?"

"Tom Mudd is the name I have traveled under in recent months. But my name is Thomas Senlin."

"And was Thomas Senlin also a captain?"

"No, he was—*I* was the headmaster of a small village school."

"A teacher?" She seemed to find him more interesting now. When two new beads emerged from the pipe in the ceiling and slid down to her nest of yarn, she let them collect at her feet, unopened. "What did you teach?"

He wanted to pretend they were engaging in small talk rather than an interrogation. It seemed the only way to keep his nauseous fear in check. Of course, it was difficult to sound at ease while tangled up like a fly. "Oh, the usual, I suppose: reading, writing, mathematics, the natural sciences, history—"

She pounced in here. "Which history?"

"Which? The history that happened, I suppose," he said, laughter in his voice.

She was not at all amused. "History has nothing to do with what happened."

"How can you say that? It's apparent to me that you are responsible, at least partly, for the tapestry that holds the cove together. I've not been able to make sense of its pattern before, but those beads that slide down to you, they carry receipts, don't they? They tell you what to add to the record. So, the tapestry is like a ledger. An account of—"

"—of births and deaths, losses and sales, seasons and storms, debts, oaths, black scotches, marriages, adventures, songs, even jokes. Everything that is important to us."

"Incredible, incredible. You catch all of that with your thread?"

"Yes."

"Now it makes sense why the tapestry is full of symbols, little pictures, and hatch marks rather than letters and numbers. It's so the locals can read it, so it is of some use to them. You are their historian."

"I am not!" she said sharply. She wagged her bone comb at him. "I am a recorder. A recorder takes things down. A historian makes things up."

He saw that he'd goaded her, and though he was clearly at her mercy, he couldn't stop himself from arguing the point. "Well, that's hardly fair."

"I agree. It is unfair. A historian begins with an ending, and then he concocts a pleasing cause. It's a fairy tale."

"That's a ludicrous accusation. History is the narrative of time, and like any narrative, any story, there are some details that are necessarily glossed over, some that are included under the umbrella of anecdote and analogy. But the thrust of the story is not perverted by small omissions. If anything, it is clarified."

"Of course it is clarified! That's because all the confusing and muddling and disagreeing parts have been removed. It's clear because it's untrue! Who are these pious men writing the story of time anyway? To whom are they devoted? Every historian I've ever heard of has a benefactor or a master or a duty to his country. History is a love letter to tyrants written in the blood of the overrun, the forgotten, the expunged!" Her former decorum had fallen away entirely now, and Senlin glimpsed in her vehemence her son's passions. There was a little of that mania in her, too.

Senlin had had many philosophical debates in his time, but never while dangling in the air, safe as a man in a noose. The conversation felt surreal and also oddly nostalgic. He found he was nearly enjoying himself. "It is an unhappy but not a new notion that history is written by the victors. Yet I think it is the height of cynicism to throw out an entire discipline for a few errors."

"It is not cynical to admit that the past has been turned into a fiction. It is a story, not a fact. The real has been erased. Whole eras have been added and removed. Wars have been aggrandized and human struggle relegated to the margins. Villains are re-dressed as heroes. Generous, striving, imperfect men and women have been stripped of their flaws or plucked of their virtues and turned into figurines of morality or depravity. Whole societies have been fixed with motive and vision and equanimity where there was none. Suffering has been recast as noble sacrifice! Do you know why the history of the Tower is in such turmoil? Because too many powerful men are fighting for the pen, fighting to write their story over our dead bodies. They know what is at stake: immortality, the character of civilization, and influence beyond the ages. They are fighting to see who gets to mislead our grandchildren."

"Well, that rings a little true." Senlin frowned deeply. "I was misled by a false account of the Tower, once. I have often wondered why a man would write such a gross fabrication."

She smiled. It was a kind and sad expression. "You came, didn't you? You left your life, your school, your students, and you came to the Tower. You brought money, I suppose? You spent more than you could afford, perhaps? You brought your little fortune to the Tower and laid it on the altar, you and scores of other men and women like you. Can you really not imagine why someone would write such glamorous lies?"

It was a revelation, and as is so often the case with revelations, the thrill of discovery was quickly followed by embarrassment. Why had he not come to this conclusion earlier? The *Everyman's Guide*, which duped and flattered and dribbled out just enough truth to be convincing, was no nobler than an advertisement. He had been fooled into coming to the Tower and giving up what riches he had, and someone had profited from it.

"You are right, Madame Bhata. I have lost more than I can afford."

"Ah. So we come to it at last," she said, and for the first time she set aside all her work and paid him the full weight of her attention. "Tell me what happened."

Senlin told his tale as briefly as he could, though Madame Bhata interrupted frequently with questions. These, Senlin answered honestly. He laid bare his shortcomings and crimes, his alliances and enemies, and his hope for finding his lost wife. He even shared his strong suspicion that the commissioner of the Baths had placed a bounty on his head for the theft of a work of art, a confession that invited her to test his worth, to turn him in, as well she could and might.

But what was excruciating at first turned cathartic the more he talked. In telling his story, he discovered that he had developed definite ideas about his own motives and decisions. These ideas seemed to have formed in the ether of emotions and dreams, that woolly fog that lay outside the footlights of the conscious mind. They were not large revelations, but were rather like the little epiphanies one suffers and enjoys over a morning cup of tea.

For one, he had never understood why he had adopted the pseudonym Mudd. Mud was an obscenity and a pejorative in the Tower. It was a joke, and so he had assumed it was only archness and self-deprecation that had suggested the name to him. He had chosen it, after all, in a bleak moment. But that was not it, not really. His associations of mud, unlike the Tower's, were positive: It was the thing that announced spring, the thing that nursed life into blossom. It was the thing that could be turned into bricks, and those bricks made into homes and schools and libraries. It was mud that Marya had liked to stamp her boots in, just to tease and bait him. He had chosen the name because it embodied the Tower's unreasonable loathing of the lower world.

This and other little revelations whipped his narration along, and when he was done, he felt invigorated and also exposed.

"I hope you understand why I have been careful with my name and my story," he said. "If the wrong parties found out, my crew and my wife might suffer for it. I hope you will be discreet with what I've shared."

"It is a part of the record now. I will not hide it, Thomas Senlin. But I can console you with the fact that the men you fear never trouble to read the inferior lore of the inferior races. I think the secrets of Captain Mudd are safe enough, even though they stand in the open."

He knew she wouldn't offer him a better consolation, and so he moved finally to the purpose of this daring, draining visit. "Now that you know me, you know why I have come."

"You wish to seek your wife in Pelphia."

"Yes."

"You can enter Pelphia by the ringdom above it, by the Silk Reef."

Senlin was both puzzled and disappointed by the simple reply. "I read that it was sealed up after the war between Pelphia and Algez broke out. All the stairways were filled with rubble."

"What did I tell you about believing those histories? They are so full of holes! Did your book say anything about the trail of the hods? Nothing? Of course, nothing! Listen. At the heart of the Silk Gardens is the Golden Zoo. It is a relic of the world before the war."

"A zoo? Are there animals there?"

"Perhaps. I'm not sure. But there is a man there who may help you. His name is Luc Marat. He is in charge of what little there is to be in charge of. He rescues hods, I've been told, and has turned the zoo into a kind of mission. He knows the trail of the hods very well. He can show you a way into Pelphia."

"Is he dangerous, this Marat?"

"He is a mystic, and they are naturally pacifistic. But he is also a zealot, and they are not slow to anger. His ideas are unpopular, and there are many in the Tower who'd like to see him hanged. So, to many he is a criminal. He is suspicious of strangers, naturally. I don't know what he'll make of you. Not everyone is as friendly as I am."

The information sounded plausible: a hideout, an outlaw of some compassion and influence, and an overlooked entrance into Pelphia. It might be tricky to navigate the portals of the hods, but could it really be any more difficult than piracy?

Senlin's heart began to pile hope upon the possibility, consecrating the rumor, until it seemed to him a virtual certainty: This mystic, this Luc Marat, would lead him into Pelphia.

"Will he expect to be paid?" Senlin asked.

"It would be wise to go with a peace offering, yes. I understand his mission has a great appetite for books—all sorts."

Senlin was surprised. His time in New Babel had shown him how relatively rare literacy was among the Tower's working populations. A mission that had a need for books could only mean one thing: Marat was trying to educate the hods. It was a noble aspiration, and Senlin wondered if he might not find a kindred spirit in the zealot Marat.

His reverie was interrupted by what he mistook for the cawing of a crow. He turned in time to see a shrieking man plunge past the naked frame of the cove. The spectacle was not sufficient to rouse Madame Bhata's interest. Her shuttle swam on, cutting through the weft like a fish through reeds.

"I have one more question," she said, now absently and to an even more absent Senlin, who continued to stare at the sky. He was trying to convince himself that he had imagined the falling man, that it was another hallucination. Then her question brought him back to the present: "Why do you take Crumb?"

He hardly hesitated; it was the scantest whiff of a pause before he got his answer out. "I do not." He sounded indignant; he sounded convincing. But she was not convinced.

"I am surprised you would lie about such an obvious weakness after telling me so many secrets."

"Madame, I am not lying. I was exposed to it twice, unwillingly, and the last time was months ago."

"And yet you are under its sway now. I recognized it as soon as I saw you flopping about in my web. Oh, you addicts are all the same; you deceive yourself so well you think everyone is deceived."

"I swear on my life: I am the victim of an overdose. I do not take Crumb."

She stared at him, her bearing frigid. The blade shears emerged again with a chilling nonchalance. Senlin thought of the six empty coats that turned in the wind; he thought of the six lost souls. She had snipped them from the thread of history to keep their dishonesty from coloring her account.

The shears in her hand rasped open. He was as pale as she was serene.

Then, unaccountably, she stopped. Madame Bhata sighed and said, "Go. Go look for your wife, Thomas Mudd Senlin. What good does it do to punish a man who so stubbornly punishes himself?"

Chapter Eight

I knew a boy in school who rolled out of his bunk in his sleep, struck his head, and never woke again. I console myself with this terrible memory whenever I look down at the chasm that follows me like a shadow. We are, all of us, living at a deadly height.

—The *Stone Cloud*'s Logbook, Captain Tom Mudd

A ship's rigging is as expressive as a violin. The jute and block instruments are capable of performing happy minuets when the crew is glad, reveries when they are contemplative, and nocturnes when they are melancholy.

Presently, it seemed to the crew of the *Stone Cloud*, the rigging sawed at the minor chords of a funeral dirge.

They stood with heads hanging in the furnace glow of the afternoon sun. Their captain paced before them in a state of great frustration. Despite his black mood, they could not help but wonder where the tricorne hat on his head had come from.

"Over a rat?" Senlin said, coming to a halt before Voleta.

"A squirrel," she corrected, and with her hair still over her face, raised the little animal in a cupped hand for her captain's inspection. The creature, which had recovered from being bounced upon the floor, blinked its black eyes at him with a quiet sentience.

"So, you stole a squirrel," he said, pointing at her. "Then when the owner came to claim it, you"—his finger turned to Iren—"threw him through the wall." Iren looked uncharacteristically abashed. "And where were you during all of this, Adam?"

"Holding a pistol under the table."

Senlin rubbed the back of his neck. "Of course you were."

"What would you have had us do? That jobber was threatening her," Adam said, nodding at his sister. "Who knows what he might've done."

"This is your justification for killing a man and earning us a black scotch from the one port—*the one port*—disreputable enough to let us in?" Senlin said, looking to his first mate for support. She stood with her arms crossed, staring resolutely at the distant saw of mountain peaks. She looked like she was holding a bee in her mouth. Senlin frowned and soldiered on, unaided. "Has it come to this? Are we now resolved to either surrender or murder when faced with adversity? Are there no degrees between the two disgraces?"

Senlin turned to Iren, who drew herself to attention and stood with her chin raised, basking in the shame like a stoic. "They are young and impetuous, but you are old enough to understand the heavy consequence of decisions lightly made. You..." Senlin's agitation abruptly crested, and he pulled back from saying any more. He composed himself and concluded, "Iren, we will continue this in my quarters."

Hoping to make amends, Adam retreated to his formal duties as pilot. "What's our destination, Captain?"

"I'll have a course for you shortly. For the time being, find us a quiet cloud to stick our heads in. And please, let's all try to keep the killing to a minimum."

Senlin opened his cabin window to invite the light and the passing chatter of flocking birds. Books and charts, a collage of research, lay upon the table. He stamped two cups atop the sprawl and poured a share of rum.

"There are many pirate customs I do not understand," he said, inspecting his pewter cup. "For example, the hanging of chimes and rattles to scare away gremlins, who for some reason require absolute quiet to work their mischief. Or the belief that blue is bad luck, and yellow, good. Or the widespread phobia of whistling, which apparently taunts the wind into blowing harder." He sipped the potent liquor. "But reconciling disagreements over a dram of rum—that is a custom I can appreciate. If I ever get home again, I think I will introduce the practice to the county school board."

Iren took her seat like a rockslide takes a road. She looked miserable and defeated, an uncomfortable expression on such a formidable frame. Her iconic square jaw hung loose as a jowl.

"I remember the moment when I decided I liked you," Senlin pressed on with an amiable tilt of his cup. "We were on our way to see Finn Goll, and you confessed that you might be compelled to strangle me if it turned out I was a thief. If it came to that, you said you hoped I would fight back.

"At first, I thought you were being droll, but then you reminded me of our lessons—you told me not to lunge, told me to keep my head— and I realized you were in absolute earnest. I thought to myself, 'Here is a person of conscience. Here is a person who believes in fairness.'"

Senlin waited for her to comment, but she only lifted her shoulders and let them fall.

"Iren, you are not a murderer." Huddling over the table, he tried to interrupt her downcast gaze. "Tell me, what happened in the pub?"

"I lost my head," she said, her voice full of puzzlement. "He was terrorizing someone I love, and I . . ."

Senlin sat back in amazement. "Someone you love?"

"Voleta." She looked up to see if he understood.

Marya appeared at his elbow, the soft curtain of her hair grazing his neck. "Will wonders never cease? Finally, a little romance has bloomed upon your ship, Tom."

"I don't miss much about the life I left, but I miss Finn Goll's children." Iren spoke without emotion, but she could not keep her turmoil from creasing her brow. "The way they looked at me—that's how Voleta looks at me. She sees through the scars and the scowling; she doesn't see the bloody trail behind me. She doesn't know what I did with my life."

"No, not a romance," Marya said, drawing a fingernail lightly down his cheek. "Old mother hen sits upon an empty nest."

"Shut up!" Senlin snapped. Marya evaporated like a splash of water upon a hot stove.

Iren's wide-eyed expression of shock pierced him, and he quickly washed the words from the air with a wave of his hands. "Do not talk like that, like our lives are published and done, as if we cannot change. You are in the prime of your life."

"Either the flies are speeding up, or I'm slowing down." A distant caw drew their attention to the window, and through it they observed a spatter of black stars cross the white sky. They watched the constellation of birds dissolve into the sun's glare in silence. "She's not like us," Iren said firmly. "I would very much like to keep it that way."

Senlin reached across the table to touch her arm. The amazon began to recoil but stopped. She let his hand remain. "Iren, you are the only reason I haven't slipped and fallen on my sword. I am alive because of you. That is one and only one of the many admirable things you have done with your life. You are an example of courage and experience, which I have benefitted from, and which I know Voleta benefits from, too. She is better off in your company than out of it."

Senlin could see her expression begin to harden again like a lake in winter. The moment of tenderness was ending. "Perhaps," she said.

"We just need to find a better way for you to express your feelings than hiking men through walls."

"Aye, sir," she said. "May I be excused?"

"Of course."

Once she was gone, Senlin reflected on her confession with a mixture of relief and worry. The fact that Voleta held so much sway over Adam and Iren might one day pose a problem. The girl might split the crew. Conversely, if ever their inhospitable circumstances began to fray their spirits, she might be the binding that held them all together.

Feeling disquieted, he turned to his research for distraction if not comfort. He consulted the ribs of his aerorod and began to study a ringdom he'd dismissed in the past as a defunct and unapproachable port: the Silk Reef.

According to the works in Billy Lee's modest library, the Silk Reef was once a splendid park and silk farm. Before decay and rumor had rechristened it the Silk Reef, it had been known as the Silk Gardens. The silk it produced was unparalleled in strength and lightness and was the preferred material among the elite makers of airship envelopes—

A violent drumming on the cabin door startled him from his research. Before the rattle had left the hinges, Edith charged into the room. He came to his feet, readying himself for news of some new calamity, but she made no announcement. In fact, she hardly looked at him. She stamped about in a circle as if looking for somewhere to spit.

"Well, Mister Winters, what does half a dozen beats on my door signal?" Senlin said. "An argument, I suppose."

He said it in jest, but the years she had spent managing foremen and field bosses had left her sensitive to patronization. Her subordinates had often resorted to mockery since they could not defy her openly. When she brought up a botched job a foreman didn't wish to take credit for, he might loudly ruminate on a woman's aptitude for melodrama. He might call her *miss* or *girl* or, woe-unto-him, *dolly*.

Fighting to contain her misplaced ire, she cleared her throat and said, "How are you?"

Senlin could not imagine a more baffling question. To bolt into a room, red-faced and seething, only to propose weak small talk seemed the height of absurdity. He chuckled, and this tweaked her last nerve.

She spoke in a furious rush: "Why would you hide the fact that you're seeing things? Not just things, but your lost wife. No wonder you can't hold a conversation or finish a thought. You're addled! You pretend to be with us, but you are not. You're off with her. And perhaps you can't help it, perhaps it is the Crumb poisoning you still, but you should not have hidden it from me."

At first, Senlin's gaze darted about like a man absorbing an ambush. His natural guilt nearly propelled him into a blubbering apology, but he was momentarily diverted by a different revelation. "You read my journal."

"It's not a journal, Tom! It's the ship's log. It is a public document."

"That—" he began in a shout, and immediately realized he had no defense. Moreover, he had no sense of why he'd personalized something so procedural. He hadn't set out to turn the log into his confessor. In the beginning, he just felt compelled to explain the reasoning behind some of his more...*unusual* orders. That explanation required he disclose his intention to dock in Pelphia, and that required him to relay some details about Marya. The rest of the confession, the fact that his lost wife haunted him, had just slipped out. "That is a valid point," he concluded mildly.

"Is she here now? Is she in the room with us?"

"Yes." His expression was as inscrutable as spilled ink. "She is not always with me. The torment ebbs and flows." He glanced at Marya seated across the table from him. Marya, donning her red sun helmet, gave a coquettish wave. "Presently it flows."

Edith chewed and swallowed a few passionate words. She reminded herself that he was not just the captain. He was her friend. And as her friend, he was suffering. The recriminations could wait for the moment.

She took a deep and composing breath. "What is she doing?"

"Tell the hussy I'm playing the bassoon," Marya said.

"She's calling you names."

"Which ones?"

"I'd rather not say."

"Is she usually like that, your wife?"

"No, not at all."

"Has it gotten any better?" Edith slid into the chair Marya occupied.

"I'd call it 'wedded bliss,' wouldn't you?" Marya said, sliding out to make room. She threw an arm around Edith's neck and put on a conspiratorial smirk, as if she and Edith were old friends. Senlin wanted to clutch his head and run from the room.

"Not really," he said.

Edith looked him squarely in the eyes. "Has it gotten any worse?"

He did not glance away. "No, it's about the same. I'm still hopeful I'll improve. The overdose can't last forever."

"Hopeful," she said in a tone that seemed to oppose the word. She was not without sympathy, but his secrecy had left her feeling a little betrayed.

She tried to think of a question that would give her some clearer sense of his state of mind without making it seem like an inquisition. "Do you talk to her, to your ghost?"

"No, I've made a concerted effort not to converse with the figment."

Frowning at the offense, Marya stamped over to his wardrobe. She threw open the doors and dove her arms inside. To Edith's eye, nothing shifted in the room. He alone witnessed the geysers of silk robes and bedding she flung into the air.

He tried his best to appear unperturbed. "Will you tell the crew?"

"How can I? If I told them, I would...I would have to take command," she said.

Senlin nodded at this as if the statement were an unmanageable but anticipated bill. He knew what course his affairs would take if he were deposed. He would be an obligation at first, then a hardship, and then he'd become a millstone cracking the necks of his once-crew. His farcical quest for his lost wife would end. The ghost of Marya would haunt him into madness. Eventually, the crew would have no choice but to strand him upon some dire crag and seek a better future for themselves.

The self-pity of this vision was as repugnant to him as it was visceral. He shook his head and said again, "Will you tell them?"

"No," Edith said cautiously. "I don't think they'd follow me. They still have a lot of warm feelings for you, Tom. I told you when we started: I don't want to be captain. But I also don't want to die. If you're seeing devils, then you're a danger to us all."

"Yet, while bedeviled, I have kept the crew fed. I have kept the ship whole. I may be haunted, Edith, but I am not defective," Senlin said, rallying some pride. "You say the crew is still with me, but what about you?"

"It's not a question of loyalty; it's a question of leadership. We seem to be wandering about, waiting for a miracle, and I'm not sure it's coming, Tom. How long must we tread air and wait?" She realized she was saying too much. She was putting herself and the crew between Senlin and his wife, which was not fair. And yet the impropriety of it did not make her concerns any less legitimate.

"Someone has to lead," she said as neutrally as she could.

"And it will be me. I have found a way into Pelphia. I know where we must go and what we must do. Our days of wandering over the desert are almost at an end."

He related what he'd learned from Madame Bhata about the Silk Reef and the mystic-zealot, Luc Marat. He told her of Bhata's advice that Pelphia could be reached through the tunnels the hods used, and that they only needed books to bribe Marat into showing them the way.

"You're going to give him our books?"

"Our books?" he said, picking up one of his inherited aeronautical texts. "No, no, no, if we lose these, we'll be left fumbling in the dark. They're essential to our navigation, and besides, there aren't enough of them to fill a schoolbag. They wouldn't make much of a peace offering."

"So, where do we get more?"

This was the question that had troubled him since he had crawled out of Madame Bhata's web. He sensed where the question would lead, and he didn't want to follow it to its conclusion. But it couldn't be helped. The fact was, they were entirely without refuge, and the sky was rapidly shrinking now that Captain Mudd's game was known. They couldn't pretend to be half pirates anymore. They couldn't afford to be patient, and they hadn't the resources to be daring.

There was only one type of vulnerable target that reliably carried books: the ships whose captains had been inspired by the literature to come to the Tower.

He knew what they must do, and he had no illusions about what it meant. He would not be the same man when he met his wife again.

He said, "We're going to rob a tourist."

Chapter Nine

One need not be royalty to be in high demand. Even the plowman and the dairymaid are thought exotic in the ringdoms of Babel.

—*Everyman's Guide to the Tower of Babel*, IV. X

Senlin, Edith, and Iren crowded on the narrow porch of the picturesque cottage. Blue and purple pansies, frozen by the mountain passage, thawed in window boxes under painted shutters. The jute welcome mat underfoot was clean and squared to the door, and the brass knocker was so polished it beaded with the midday light.

Senlin had to fight the urge to take off his hat.

He knocked again, and they listened to the sound of someone—two someones—trotting back and forth inside. Beneath the pressed-tin house number, someone had drawn in a fine cursive, *Seventeen Locust Lane*.

Iren's harpoon had passed halfway through one of the porch's posts. At the end of the tether, the *Stone Cloud* bobbed, looking no larger than a kite. The *Seventeen Locust Lane* was an uprooted chalet, rigged to a quilted sack that was fired by a tar-paper duct running from the chimney. To call the thing a ship was quite generous. Beleaguered as his own vessel was, at least Senlin could take pride in the fact that it would never be confused for a flying tearoom.

Most tourists were easy to pick out. Their ships were cobbled and converted, pasted and pinned together. They rode in gondolas that had once been hay wagons, brewers' vats, and bathtubs. Once, Senlin had seen a tourist flying on a living horse that dangled under a balloon in a harness. The horse looked entirely humiliated and a little airsick.

For every hobbyist who made it over the mountain range, a dozen others were rebuffed by the wind or done in by the cold. The ones who lasted long enough to break upon the valley rarely survived long. Most fell victim to pirates. The stouter tourists soon discovered no port would have them, and they had no choice but to crash-land in the Market or worse: begin the mortifying, and still perilous, voyage home.

Senlin had always made a point of leaving these intrepid, albeit misguided, souls alone. It seemed poor sport to harass such defenseless dreamers.

But that was before Captain Mudd had made a name for himself; that was before a stack of books was all that stood between him and his wife.

It was taking too long for whoever it was inside to answer the door, and the delay had begun to make him nervous. Visions of a loaded cannon being wheeled around danced in his head. He was about to direct Iren to break the door in when it flew open on its own accord, startling them all.

The woman in the doorway had a waist as slender as a sheaf of wheat. Her hair was rolling and golden, and she wore a pinafore that evoked a pastoral innocence so intense, he nearly mistook it for dim-wittedness. She had a serene, slim face that made her age hard to guess, but Senlin supposed she was perhaps twenty-five years old. She had a pleasant smile and a better curtsy. "Please, come in," she said. "We were just sitting down to tea."

Surprised by this cordial reception, the trio of pirates filed silently into the cottage. Iren, who'd been holding her chain belt like a garrote, discreetly rewrapped the weapon about her waist. The interior reminded her of Finn Goll's home, and something about that association made her feel a little ashamed of what they were preparing to do.

The parlor had paintings on the walls and candlesticks on the mantel and many other domestic touches that signaled it had been a home long before it had become a ship. A worn but colorful rug lay under the rustic dining set, which held an heirloom teapot, cups, and a pristine doily skirt. At the head of the table in the highest-backed chair sat a man with a plump and dark mustache. It was the mustache of a pensive but proud character. His shirtsleeves were starched, his vest fitted, and his watch chain gold. He seemed accustomed to pleasantries and respect.

"Nancy, I see you have found some company," he said, rising from his seat with practiced poise. Senlin had heard him and the woman dashing about a moment before, preparing both the tea and this reception, and so it seemed a funny piece of theater to feign such composure now. Though of course it wasn't theater: It was polite society, a thing Senlin had almost entirely forgotten. Still, he knew what to do when the mustachioed man offered his hand. "I am Dr. Louis Pencastle from Milford."

"Captain Thomas Senlin from Isaugh."

"Captain Senlin?" Edith said.

"Oh, there's no point in lying. I know Milford. It's only two hours by train from my old stoop."

The doctor looked confused, though he did not pull his hand from Senlin's too quickly. "And I know Isaugh. But what is all this about lying?"

"I've made my name something of a liability. So I often go by another."

"Well. Travel does strange things to a man, I suppose," Dr. Pencastle said affably. "Whoever you are, wherever you hail from, you are our first visitors, and so we welcome you to join us for tea."

"That is quite generous. But I'm sorry, we can't stay long."

"Come, come! You staved my porch with your anchor. You can drink a cup of tea," he said, spreading his arms toward the slim woman who had already begun to pour. "Besides, we are celebrating. We are at the end of a long journey. This afternoon, we'll be tying up in a Tower port for the first time."

"Which port?" Iren asked, and though she wasn't trying to be particularly gruff, her voice was enough to make the woman flinch, as if something had just been thrown very near her head.

"New Babel," the older gentleman said, making a good show of addressing Iren without cowering, though no one would have blamed him if he had. "There is a thriving industry there, which I have reason to believe includes the production of a formidable narcotic called Chrom. Since I read of it, I have imagined all sorts of possible applications for such a drug, from surgery to toothaches."

"New Babel will eat you alive."

"Much as a city of any size might devour an unmindful visitor, I'm sure. And we haven't decided for certain on our destination. We might dock in Pelphia. I've read that travelers can expect quite a fine reception there," Pencastle said.

Senlin bit down on a smirk, but not before the doctor recognized the pitying expression. "Oh, don't mistake me; I'm not reckless, Captain Senlin. I am not one of those lads who jumps in a barrel and flies to the Tower to find fortune and fame. I am a physician of twenty years. Last week I removed my shingle from a thriving practice, and I did so for the express purpose of furthering my education. I have read of the many innovations in medicine unique to the Tower. I have come to learn for the benefit of my patients and my peers. I am determined to go home a better man than I came."

"I once shared a similar aspiration," Senlin said. "But I think you may be surprised by how swift and morbid your education will be. You and your wife—"

"Oh, no, no, this is my daughter," the doctor said.

Flustered by this mistake, which seemed to reveal much about his own character, Senlin apologized to the blushing and downcast young woman. "I'm so sorry for the error. My eyesight is poor. I'm sure you are a lovely and youthful and..."

"Tom," Edith interrupted his dithering. She removed the square of burlap that had been tucked in her belt and shook the sack open. "I think it would be kinder if you just got to the point."

"Yes," he said, and composed himself. "I'm afraid I'm going to need to borrow some books."

Senlin gave Iren and Edith a discreet signal. The two left the parlor to go through the other rooms in the house. Nancy ran after them saying, "Oh, I'll show you my room."

"What is this?" the doctor said, marching from foot to foot, trying to decide whether to stay and reason with the visitor in his parlor or chase after the two aeronauts taking liberties with his home. "What do you mean 'borrow my books'?"

"I imagine you have a copy of the *Everyman's Guide*?"

"All eight volumes," the doctor said, tugging at the points of his vest. "And the index. How could I have come without them?"

"What about Tolbert's *Oral History of the Tower*?"

"I own a first edition."

"And Franboise's *Anthropologies of Babel*?"

"Of course! And since you're quizzing me: I also have John Clark's *Reflection on a Pillar* and Phillip Borge's *The Stylus of Nations*. As I said, I'm no boy in a barrel! I come prepared. I have brought scores of books that elucidate the Tower from every angle, every approach."

"Well, I am taking them."

"You cannot. I need them; I need them for reference. How am I to know the customs where we alight? How am I to navigate the courts of nobles and the institutions of learning without a guide? You would leave a blind man in a strange forest?"

"I would send a blind man back home," Senlin said, trying for calm amid the doctor's growing distress. "This may be difficult to believe, but I am saving you and your daughter from disaster. The Tower you expect to find and the one that stands just there outside your sills are not twins but opposites. I was like you once. I came to the Tower expecting to improve my knowledge of the world. But truth is not something the Tower parts with gladly. Certainly none of it seeped into those treacherous guides and philosophies."

"Please don't insult me! If they're so valueless, why steal them? No, you are pleading with your own conscience here, and I won't let you use me to assuage your guilt. I opened my door to you. I extended my hand, and this is my reward?" The doctor's collar strained about his swelling neck. He raised his chin to Senlin, standing nearly on the toes of the captain's boots. "You are a thief. A pirate! And like any pirate, you were not born to the life; you were driven to it by your own cynicism. You act as if you deserve enrichment at my expense, and then you have the audacity to excuse this, this—*narcissism* with the feeble assurance that you are doing me a favor?"

"Believe me, if you approach Pelphia, you will be shot down."

"Bah! You pose as some sort of scholar, reciting book titles and speaking of knowledge. But what sort of scholar goes around ruining and changing his name? A charlatan, that's who!"

A short cry sounded from a room in the house, and the doctor lurched toward the door, crying, "Nancy! Nancy! Don't you lay a hand on her!"

Senlin caught him by the shoulders before he could leave, and the panicked doctor wheeled about and slapped Senlin fiercely on the cheek.

The blow sobered the doctor more than it hurt Senlin, who merely exercised his jaw and tightened his grip on Pencastle's shirt. When their eyes met again, the doctor saw in the pirate captain's gaze a challenge he did not feel ready to meet, and his posture softened.

For his part, Senlin found the doctor's argument convincing. He had tried to remain as he was and become only what he must. He had tried to be the gentleman pirate, the scholarly cad, and had failed on both counts. Perhaps his stubborn duplicity had contributed to his sickness, had stoked his tormenting visions.

Senlin didn't know whether he wanted to congratulate the doctor on his diagnosis or throttle him for the insult.

Nancy rushed into the room, followed closely by Iren and Edith, both carrying sacks that bulged with the corners of books. "Please, please," Nancy said through tears, clutching a thick little book, "don't take my diary. It is my confidant; it is my little soul. Take the silver! Take the china! *Please* leave my book."

Her pleading pierced Senlin. He dropped his hold on her father. "I'm sorry we have traumatized you. You may keep your book, Nancy."

"I'm sure my daughter is much consoled. Don't pretend you have been reasonable. This is not reason. This is violence!"

"It is exasperation," Senlin said, looking sick with loathing and anger.

"You robber! You bully! I don't believe you were ever anything else."

Edith stepped forward briskly and boxed the man on the ear. "That's enough," she said as Pencastle swung back around, cradling his ear. "Just because you don't recognize mercy doesn't mean you haven't been shown it."

"But why must he take my books?" the doctor pleaded, his chin gleaming with spittle, his composure utterly shattered.

"Because the Tower has asked for them," Senlin said.

Chapter Ten

In the natural world there are two varieties of awe:
the carnal awe associated with reproduction, and
the hypnotic awe experienced by the prey of certain
predators, such as the stoat.

After years of observation, I am still not sure
which variety of awe the Tower inspires.

—*Reflections on a Pillar*, John Clark

Voleta Boreas had never been one for daydreams or idle reflection. Why anyone would pretend to be elsewhere when there was so much of the present to experience was an absolute mystery to her. She disliked sleep, too, for similar reasons. Sleep was like an eclipse: an unsettling interruption of a perfectly good day. She did nap, but only in precarious spots, on rails, prows, and in the rigging, because it was impossible to sleep deeply while balanced on an edge. She was vigilant, tireless, and constantly seeking novelty.

In short, she was the perfect lookout.

From the moment they had alighted from the Port of Goll, she had made it her business to keep the crew of the *Stone Cloud* safe from ambush. She possessed a singular talent for peering into the gnat swarm of merchants, cruisers, warships, and tourists and identifying trouble while it was still distant and evadable.

Spotting pirates was an art. Just as any shell could be home to a hermit crab, any ship could be a pirate ship. (They were proof enough of that!) Despite the insistence of countless adventure stories, pirates never flew black banners or bony flags. They often looked quite innocent. The only reliable way to separate the pirates from the law-abiding public was to mark their course. Ships that prowled in circles, or shadowed other ships, or leapt rapidly between currents made her suspicious. If such a vessel ever veered to intercept the *Cloud*, Voleta would call for a course change, and they would escape before the trap could be sprung.

Though it wasn't just pirates she had to worry about.

A trail of looted merchants lay in their wake, any of which might like a crack at them. And then there was the *Ararat*, the commissioner's flagship, which carried enough guns to decapitate a mountain.

The captain was convinced Commissioner Pound would stop at nothing to get his stolen painting back, and he exhorted Voleta on a near daily basis to keep an eye out for the dreadnaught. She needed little goading to be vigilant; they were all well acquainted with Pound's brutal tactics. He had sunk an innocent merchant and devastated an entire port just to get at the captain.

Early in their voyage, Voleta had asked why they didn't just sell or dump the painting since it was such a trouble. The captain replied, "I would throw it overboard in an instant if I thought it would make an end to the commissioner's chase. But, unhappily for us, the painting is both a repellent and a lure. Pound won't blast us from the sky so long as he thinks we have it, but neither will he call off his pursuit until he has pried it from our grasp."

Fortunately for them, the *Ararat* cast a unique silhouette—like a pillbox hanging from three black plums—which made it easy to identify. The *Stone Cloud*, on the other hand, was innocuous and easily overlooked. Voleta had spent many hours on the soft crown of the ship's envelope seated in a dimple of warm silk, watching the skies for that awful profile. She had spotted the *Ararat* in the distance on several occasions, and they had taken the precaution of ducking inside a cloud for a few hours. The evasions had become almost routine.

Yet, today was far from routine. Today, for the first time in memory, Voleta daydreamed.

It was Squit's fault. The squirrel loved to be chased, and Voleta loved to oblige her, especially when everyone else aboard was in a foul mood, which they inexplicably had been since returning with sacks of books from the flying cottage. While the rest of the crew grumped below, Voleta pursued the flying squirrel through the rigging.

For nearly a half hour, Squit eluded her with ease. After a great deal of effort, Voleta managed to herd the wily thing onto the top of the envelope. The squirrel's paws drummed across the balloon like fingers on a tabletop. Voleta reached for her, but rather than retreat, Squit darted forward, ran up her sleeve, popped out her collar, and tickled up her neck into her hair. It felt like an electric jolt had run up her arm and out the top of her head.

Exhausted and exhilarated, she threw herself down onto the voluminous mattress. Squit curled into a ball inside her tresses and quickly fell asleep. Voleta lay in a daze, staring up at the naked sky.

She wondered how long Squit had been in the little rattan crate she had liberated her from. Days? Months? Had she been bred or had she been captured? Voleta pictured the tender creature pacing back and forth for hours, bumping her head against the same limit like the pendulum of a clock. How had she not gone mad or lame? Voleta imagined herself shrunken down to the size of the squirrel. She imagined digging at the floor of the crate, digging until her fingers bled and the board was stained and gouged, digging until that exercise was all she had and all she was, digging without hope of escape.

She saw Rodion, her old ringmaster and pimp, standing over her in the dark while she pretended to sleep in her cot. The other girls slept in big, plush beds with fine linen sheets, but they had to share them with horrible men who seemed to be digging at the floors of their own hidden cages. She did not envy those girls. Her own cot, tucked in a corner of her changing room backstage at the Steam Pipe, was a privilege of her stardom. But her fame did not protect her from Rodion's lust. She knew what he was thinking as he lurked in her room because he had often told her of his vile dilemma. He'd say, "I can't decide if I should sell you or spend you myself."

She had lain listening to him pant for hours.

Then a familiar shape broke through the glaze of memory, and she realized she was staring insensibly, blindly at the *Ararat*.

She could not believe it. She stuck out her arm, blocking the fortress-like gondola with her thumb, and then blinked her eyes back and forth, calculating the distance: half a league. Impossible. The rim of the ship sparkled where helmets, guns, and grappling hooks refracted the sunlight.

The *Ararat* was preparing for battle.

They had been spotted.

Knowing that the *Ararat* would not immediately blow them from the sky was cold comfort. The crew of the *Stone Cloud* would be spared a guttering meteoric death only because Pound meant to cripple and board their ship.

Senlin knew the commissioner was a vindictive sort. Pound had taken great personal satisfaction in seeing Tarrou, a once beloved fixture of his galas, publicly shamed, beaten, and condemned to the life of a hod. And Tarrou had just been a little tardy on his bills. Senlin had burgled and humiliated the tyrant. Their fate would be far worse than slavery, of that he was certain.

Senlin was resolved to preserve his crew from capture and torture at the hands of the commissioner. If that meant scuttling the ship and killing all aboard, he would. He couldn't say whether this determination was cowardly or merciful. He tried not to dwell on it.

"It's coming on us fast," Edith said, shielding her eyes. The *Ararat* had the sun behind it. The *Stone Cloud* hung unprotected in the glare. "Up or down, Captain?"

He finished buttoning his coat and straightened his tricorne as if it were the rudder of his thoughts. The sky was spotless. It was the sort of crystalline day that precedes summer, the sort of day that would've once transfixed his students, ruining even his best lesson. Now, as then, he would've paid any sum for a cloud.

There was nowhere to hide, except the pinnacle shroud of the Tower, the so-called Collar of Heaven, which was by all reports a lethal fog. It was far too distant for them to reach in time anyway.

No, they had to descend. The *Ararat* could keep pace with them in a descent, of course, but Senlin suspected the big warship would not be able to rebound and climb again as swiftly. If he could get the *Ararat* to pursue them to a shallow enough altitude, the commissioner's dreadnaught might even be driven into the ground. The *Stone Cloud* would play the matador's cape.

"Mr. Boreas, close the flue and open the vents. We're going down. How much ballast can we spare?"

"The tank is full," Edith said. "Otherwise, we're running light. We may have to jettison the furniture."

"This will be exciting," he said. "Voleta, Iren, get your hatchets. You're on line duty. If they get a hook in us, cut it loose."

"Aye, sir," Voleta said but didn't move. None of them did. They stood as if bolted to the deck, staring over his head at the closing warship.

The *Ararat* shared one thing in common with the ships of tourists: It looked nothing like a boat. The ship's designers had rejected any fanciful homage to a nautical cousin in favor of a more utilitarian and fearsome design. It was a castle: crenellated, hatched for gunners, and possessed of a drawbridge door. It was as black as tar, but beneath that lacquer stood the bones of a forest—hundreds of trees had been stripped and bent and banded together into a hull so toughened it could rebuff a five-pound cannonball. Its belligerent size made it capable of driving another ship into a wall or hammering it to the ground. It couldn't be fended off, and once seized by its hooks, it could not be escaped.

Senlin stamped the deck with his aerorod. His sometimes map, sometimes club rang like a gavel. Everyone startled at the noise.

"Where is my crew?" he said, searching their eyes that turned and shied and blinked. "Where are the brave souls who once drove off the *Ararat* without a ship or a single cannon to assist them? Where is that audacious gang who shrugged off their masters and reclaimed their right to pursue their will and whim? This company of mercenaries we face today fight for nothing. They stand for a wage. They stand for ambition, for promotion, for medals on their breast. They fight for a man who commands no respect, a man who must wear a mask because he is allergic to the world. He hides because he is afraid—afraid of us, and well he should be! We fight to be free, and we war for one another. Our friendship makes us dangerous; we take courage in our fidelity. So, I ask again: Where is my crew? Where is my crew?"

His speech broke the plaster of fear that had hardened about their hearts and limbs. They sprang to the helm and the rails. Iren uncrated their motley collection of weapons, their cutlasses and sabers, pistols and muskets. Voleta fetched the line axes and refilled the coal pail, while her brother studied the barometer and anemometer at his station, divining from those antique instruments how far they could fall before the ground would catch them. Edith sealed the hatches and locked the great cabin, and then set about helping Iren load the guns with swift and steady hands.

There was a fluttering sensation in Senlin's stomach as the ship began the aggressive descent. The wind whistled up about them and the lines groaned with the lightened load. Adam was a reliable pilot, but even so the drop felt a little too precipitous. Senlin hoped he hadn't cheered the young man into recklessness.

Below, the Market looked like the cross section of a lung: the branching aisles, the dense tissue of tarps and tents, and the wider passages of the railroad divided and forked and halved again. Their descent had set them in a sluggish southern current, and the *Ararat*, on a higher, fleeter draft, was moving quickly to overshadow them. Watching the birds swoop and flock between the narrowing ships, Senlin waited for any sign that the wind was changing in their favor. He saw none. He wished they were a bird, turning and climbing as they pleased, rather than this tumbling leaf!

"It was a fine speech, Tom, a classic bit of rhetoric. You could've been a statesman if you weren't such a sentimental fool," the specter of Marya said from his side. Her cheeks were flushed and her mouth full as if she'd just drunk something that was very hot. She petted him as she spoke. "But you can't talk the wind into changing. There's really nothing else to be done now."

He was disturbed to see she had begun to saw at one of the thick jute cords that tethered the ship to the hydrogen envelope. He recognized the knife. It belonged in a drawer in the kitchen of his cottage; it was his knife, a knife that he'd used to scale fish and slice fruit. The jute frayed as she worked. "You promised you'd keep them from falling into the commissioner's lap. Keep your promise. Grab a knife, Tommy, and start sawing. We're running out of sky."

"Please. Please leave me alone. I can't—" Senlin said in a strangled whisper.

"Oh, so you can hear me?" She stopped sawing for a moment and considered his face, wrinkled from pleading. "This is your good knife. You scolded me for using it to trim the broom, once. Do you remember that? You treated me like a child. I wasn't your wife, really. I was a pupil. We should face that fact together. It was all a little sick, what you did, Headmaster Senlin, taking a wife from your class roll."

"Please!" he hissed. "I am sorry. I will tell you how sorry I am in a little while. But please, leave me alone for today. I want to save us, and I cannot, *I cannot*, if you're here. You will kill me."

The wind scraped at them. The deck quivered. She turned the point of the knife on one fingertip and gave him a speculative look. "I like it when you talk to me, Tom. But you have to promise to do it more often. One day. I'll give you one day. If you ignore me later, I'll be very cross."

"If I ignore you, it will be because I am dead." Senlin glanced about before he locked eyes with the figment and said, "I promise. We will talk tomorrow."

Voleta, who leaned out from the rigging, called down some alarm that was gobbled up by a gust, and Senlin looked away. When he glanced back, Marya was gone.

"They're getting over us, Captain!" Voleta repeated. The black *Ararat* had nearly passed from view, hidden behind the ship's envelope.

Senlin peered down. They were perhaps a thousand feet from the floor and still descending too quickly. "Fire the element, Mr. Boreas. Slow us down."

"Aye," Adam called back.

"If we don't blow the ballast, we won't get out from under her," Edith said, straining over the ship's edge.

"She'll get a dozen hooks in us when we pass her," Senlin said.

"Then we'll have work to do. Right now we're the spike, and they're the hammer. We're going to be driven into the ground, Captain," Edith said.

Senlin wanted to keep their course, to wait for a low current to separate them from the shadow of the warship. But the hope was too slight to hang all their lives upon. He beat his palm on the rail and gave the order to blow the ballast.

At the helm, Adam pressed the throttle forward, but halfway through the motion, the lever lost all resistance. The lever fell back, loose as a broken limb. He pumped it with growing agitation but to no effect.

"The ballast, Adam!" Senlin said, bounding up the stairs to the quarterdeck.

"It's not working." Adam squatted and threw open the cabinet under the helm. "There's a pool of oil."

"What does that mean?"

"The hydraulic line has a break in it somewhere. I can't fix it."

"Iren!" Senlin called through cupped hands. The giantess looked up from the main deck where she stood churning a ramrod in the barrel of a musket. "The ballast hatch is stuck. Can you open it?"

She gave a final tamp of the rod and flipped the loaded gun, stock-first, at Edith, who snatched it from the air. Iren mounted the forecastle and pulled up the planks that covered the reservoir. A plume of water shot up when she leapt into the tank.

"I can't see them anymore, Captain," Voleta said, sliding down a line back to the deck. She ran from the port to the starboard rail and back again. She pointed at the ground to the east. The shadow of the *Stone Cloud* swelled and drew nearer, marking their descent. The silhouette raced toward them across the canopies of the Market. The much larger shadow of the *Ararat* was directly over theirs. The two shadows closed, pinching the narrow crack of light that separated them until they finally merged.

The planks bounced beneath them and the rigging leapt. The hull twisted and bucked like the board of an unevenly pushed swing.

"They're on top of us," Voleta said.

A rope uncoiled out of the sky. A second line followed, and then more on every side. The ends of the ropes began to strain and bounce like snakes held up by their tails. Men were climbing down. In a moment, the commissioner's agents would begin swinging onto the ship. A moment more, and the crew of the *Stone Cloud* would be overrun.

Chapter Eleven

The clan of the Pells is distinguished by their courtly manner. A Pell is always well dressed, sweetly perfumed, and arrayed in the most current fashions. They are harmless in general, but loquacious to a fault; if ever cornered by a Pell, one is in reasonable danger of being charmed to death.

—*Anthropologies of Babel* by A. Franboise

The young nobleman could not stop fussing with the blue cravat at his neck. He pinched it, dimpled it, pulled and tucked it back into his silk shirtfront each time he caught his reflection in the casement window. Since he could not stop pacing his cabin (which the provincial airship captain had optimistically declared the Marquess Suite), his reflection appeared with maddening regularity. And there was always something amiss with his blasted cravat.

The truth was, the girl had spoiled the entire outing. He was an aspiring ornithologist, and this three-day scientific expedition had been chartered by his father, the influential treasurer of Pelphia, for the express purpose of establishing his son's credentials in the field. The young nobleman was supposed to be identifying and recording the passage of migratory birds, in particular the honey buzzard. Instead, the maid who brought his breakfast, tea, and dinner had bewitched him. Her schedule of entrances and exits allowed him just enough time to recover his wits before she appeared again and re-invigorated his desire at the expense of his research.

He'd never seen anyone quite like her. She was as dark as a coffee bean and broad of mouth. Her figure was so extravagantly turned it made the girls of Pelphia seem as voluptuous as broomsticks.

She obviously was not so taken with him. She rose to none of his baiting flirtations. He had tried at first to impress her with the scope of his ornithological knowledge, but she had only shown him the glorious white orbs of her eyes and replied that she "didn't know a thing about chickens." He'd showed off the tools of his science—his field glasses, telescopes, and calipers (which he would use to measure the skull and beak of the honey buzzard if he was ever fortunate enough to snare one)—but his fine instruments had seemed as wondrous as spoons to her.

These failures, rather than pouring water on his passions, only fired his lust. If this had been his ship or a vessel in his father's fleet and not some chartered sloop, he would have boldly impressed upon her the depth of his infatuation. But she purportedly had some family among the crew, and he was too exposed to risk an aggressive romance. He had no choice but to woo her. But how?

There were two minutes until teatime. He absolutely had to have something to say. The weather? Too drab. His heritage? Too imposing. Her heritage? Too depressing. What then?

He allayed his anxiety by tearing off and then completely rewrapping his cravat. He was in the midst of perfecting the scalloped edge when his gaze was drawn to something beyond his reflection in the window. Two ships appeared to be mating in the distance, one small and one vast. He recognized the dominant ship immediately: It was the *Ararat*, the flagship of the commissioner's armada. The commissioner of the Baths served the Pells, of course, and so, by way of transitive property, this ship flew partly in his father's service, and so was very nearly the young ornithologist's own command. Or so it seemed to him.

He threw open the window and trained his field glasses on the paired ships. His sloop was flying low at the moment because the higher currents had developed a chill, and he had complained. How right he had been to complain! Now he had a perfect view of this bit of aerial theater.

It was apparent that the *Ararat* had accosted a grossly inferior vessel, probably pirates, and was in the process of boarding her. Already a dozen lines encircled the ship, and gallant agents in tidy, navy-blue uniforms descended on all sides. The pirate ship was undermanned: He counted a crew of four. They looked as small as music box figurines through his binoculars. A tuft of smoke broke from the muzzle of one of their toy guns, and an agent shinnying down a line lost his grip and fell, clutching his chest.

The young ornithologist reared from his glasses excitedly. "The commissioner has caught a lively gang. What fun."

The bell over his door rang, and he called, "Yes, yes, come in!" before he remembered who it was that stood behind the door. The comely maid entered with a silver tray on her arm, her eyes trained on the table for which the tray was bound.

"Oh, set it down! Set it down, and come here," the ornithologist said excitedly, returning to his glasses. "One of my warships has caught a tub of thieves!"

The agents on the ropes swung onto the deck while the crew of the *Stone Cloud* attempted to reload their aged firearms. Adam was tipping black powder into the muzzle of his musket when an agent with a trim beard stomped onto the quarterdeck behind him. Adam slung the black powder sachet at the man while he was drawing his sword. The gunpowder flew into the agent's face, making him flinch and sneeze. His cutlass clattered to the deck. Adam kicked with his boot heel, and the agent staggered blindly over the balustrade.

Adam turned to see another agent swing onto the main deck. Voleta hung in the canopy of ropes by her knees. She wrestled with a rusted pistol that had broken before she could fire it. The frizzen had come unhinged from the pan. She was determined to reattach it, even as the black powder drained from it. The agent drew a bead on her with his new sidearm, his hand tracking Voleta's distracted swaying.

Without a thought, Adam snatched up the cutlass at his feet, leapt onto the helm, and launched himself from the quarterdeck.

Edith dropped her spent flintlock and counted the surviving first wave of agents: five in all. She knew the furnace would be the first target of the boarding party, who would want to cripple the ship, so she stationed herself before the burner and drew her saber. Three men rushed her at once, their swords forming a trident. She parried the first sword and cycled it around past her shoulder. The second blade she grasped with her steaming gauntlet and snapped three-quarters down. The third prong of the attack she narrowly fended off with this broken shard.

Their assault foiled, the men sprang back.

Edith threw the steel fragment at the man who'd surrendered it to her, and his reflexes compelled him to try to catch it. The burnished sliver passed through his hand and lodged in his neck with a bloody spurt.

His compatriots watched him fall and then turned round in time to discover that they were about to follow him down.

"You see, the *Ararat*, that's the grand black ship flying all those pretty gold banners, has the little ship pinned. It can't go any lower or it'll be dashed upon the ground, and it's too small to lift the warship," the young ornithologist said to the maid, who was staring openmouthed through his field glasses. At last he'd discovered something worthy of her attention. "So, they have no choice but to yield or resist and be killed."

"Who are they?" she asked.

"Pirates, of course."

"How do you know?"

"Because they are being pursued by my commissioner, and because they were running, and because they are fighting back. Pirates are quite stupid." He gazed through a spyglass and surreptitiously shifted behind the maid, who leaned out upon the sill. She seemed unaware of him. He felt slighted by her indifference toward his intimate presence, but he could hardly blame her. The scene was absorbing.

A pretty pirate girl hung in the tub's rigging like a cherry in a tree, and beneath her, a pirate lad had leapt onto one of the commissioner's agents. "Look at that one! He has an eye patch and everything. I can't wait to tell my brothers. A real pirate. Look at how he flails about. It's obvious he hasn't a spot of military training."

"Maybe he loves her," the maid said, watching the desperate pirate lad wrestle with the agent. The two rolled on and over each other, fighting for control of a single pistol.

"I'm sure he does, a dolly-mop like that. I'm in love, too. Ah, to be pet by a pirate girl." They watched the girl with the wild, black hair drop onto the back of the uniformed man who had pinned the one-eyed lad to the planks. She had a hatchet in her hand, and she did something horrible to the back of the agent's head with it.

The ornithologist gasped.

The maid did not.

"If only she were here to pet you," she said in a low but audible tone.

He lowered the glass and wasted a most sincere and hungry leer upon the back of the maid's head. She was spirited. He liked that. The ornithologist licked his lips and peered into his scope again. "Here come reinforcements," he said.

Somewhere inside the flying fortress that hunkered upon them, somewhere among all those squadrons and cannons, Senlin knew the commissioner was smirking behind his black rubber mask. Senlin was also certain that Pound would not put himself into the fray again, not after their last encounter, which Pound had so narrowly survived. No, if he ever saw Pound again, it would be at his own execution.

Senlin watched from the forecastle as the next wave of agents slithered down the lines from the shadow of the *Ararat*. He had already fended off a pair of men, batting them from their ropes with his navigation rod. This violence had affected him like a shot of brandy, leaving him clearheaded and vigilant. It was a surprise to find that violence could work in such a way, and he wondered if it was like brandy in other ways: Was violence clarifying in doses but intoxicating in excess? Could one deal out murder responsibly, even civilly? Was violence, like wine, the midwife of philosophy?

A gunshot from behind drove the illusion of lucidity from him. He turned to see an agent facedown upon the forecastle stairs, a smoking hole in his back. From the main deck, Edith looked up from the bead of a pistol and saluted Senlin with the gun. Senlin returned the cool gesture and came around in time to discourage a man who'd just gotten his boot toes on the rail.

He knew they couldn't go on like this forever. Pound had more men and powder to spend than they had strength to resist. Senlin guarded the open reservoir from which Iren had yet to emerge. Feeling she had been submerged for too long, Senlin crouched down to look for her. He could see nothing but the sloshing ink of the unlit water and the occasional boil of her breath. If he went in after her, it would leave the bow undefended, and they would be overrun—though that was inevitable as long as they were pinned under the dreadnaught. They were trapped in the same dead wind as the warship with only a few hundred feet of air between them and the Market below. Senlin had seen how the inhabitants of the Market greeted crashed vessels: They took to them like beetles to a carcass. His corpse would probably still be warm when some tourist began pulling at his boots.

Iren broke the water's surface with a gasp. Her hands were green with algae; Senlin gripped one to help her out of the reservoir. "I can't open it from here. The latch is stuck fast." She was shivering, and her lips were pale. "I'll have to break the hinge from the outside." She snatched up the short-handled axe Voleta had left to cut grappling lines. She passed the hook end of her chain through a sturdy cleat in the deck and wrapped the other end about her forearm. "I just need a minute." She was about to leap overboard when Senlin stopped her.

"Wait! We can't buck her yet. We have to get out from under her first, or it'll be a waste of ballast."

They ducked reflexively when a shot seethed through the air over their heads. The responsible agent, seeing that he'd missed, attempted to clamber back up the line he dangled from. Iren plucked a belaying pin from the rail and hurled the wooden club at the invader. It struck him in the forehead and he dropped like a stone. "How are we going to do that?" she asked.

Senlin looked down at the Market. They were low enough now that he could distinguish individuals. Camels, litters, and palominos clogged the narrow lanes of the slum. A rotten smell was subdued by the scent of fresh linens. A train approached under a white scarf of steam.

"We have to go down."

"There isn't enough air."

"It's not air we need, it's wind!" Senlin said, and pulled the harpoon from the cannon.

"There's a fifth pirate now. A big one! I can't tell if it's a man or a woman. It just crawled out of the bow. Oh, it's beaned a man!" The ornithologist had been narrating in a nervous stream for several minutes.

It had dawned on the maid that her curiosity had put her in a vulnerable position. But the scene was so enthralling. She could not look away. The woman with the clockwork arm had beaten back a dozen of the gussied men without assistance. Whenever one of the commissioner's aeronauts fell under her gleaming fist, the maid wanted to cheer.

"Are you watching? Watch the bow, dolly," the ornithologist cooed. "I think the admiral is up to something." As they watched, the man in the black tricorne hat threw a harpoon into the underbelly of the ship's envelope. The barb of the harpoon snagged upon the silk and the pirate jerked the line down, opening a gash. The balloon began to roil and deform about the tear.

"It's like watching an adder strike itself," the ornithologist said. "But oh, the desperate acts of desperate souls." He closed the already narrow space between them, pressing against her as if she were a stubborn door.

The maid stared rigidly ahead, wishing she could pour herself through those binoculars and travel the distance to that heroic ship even as it slouched to its ruin.

*   *   *

When the captain threw the harpoon into the envelope, Iren was sure he had gone mad. She had to restrain herself from grabbing him by the neck and shaking him, though perhaps it was as much shock as restraint that stayed her. The gash he opened fluttered, riffled and, after a moment, resealed itself.

A gap opened between the ships. The *Stone Cloud* slid half-free of the *Ararat's* shadow before the *Ararat* pressed down again, though not as evenly as before. Pinched under the heel of the warship, the *Stone Cloud* pitched astern, then rolled aport.

The dead were carried by the incline to the rails. The aged balustrade creaked with each additional body, then a pilaster snapped and that started a chain reaction down the length of the ship that ended with the entire rib peeling away. The bodies spilled overboard and crashed down onto tents and jitneys and unprepared tourists. Senlin clung to the mounted cannon and watched the bombing. It was a queasy thing to see men turned into missiles, to watch the dead make more dead.

His plan was only half done, and yet all hope ran out of him. He braced himself on the foot of the cannon and reloaded the harpoon. He felt a sudden suspicion that this was not an elaborate escape attempt: It was suicide in a state of denial. Perhaps he was even now acting on that determination that his crew would die before he allowed them to be captured by the sadistic commissioner. Or perhaps Edith's misgivings were right, and the bedeviling ghost had so poisoned his mind that he could not be counted upon to distinguish between salvation and self-destruction. He couldn't distinguish between hope and delusion any longer.

Though it didn't matter. Even if it was all folly, there was no stopping now.

Without a wind to pull them free, they would have to rely on a mechanical gust. He could only hope that his ship had slipped far enough out from under the *Ararat* that it might be tugged free without coming to shreds. It all depended upon the train coursing through the Market below. Already the engine was behind them and moving away.

Iren called him back from his thoughts. "What are you going to do?"

"I'm going to spear the train. It will tow us out from under this beast, and then you must open the tank or we'll be dragged into the ground."

"You don't have a shot," Iren said, pointing where the train had passed behind the quarterdeck.

Senlin swiveled the cannon around, pointing it over the main deck directly at the door of the great cabin. "I'm going to have to make one." Iren opened her mouth to argue, but Senlin barked at her as he never had before. "This is our only chance. You must open the tank!"

Iren looked as if she might lunge at him for speaking to her so forcefully. He did not spare her the emphasis of his gaze. Somewhere in the hull, a breaking beam raised a mighty crack. Iren stuck the handle of the axe between her teeth like the bit of a bridle and hurdled the railing. Her chain rang fast upon the cleat. She bounced against the hull until she caught ahold of it.

Cupping his hands, Senlin called to Edith, who had slid down to one corner of the deck. "Open the cabin door!"

Edith scrambled over to the door but kept her alarmed expression turned toward Senlin. She realized that he was not only clinging to the cannon, but also attempting to aim it, apparently at her. She rattled the latch of the door, found it locked, and began patting herself for the key. "What are you doing?"

"Open it now!"

Ducking to the side, Edith pounded the door once with her engine arm, emptying the hinges. Senlin triggered the flint that sparked upon the plate, touching off the load of black powder. The harpoon fired, carrying its line down the spine of his ship. It passed through his cabin and exited by the bay window of Edith's chart house in the blink of an eye.

The desperate arrow plunged toward the Market amid a shower of broken glass, flying over the heads of merchants and tourists who had all begun to panic and bolt from the shadow of the falling ship. The harpoon found its mark. It struck the roof of a dining car, piercing the ceiling within and startling the waiters who were setting up for tea. The spur tore the roof open, popping lanterns and shattering plaster as it gouged a path to the rear of the dining car where it finally snagged upon the iron frame.

At the end of the taut line, the *Stone Cloud* leapt like a startled horse. The two airships broke from each other, the smaller ship descending sharply as the train hauled it into the wind.

The violent lurch of the ship propelled Senlin over the bow. He caught the gunwale by little more than his fingertips, his legs turning and kicking in open air. He pulled his head level with the deck in time to see the cannon crack free of its moorings and tumble along the length of the deck. The barrel caught and snapped the umbilical, narrowly missing the furnace, and bounced through the threshold of the great cabin, breaking the lintel. The gyrating gun pulverized a linen chest, a bureau, and one corner of Senlin's bed. It gathered and carried a coma of debris. By the time it struck the partition of the chart house, it had become a comet.

The cannon blew out the aft of the ship, taking Edith's room with it.

Clinging to the ribs of the keel below, Iren had continued to chop at the hinge of the ballast tank through it all. She was in the midst of her second swing when the ship surged after the train. She was in the midst of her third swing when the unmoored cannon destroyed the chart house. And when the fourth swing bit into the hinge, the cloud finally burst.

Part II
The Golden Zoo

Chapter One

We are, each of us, a multitude. I am not the man I
was this morning, nor the man of yesterday. I am a
throng of myself queued through time. We are, gentle
reader, each a crowd within a crowd.

—*Folkways and Right of Ways in the Silk
Gardens*, Anon.

During the honeymoon days after their escape from New Babel,
the *Stone Cloud* had seemed as glorious as a pleasure cruiser to
her rescued crew. They were not blind to her flaws, of course.
They perceived the knot repairs in her rigging and the subtle tilt of
her deck. Her furnace was as intemperate as a two-year-old. Yet, from
her filthy orlop to her frayed telltales, she was every inch their savior,
and they loved her.

They spent a day tumbling in the blizzard that blew them out of the
commissioner's reach, then broke from the great wall of snow upon a
bucolic scene of flocking sheep, a drowsy hamlet, and fields combed
for their winter rest. Without intending to, they had traversed the
mountains that encircled the Valley of Babel.

This glimpse of farmland made Edith quite nostalgic, but Senlin's
first thought upon seeing the old world again was, *We mustn't stray too
far from the Tower.*

He needn't have worried. The wind perished, and the ship fell into a fog that lapped upon the foothills like a milky sea. As they sank, the sun shrank and blackened like a raisin, inviting a gloom that thickened into night. Senlin had never experienced such profound silence before. He could hear the others stir and breathe, could hear the murmur of his own heart. They lit the deck lamps, though the light only swapped one opaque medium for another—black for white, dark for fog.

Rather than feel socked in or blinded, they felt embraced by the mist, because if they could hardly see one another standing upon the same deck, what chance did anyone else have of seeing them?

It was such a luxury to be unafraid.

They took advantage of the respite to clear out what Lee's crew had left behind. Like a bird brings new threads to an old nest, they began to make the *Cloud* their own.

In his great cabin, Senlin tried to solve that most ancient of domestic puzzles: the arrangement of furniture in a room. The goal, of course, was to please the eye without terrorizing the shin, which seemed simple enough on the face of it but was really quite a riddle. Captain Lee had been unencumbered by any aesthetic sense; the proof of that showed in his decision to push every stick of furniture to the wall. The great walrus of a wardrobe, the leather-trimmed chest, the dining set, and the prissy four-post bed all lurked at the perimeter of the room.

"It's like being surrounded, isn't it?" Marya said, turning about in the center of the floor. "That wardrobe looks like it's plotting something." She thrust out her chin and smiled at him, just as she once had from the carriage window of a train the day she returned from the women's conservatory. She beamed at Isaugh's humble station, the aging porters and the ladies in their ponderous, out-of-fashion hats. Her auburn hair swam about her face, blown by the waning steam, and he, having come on some business he at once forgot, stared up at this winsome woman, his former pupil, and was hopelessly smitten.

He suspected the figment would disappear soon enough, and in the meantime she wasn't any great bother. It was a time of transition for him, a time for adapting to his new function as captain, a role that seemed at once ill-suited to his talents and yet impossible to refuse, a role which left him to wrestle with the morality of imperiling his friends for the sake of his wife. Out of this inner turmoil, the specter of Marya had emerged. She let him recall the man he had once been: the sincere headmaster, the bore of parties, the awkward fiancé.

Of course, he knew better than to form an attachment to the figment. He decided at once he would not converse with her, but that did not mean he could not enjoy this nostalgic specter. When the Crumb ran its course and she vanished again into memory, he would heave a great sigh and carry on.

Marya set a knuckle to her chin and squinted thoughtfully as he shouldered the wardrobe out of the cabin's corner. "That's better. He seems more friendly there. Now, what's to be done with this chest?"

A quick knock sounded, and the heavy door to the main deck flew open upon a cloud. Voleta emerged from the fog, her eyes trained on the tea tray she carried before her. She wore a fanciful assemblage of ill-fitting clothes; her boots swamped her legs past the knees.

She closed the door with her hip and said, "Edith, I mean Mister Winters—my, that does sound strange—she said you should eat."

Senlin quit pressing upon the wardrobe and took the tray at once. "Goodness, you don't need to serve me. Please, tell Mister Winters in the future I will take my meals with the rest of you in the galley." He made a space on the table for the tea set, cup and saucer, and a bowl full of something quivering and gray.

"Could it be pudding?" he asked.

"It could be pudding," she said, and clasped her hands behind her back. She looked about at the shuffled furniture, the stacks of books, the sad tangle of bright scarves and beads that lay in a clump upon the bed. "It's quite nice in here," she said.

He had seen the other quarters and felt abashed at the relative luxury of his cabin. It certainly hadn't been his first choice of lodging, but Edith had insisted, and he had acquiesced. "I was going through Lee's effects and found a collection of . . . trinkets, I suppose you'd call them. I doubt they're worth anything, but would you like them?"

"No, no, thank you. Those are like fishing lures for silly girls. Besides, I don't think pirates wear trinkets."

He chuckled as he swept the sparkling clump off his bed and into the trunk. "We're not pirates, Voleta."

"Said the captain of the pirate ship."

It was something of a pleasant surprise to discover that Adam's sister was so quick-witted, if not a little impertinent. Adam had many admirable gifts; he was an able mechanic and a tireless worker, but he was not gifted in the conversational arts. Senlin perceived in this young woman a sharp and inquisitive mind. "We really haven't had a chance to talk."

"Been too busy screaming and chewing our nails. That was an awful storm."

"It was, indeed. Please"—he gestured at a chair—"since you're already here, why don't we have a spot of tea?"

She curtsied, immediately looked annoyed with herself, and then plopped down upon the chair. "There'll be no more of those, Captain. No more curtsies. Salutes, certainly. Handshakes, if you like. But I left the rest of my curtsies in New Babel."

"As you should have." He retrieved a second cup from the china rack and poured them both a cup. "What do you think of our little arrangement?"

"Being an aeronaut, you mean? Living on a ship? Having you as a captain? All that?"

"Yes, all that exactly." He took a spoonful of the colorless porridge, swallowed with some effort, and chased the bland lump with a sip of bitter tea.

"It's grand," she said, opening the sugar bowl and peering inside. "I like adventure, and I like you, too. I especially like that you shot Rodion."

Senlin saw the jailor's key in his hand, the tuft of gun smoke and the tear of blood running down Rodion's face. The pimp's expression turned transparent, showing the boy inside the hateful and angry ego. And it was that person, that open-faced and hopeful lad, who fell dead at Senlin's feet.

"I think it's right to defend yourself and your friends," Senlin said in a constrained tone. "But I don't think I'll ever feel proud about shooting anyone."

"He was not anyone, sir. He was a villain of the first degree. He was a predator who liked to, who liked to..." She had begun to shake her head, her gaze transfixed. She shuddered and recovered her smile. "Thank you, anyway, for getting me and Adam out."

He sustained a pleasant expression, but the mention of her brother's name set his thoughts to warring. He would never admit how deeply Adam's betrayal had wounded him. It wasn't just the deceit that cut him; it was the honesty of Adam's calculation. Rodion, vile as he was, was the sensible choice and the more valuable ally. The boy's decision wasn't wicked; it was self-preserving. How could the adopted bonds of friendship compete with the bonds of family and the impulse to survive?

He could think of nothing to say, and so only smiled and sipped his tea.

"I don't think you and he can be friends again," she said, turning the cup slowly upon the saucer, looking at its steaming contents rather than his frozen smile. "We know that. It may take Adam a while to come to the same conclusion, but I think he will, too."

A little surprised by the acuity of her statement, Senlin tried to be diplomatic. "I don't blame him for choosing you over me. Family takes precedent. I understand that, and I'm sure he thought he—"

"You needn't defend him. I certainly won't. I think he made a mistake. He didn't include me in the decision, I can tell you. I would never have chosen Rodion. Never." She put three spoonfuls of dingy sugar in her tea and began to stir it vigorously. "But the real question is, if you can't be friends, what can you be?"

It didn't take much reflection to know she was right. The fact that he couldn't trust Adam didn't settle the question of whether he could coexist with him peaceably. He hadn't spoken to Adam since their escape, but he knew he would have to eventually, and it would be better for all concerned if the silence was broken sooner rather than later.

"I suppose we could just rely on the stations we've assumed. I will be his captain, and he will be my crew," Senlin said with a mixture of relief and regret. "Perhaps some formality will do us both good—"

A knock at the door interrupted him. Adam emerged from the fog, his face turned down. His arm was bandaged, and bruises showed on his handsome face, but his worst wound was not the visible sort.

"I dropped a plumb bob to check our clearance. I ran out of string, so we've got at least a hundred feet of air under us." Expecting no reply, Adam turned to leave.

Voleta gave Senlin an expectant look.

"One moment," he said, rising from his seat. "Do you think we're safe enough as we are?"

Adam lifted his gaze long enough to scan the captain's expression, which was admirably composed. He cleared his throat and straightened his back a little. "We're all right for the moment, but we should think about poking our heads out to have a look around. Get our bearings."

"That sounds reasonable. Consult with Mister Winters, and if she agrees, take us up for a look."

"Aye, sir."

"And, Adam..." The young man paused, his hand upon the doorknob. "Good work."

The *Stone Cloud*'s bones were showing.

The cannon had split the forecastle, gouged the main deck, savaged the great cabin, and obliterated the chart house on its way out. Senlin stood middeck and stared through the aft of his ship, waiting for the devastation to seem real.

He was doing his best to hide his shock from the others, but the fact was they were lucky to be alive, and he was luckiest of all that his mad gamble hadn't ended with them being driven aground, or dragged behind a train, or blown from the sky.

The torn flue lay in coils about the deck like spilled intestines. The envelope was a warped and puckered mass. The tilt of the deck was no longer slight. In fact, the whole ship seemed ready to tip.

He wondered what Marya would say about the state of the *Cloud*, something biting and pert, no doubt...But what madness! He was thinking of her as if she were real, as if she were anything but a crumb of the Crumb...

"The wind is still with us," Adam said, stepping into Senlin's line of sight. The captain was scowling so savagely that Adam hesitated a moment before he finished, "It's blown the *Ararat* off. Voleta hasn't seen a speck of her for two hours."

Voleta was in the netting, crawling all about the curdled balloon, listening at the self-sealed wounds for any lingering leaks. Whenever she heard the telltale hiss, she painted the spot with glue, then patched it with a square of silk.

Senlin's head was so full of other things that it took him a moment to absorb the news. "I doubt he'll stay away long. We keep heaping humiliations upon him, and he's not one to forgive embarrassment."

"By my count, that's three times you've scoffed him. Maybe he'll learn his lesson. Captain Mudd isn't to be trifled with."

Senlin laughed without smiling. "That's not the lesson I took from it. Next time you ask to work on the ship, I should let you. That faulty lever nearly killed us."

"I could never have guessed where it would break. There's a hundred feet of dry-rotted hydraulic tubing running underfoot. The only thing holding us together at this point is hope."

"Apparently we ran out of that."

"Impossible. We have you."

Senlin had the aggrieved expression of one unaccustomed to compliments. "I think you're confusing hope with stubbornness, Adam."

"I'm pretty sure that's what hope is. Stubbornness. Refusing to go down. You harpooned a train, carved up the ship, and nearly sent the *Ararat* to the ground. Call it what you like, but it feels like hope." Adam smiled, a rare enough sight, and Senlin glimpsed the friend he'd lost.

Adam's encouragement warmed him, and when he looked again at his ship, he saw the miracle lurking beneath the disaster. For all its holes, the *Cloud* was still afloat. Adam was right: There was hope yet.

When Edith approached, dragging a remnant of her room's partition, she found Senlin and Adam smiling at the mess that lay all about them. "Good news, I hope?" she said.

"The *Ararat* is away, and we're still afloat," Senlin said, and helped her shift the load onto the growing pile of scrap wood. They would pull the redeemable nails, salvage the better planks, and the rest would go over the side. He found it curious that she hadn't used her engine arm for the chore. Perhaps she wanted to exercise the muscles of her other limb.

She wiped the sweat from her chin onto her blouse. "What about the umbilical? Can we repair it?"

Adam was no longer smiling. "Wherever we light next, we'll be stuck there until we find a replacement. And I'm sure I don't have to tell you we are not long for the sky. It may not be a gentle landing."

She soothed the mechanical joint of her elbow as if it pained her, as if it could pain her, and only stopped when she caught Senlin looking. "Do we have any choices, or are we just picking our spot on the ground?"

Senlin had his answer ready. "We make for the Silk Gardens. We still have our peace offering. It's time to find out whether Luc Marat is willing to extend his charity for the hods to a few wayward souls."

"I'm not sure I can put us on the Reef. All the reliable charts were in the chart house. We'll have to fly by feel."

Senlin mistook her flat tone of voice for fortitude, and so unintentionally goaded her on the sensitive subject of her destroyed room. "The charts weren't half the resource you are, Mister Winters."

She gritted her teeth. "We're out of ballast. Once this scrap is gone, we'll be pulling up boards."

"If it comes to that, start with my cabin," Senlin said with a little too much munificence. "I'm going to see if the good doctor's library has anything useful to say about the Silk Gardens."

He was feeling encouraged, and so was blind to Edith's frustration as she began pulling apart the boards of her bedroom wall.

Edith was not at all enthusiastic about visiting the Silk Reef, which she refused to call a "garden." She had spent enough time with experienced airmen to know the Reef was an inhospitable, uninhabited wasteland. Superficially, it was a demilitarized zone between unfriendly ringdoms, but Edith considered its true purpose to be as a cap to foot traffic, because no tourist, no matter how intrepid, could pass through the Reef. The Reef kept the riffraff out of the upper ringdoms.

And everyone knew it was infested with spiders.

The Silk Gardens lay squeezed between the rival ringdoms of Pelphia and Algez and had served as the trophy and theater of their war-making for centuries. As their guns grew more titanic and the two armies swelled their ranks, the east portal of the Reef had to be expanded by pick and chisel to accommodate the growth. Eventually, the tunnel was wide enough for an airship to pass through it. And that was the moment when the old feud turned into a mutual suicide. The two enemies stuffed their armadas inside the Reef's little pocket of sky and soon discovered that sacks of hydrogen and great volumes of gunpowder, when tamped inside the Tower, make a bloody rain.

Then, a hundred years ago, Pelphia and Algez signed an armistice, which included transforming the sixth ringdom into a shared park, symbolizing a final end to generations of animosity. The historic peace lasted all of five years, but it effectively shifted the war to the open sky since neither side wished to destroy the park they'd built together but considered their own. So the neglected gardens eventually became the overgrown and ungoverned Reef. A place whispered of and avoided; a port of last resort for the haggard and the hopeless.

Reading had always been a reliable retreat for Senlin. He was blessed with a constitution that allowed him to read on trains and in carriages. He had spent many evenings reading essays in the Blue Tattoo while sailors and fishwives sang in perfect cacophony to Marya's piano. Once, he had missed the entire passage of a hurricane because he'd been so absorbed by a typographer's history of the tittle. He only realized a storm had passed when he rose the next morning to discover his fence, hedge, and flowers had been shaved from the hill face as if by a straight razor.

But for the first time in his life, he felt thwarted by the books before him. He wondered if he wasn't just distracted by his devastated cabin. His sloping bed had lost two of its posts. There was nothing left of his tin chandelier but a few lengths of chain, and Captain Lee's collection of flamboyant robes had been tossed into every corner where they lay turning in the unmitigated wind like restless cats.

No, these distractions weren't the real source of his unease. If he was honest with himself, he was having difficulty overcoming his revulsion at reading more of the same twaddle that had misled him in the past.

Still, it had to be done.

He sorted through the books, marshaling them into stacks according to their potential. The fiction and volumes of verse were, for all their efforts at profundity, useless to him. Nearly as impractical were the natural philosophies, which included some very fine illustrations. The gold-leafed histories, which after his recent audience with Madame Bhata seemed conspicuously preoccupied with wealthy men and their wars, might contain a chestnut. Outside the usual selection of malignant guides, there were only two books in the doctor's collection that were entirely devoted to the subject of the Silk Gardens.

The first volume, *Folkways and Right of Ways in the Silk Gardens*, was a book of manners. The anonymous author had the tedious habit of addressing his audience as "gentle reader," and his advice often lapsed into metaphysical non sequiturs, which were further disrupted by amateur drawings of the different features of the Gardens. Senlin made it through the first chapter before concluding the book was an intellectual spittoon overflowing with dribble.

The other promising title, *Inaugurations of the Silk Gardens*, was authored by a "royal envoy" named Niccolo Salo. Salo had attended the grand opening of the Silk Gardens during the brief truce between Pelphia and Algez. Much of the record was dominated by Salo's fawning over the duke, his original audience, in a thinly veiled bid for a knighthood.

Senlin began reading the fourteen-page dedication to the Duke of Pelphia with a sigh that quickly deepened into a groan.

An hour later, Voleta found the captain beating an open book upon his table. He was so earnest in his punishment of the dead volume that he did not notice Voleta had entered his cabin until she began to cheer him on.

"That's it, Captain! Teach it some manners!"

Senlin halted midthump.

His first impulse was to justify his rough handling of the book, which he'd gone to with the earnest hope that it would give him clear and succinct direction. He wanted irrefutable fact. He wanted an *X* upon a map. He wanted to know where the Golden Zoo was inside the perilous ringdom. Instead, he had gotten a lot of snobbery, some xeno-phobic philosophy, and endless political "intrigue" that was not at all intriguing.

Even so, what good did it do to abuse a book?

"I'm sorry you saw that, Voleta. That is not how I aspire to conduct myself," he said, with a show of great calm. "What do you need?"

"All the food is gone," she said.

His brief beatific smile broke into a frown.

"There's a hole in the galley about this big." She made a hoop with her arms. The galley lay under the quarterdeck that the harpoon gun had blown out.

"Nothing's left?" he asked.

"There's some mustard."

"Mustard?"

"About two spoons' worth. And a jar of pickled beet juice, but no beets."

"Well," he said, steeling himself against this pitiful news. "Put out the nets. We'll have to catch our dinner." The bird nets were unlikely to catch much so high from the ground and so late in the afternoon, but what choice did they have but to hope for the best?

"Is this her?" Voleta said, picking up the small painted board that lay on the table among the leather-bound stacks. "Is this your wife?"

He had forgotten that he'd brought out Marya's portrait to keep him company while he read. Usually, he made a point of keeping it tucked out of sight. "It is."

Voleta studied it closely, glancing up at her captain and then back at the portrait as she tried to marry the two of them in her mind. Senlin felt terribly self-conscious, recalling again his old insecurity at having such a young and pretty wife. "Is it a good likeness?"

"It is."

"She's very handsome."

"Yes."

Voleta grimaced. "But it's terribly filthy."

"I'd hardly call it filth. It's a tasteful nude. You have to understand, she was more than a little desperate when she met the painter, who I really don't think meant to be exploitive. I think he saw her purely as a subject, and not..."

"No, no, I meant it's got a film all over it. It's dirty."

"Oh. Yes. The paint was a little spoiled by the White Chrom and the snow."

"You should clean it."

"I can't just run it under water and put a brush to it. It would scrub off the picture."

"And it's very dear to you."

"It is." He held out his hand with a stoic smile, and she gave him back his board. "Was there something else, Voleta?"

Now it was her turn to look a little abashed. "Iren says the Silk Reef is full of spiders and bears and that nobody ever goes there."

"And you're nervous," he concluded.

"No! I've never seen a bear before," she said, her excitement making her radiant. "I want to know if we're going to see bears."

Senlin laughed, partly at himself, partly at her insatiable appetite for adventure. Only a few hours earlier, they were crossing swords with a raiding party, and already she was thinking of bears. "I hate to disappoint you, but I don't believe there are any bears in the Silk Gardens. There are spiders, though, cultivated for the silk they produce, and there are spider-eaters—"

"What's a spider-eater?" Voleta asked, her disappointment about the bears softened by her curiosity in this new creature.

"If this is to be believed," Senlin said, hiking up the tome he'd recently spanked upon the table, "they're similar to anteaters. Spider-eaters were bred to graze on the spiders, so they wouldn't run rampant through the park. But don't get any ideas, Voleta. You're going to stay on the ship while I pay Luc Marat a visit."

"Of course!" Voleta leaned forward on the table and gave him her most sober expression. "That's why I'm asking you to describe it: because I won't see it for myself. Only, it's called a garden. I haven't seen a garden in..." She trailed off, counting the many long months she'd spent penned up in her old dressing room. Nothing green grew in New Babel. Sometimes men would, at great expense, import roses or some other blossom to bait the girls with. She'd received more than a few bouquets in her time, some quite excessive, sent by wealthy gentlemen who wished to buy her away from Rodion. She had grown to enjoy watching the flowers die because she knew the gentlemen's hope wilted right along with them.

"Are there trees?" she asked, finding her voice again.

"There are many trees. A whole forest worth."

"Please tell me about them."

Senlin could not help but be infected by her enthusiasm. "Only one variety grows there: the porcelmore. They're white as bone, brittle as a teacup, and they haven't any leaves. They're a kind of cave tree. Isn't that interesting? I hadn't known there was such a thing." He sorted through the books a moment. "I found a drawing of one. It's not very good, but it—" He fumbled the copy of *Folkways* and the book spilled open on the table. When he picked it up, a folded sheet of paper fell out and drifted to the floor.

Voleta retrieved it and unfolded it while Senlin watched. "Looks like you had the right idea to begin with, Captain. Sometimes you have to beat it out of them," she said, looking up from the page with a smirk. "It's a map."

"Don't be silly, Voleta. Let me see," he said, sounding not at all convinced.

But it only took a glance to confirm that she was right. There was a compass rose and a legend in the page's corner; there were snaking paths and small bodies of water filled with delicate little waves. At the center of all the trails was an icon that resembled a bird's cage. It was minutely labeled, "The Golden Zoo."

In his trembling hands, he held a map that might lead him to his wife.

Chapter Two

Civilization first came into being when two of our ancestors knocked together at the mouth of a cave, and one brute or the other uttered the immortal phrase: "No, no, I insist, after you."

—*Folkways and Right of Ways in the Silk Gardens*, Anon.

P ort lights appeared upon the Tower's shaded face like the shining eyes of a swamp. Hundreds of yellow, white, and green lamps, some twinkling, some stark, hinted at the beastly forces secluded in the dark. The port lights seemed to watch the *Cloud*, seemed to calculate whether it was worth the effort to rise from the gloom and snatch the wounded sparrow from the air.

Alone on the quarterdeck, Edith gazed at the monstrous mire of stone and wealth and felt an apology was due. First the Tower had taken the last of her youthful exuberance, then her arm, then her freedom, and now it had circled around to rob her of her ship. No matter how much she gave it, the Tower's appetite for misery seemed inexhaustible.

She could hear Tom and Voleta in the cabin below talking about the Reef. They sounded excited, giddy, the poor fools. The consensus regarding the Reef was uniform and damning. Pirates shunned it, and that was proof enough for her that only trouble resided there.

But what choice did they have? And what good did it do for her to cast her shadows of doubt over the captain and the girl's glimmer of hope? They would see for themselves soon enough.

She had her hands full in the meantime trying to recall from memory the currents that would be active this time of year at this time of day. Wings of orange sunlight broke about the eclipsing spire. She watched a great school of starlings break around the Tower's edge and turn into sparkling coal dust amid the shadow. She tried to follow them to see what current they clung to, but the murk was too deep and she lost their trail.

Spanner's Zephyr was too high—she knew that much at least—and the Bitter Chappie and the West Monte Ponds descended too sharply to be any good to them. The Northern Steady was a reliable current, but it broke up in the chill of the Tower's umbra, which was unlucky, because it would've been perfect. She believed she had put them in Chaucer's Crook, which was a reedy little puff of air that wound about the Three Brothers thermals and snaked about the Tower just at the cusp of the sixth ringdom. At least, it usually did, when the Brothers didn't squeeze the wind to death.

The truth was, she was only half-sure she had found Chaucer's Crook, but half-sure was as good as she could do. She could recommend that they carve another cabin off and extend their orbit, but that would carry them around to the setting sun where their shadow would make them an obvious target, and there was no guarantee they'd survive long enough to circle around again. If her course was wrong or if the ship fell from the Crook, the guns of Pelphia would soon inform her of the error.

Really, there was nothing to do but wait for the ship to turn.

Which unfortunately left her with a moment to think, something she'd been trying to avoid for days—really, ever since she'd learned that Tom was seeing things. That discovery had left her feeling like the last adult about the ship. Voleta and Adam were hardly more than children, Iren was, well, *Iren*, and Tom was hiding things like a scolded child.

Though she couldn't really claim the high ground where secrets were concerned.

No, the real trouble was that none of the others understood the danger they were all in, the danger she put them in. None of them knew, not really, what the Tower was about, and who ran it, and what he was willing to do to get his way. In this knowledge, she was alone, and it weighed upon her; it made her envious of their ignorance.

She felt a sudden thrill of relief when the bow swung to point at a hole in the facade, a deeper shadow amid the shadows. She had found the Crook after all. She called to the others so they could witness their approach of this, their last haven and hope, black as it was.

They crowded onto the main deck and leaned out upon the rigging as far as their courage would allow.

Soon, the mouth of the port swelled before them. The once grand entrance of the Silk Gardens was now a ruin, though not the sort brought about by the slow erosion of wind and rain. No, the port had been aged by the abrasions of war. The scorched marble ribs of the archway were cracked and studded with cannonballs. Rust trailed from these old wounds like dried blood. Of the six pillars that once stood in file about the entrance, only one remained, and it resembled a gnawed bone.

The *Stone Cloud* cruised under the soaring, ragged arch into the darkness.

This was not a thing Senlin had ever expected to do. It felt unnatural—like riding a horse into a house. Yet, here he was: flying an airship into the Tower of Babel.

It was a binding gloom, and the quiet seemed to gag them. Senlin had to clear his throat before he could raise his voice sufficiently to deliver the order to light the lamps. He had known the ringdom was deserted—the Silk Gardens had been abandoned for decades—and still he was unsettled to find such a dead cavity inside the vital Tower.

The *Stone Cloud* hovered over the sandy floor of the tunnel as close as a dragonfly skims the water. On either side of the ship, their lamps drew long shadows from the legs of immense statues, spaced like columns in a colonnade.

Salo had exhausted several pages of his *Inaugurations* describing this hall of monuments and cataloging the noblemen embodied herein.

The treaty between Pelphia and Algez stipulated that both ringdoms be represented equally in all decorative embellishments, and yet Salo boasted that he had taken great pains to measure the height of the duke's effigy and that of his terrible rival, the Marquess of Algez. Salo was pleased to report that the duke's tribute was subtly but undeniably taller.

All Senlin and his crew could see of the colossal lords were their knees, shins, and feet. The remainder was hidden by the ship's envelope, which fairly filled the airway. What Salo called a "fitting tribute to our aristocracy" seemed to Senlin an architectural bungle. The monuments were too large to be observed by passing ships, and from the knees down, all those dukes and marquesses were indistinguishable and only as noble as their toes.

A pale, blue light shone ahead of them at the tunnel's end.

"Where is that light coming from?" Voleta asked.

"I think it's the gloamine," Senlin said. "Salo wrote about it. Gloamine is a kind of lichen that glows in the dark. It grows on the trees and the ground covering. They used it as an alternative to gas lamps, which were too dangerous to burn in a forest."

"It's beautiful," Voleta said.

They crowded onto the ruined prow and peered into this mounting light. Then the colonnade ended, the Silk Gardens opened before them, and they discovered that despite all they had seen, they hadn't yet exhausted their awe.

In his *Inaugurations*, Salo described this place of disembarkation as a sugar-white beach embraced by a glowing forest. Lively crowds cheered the arrival of stately ships. Musicians and dancers filled lily-white gazebos. Flower girls cried, "Carnations for your collar; roses for your posy!" and shook bouquets over their heads, filling the air with petals and perfume. Weddings were so common in those early days that one could traverse the beach by leaping from bridal train to bridal train without ever touching the sand.

Most remarkable of all—indeed the main attraction for many— were the host of fantastic clockwork animals that populated the forest, ornamented the paths, and served as whimsical landmarks to visitors. Some of these mechanical beasts resembled ibex with hinged mouths that seemed to graze. Others resembled giraffes with long plated necks that turned and reached. Copper zebras leapt on rails, silver peacocks trumpeted and fanned aluminum tails, and gold-bellied elephants raised their trunks in welcome. The Silk Gardens were, as Salo put it, the toy chest of a genius.

But that was the world that was.

The beach before them was littered with shipwrecks. There were dozens of them, ships of all cuts and sizes. The wrecks lay amid the devastated bleachers and caved-in gazebos. They were shrouded in their deflated silks like corpses in a morgue. The derelicts and debris had been pushed to the edge of the beach by the force of storms that howled through the tunnel a few times a year. Behind this reef of wreckage, the spiny forest seemed an impenetrable bramble that rose nearly a hundred feet to the grand dome of the cavern. The trees glowed like an alcohol stove with an otherworldly light.

"I don't like it," Iren said, noting all the opportunities for ambush.

"What do you think all those wrecks mean?" Voleta asked.

"They mean parts. Salvage. We can repair the *Cloud*," Adam said.

"Well, that's one good turn, at least." Senlin nodded, trying to shake the feeling that their ship bore a striking resemblance to the derelicts before them.

"None of them look very fresh. The wind has had time to bury them," Adam said.

"What about the people aboard?" Voleta asked. "Do you think they were rescued?"

Iren snorted.

"It doesn't matter what happened to them. What matters is what will happen to us," Senlin said, trying for confidence.

He pressed past his crew, descended the forecastle, and retreated to his cabin. When he returned, he carried the two sacks of books, one over either shoulder. He sat these down by the edge of the ship where the rope ladder lay rolled in its box. He made a second trip to his stateroom and returned in the process of buckling a sword belt, with a rapier that had been surrendered by one of the commissioner's agents. His aerorod, which he'd all too often swung as a club, would stay aboard.

"I don't need to tell you what sort of trouble we're in," he said, donning his tricorne. "We have little water, no food, and a limping ship. We must divide and conquer. I am going to trek to the Golden Zoo. Hopefully, I can talk Marat into parting with some information about the hod trail and some of his stores."

"Asking for directions is one thing. But asking for a handout is just m—" Edith bit down on the word *madness* before it escaped. "It seems a little optimistic, Captain."

"*Optimistic* is the word for it, Mister Winters. Optimistically, Marat will make me tea, fill our pantry, and throw open the doors to Pelphia. I hope that is the case. But I have a pessimistic solution as well. If it comes to it, I'm going to facilitate his generosity in our favor."

"You're going to rob a missionary?" Voleta interjected with a zest that dismayed Senlin.

"Yes, Voleta, but only as a last resort. And if it comes to that, I may be returning in a hurry," Senlin said, turning to Adam. "The ship must be ready to fly. It doesn't have to be handsome, but it needs to hang in the air. Do you think it's possible?"

"Aye, sir," Adam said.

"You're not suggesting that you go on your own?" Edith said, shaking her head. "No, I'm coming with you. Permission to come with you."

She knew it was not a good idea. For one thing, it was against procedure, which held that while ashore, either the captain or the mate should remain aboard, partly because a crew needed leadership and partly because nothing prevented them from sailing off on their own.

But the fact that Senlin was delusional trumped any protocol. She couldn't send a man who was seeing things into a forest that was probably infested with beasts and spiders. Edith pictured him wandering about in circles, turning his map this way and that, and ranting to his lost wife while the rest of them starved on the boat. If Iren went with him, she'd have to be told what, exactly, he needed protection from, and Edith wasn't ready to tell the crew their captain was haunted just yet. Once that news was out, there would be no going back.

Senlin saw in Edith's expression a determination that he had no hope of discouraging. And, truth be told, he didn't relish the idea of going into the woods alone. He surprised her with a smile. "All right, Mister Winters. Don't forget your sidearm."

"We haven't any powder," she said.

"But it makes a good impression, don't you think?" he said, and turned to Adam while Edith went to fetch her pistol. "Adam, I leave the *Stone Cloud* in your capable hands. Fix her for me, would you? Iren, I dare say you have some heavy lifting ahead of you. Voleta, you're my little owl. If trouble comes, and I may bring it with me, I'm counting on you to see it a long way off. Keep an eye on everyone, please."

The crew made their promises to do all they could while Senlin uncrated and unfurled the ladder. Edith returned with a sword on one hip and a pistol on the other. She'd also tied a yellow scarf about her neck, her version of dressing for a social call.

"Mister Winters and I will be back tomorrow morning with breakfast," he announced with a little more confidence than the circumstance probably deserved. Yet Voleta was not one to pass up an opportunity to raise a cheer, which she did while prodding her brother in the ribs until he finally gave in and helped finish the hurrah.

Senlin gestured for Edith to lead the way down to the dusky beach below. Before following, he leaned into Iren and spoke with a neutral expression to keep from stirring Adam's or Voleta's suspicion. "If the commissioner finds you, and I pray he doesn't, betray me at once. Tell him I have his painting," Senlin said, patting the breast of his coat. "Tell him you are saboteurs left behind for your crimes. Say whatever you must to survive. And if we aren't back in a day, take the ship as soon as it will fly and go. Sell it for scrap if you have to. Don't let them starve."

"Aye, sir," Iren said, her broad face tight as a drum.

Chapter Three

Gentle reader, do not make yourself an arbor under which other pedestrians must pass. Move your embraces and glad reunions to the shoulder. Even a great romance is but a stumbling block when it happens upon the road.

—*Folkways and Right of Ways in the Silk Gardens*, Anon.

If there were forests on the moon, Senlin imagined they might well resemble the eerie landscape of the Silk Gardens.

The trees were hard, barkless, and pale as mushrooms. Glowing moss bearded the sandy ground between the disheveled cobblestones of the winding trails. Everything seemed to be pressing up and crowding in. Spider silk laced between branches and swooped over their heads, growing so dense in the high bowers that the fine threads merged into a single, unbroken canopy. The air was parched and cold, and it tickled their nostrils with minerals as pungent as potpourri. Very quickly, the ship and crew seemed far behind them, and they felt quite alone.

It was strange to think that such a wilderness had been allowed to grow inside the vital Tower. The dissolving relics of the abandoned park only made the scene more surreal. They passed smashed bowers, empty signposts, and booths that had once been filled with edibles and mementos that now bowed under mats of shining lichen.

"Did we take another wrong turn? I don't see a bird anywhere," Edith said, setting down her sack of books alongside Senlin's. The forest was chilly, and still she'd begun to sweat from the exercise. She tied up her hair with her yellow scarf and relished the cool air on her neck. "Are you sure it's a bird?"

"It looks like a bird," Senlin said. "An ostrich, I think. It's drawn very small." He squinted at the map. "I suppose it might be a chicken."

"Here, let me look. I can't imagine why you thought this map would be reliable." She had a point. Even after a century, the map had acquired none of the dignity of an antique. It was garishly colored and crowded with animal caricatures. It was the sort of thing that cried out to be folded into a hat and given to a child. "Your giraffe turned out to be a llama, and I'm still not sure what that last landmark was," she said, referring to the rusty beast they'd passed earlier. "A large dog? A small bear? This map is hopeless."

"It has gotten us this far," Senlin said, taking the map back before she could horribly misfold it. He wasn't blind to its flaws, but he'd already invested too much hope to give up on it now. "If you overlook the general aesthetic, which is admittedly silly, it does have all the marks of a map: There's a compass rose, a scale, a legend..."

"It's covered in hearts, Tom."

"Yes, I see them. The legend identifies those as areas that couples might find—"

"—enabling."

"I was going to say 'of scenic interest,'" he said.

"So, which way?"

They had stalled at a fork in the winding path. Senlin peered in one direction, then the other. Both ways were as narrow and tortuous as animal trails. Unlike other ringdoms he'd seen, which were uniformly flat, the ground here rolled and pitched over modest knolls and valleys, all of which were a little too constrained to be convincing. As wild as the Gardens were now, the original landscaping had not been entirely erased.

But the porcelmores grew so tightly and their branches were so tangled, the forest off the footpath was virtually impenetrable. This had been a disappointment to Edith. She had hoped to forgo the meandering lanes outlined on Senlin's map in favor of a more direct route. If they traveled in a straight line, the Golden Zoo was only a mile and a half away.

When they first entered the woods, after snaking through the abysmal graveyard of airships, she had been able to forge a path with relative ease. The brittle, white branches shattered under her cutlass like fine china. But the work quickly turned difficult. The saplings grew thicker, their growth denser the farther they went. Worse, the shattered wood proved to be as sharp as quills, and it wasn't long before they began to feel like a pair of pincushions. Her efforts also disturbed the gloamine, which fell on them as a fine, luminous powder. The silt clung to their clothes and hair as stubbornly as pollen and soon turned them into a pair of glowing ghosts thrashing through the undergrowth.

And that was when she had agreed to give the map a try.

"Look, there it is," Senlin said, pointing to a half-covered form on the side of the path. He cut aside a few saplings with his sword to get a better look at the mechanical beast. Like the others they'd seen, it must've been splendid once. But rust had eaten away at the machine's polish, and many of its plates were corroded through. "It's an emu."

"How can you tell?"

Senlin scuffed aside a clump of moss so she could see the machine's planted feet. "See, it has three toes. An ostrich only has two."

"How in the world would you know that?"

"I had a student ask me once what the difference was, and so I went home and read everything I could find on emu and ostrich anatomy, which to be fair wasn't much."

Edith shook her head in amazement, though her patience quickly thinned. "What are you looking for now? Come on, we don't have time for this."

"This one is stamped, too," he said, reaching around a thorny branch to read the plaque on the bird's breast. "It says, 'The Emu of the Sphinx.'"

"Fascinating."

"It is. Don't you see what this means? When I was in the Basement, I rode a machine called something like...like...the Many-Handled Pump of the Sphinx."

"The beer-me-go-round."

"You've heard of it?" he said.

"You lived with students; I lived with pirates. If beer comes out of it, I've heard of it."

"Well, then you know the pumps and all that plumbing must be very old, as old as the Tower itself, perhaps. And this emu is at least a century old. But, em..." He trailed off when he saw her expression. With her hair pulled up and her neck stretched, she looked quite severe.

"My arm is new," she said.

"Exactly. Obviously, it can't be the same man responsible for all these inventions. He'd have to be hundreds, perhaps thousands, of years old."

"What does it matter?"

"What does it matter? Anyone that involved in the design, perhaps even the construction, of the Tower must be unimaginably knowledgeable."

"But you just said it couldn't be the same person."

"It can't, of course, but he must be someone with access to that knowledge. Your Sphinx, whoever he is, must know the Tower intimately: its secrets and inner workings. Think of the questions he could answer. Here we are desperately scrounging for a little information. Meanwhile, the Sphinx—"

"Let's move on."

"You know, if there's something you want to tell me, Edith..."

"Come on, Tom. You promised Voleta breakfast."

After an hour of slow, meandering progress, they came upon a small clearing with a collapsed bench and a perfectly round pond at its center. The pond held the gloomy light like a mirror.

"Those book corners dig into you like a spur," Senlin said, dropping his sack on the sand. He tried to massage his back, was foiled by his long coat, and so removed it, folded it in half, and set it upon the bag of books. As he kneaded his back, he said, "I feel like a monster for having made my students carry their books to school every day."

"Young backs have short memories," Edith said, and knelt to inspect the water. She stirred, sniffed, and peered into the basin like she was reading tea leaves in a cup.

Senlin cleaned glowing silt from his compass crystal and consulted it alongside the map. He neglected to mention that they were presently camped upon a heart. "How deep is it?"

"It's more a cistern than a pond. It drops right off. I can't say how deep."

"The real question is can we drink it?" Senlin asked as Edith craned down to smell the water.

"Be my guest," she said.

"Don't be absurd. Testing for poison is a first mate's job," Senlin said. Edith gave him a strained look. "I was only joking! What is the matter? Really. This has gone on long enough. You've been frowning and huffing all day, and I suspect that I'm at fault, but blast it all, Edith, if I can guess how. You must tell me. What is the matter?"

She stood up and slapped the grit from her palms; that light clapping resounded like applause through the silent grove. "You blew out my room, Tom. I know you had to do it. Perhaps I would've done the same thing. But that stupid little chart house, with all its stupid drafts and splinters, meant a lot to me. I lost everything with it."

Senlin crossed the glade and took her by the shoulders. "Edith. You have every reason to be upset. This is the trouble with running for your life—it's easy to lose perspective of what accounts for a life." He gave her a reassuring shake, a sort of telegraphed embrace. "As soon as we're out of this, we'll rebuild the chart house. You can be the foreman, and Adam and I will be your carpenters. I promise."

"I lost my vials," she said, shrugging under his hold. "Every last one. They flew out the back with the rest of my things."

Now Senlin understood. When the Sphinx first fitted her with the engine nearly a year earlier, he had given her a stock of the mysterious batteries for her arm. She had jealously guarded these because there was only one source for replacements. He knew she had no desire to hurry back to the Sphinx. She could hardly stand to hear him mentioned.

"How long will your arm last?" he asked in a thin voice.

"Days. Hours. Depends on how much I press it," she said. "Then it'll be a millstone."

"So, in one fell swoop, I destroyed your sanctuary and robbed you of your arm," he said soberly. "I'm sorry. I'm so very sorry."

"It had to be done. I don't blame you. I'm just angry. No, that's not it, I'm . . . to be honest, Tom, I'm a little . . ." She wanted to say that she was afraid—afraid of what would happen to her when she returned to the Sphinx, and afraid of what the Sphinx would do to her friends if she brought them with her. She feared the day might soon come when she would have to leave him and the crew. But she couldn't bring herself to confess any of this now.

"What is that sound?" Senlin said, interrupting her deliberation. He turned sharply and stared into the milky light of the forest.

She heard it, too. It sounded like wind moving through dry leaves, but there was no wind and no leaves to stir in it. They were still studying the rustling when a black spot, no larger than a chestnut, skittered out from the trees. It ran across the sand, passed under the bridge of their arms, and disappeared into the undergrowth on the opposite side of the clearing, all in two blinks of an eye.

"Look, there's one of the spiders. Gnarly things, aren't they?" Senlin said.

Edith was still glaring at the forest. "The woods are going dark," she said.

Senlin saw she was right. The glow of the forest was being snuffed out. The edge of the eclipse rose high into the bowers, and the darkness moved quickly toward them. A few more inky spiders trickled from the forest and scrambled across the sand.

A shrill cry broke over the droning rustle. It sounded like the squeal of a boar, but more resonant and chilling. Senlin shortened his hold on Edith.

The awful note blared again, seeming now to rise up from another side of them. Then the darkness poured into the glen.

The mass of spiders was so dense it obscured everything beneath it. The trees vanished, then the clearing, and then the sand at their feet disappeared under the curdling black swarm.

"Into the water!" Senlin said.

They took a breath together, and still locked in an embrace, leapt into the deep, dead pool.

Chapter Four

I admit, your lordship, to having had my doubts about boarding spiders and spider-eaters in a public park. It seemed to my admittedly meager imagination a bit like inviting rats into your home and then adopting tigers to keep them in check.

—*Inaugurations of the Silk Gardens*, Salo

In the cove of shipwrecks, a terrible squeal echoed across the domed ceiling and bounced through the alleys of wrapped ships. It sounded like the desperate complaint of a wounded animal, Adam thought, and in many ways, it was.

Down on one knee, Iren pried nails from broken boards with a crowbar. The spikes emerged slowly and with a piercing squeal. She dropped the nails into a zinc bucket, so each scream concluded with the rat-a-tat of a snare drum. It was slow going because she was trying not to bend them. They would need straight nails to rebuild the ship.

Adam cringed at the noise and tried to focus on the sled he was building. When he realized that they needed a fair amount of salvage, he had decided that a sled was only practical. The forward hatch formed the base, and the captain's bedposts formed the runners.

"Done with your list?" Iren asked, palming sweat from her brow. The work had invigorated old scars on her arms and face. She looked nearly as battered as the ship.

"Just. We lost a quarter of our tethers. It's a miracle we didn't fall from the sky. So, we need rope—a lot of it. There's the umbilical, of course, and we could use some gas. Ballast should be easy enough. If we can find sacks, we can fill them with sand right here." Adam stood up from his work and gave the sled a soft kick. "That'll do. Where's Voleta?"

"In the galley," Iren said.

"Still counting crumbs, hmm? I'll tell her she's in charge of the ship while we're on our raid. She'll like that."

Adam went below to find his sister. Left alone, Iren's thoughts turned to questions of violence, as they often did in moments of quiet. She thought about the likelihood of an attack, which seemed middling, and the defensibility of their position, which was poor. They were surrounded by open beach. If the *Ararat* cruised in behind them, there would be nothing to do but jump ship and run for cover. If an attack came from the forest, she'd see them coming, but without any gunpowder, there'd be nothing she could do to discourage them. The ship's keel hung about six feet off the ground, which was high enough to keep an enemy from swarming the ship, but low enough to be scaled or, if their attackers were sufficiently numerous, pulled down.

She imagined the ship's deck swarming with armed brutes. This was usually her favorite part of the daydream because now she could watch as she dealt out mortal blows, dismembering the horde one soul at a time. She reveled in the vision because it was always immaculate: Every one of her parries was successful and every attack was true.

But an odd thing happened on this occasion when she imagined herself sparring on the deck of the ship. She saw herself stumble, and a brigand's rapier pierced her between the ribs. Then she didn't see the man lurking behind her, and when he kicked her in the back, she staggered and nearly lost her feet. Then a big brute with arms as thick as roof beams grabbed her, pinning her arms to her sides. This vision of herself being methodically beaten confused her, and she tried to reset it or overcome it, but the tactician in her head refused to cheat. Her defenses had been slow, her attacks incomplete. She had been drubbed, fair and square. Her pitiless imagination played out her grappling, panicked death in gory detail.

Her usual frown deepened.

A distant squeal interrupted her thoughts. It came from the forest. She squinted at the trees expectantly, but the cry did not repeat. It could not have been an echo of the pulled nails. It was far too late.

She was still trying to identify what she had heard when Adam pounded up the stairs from the hold and popped out of the hatch in a panic.

"I can't believe she'd be so stupid at a time like this!" He snatched up the scabbard of his rapier and began buckling it on with trembling hands.

"Where are you going?" Iren said, stepping in front of him.

Adam hardly seemed to see her. He tried to slip past her, but she pulled him back. His eye was fixed on the gloomy forest.

Why had he imagined, even for a second, that Voleta would resist the call of such a playground? These were the first trees she'd seen in years; of course she'd have to climb them. All the world was her trapeze!

"She's gone," he said.

"You have to fix the ship."

"I'm not going to sit here tinkering while my sister's lost in the woods."

"You have to fix the ship," Iren said again. Her broad face was as set as a casting mold. "We've no food and little water. We are stranded. Voleta is stranded, too."

"I know! I just need a minute to find her and drag her—"

Grabbing him under the arms, Iren lifted Adam into the air. She brought him in until their noses touched, then smashed, then rolled together. She smelled like iron chains and sweat. When she spoke, her foul breath warmed his face. "You want to be trusted? You want to save your sister? You want me to set you down on your feet and not your head? Do what you promised the captain you'd do. Fix the ship."

Though his devotion to his sister bucked against the reasoning, he knew Iren was right. Voleta had been impulsive, leaving him again to be the prudent one. He recalled the pragmatism of his days in the port and remembered that rescue sometimes demands preparation rather than action. No matter what happened next, they would need the ship.

Adam nodded, grinding their noses together, but Iren did not loosen her hold. He understood the moment required more than a tacit agreement; he knew what she was waiting for, and so he delivered the words in as firm a tone as he could muster: "I will fix the ship."

Voleta moved through the high branches of the porcelmores under a cloud of webs. The forking, glowing trunks below resembled lightning, frozen midstrike. It was an astonishing view. She was glad not to have missed it. She leapt to a new limb, then walked out to another on tiptoe, crossing with a swiftness impossible on the ground where the undergrowth was as thick as a bramble.

She had tried to be good. But the ship had become such a depressing place. She didn't feel like she could've stayed aboard another minute, even though she knew her disappearance would test her brother's nerves.

Before she left, she had been scouring the deep cabinets of the pantry for anything edible. She found an old soup bone tucked in a corner and a rusty pot of hardened molasses, which she at first mistook for some sort of patching tar, and she swept from the cupboard shelves enough loose tea to color a cup of hot water.

It was boring work.

In her boredom, she had begun to hum a stupid, sticky melody. The tune just popped into her head and refused to leave. She hummed and hummed it, until slowly, the song teased a memory to the fore of her thoughts, and she saw the specter of an organist, dramatically caped and leering over his shoulder as his hands ran up and down the keyboard with automatic grace.

In a flash, she recognized the song coming out of her own throat. It had been her musical accompaniment on the stage of the Steam Pipe for many, many nights. It was a tune written and named just for her: "Voleta the Flying Girl."

She struck out from the ship shortly thereafter.

There was nothing better for clearing the head than a little adventure.

Squit went with her, of course, though she kept her tucked in her sleeve because she was afraid the squirrel might get bitten by one of the black spiders that were everywhere in the treetops. They were compact like crabs, and they darted around the trunks and through the cloud of silk above her. They generally tried to avoid her, but it was hard not to step on them or accidentally clutch one when she gripped a branch. Despite her heavy gloves and leather boots, one of the spiders had gotten onto her neck and bitten her. It smarted like a bee sting, but the venom didn't feel fatal.

She had gone in the same direction as the captain with half a mind to keep an eye on him and half a mind to leap out and surprise him for the sport of it. He and Mister Winters made so much noise talking and arguing, they were easy to keep track of.

She hadn't quite caught up with them when she heard something new. It sounded like a rustling wind, then a spattering of rain falling through leaves. The noise swelled all about her, and for a moment she thought a storm was breaking. But of course that was absurd. She was inside the Tower.

But it wasn't rain that was falling.

The spiders no longer scattered before her or wandered aimlessly in and out of the web cloud. They changed direction all at once like iron shavings in the presence of a magnet. First the spiders ran in singles and then in streams. Then they poured from the cobwebs in a great black cascade, tumbling, falling through the branches and over her.

She hadn't time to get out of the way. She clung to a willowy treetop and tried to make herself very small. The swarming spiders crested over her.

She expected to be stung to death. But the spiders were apparently not in a biting mood. This fact might have consoled her more, if the exposed skin of her neck and face did not tingle so terribly under the pricking of thousands of legs. She clenched her eyes shut and held her breath.

Something of the sensation called up a memory, and since she was in need of a distraction, she indulged the nostalgic fancy that carried her back to her old home.

In the Depot of Sumer, where she had been born and grown intrepid, there was a narrow beam that crossed a particularly active portion of track. Adults would never think to cross the beam, and if they had suspected that it tempted children, they would have surely taken it down. The beam had once been part of a grain chute that filled open hopper cars, though it was all that remained of the dismantled machine.

The depot children, the rough ones at least, bragged about crossing the beam, though of course no one had seen anyone do it. The bar was forty feet across, about as broad as a boot heel, and rusted orange. Even if the beam held, the steam of a passing train might cook you or blow you off.

Voleta, who often took pains to prove her fearlessness to the condescending depot boys, began to think of this unremarkable rusty beam as the single greatest test of courage in all of Sumer and perhaps the world.

So, one afternoon she marched up and down the neighborhood boardwalks, collecting a mob of jeering, teasing children, who would bear witness to her transit of the beam. Since it was the steam that frightened the boys most, Voleta decided to wait until a train approached to begin her crossing. That way, no one could say she had been lucky. When an engine began to chug up the track, belching great piles of sooty smoke, she left the surety of the boardwalk and sidled out onto the beam.

The edges of the iron were so soft they crumbled under her shoes. The metal groaned but did not break.

She had to hurry to reach the middle of the beam before the train passed. The smokestack seemed to be choking. The steam puffed and pinched and puffed again. She turned to face it. She closed her eyes and put out her thin, bare arms.

Under the bellow of the engine, she heard the voices of adults rise in alarm. But they hadn't time to stop the train, and they were afraid to venture out after her and break the beam with their weight. First they commanded her to come in, and then they cursed her because they saw *the little tart was smiling*.

The indifferent engine passed, loud as a gale, and the smokestack blew at her with such hot violence it made her hair stand straight up and her clothes pull at her like a sail. She was instantly soaked, her skin nearly poached by the blast of boiled air. But when the train passed, she had not been cooked, and she had not been knocked off her beam.

She returned to the boardwalk, still smiling, though she was as pink as a piglet. The crowd of adults who'd gathered were so exasperated they couldn't decide whether to throttle her or coddle her, so they just took her home. She survived her mother's horror and the blisters that formed and the cough that lasted a month with absolute, insufferable smugness. At last she and everybody else had proof that she was brave.

When her mother finally allowed her to go out and play again, she discovered a funny thing. The depot seemed smaller and safer and dull. The narrow beam that had captured her imagination for months now just looked like an old bar. Soon, she couldn't remember which beam had been the focus of her obsession. She crossed them all, crossed them all twice, just to be sure, and found them all the same. Then she knew she would have to leave the depot and go somewhere with higher wires and hotter steam...

When Voleta opened her eyes in the boughs of the Silk Reef, the wave of spiders had passed.

The mass fled before her like the shadow of a fast cloud. To her surprise, she found that she hadn't been bitten, not even once. Wherever the spiders were going, they hadn't time to waste on her.

She looked down and saw the cause of the spiders' agitation at once. A herd of enormous, shaggy beasts were pressing through the undergrowth. These had to be the spider-eaters the captain had spoken of. They were driving the spiders into a swarm.

One of the beasts raised an earsplitting cry, and the others soon trumpeted back. Voleta counted eight in all. Then one, a big straggler with an impressive gray mane, stopped and turned around as if harkening to some other call. She heard in the faint distance a shrill squeal. The gray-crested beast let the pack go on without it. He sniffed the air and lumbered away.

It was going toward the ship.

Voleta hesitated. She thought of her brother. He had Iren and the ship to protect him against one monster. The captain and Mister Winters were about to be overrun by a swarm of spiders and the beastly herd that chased them.

She hadn't any doubt what Adam would do if their positions were reversed and it was she who was waiting on the ship. She loved him dearly, but he could be such a marm sometimes.

Chapter Five

Should you ever be tempted to dip your toes in the Garden's aquifers, just remember where the water flows. One man's bath becomes another man's broth.

—*Folkways and Right of Ways in the Silk Gardens*, Anon.

The water was as cold as a springhouse. It needled their skin and made their muscles seize. Edith had been right about the pool: There was no tapering of the shore, just a sudden, severe drop.

As they sank, still clinging to each other, Senlin watched the blue glow of the forest ripple overhead. Spiders cascaded across the surface, their fat bodies buoyant as corks. The darkness that followed, quick and complete, stole his sense of direction. It occurred to him that the cistern might be as deep as the Tower; it might flow into the plumbing, which might connect to the subterranean seas. The two of them were sinking to the center of the earth. There was nothing inside the perfect dark to orient him except for his hold on Edith.

A moment later, his feet touched the rocky bottom, quelling his disorientation. The full weight of the water bore down upon him. He didn't let go of Edith, though he knew it was her arm that had brought them down so quickly and that held them to the floor so firmly. He knew, too, that even if it meant he would drown, he would not leave her behind.

Then the surface above them was lit again by a great commotion. Legs and long-trunked bodies shattered the water and thrashed across. The passage was so violent and swift Senlin hadn't time to really observe the animals, but he was certain he had just seen his first spider-eater. A pack of the beasts had made the spiders swarm.

Senlin peered up at the stormy surface, glowing again with the light of the forest. The chopped water began to calm. There was no sign of the spiders or the eaters, though for all he knew, the beasts might be waiting by the waterside.

It didn't matter. He was running out of breath. He began to swim toward the light. Only then did he understand the full burden of Edith's engine. She kicked along with him, but her boots were taller and heavier than his, and these, combined with her armored limb, hampered her terribly. She began to flail. He redoubled his grip on her belt and beat his legs more fiercely. No, not fiercely—*fearfully*.

It felt like swimming back up a waterfall. He strained until his neck ached, and still they made little progress. When he slowed his frenzied kicking, even for a moment, they sank back down twice as fast as he'd raised them. His legs burned despite the chilly water. Edith nudged him to the wall of the pool where she could use her arm to help pull them up. With her help, they began to ascend more quickly, though still not fast enough. His panicked lungs pushed on his mouth to open; his throat spasmed, swallowing again and again. He wanted so badly to breathe the water in.

They broke the surface with a gasp that hurt when it filled them.

They hauled themselves ashore, too exhausted to appreciate the absence of spiders and spider-eaters. At that moment, Senlin would've been happy to roll around on a bed of broken glass: anything so long as it was dry.

Both felt pressed beyond exhaustion. They hadn't slept in days. They had been beaten, starved, and now nearly drowned. It was too much. Their panting slowed. The sand felt as soft as goose down. Lying at arm's length from each other, they closed their eyes just for a moment, just to catch their breath, and without meaning to, they fell quite asleep.

*   *   *

At a distance the shipwrecks reminded Iren of presents waiting to be unwrapped. Inspired by visions of full pantries, kegs of rum, and powder to load their guns, she enjoyed a little burst of energy while dragging Adam's cobbled sled across the beach.

But it didn't take long to realize they were not the first to unwrap these gifts. The silk of every wreck was slit open like a tent. Because many of the vessels lay on their decks or sides, crude entries had been chopped in the hulls. Adam lit lanterns for them, and they began to search the wrecked, crazily turned cabins for salvage and supplies.

Amid the detritus of shattered lockers and kitchen cupboards, they found no sign of food, liquor, or black powder. They did find rope, lumber, a tank of hydrogen, and most miraculously an undamaged umbilical duct tied up neatly in one corner of an engine room. These much-needed materials gave them hope they would be able to repair their ship, but it did not make them feel any better about breakfast, which seemed again to retreat from them like a desert mirage.

They scoured the places that months of piracy had taught them not to overlook and discovered under the stairs of one cargo hold a chest that had been boarded up inside the hollow. They cracked the feeble lock and found six ornate pistols lying on a bed of straw. They were the sort of weapons more suited to formal duels than battles, with butts of carved horn and pearl-pointed ramrods, but they appeared quite functional. Included in the chest were two horns of powder, bundles of wadding, and cases of shot. It was a thrilling discovery, but the only one of its kind.

After another hour's work, they were at the end of their list of supplies, and the sled was full. They had what they needed to repair the *Cloud*.

But uncovering the pistols had whetted Adam's appetite for treasure. He still had a mind to return to Senlin's good graces, and what surer way was there to recover a man's faith than with treasure? He had his eye on a particular round-bottomed schooner that lay mostly submerged in the sand. He hoped that its state of interment would've discouraged foragers. Iren was keen to get back to the *Stone Cloud*. Lingering between open beach and a stand of trees made her nervous.

But she had just begun to load the pretty guns, and the activity was so pleasant she wanted to finish. She agreed to give Adam five minutes (not one minute more) to search this one final wreck.

The wrapped ship lay almost perfectly upside down. He entered through a breach in the side of the forecastle. The craft had sunk so deep a little dune had poured into the great cabin below. In another decade or two, the beach would probably fill the ship.

Inside, he raised his lantern against the darkness and felt a swerving sense of disorientation. All of the furniture in the room was above him, clinging to the ceiling that had once been the floor. A four-post bed, a chest of drawers, two bookshelves, and a nightstand stood perfectly squared overhead. It was not unusual for airmen to fix their furniture to the deck, especially in the captain's quarters where the furnishings had some value, but these pieces had been so ruthlessly bolted that even a violent tumble and an era of rotting hadn't uprooted them.

The room beneath the furniture was another matter. Broken crockery, navigational instruments, and linens lay in a great haystack. The whole space was sprayed with playing cards, cutlery, papers, books, and maps that had spilled out of the open chart house at the rear of the room. Amid this domestic rubble, skeletons were strewn in undignified poses: head between legs, or tailbone in the air, or nosed into a corner like a naughty child.

Adam forced himself to look past the ghastliness. He hadn't any time to waste.

Searching the other wrecks had taught him he'd find nothing of value in the open, so he began tapping on the walls and feeling for misplaced seams in the paneling. After a little hunting, he found what he was looking for: a secret alcove behind the shelf of a suspended bookcase. The back plate opened when he pressed it. Inside he found what he took to be the captain's private cache. And what a pitiful captain he must've been. Two thin gold chains with painted tin charms, eight shekels, and a few coppers made up the entirety of the captain's fortune. Adam swept all into his palm and pocketed the woeful prize.

He was about to slam the panel back in disgust when he spied a leather-bound book discreetly stuffed to one side of the compartment.

When he removed the book, something fell out of its spine. He caught it in the air and turned it toward the sallow lantern light. It was a bar of gold: six inches long, narrow as a thumb, and no thicker than a coin. But it was pure gold, heavy and lustering.

Adam opened the book and began reading where the ribbon marker lay. The account was written in an educated hand. The final entry read:

I have done it. I have scrabbled into heaven. I have broken through the Collar and touched some of her riches. But the sparking men pursued us, and we had to flee. I must console myself with this taste of my future fortune. I am resolved to return with a fleet. I have seen things I can hardly believe: posts of silver and roads of gold. All the Tower under the Collar now seems little better than a poorhouse.

The words brought to mind the old airman from the Ugly Rug and his apocryphal description of the fortune that lay beyond the Collar of Heaven: "Trees of silver and rivers of gold. All you have to do is run up, stick out your arm, and pull treasure in by the handful." Here in his hand was some proof of that impossible promise.

Iren's muffled voice interrupted his excitement.

Assuming his five minutes were up, he stuffed the gold file back into the book's spine and secured the volume in his waistband under his shirt. He'd just begun to scale the slope of sand at the entry when the crack of a pistol froze him in his tracks. A second shot quickly followed, and then a third, each progressively farther away.

Hurrying up the unstable slope, he found the sled abandoned. A confusion of tracks pitted the sand. One of the ceremonial pistols lay on the ground. He picked it up, and a wisp of acrid smoke twisted from the barrel.

The angle of the wreck obscured his line of sight of the *Stone Cloud*. He rounded the silk-wrapped aft of the ship just in time to hear a fourth pistol report. A split second later, the shot thudded into the wood by his head. Someone was shooting at him.

Then he saw the beast, charging away. From the back, it looked like a stretched-out bear striped with swaths of gray. It nearly galloped. Iren ran ahead of the beast, dodging left and right. Her feints did not seem to confuse the animal in the least. It charged at her headlong, narrowing the gap. She threw a pistol at it, the very one that she'd blindly fired over her shoulder and nearly struck Adam with. The beast wagged its long neck and snorted when the butt of the gun bounced off its head.

She was running for the refuge of the ship.

Adam knew at once she would never reach it in time.

Chapter Six

Without military experience to shape and temper them, young men turn into idlers, my lord; they turn into bards. The Gardens are full of them, lounging on elbows with their shirts open, spewing poetry at plain-faced girls. I shudder at the waste of it. We will owe this generation a war.

—*Inaugurations of the Silk Gardens*, Salo

Senlin woke feeling like the tea bag at the bottom of an empty pot: wet, heavy, and used up.

The forest shone on him lying on his back in the sand. He had the strange inclination to gather up a pile of the glowing branches to build an absurd campfire, one that glowed blue rather than orange and cooled rather than warmed. He and Edith could sit about it and sing songs and roast ice cubes.

He tried shifting his arms, but they seemed reluctant, and he didn't see why he should insist. He recalled his near drowning with the same dreamy apathy. He still tasted the mineral-rich water. At least he knew it was potable now.

He closed his eyes for a moment to gather his wits, and when he opened them again, a pale face was hovering very close to his own.

It took Senlin a long moment to realize that this pasty face belonged to no one he knew, and that he, a stranger to these woods, should be alarmed by this fact.

The face retracted from view, and Senlin sat up quick enough to make his head swim. He found Edith sprawled at his side, wet hair curtained about her sleeping face. He shook her shoulder until her eyes opened and she too popped up, coughing to clear her lungs.

The peering face belonged to a small bald man with a dramatic underbite that had the unfortunate effect of making him appear simple-minded. He looked ready to dart off at the least provocation. Senlin took him for a hod, though he didn't wear the iron collar or carry the load that generally distinguished them. He wore a white sarong and carried a flat basket piled with perilous-looking mushrooms on one arm.

"Hello," Senlin said. He pulled at his soggy lapels, releasing streams of water.

The hod said something slurred and strange in return. It reminded Senlin of the dialect unique to inebriated men. He understood not a word of it.

"I'm sorry?" Senlin said.

The hod repeated the drunken sentence exactly as he had before, and still it made no sense.

"Maybe he's been in the woods too long," Edith said. She clapped the water from her ears. The hod maintained the anxious expression he'd come with and glanced all about even as he repeated for a third time the same babbling mess.

Undaunted, Senlin extended his hand. "I am Captain Tom Mudd. I am looking for a man named Marat."

As soon as the word *Marat* was spoken, the whole aspect of the hod changed. A moment before, he'd seemed ready to skitter off, and now he seemed quite self-possessed. He bowed at the waist. When he came up, his expression was almost pious. He said, "Marat, Marat, Marat," and with a series of sweeping gestures, urged them to follow him down a narrow path into the forest.

"Oh, I don't like him," Edith said. "He's exactly the sort of lunatic you warn children about following into the woods. Or don't you have those stories where you come from?"

"We have them. But for us it was grottoes. Never trust a man who sleeps in a grotto."

"What's a grotto?"

"It's a sea cave. They're quite interesting, actually. You can find all sorts of urchins and crabs and octopuses in them," Senlin said in an agreeable tone, which the hod smiled at gamely, though he didn't seem to understand a word. "Look at him, though; he's harmless. And I don't think there's any doubt that he knows Marat."

"Marat!" the hod said, and swept his arm at the glowing forest.

"He does like that name," Edith said.

"If he makes any trouble, you can bop him on the head." Senlin collected his coat and sack of books. "Let's see where this goes."

"You're both mad." Edith exercised her engine arm. She frowned at the water that drained from it. "Are you sure you've never slept in a grotto, Tom?"

"I may have dozed off once or twice," Senlin said, smiling.

Unobserved in the treetops over the little clearing, Voleta watched the trio move into the forest. The fat-cheeked squirrel sat on her shoulder, methodically preening her tail.

Voleta said, "Look at them, Squit. They're going with him. It's like no one ever told them about following strangers into the grass. And they call me reckless."

When the beast first emerged from the forest at a gallop, Iren had been loading the last of the six pistols.

It had been such a happy and absorbing little chore. These arms were nothing like the thick-barreled, graceless pieces she'd used all her life. These guns were like a lady's fingernails: painted, manicured, and fine. After she prepared each one, she stuck it in her chain belt where it hung like jewelry. For a moment she forgot her hunger and weariness. She felt like strutting around. For the first time in memory, she wished for a mirror.

Then the animal appeared and the guns were just guns again.

It looked like a narrow bear with the stump of an elephant's trunk and shaggy, long legs. She guessed it was a spider-eater, which the captain had told them to expect, though she had been picturing something smaller. Captain said they were like big anteaters, which didn't help her imagination at all since she'd never seen one of those, either. She had reasoned that since ants were so small, an anteater would be no larger than a hamster. A spider-eater, her logic continued, would therefore be about the size of a guinea pig.

The behemoth that bolted at her now was very disappointing. She had a pistol in either hand and four more stuffed in her chains and still felt underprepared for this introduction to the species.

The beast was fifty paces out when she fired her first shot, which thumped in the sand well short of the mark. The crack of her pistol seemed to only invigorate the beast. It gave a terrible cry and tossed its head in an ecstasy of rage.

She should not have showed it her back. She knew it even as she did it, knew it even as she began to run. If she had stood her ground, dropped to one knee, and worked through her battery of pistols, she would have almost certainly felled the thing. Instead, she'd let herself be startled into fleeing. She'd allowed herself to become its prey.

Taking potshots over her shoulder, she ran toward the *Stone Cloud*, dropping the guns as she spent them. One of her shots, she was sure, had struck the spider-eater in the chest, but the creature only jerked a little, then thundered on. It was more sure-footed on the sand than she, and its legs were fresher. Captain had told them that the beasts would probably have claws, which hadn't seemed so awful while they were as big as a guinea pig but was now considerably more troubling. She had no interest in wrestling the thing. She fired her last shot, but her arm shook and the ball flew wide.

She ran in a serpentine fashion, hoping to juke the beast off her tail, but it wasn't fooled. She could smell it now; it smelled like foul meat and turned earth. She felt the familiar frisson of adrenaline, but with it came the unfamiliar feeling of grief. It seemed unfair that this would be her final test. Her usual courage competed with a desire to not be there, to not be hurtling toward this lonely end. She would, if she could, try the whole thing again.

The skulking *Stone Cloud* was only twenty strides away, but it might as well have been over the horizon. She could hear the beast's wheezing.

She must turn around. She must stand her ground. There was no reason to refuse the confrontation. There was no benefit to being dragged down from behind. And yet, she could not make herself stop.

Her confusion was interrupted by a sharp crack that rang against the bowl of the cavern ceiling. The crack sounded again and again in quick succession, and she sensed the beast was no longer closing on her. The dangling rope ladder to the hovering, listing ship was nearly in her hands. She lunged for it, caught it, and dragged herself up.

Safely on deck, she flew to what remained of the ship's bow. The spider-eater had turned around and was retreating from the *Cloud* with the same speed that it had come. It ran toward Adam, who stood hammering the hull of his lucky wreck with the butt of a pistol.

He had called the terror back to himself by beating the gavel of an empty gun.

It was a miserable march. Their small guide seemed determined to take them down the most cramped and overgrown trails. The sacks of books they carried, which had been spared their dunking, seemed to grow heavier by the minute. The trees nipped at them. Grit from breaking branches stuck to their wet clothes, turning their cuffs and collars into sandpaper that sawed them raw. Still, they were happy to have an escort, even a simple one. Anything was preferable to bickering over a flawed map.

Occasionally, their guide would discern something in the character of the woods that disturbed him, and he would crouch low, gesturing for them to duck alongside him. Then, before long, a foul stench would waft in, and something large would crunch through the none-too-distant underbrush. They would wait until the commotion passed and then wait a few moments more to make certain the spider-eater was well and truly gone.

An hour after their trudge began, the forest abruptly stopped, and they found themselves at the edge of a grand clearing nearly as vast as the beach they'd landed on. The ground here was carpeted in a spongy moss that glowed like a gaslight.

In the center of the clearing, rising to the very limit of the ringdom, was the Golden Zoo. The vision stopped Senlin and Edith in their tracks, and their guide had to come back and wait for them to digest their amazement.

The Golden Zoo resembled a birdcage, but to say so was inadequate to the point of being misleading. It was roughly bell-shaped and round in footprint, and it cast an elegant silhouette, but the resemblance ended there. The Golden Zoo was a lustrous fortress, a gilded citadel whose bars were as numerous and varied as the strings of a harp. The simplicity of the Zoo's broad shape was not reflected in the intricacies of its interior, which included several floors and numerous cells, some glowing with lamplight, some shrouded by curtain, and many churning with the activity of the people inside. Indeed, the effect reminded Senlin of an industrious beehive.

The sheer number of hods was startling. There were hundreds of them, perhaps thousands. And they were not idle. They emerged from the forest carrying baskets of wood, great kettles of water, and laundry draped over poles. Sentries stood at the gates of the Zoo, armed with capable-looking rifles. The hods were dressed in an assortment of dishwater sarongs and shabby tabards, none of which were pretty but all of which seemed practical and warm. The camp was militant in its orderliness, a quality Senlin had not anticipated when Bhata referred to it as a mission.

Though he was a little surprised by their numbers, the sight of so many hods stoked his courage. Because where there were hods, there must also be an open path between the ringdoms. Which meant there was a way into Pelphia. Which meant there was hope.

Still, Senlin thought it wise not to presume they would be given a warm welcome. Despite their guide's apparent inability with the language, Senlin did not entirely trust their privacy, and so when he spoke to Edith as they walked across the queer lawn, he was purposefully oblique. "We are two lonesome travelers come to beg for our supper and some direction. We will accept whatever hospitality is offered; we will present our modest gift without condition; and we will forgo any discussion of our dependents until we are certain we aren't bound for trouble."

Edith gave a diplomatic smile to show she understood: They would not mention the crew.

They followed their guide past a pair of sentries and through a tunnel that was walled in gold tiles with a ceiling of hazy quartz, which let them see, though foggily, the figures passing overhead.

"I doubt the architect ever wore a skirt," Edith said dryly.

The atrium inside the Golden Zoo was as big as a town square. Walkways of pale crystal ringed each of the floors above them. Elevators, pulled by steam engines on the roofs of the cars, transited the levels. Interspersed across the floor of the atrium and inside the cells he could see stood the remnants of numerous mechanical animals. Many had been stripped to their skeletal gears, rendering their original form unrecognizable. Even in their state of disassembly, they were wonderful.

Senlin had never seen anything so fantastic, though the glowing spectacle of gold and crystal was made strange by the trooping about of men and women in rags.

There were cots everywhere. They stood in ranks in the open court and in every cell. About half of the hods were busy with some domestic work: They cooked and sewed and braided rope. The other half of the population sat stooped in study, books open on their laps. They made feverish notations with nib and ink.

Now that he was looking for them, Senlin saw that there were books everywhere. They stood in stacks under beds and up against the walls of cages. He had never seen so many books outside of a college library, and it made him a little hopeful.

After their soggy introduction beside the well, Senlin had concluded that their guide suffered from a defect of birth or was perhaps the victim of some traumatic accident, and it was to this that his gibbering could be attributed. But Senlin now discovered that his guide's infirmity was not unique. The babbling was endemic. When Senlin tested the name "Marat" with the hods they passed, he got only nonsense in reply. The hods who labored over books didn't even pay him the courtesy of looking up when he spoke to them, and he couldn't help feeling a little foolish, like a latecomer to an exam.

Their guide led them to an elevator. From inside, the car seemed as delicate as a champagne flute. The hod closed the accordion door and worked the ornate throttle. The engine above them chugged and shook condensation onto their shoulders. The car began to rise. Senlin had never ridden in an elevator before, and he found the sensation a little unsettling. Then he looked down, and his disquiet turned to nausea. The floor was made of a thin pane of quartz through which the ground was distinctly visible. Startled, Senlin instinctively reached out for something to hold and grasped Edith's clockwork hand. She gave him a consternated look, as if he had called her by the wrong name, and he dropped her hand as speedily as he'd taken it up.

They debarked on the top floor of the Zoo, where long curtains blocked their view of every cell they passed. Their journey came to an end inside an open cell with thick stage curtains drawn over the adjacent rooms.

In addition to the ubiquitous stacks of books, the room held two small beds and a table set with chairs. The atmosphere was quite cozy, yet still insufficient to make them forget that they stood inside of a barred cell.

Edith gave Senlin a pointed look and set her hand upon the hilt of her sword. Her unloaded pistol had been lost in the well, but it hardly mattered. She wasn't making a hollow threat; there was no bluster to her bearing. She would not let their babbling guide close the door to the cage no matter the result. Knowing what had happened the last time she'd been imprisoned, Senlin could hardly blame her.

The hod must have sensed her unease because he held up both hands like a man surrendering and said, "Marat, Marat."

For a moment, Senlin thought the hod was announcing that he was Marat, and Senlin despaired at ever communicating their need to their babbling host. Then they heard an approaching squeak, which brought a smile to the hod's face. The squeak played a phrase of three ascending notes that repeated again and again like a lovesick bird.

Then the source of the squeak came into view on the skywalk outside the cell. It was a man in a wheelchair. His head was shaved, his shirt was plain, and in this way, he resembled any other hod. His smile radiated surety and good humor. Though middle-aged, his pale skin glowed with vitality, an impression that was not diminished by the presence of the wheelchair or the afghan that covered his legs. His face possessed those perfectly symmetrical features that are often reflected in art but seldom found in nature.

"Welcome," he said warmly. "I believe you are looking for me. My name is Luc Marat."

That a brave impulse could be followed so quickly by cowardly regret came as a surprise to Adam. When he'd first called the monster back by drumming upon the hull of the wreck, he'd felt suffused with courage. But the moment the beast reared about and began loping back to him, his heroic spirit evaporated, and he was left with a strong desire to run and hide.

He retreated to the breach in the wreck. His lantern swung before him as he slid back down the little dune into the upside-down cabin. The skeletons that had seemed a macabre artifact before now seemed like sinister observers.

He cast about for something large and heavy to throw over the entrance.

Why had he not run into the woods?

There was nothing he could use as a barricade. There was nothing here but a dead man's confetti.

A heavy thud reverberated through the timbers of the cabin. He climbed onto the lintel of the door that led to the deck and tried to wrench it open, but it had been crushed shut by the reversal of the ship and wouldn't budge.

Why had he killed himself to save Iren, a woman whose death, only a few months earlier, he would have thought unremarkable and, given her violent profession, inevitable?

He smelled it before he saw it—a putrid, earthy stink. The black snout, pointed as a finger, appeared around the ragged edge of the breach. A tremor ran up Adam's legs and out his arms. The glass shade of the lantern chattered against its collar.

The fright at seeing the thing so close gave him an unexpected moment of lucidity. He knew why he had called the beast away from Iren. The old amazon, gruff as she was, loved Voleta. And though he didn't understand her affection, he had seen the force of it more than once. If he had to choose, he knew his sister would be safer with Iren than she'd ever be with him. He had to confront the uncomfortable fact that every older brother must one day face: His sister didn't need him, not anymore.

It was a grim revelation to have just moments before death, but it brought with it a firm resolve. If he somehow managed to escape, he would not waste the rest of his life chasing after Voleta. He would change. He would chase something new.

The spider-eater was quite unimpressed by Adam's epiphanies. It ducked its head and lumbered down into the cabin.

Chapter Seven

When the gilded birds of the Zoo trilled their fantastic song, women swooned, fops moaned like doves, and old men mopped their rheumy eyes.

This is the trouble with the man of the masses: show him the sublime, and he is reminded of himself.

—*Inaugurations of the Silk Gardens*, Salo

It was hard not to be charmed by their charismatic host. He listened attentively to the account of their stranding (which was largely true except for the glaring omission of a crew and the pursuant commissioner), and he gasped as if on cue when Senlin related their ordeal with the swarming spiders and the deep well. Marat's shapely brows were as expressive as a pantomime, and they rolled and stretched in sympathy with the details of Senlin's tale. If he was at all suspicious of them or their intrusion upon his mission, he showed no sign of it. When Senlin presented his offering of stolen books, a somewhat awkward gesture considering the profusion of literature around them, Marat received the tribute with perfect grace, saying, "We are always in need of new material. My friends have an insatiable appetite for meditating upon the written word."

Their original guide, who Marat called Koro, returned with sweetened barley tea and hardtack biscuits. After serving them, Koro pointed to their feet and then pulled at his sandals until they got his meaning and gave him their soaked boots. Koro stuffed these with straw to help them dry and then set about the business of brushing them clean. It was the most hospitality Senlin had been paid in months, and he could not help but feel it was a promising sign. Perhaps at last they had found someone who would help them.

Yet, what softened his defenses only seemed to harden Edith's. She didn't like any of this: not the living in cages, or the insensible babbling, or the conspicuous number of armed hods standing in doorways and stalking the halls. In her experience, a mission was a roadside lean-to where one could find water for their horse, a pit for their fire, and perhaps a little direction from the local hermit. This was no mission, and their host was no hermit.

She liked him least of all. He looked like the sort of man who was unaccustomed to being told *no*. The more he flashed his glamorous smile, the more she scowled at Luc Marat.

Though not even she could resist the offer of food.

While they tried their best not to gulp their tea and gobble their biscuits, nor to feel terribly guilty for eating and drinking while their crew waited with empty stomachs, Marat talked about his mission.

"We've been here nine years," he said. "There were only a handful of us in the beginning. Koro was one of those brave few."

The hod looked up from his work at the sound of his name. Marat spoke a few words of gibberish to him, and the hod laughed at the inscrutable joke. "I asked him if he missed the good old days when we first arrived. You should have seen the Zoo then. The spiders had moved in. You've never seen such cobwebs. It was like cutting through a mattress." He shook his head, knitting his perfect brow. Koro moved on to another boot. The swishing of his brush accompanied Marat's dulcet voice. "There's always that point when you undertake something new, that moment when everything is tentative and fragile. In our case, that period lasted for years. You might not suspect it to look at us now, but we came very close to extinction."

"There certainly are a lot of you," Senlin said, and ate another biscuit. He thought they were quite nice, though they undoubtedly benefited from the seasoning of hunger.

"There are. There are. And we still turn thousands away every month. The black trail is never empty."

"The black trail?"

"That's what we call the tunnels we were imprisoned in. The black trail snakes for miles and miles through the walls of the Tower. I'm sure the architects thought they were being clever by building such a gradual slope, but it feels endless when you're on it. And bleak. I've seen old men with ruined lungs carrying open buckets of stinking pitch. I've seen a girl dragging a sack of gunpowder that exploded when a spark fell from her headlamp. I've seen men broken in half under blocks of stone. What a life—to live as a footman to a rock!"

Marat paused to speak to Koro, and whatever he said made the hod look terribly grave. "They die, Captain Mudd. They die in droves from exhaustion, injury, illness, thirst..." Speaking of these injustices soured their host's mood. A moment before, he had been enjoying his tea. Now, he seemed embarrassed by even this humble luxury. He pushed the cup away.

Senlin thought of his friend Tarrou, who had been ripped from his lounge chair beside the shining reservoir and thrown onto the black trail after a brief, bloody baptism. Perhaps Tarrou had succumbed to his wounds and was already dead. And perhaps death was preferable to the alternative Marat described.

"We haven't the resources to free them all. We save the weakest, the most frail. The rest we encourage with the hope that they will one day be free."

Though Senlin was trying his best to be agreeable, he didn't believe this for an instant. The hods he'd seen marching around the perimeter and the workers in the Zoo appeared generally vital and energetic. This was no field hospital.

"Free to get your tea, you mean?" Edith said, revealing her own doubts.

"Perhaps the concept of hospitality confuses you. These little rituals of service are how we show respect and admiration for one another and for our guests," Marat said, bristling. Senlin thought he glimpsed in his flared expression a carefully concealed reserve of anger.

Senlin had been discouraged by Marat's dire description of the black trail, but he wasn't ready to give up on the idea yet. Pelphia was just underfoot, and he imagined that they could endure a miserable but brief march through the walls. It was still a viable plan, but only if Marat liked them well enough to show them the trail. The prospect of this seemed to shrivel the more Edith talked.

He changed the subject. "I've encountered a few novelties in my travels, but I must admit, a new language is something quite extraordinary. It's like nothing I've ever heard. I have to ask, who was the author of this curious warbling?"

Marat relaxed a bit at the diversion. "I don't think anyone would claim to have authored it."

"Are you saying the language arrived spontaneously?"

"It evolved over years," Marat said. "Hods discovered they could speak more openly if slavers and constables didn't know what they were saying. It began, I suspect, as a few coded phrases shared by friends, and grew from there. This *curious warbling*, as you call it, has given us a reputation for raving, but you must admit—it is an elegant solution."

"What do you call it?"

"Hoddish. The powers that be call it a blight upon the Tower. So much the better."

"You're a mystic," Edith said, an accusatory note in her voice. Senlin tried to dissuade her from saying more by a subtle narrowing of his eyelids that was entirely wasted on her. She was determined to speak and oblivious to his cues. "You think the Tower is to blame for all of your troubles and all the injustice in the world."

This time, Marat's smile was not chased off by her frankness, though it did turn a little, like a candle flame moved by a draft. "The Tower is a straw that draws blood from the earth. And who sucks upon this straw? All those happy souls sitting in the clouds—the Sphinx and the like. I realize you are obligated to defend the Tower even though it took your arm. You are a friend of the Sphinx."

"I wouldn't call him a friend," Edith said.

"No, he doesn't have friends, does he? He has enemies and he has machines. Everyone he meets he turns into one or the other," Marat said, rubbing the arms of his wheelchair. "I'm sure you like to think you're living some sort of autonomous life, Edith Winters, a life of possibility and consideration. But we both know you are not in charge of that terrible machine hanging at your side. It is in charge of you."

An expression swept over Edith's face that Senlin had never seen before. He had seen anger, fear, even disgust, cross the stage of her face. But this was an entirely new actor. This was the look of hate. It made him very nervous.

When she finally spoke, her voice was as dry and sharp as flint. "I know what I gave up when I accepted this arm," she said, rapping the shoulder plate with a knuckle. Her arm gave a shallow gong. "I know I am indebted to a man who isn't safe or sane, a man who preys upon the desperate. I will spend the rest of my life dreading the moment when I am called to heel to him. But I wouldn't be alive if it weren't for the Sphinx, if it weren't for this machine. Believe me, I understand what I am, Luc Marat. What I don't understand is why you think you have the right to judge me."

"You're not like the other Wakemen, are you? I can see you're right on the verge, teetering between loyalty and revolt. Wonderful. That's such an exciting place to be. Let me show you something," Marat said with a delicate expression of arrogance that a less attractive face would've turned into a sneer. He spoke to Koro, who had finished with their boots. The hod smiled like a bulldog, then scuttled from the room.

"You've probably figured out by now that there were never any animals here. The Golden Zoo was a collection of the Sphinx's windups. They once filled these cages."

"But why put bolted-down machines in cages?"

"That's a very good question, Captain. Perhaps it was because, even then, even among the aristocratic elite, there was a niggling distrust of the Sphinx's engines." Marat gave Edith's arm a little further scrutiny. She crossed her arms to disrupt his staring, and he broke it off with a wistful smile. "We spent years dismantling and removing the monstrosities, though we spared one to remind us of the genius and lunacy we face."

The curtain that blocked the adjoining cell parted, revealing Koro at work on a pulley line. What lay behind the curtain was perhaps the most elaborate machine Senlin had ever seen.

It was an aviary, a gold ladder filled with dozens of clockwork birds. They perched in tiers, the largest birds on the bottom rung, the smallest on the top. Their precious-metal shells were engraved with feathers and crests. Inlays of opal decorated their beaks and filled their eyes. A bank of cogs and rods backed the menagerie. Koro laid his hands to the crank handle at the base of the machine and awaited his master's signal.

"This carillon was once the pride of the Golden Zoo," Marat said. "The Sphinx built it to demonstrate the beauty of his machines. Here, listen to its rapturous song."

Marat nodded at Koro, who began to turn the crank.

The noise was abrupt and unbearable. A lurching, uneven knelling of soup pots rang out, and then a metallic shriek joined in with a voice like twisting steel. Deep, detuned bells clanged like a forge. The birds flapped and convulsed in a tortured routine propelled by Koro's mad turning of the wheel. Wings sheered as they flapped, heads popped free as they twisted, and bolts and screws fell from the flock in a jangling rain.

Senlin and Edith shuddered in their chairs, cringing as if it might seal their ears. All the while their host beamed at them with a sadism not even his beauty could conceal.

At last, he signaled Koro to stop.

"I know what you're thinking," Marat said. "What a cheap trick to let a windup rust away and then deride it for not running properly. But that is the point. Machines do not serve us; we serve them. If they all vanished from the earth tomorrow, our race would carry on. But when we remove our hand from the machine, it dies." Marat seemed to relish those two words. "The Sphinx builds us masters we don't need. The very heart of the Tower is a machine, a dynamo that leeches energy from men and women, turns it to lightning, and funnels it to his workshop to make more masters, more machines. How could anyone serve such a man?"

Edith was holding her temper in check, though Senlin could sense her straining. Marat was clearly waiting for her to speak, and at last she formed a few clipped words: "It's easy to judge a life not led."

"It is," he said. His chair played three descending notes as he wheeled back from the table. He pulled the afghan from his lap. His legs gleamed golden in the lamplight, illuminating his face like a reflection pool. Elaborate gears and rods showed between the thigh plates and the round shields at his knees. The armor was etched in fine arabesque scrawls, like those that decorated Edith's arm. But unlike her arm, Luc Marat's legs were silent and still.

"The Sphinx has seduced many, many men and women with his pretty machines that are full of terrible screams. He is convinced that his work is the fruit of progress and that it must be protected from anyone who disagrees. Nine years ago, I chose this chair over taking orders from that ruthless tinkerer, and I have never regretted it."

Though Senlin felt the utmost sympathy for Edith and would, were he able, erase the Sphinx from her life, he felt a terrible sinking feeling that was not at all empathetic. It was entirely selfish. He realized that he was, once again, being pulled into a dispute that did not concern him. Ogier's obsession with the painting had resulted in Tarrou's ruin and nearly his own death. When he had been drawn into the politics of the Port of Goll, he had made such an enemy of Rodion, he was ultimately compelled to kill him.

Senlin had become a thief and a murderer because of the ambitions and disputes of other men, none of which had brought him any closer to reuniting with Marya. Senlin had to stop this before Marat insinuated them into his struggle.

"I assure you," Senlin said in a candid tone, surprising his host, who seemed to have forgotten him, "I am not here to argue over the Sphinx's influence, or his designs, nefarious or just. I don't know the first thing about the man, and that arrangement suits me just fine. Frankly, we are too insignificant to make any difference to your cause or his." At this, their host gave Edith an incredulous smirk. "I only came because I need to get into Pelphia, and the ports are closed to me. All I ask is that you point the way to the black trail, and we will be on our way."

Marat threw the afghan back over his dead mechanical legs with a laugh. "Captain Mudd, this may be the first time in history that someone has asked to be shown the black trail." He turned again to Edith. "Do you mean to accompany him, Wakeman?"

"I do," she said, and obviously enjoyed his surprised expression.

"Interesting," he said.

"So, you will help us?" Senlin said.

"Absolutely. I live to serve my fellow hod."

"Fellow hod?"

"You don't seriously believe that you can walk the trail as you are? You wouldn't survive the night. Not all hods are as magnanimous as I am. Some of them hold grudges against free men in general and Wakemen in particular. Even if you survived the walk to Pelphia, the moment you popped out, the local constabulary would arrest you and conscript you into hoddery."

Senlin's expression darkened as Marat spoke. "So, you propose that we become hods willingly?"

"You said you wanted to travel the black trail. That is the only way to do it. I can even furnish you with shackles and a load."

Senlin had been straining forward in his chair but rocked back now in bodily defeat. It was a moment more before his thoughts came to the same conclusion: The plan was spoiled. He could make no progress to Pelphia here.

Marat was unmoved by his guest's visible disappointment. "Perhaps on the black trail," he said, turning his statuesque features back to Edith, "you will discover that living with your loss is better than living for another man's gain."

Their host wheeled toward the exit. "Consider this a crossroads. You have seen what life is like in the Tower when you are alone. You end up lost, maimed, shipwrecked, and—forgive me for saying so—begging. You can go on living at the whim of the wind and the direction of your master, or you can share a life with friends who are fighting to reclaim their dignity and liberty from the institutions that robbed them. Consider it. Sleep on it. Tomorrow, you can join us and be free."

He went as he had come and left the door of the cage standing open behind him.

Chapter Eight

Please do not saddle the clockwork beasts. Do not pet or tease the spider-eaters. Reserve such familiar activities for other, more receptive subjects.

—*Folkways and Right of Ways in the Silk Gardens*, Anon.

Adam had never thought of himself as a runt. True, he'd always been a little shorter than his peers, but his shoulders were wide enough to push through a crowd, and his bearing was sufficient to discourage bullies from taking an interest in him. He had faced down his share of bigger men. On his best days, he even fancied he possessed a menacing stare, monocular though it was.

But when the spider-eater reared onto its hind legs, its head scraping the furniture riveted to the ceiling, and glared down the barrel of its snout at him, Adam felt every inch a runt.

The beast's claws were like the horns of a ram. Its breath came in great heaves that turned to dripping slaver. It stood stock-still with its arms stretched wide, waiting it seemed, though Adam couldn't imagine what for. He had heard of beasts that could be intimidated into retreating, and he wondered if that might be the case with spider-eaters. Of course, he'd heard of other large animals that were antagonized by sudden movements and could only be repulsed by prey that played dead.

There was no one here to see him, no one to impress in these last moments of his life. Adam could go out flailing and raving, or he could lie down, close his eye, and hope for the best. He only had himself to please. It seemed an easy choice.

He threw out his arms and screamed with all his might. The cry stung his throat. The light of his lantern flashed up and down the walls and over the beast standing with its own arms stretched out like the spars of a mast.

Before Adam could exhaust his breath, the spider-eater swung at him with a laziness that seemed almost playful. Then the blow caught him on the ribs, and the cabin turned sideways as he was propelled through the air.

The lantern leapt from his hand and popped upon the floor. The spilled oil burst into angry flames that spread in every direction at once, fueled by bedclothes and playing cards and the rags that swaddled the skeletons. The fire grew without deliberation, turning what had been a gloomy cabin a moment before into a spotlighted stage.

Where Adam had failed to impress, the fire now succeeded. The spider-eater shied, stamped tentatively at the fringe of the burning spill, and whined at the heat of it. The beast deliberated a moment, swinging its long neck across the fire toward Adam, who lay prone and holding his ribs. Then the fire touched upon some ancient pocket of sap in the wood and gave a little explosive snap. The beast startled. It was inside the breach in two strides, then out and gone before Adam could get to his feet.

Any relief Adam felt at having driven the monster off was short-lived.

The fire stood between him and the gap in the hull he'd come by. Even as he rallied the courage to dash through the wall of flames, it thickened and forced him farther from the exit. The planks were so desiccated the floor burned like a fuse. He backed into the bookshelf he'd lately scavenged, his face streaming sweat, his skin tingling from the violent heat. Beside the shelf was the shut door of the chart house. A chart house meant windows, and windows meant escape.

The door stood level with his knees in the upside-down room, and he was grateful to find that rot had softened the boards. He quickly broke through a corner of the door and climbed over the lintel into the cramped room.

The floor, which once had been the ceiling, was heaped with maps and papers that slid about underfoot. He knew as soon as the fire got in, he would be caught standing atop a perfect pyre.

The panes of the casement window were missing. But where he'd hoped to see the beach outside, there was only a sheet of silk ballooning into the room. He pressed against the silk blister, but it didn't yield. It took him a moment to comprehend why. This part of the ship was below the surface of the beach. The silks tangled about the hull were all that kept the beach from filling up the chart house. He could cut the silk, but the beach would flow in and bury him. If he was lucky, he might stay on top of the sand, and if there wasn't much of it, he might find room to climb to daylight.

Looking back into the inferno, he watched as the moorings lost their ancient hold on the bed. The head- and footboards fell, cleaving the floor amid a fiery spray. The ship creaked like a tree being blown from its roots. The cabin was poised on the brink of collapse, which would smother the fire and him along with it.

Adam unsheathed his knife and, clinging to the windowsill, lanced the silk blister.

Sand flooded in under a cloud of blinding dust. It coursed around his chest like a river, forcing him back, pulling him down. If his grip on the sill failed, he would be buried alive in an instant. The smoke and sand seized his lungs and gouged at his tearing eye.

He was submerged to the waist before the flow of sand began to ebb. He pushed his arm through the window, hoping to feel the open air, but all he found was a steep, unsteady slope that loosened as soon as he disturbed it. He tried to pull himself through the sill, but he slid back, again and again, toward the oppressive heat. He wondered which would kill him first—the burial or the cooking. He reached up once more into the slow avalanche and felt air. Escape was only an arm's length away, but the beach was too deep, the fire too quick.

Amid the frozen sand, a warm hand grasped his arm.

He felt himself rising, drawn by a force stronger than the grave. For a moment he was packed on all sides by sand. And then Iren pulled him from the ground.

He was sure he would've collapsed if Iren had not held him on his feet. He coughed until he trembled. When he was able to blink the sand from his eye and see her, she looked ready to laugh.

"You're a funny-looking turnip," she said, and then picked him up and threw him onto her shoulder.

Bouncing against her hard back as she trotted toward the *Stone Cloud*, Adam did not mind feeling like a runt. If she wanted to carry him to the moon, he'd gladly ride along.

Voleta followed and watched from the trees while the hod played the prattling guide to the captain and Mister Winters.

Despite his babbling, the hod was savvy enough to duck the spider-eaters and to keep from walking in circles. Sometimes the curious little man would pause at the foot of one tree or another and select a mushroom for his basket. He seemed harmless enough, though that didn't make Voleta trust him. If all evil men only looked evil, there'd be a lot less trouble in the world, but in her experience, looks had nothing to do with character. Take old Iren, for example. Her face was as chopped up as an old butcher's block, but her heart was soft and big. Voleta wondered if this harmless-looking hod wasn't leading them all into some horrible trap.

She considered staging a rescue. She could easily leap on the hod from the trees. The idea had its appeal, but if she jumped on the mad babbler, she would never find out where he lived, and she was curious. She contemplated joining the little company—she might just stroll out of the woods with a casual, "Hullo there, Captain!"—but she suspected Mister Winters would not be happy to see she had left the ship, and Voleta didn't like being scolded. Besides, if she joined them, she wouldn't get to enjoy the treetops any longer, and they were quite nice. Stalking was so much more exhilarating than walking in a queue.

In the end, she decided to shadow them with a mind to intervene the moment things became more interesting down below.

Then she abruptly ran out of trees.

The clearing that opened before her was no picnic glen. It was as grand as an old estate. The tidy lawn of moss shone like new frost, and the cobbled avenues were lined with iron benches and rusting animals. At the center of it all stood the Golden Zoo. It reminded her of a carousel: It was round and full of poles and overwhelming to the eye. It glowed like a carousel, too, with many lamps that threw many sharp shadows. It was a pretty cage, but she wasn't fooled. She'd lived in a pretty cage before.

She couldn't see any animals, and it didn't smell like a zoo. The air smelled like a laundry room, in fact. She wasn't disappointed. She didn't like to see animals behind bars, not even gold ones.

There were a lot of hods, though, and they were all as busy as ants. They toted pails of water and marched around with rifles on their shoulders. They pulled wagons full of coal, kegs, bolts of silk, baskets of nuts, loaves of bread, potatoes, and (she could hardly believe it) apples. It was enough to make her stomach growl. Where had they gotten it all?

She was alarmed to see the captain and Mister Winters walk into the Golden Zoo like a couple of ticket holders. Was this what the captain expected: a bunch of armed and well-fed hods holed up in a barred fortress? It certainly made her uneasy. They didn't know the first thing about these hods. She thought how silly the captain and first mate would feel if the hods turned out to be cannibals. Of course, she would feel guilty if she were outside swinging from a tree while her friends were boiling in a pot. She knew she had to do something, but it wouldn't help anyone if she just jumped into the soup pot with them.

Her stomach growled again.

Keeping to the treetops, Voleta skirted the clearing, looking for some way to cross the open ground without being seen. But she found no good cover, and there were too many hods besides. She'd stand out like a caboose among all these baldheads.

She had traveled halfway around the grounds of the Golden Zoo before she noticed her arm was glowing more brightly than the limb she clung to. The luminous lichen had begun to cake upon her sleeves and upon her pants and in the wild piles of her hair, too. It made her stand out from the gloom, and if left alone, would draw attention.

She was quietly brushing and shaking out her clothes when voices in the forest below stopped her. She listened to hear whether she had been discovered. One voice was distinct above the rest, and it was remarkable because it was intelligible: Whoever was speaking now wasn't babbling like the other hods.

Four hods emerged from the edge of the wood almost directly beneath her. As soon as they were clear of the tree line, one of the hods found himself ringed by the other three. It was the hemmed-in one who was complaining loudly.

He said, "I told you, you can't have it. And stop saying goo-goo ga-ga to me. Even if I understood what you were saying, and I don't, it wouldn't matter because you can't have it." The speaker resolutely clutched a small wooden keg to his stomach.

One of the surrounding three replied with an inscrutable speech, which he animated with encouraging gestures like a man trying to coax an animal into eating from his hand. The babbling concluded with a single recognizable phrase, "Come and be free."

"See, there. You can talk sense! Don't pretend you don't understand me," the accosted hod replied. "And I don't need your help to be free. I am about to be free. I have walked the black trail for four months, and in six days, I'll have paid my debt." He straightened a little, bolstered by his confidence in his inevitable liberty, and one of the men took the opportunity to lunge for the keg. The surrounded hod was quick enough to jump back, but his evasion threw him into the hod behind him, and he shoved him roughly forward. "Quit it, you idiot! It's gunpowder."

The original spokesman for the detainers repeated his speech but without the warm gestures of before. Voleta thought it sounded grimmer now, a sort of final negotiation, though the tormented hod didn't seem to recognize the warning that filled the phrase: "Come and be free."

"I want to go back to the trail. I want to go back." He took a shuffling step toward the forest. "I thought it would be nice to get out for a minute, but I was wrong. I want to go back!"

The retreating hod didn't see the man behind him raise his club. The blow was singular but effective. The keg popped from the stricken man's arms and was caught by the hod who, just a moment before, had promised him freedom. The struck man fell, the life apparently driven from him.

The third hod in the group pulled a spade from his belt and set about cutting into the spongy sod. In a moment, he had peeled back a long strip of the glowing lawn that came up as easily as carpet. The others shifted the lifeless hod into the shallow grave. When they dropped him, he let out a moan.

The spokesman of the trio knelt on the groaning man's chest and wrapped his hands about his throat. He strangled him while the other two watched with bland, unmoved expressions. The process was neither quick nor dignified, but not even the spasms of the dying man stirred any doubt that the chore would be done.

Voleta rarely looked away from a spectacle, but she did now.

When it was over, the hods rolled the strip of moss back over the dead man, already half-submerged in the soft loam underneath. They took turns pacing over the uneven spot until it was level with the rest of the radiant lawn.

Chapter Nine

After the initial shock receded, I quickly forgot Edith's arm was at all unnatural. Much as spectacles flatter an intelligent face, the powerful engine complements her quite well. It is difficult to fathom that such an essential and vital part of her could one day run down like a pocket watch.

—The *Stone Cloud*'s Logbook, Captain Tom Mudd

The ship's umbilical lay across the *Stone Cloud*'s deck like an overgrown tube worm. Adam sat dissecting one end of the salvaged duct, cutting through layers of silk, cotton insulation, and wire. The collar was too large for the mouth of the chimney and had to be cinched in. It was fiddly work, and he hadn't the right tools for it, but he felt no urge to complain. The work made him feel capable, and it distracted him from his hunger and his worry.

The tang of smoke from the burning derelict was still detectable in the air. The lack of wind and the gaps between shipwrecks had kept the fire from spreading, and once the hull gave way, the beach spilled in and smothered the blaze. They could only hope that the fire hadn't attracted any unwanted attention. At least they had some fresh guns if it did.

"There," Adam said. "That should do it. Can you help me get this fitted onto the stack?"

Iren helped lift the cumbersome, delicate duct over the furnace.

Adam's modified collar fit well, and she held it in place as he bolted it down. The work required them to stand in a tangle of arms and elbows, which, even a day earlier, would've made Iren gruff and Adam nervous. But since their encounter with the spider-eater, the tenor of their interactions had improved. It seemed to Adam that they had become friends.

He took advantage of their newfound camaraderie to satisfy a point of curiosity. "I don't want to sound ungrateful because I really do appreciate you always keeping an eye out for her, but I can't help wondering, why do you like Voleta so much?"

The amazon grunted, and for a moment, Adam thought that was all he would get out of her. But then she said, "I saw her on stage at the Steam Pipe. I was there with Goll. I didn't like going there, seeing those poor girls. It made me feel guilty." Iren paused so Adam could shift to the other side of the chimney to continue turning bolts around the collar. She had her arms hooped over him when she resumed. "When I saw her up there, up on her bar, she looked different. Most of the girls looked drunk or like they had a mask on. Not her."

"Move your arm a little," Adam said, and she did, making room for his wrench. "How did she look?"

"Brave. She looked me right in the eye. She wasn't scared. She looked at me as if she knew me. Goll's children looked at me that way, like I was somebody they knew, somebody they liked. It felt good."

"All right. Let's see if this holds," Adam said, and they stepped back together. "It's not falling off. I guess that's a good sign."

Adam rubbed the oil from his hands with the attentiveness of one who is stalling for time. He had to say something in response to Iren's confession, but he didn't possess the captain's vocabulary or Mister Winters's authority. He was afraid that one wrong word would snuff the little candle of their friendship.

At last he said, "You're a lot like her, you know. People misjudge her all the time because of how she looks and acts—a pretty, silly girl. But she's smart and fearless, and she can be very kind. I misjudged you, too. I'm sorry I did."

The heavy folds of Iren's eyelids were so narrow he couldn't see her eyes to read them. Her breath whistled dryly from her battered nose. He was beginning to suspect that he had indeed snuffed the candle when she said, "Are you calling me pretty?"

Adam snickered. "I wouldn't dare," he said, and ducked when she swatted at him.

Muffled voices reverberated through the atrium outside; the crystal elevators chugged between floors. Though their block of cells was quiet, the rest of the Golden Zoo thrummed with the daily goings on of life.

Senlin marveled at how adept the human race was at injecting a sense of routine into peculiar environments; it seemed a certainty that once people were added, the mundane was sure to follow. He could sense the harmony of the place. Their host seemed touched with megalomania, but he had at least provided a home for these few and fortunate hods.

Edith stood in the open doorway of the cage. Something either in her posture or the dazzle of the gold bars that framed her reminded him of the girl in Ogier's painting. Edith looked similarly serene, and like the girl who stared so resolutely away from the shore, she seemed focused on something invisible, something internal. She looked unabashed and lovely and . . .

Well, it didn't matter how she looked. He pushed the troublesome thought away.

"I'm sorry we had to come all this way to learn what common sense might've told me: The hod trail is only fit for hods. Don't you think Marat was being devious by suggesting that we could just dress the part? I can't think of a more dangerous disguise. Once you put the vestment on, how would you ever get it off?"

"You wouldn't. Once a hod . . . Why did he leave the door open?" she asked, swinging around to face him.

Senlin cleared his throat. "To discourage us from leaving, I suppose." He retreated to the opposite end of the cell where stacks of books stood like a wainscoting against the bars. He idly picked up a clothbound volume with the ambitious though not particularly scintillating title *Bogs and Marshes: A Complete Survey.* Opening the book, he was surprised to discover that its entire contents had been, word by word, blacked out.

Unsettled, he took up another volume entitled *A Cobbler's Encyclopedia of Skins and Leathers.* Every character, down to the last page number, had been inked over. He quickly surveyed several more books, his anxiety growing. They were all ruined.

He had seen this sort of methodical defacement before in the Baths. At the time, he had assumed it was just the work of a local imbecile. But this wasn't casual vandalism; this was a campaign.

Then it dawned on him: The hods he'd seen scribbling away downstairs weren't illuminating the manuscripts. They were destroying them. Senlin had assumed Marat was teaching these poor wretches to read, but that wasn't the case at all. He was using them to obliterate these books.

And Senlin had stolen a man's library to contribute to the effort. The thought made him sick.

But what possible reason could Marat have for such senseless waste, not just of the knowledge and experience that the books embodied but of the effort it took to strike them out? If he loathed books so intensely, why not just burn them? Why meditate upon their destruction? Senlin couldn't fathom it. But then, he had no idea what the point of this mission was. It didn't seem humanitarian; it was too militant for that. What was the purpose of recruiting all these hods? Reformation? Criminal enterprise? Revolution? What?

He felt a tinge of mania creep into his thoughts, and he made a concerted effort to swallow it as one might an upwelling of bile. "Madness," he muttered, and then more loudly so Edith could hear: "They've ruined these books."

But she wasn't very interested in his discovery and instead returned to his previous point. "What do you mean he left the door open to keep us in?"

"If he locked us in, he knows we would try to escape."

"Perhaps, but we could just walk out the open door," Edith said.

"That's an excellent point." Senlin rebalanced the stack of mutilated books. He found the task difficult because his hands had begun to shake. "But what would happen if we tried to leave?"

"Someone would stop us," she said, frowning at the thought. "This place is swarming with hods."

"I agree." He clenched his hands to stop their trembling. Perhaps he'd caught a cold from his recent soaking, or perhaps he was just malnourished. The biscuits had hardly blunted his hunger. "What do you make of this place? It's not what I'd pictured."

"I've never heard of anything like this. He's kept it a secret, and that's not an easy thing to do in the Tower. It isn't a mission. That much is obvious." Edith probed the heavy curtain that hung behind the bars of the adjacent cell. With a windup aviary on one side of them, she was curious to see what was on the other. "Once word gets out what Marat is doing here, there's going to be trouble."

"I can think of a few librarians who'd like to see him spanked."

Edith shook her head. "It's no joke. Those guards downstairs had rifles on their shoulders. He's arming the hods. I'm sure you can see the problem some of the ringdoms would have with that."

"Why did Marat call you a Wakeman? A Wakeman is a guard, isn't it?"

"Sort of," she murmured in distraction. At last she found a seam in the curtain and parted the drapery a little. "If the point is to keep us from leaving, why not just lock the cage? That's what it's for! What's the point of leaving us with a choice?"

"Because we are uncertain, and he knows it. If we chose to walk out that door, they might stop us, put us in shackles, and post guards outside. And then we'd be well and truly imprisoned," Senlin said. "But with the door open, they permit us at least the illusion of freedom. And it's quite difficult to escape an illusion. They think we will prefer imaginary freedom to certain imprisonment."

She peered through the gap in the curtain. "But if we don't have any choice but to stay, then it's already a prison," she said.

"Not until we try to leave."

"And around we go." She craned about to get a better view of the adjoining room, then stopped and frowned. "Tom, look at this."

Senlin crossed the room, pinched the curtain where she held it for him, and gazed through. The cell was crowded with racks of rifles that stood as thick as wheat in a field.

"My word. How did a fraternity of hods manage to amass such an arsenal?"

"There's something else," Edith said.

A glass case stood against the far wall. Inside it, five identical picture frames hung in a row. The paintings in the frames were also apparently identical. Each was of a girl in a white bathing dress standing in a shimmering body of water. They were copies of the Ogier inside Senlin's pocket.

"How is that possible?" Senlin asked in agitation. "Are they forgeries? They must be. But why would anyone collect fakes?" With each successive question, his frustration mounted, and he felt a strange swinging sensation as if the floor were teetering under him. "Why does it keep coming back to this confounded picture? Don't you feel as if we are always striving to understand, on a most rudimentary level, what is happening to us? Why must everything be such a battle?"

He lurched about to face the room, almost panting with distress. His hands shook at his sides. He suddenly felt very unwell.

And there was Marya, sitting on the table, holding his tricorne hat in her lap. She was as she appeared in Ogier's painting of her: unclothed.

His wife smiled at him as if his panic was just an act, as if he was clowning for her. "It's only a battle if you put up a fight," she said.

Senlin fainted dead on the floor.

Voleta had no doubt that the captain was in trouble. He might not know it yet, but he and Mister Winters had fallen in with some bad characters. Who knew how many bodies they'd stuffed under the sod? She had to find her friends and warn them, or if they were already caught, she would have to get them out. It was her turn to come to the rescue. And maybe find some dinner along the way: a crust of bread, a nice piece of cheese, perhaps a few plump dates...though she wouldn't turn her nose up at a turnip. Or a crab apple, for that matter. Or anything, really, so long as it wasn't buckwheat gruel.

She had to stop thinking about food. The question before her right now was how could she cross the open field and break into the Zoo without being spotted by the babblers.

She had to think of something and quickly.

Inspiration never came to her so long as she was sitting still. Adam accused her of wandering off, but what her brother didn't understand was that her legs pedaled her thoughts. Inactivity made her stupid. People who could sit in a chair, open a book, and just think themselves around the world were magicians as far as she was concerned.

So, she decided to pedal her thoughts a little.

She hadn't tiptoed between three trees before she heard something interesting: It sounded like the clinking of a hammer. She followed the ringing to a nearby glade where a troop of hods scoured laundry in a sudsy pool. Clothes dried on the rusting antlers of a herd of mechanical deer that encircled the cistern, pretending to drink the very thing that corroded them. The air held the sharp fragrance of detergent. The blacksmith who had attracted her with his hammer song hunched over an anvil. He seemed to be beating the brains out of a kneeling man. Then she realized he was striking the pin from the iron collar around the man's neck. A moment later, the collar popped off with an exuberant ring. The freed man leapt to his feet, rubbing his neck with great relish. The blacksmith took the collar and clamped it about the neck of another hod, who accepted the irons without complaint. The blacksmith placed the hod's neck on his anvil, and began hammering in a new pin.

A ratty beard and stringy hair clung to the head of the liberated hod. He was ushered to a stool where a woman shaved and sheared him. Now clean headed, he was given a fresh robe to wear. It was humble hospitality, but the man's gratitude was profound. He kissed the hands of the women who dressed him and embraced the blacksmith, who hardly slowed his labor. It was a surreal little scene, and all of it occurred under the watchful eye of three armed hods. Voleta was fascinated. She understood why they would take their shackles off, but she couldn't imagine why they would ever put them back on again.

Squit, who had emerged from her sleeve, burrowed in and out of her thick, dark locks. Squit didn't seem to like the gloamine, or perhaps the spiders had just put her off. Either way, the squirrel was swimming around in her tresses quite diligently, which didn't make it any easier for Voleta to think. When she reached up, she discovered that Squit had gotten her little neck stuck inside a noose of curls. The squirrel began to thrash about in distress.

Without a second thought, Voleta pulled her penknife from her pocket, thumbed it open, and cut the beloved pet loose. Squit darted up her sleeve, leaving Voleta pinching a tangle of hair. She looked at the clump. The hair no longer seemed like her own. The moment it was off her head, the curls became almost grotesque. She patted her head until she found the divot she had cut. It felt strange. But, like the socket left by a lost tooth, it was fascinating to touch.

The solution seemed obvious. She needed a disguise, and she had everything required to make one.

She gave the blade of her folding knife a speculative touch with her thumb. It felt sharp enough.

Really, there was nothing else to be done.

Chapter Ten

The man or woman who is rarely lost rarely discovers anything new.

—*Folkways and Right of Ways in the Silk Gardens*, Anon.

Senlin woke up apologizing.

He apologized for collapsing at Edith's feet without a word of notice. He apologized for being a gangly load, which she'd had to drag across the floor and heave onto a bed. He apologized for the chill he'd probably caught when they'd almost drowned, and he apologized one last time when Edith said the apologies were getting out of hand.

"You're obviously ill. One moment you're all smiles and lectures, and the next, you're raving and flopping onto the floor."

"I was hardly raving. It was just a little fit. I feel fine now," he said, which was not entirely true. He still felt light-headed and queasy, but neither was stronger than his embarrassment. He was eager to put the whole episode behind him. He insisted that Edith let him get up, but no sooner did he rise than he saw her again.

The specter of Marya glanced up from a corner of the cell where she paged through one of the blacked-out books. There was something the matter with her skin, not just the preponderance of it, but its appearance, too. It was mottled and unfocused, and it glistened like oil. She was covered in paint, he realized. No, she wasn't covered in it; she was made of it. There were wet footprints everywhere on the floor, each print as colorful as a palette. She smiled and swept back her auburn hair. It smeared and caught the color of her hand.

"She's here, isn't she?" Edith asked.

He needn't answer. He stood like a man at a whipping post, rigid with self-control.

Edith wanted to be sympathetic, but she felt overwhelmed by Marat's baiting, and this paradoxical prison, and the inevitable decline of her arm. It seemed unfair somehow that Senlin's impairment would reassert itself now. She felt like all the patience had been wrung out of her. It was not enough for him to be stoic anymore; he had to be well.

But as she watched his expression squirm from a scowl to a grimace, she remembered how he had comforted her when they'd been caged in the Parlor. He had been a stranger, and yet, unaccountably, he had stayed with her. And was he not just as vulnerable now—a man who prided himself on the power of his mind being tormented by that very organ?

Edith drew a calming breath. "She has bad timing, your ghost," she said.

"It is inconvenient," Senlin said tightly. "I had bargained for a few hours of peace." He swatted near his ear as if dashing off a fly, though he only unsettled the air, and sat down heavily on the thin mattress. "Apparently, the grace period is over."

"Is she talking to you?"

"Yes."

"What is she saying?"

"What does it matter?"

"Look, if gritting your teeth was going to cure you, you'd be well by now. We might as well try something different."

Senlin relaxed enough to give her an exasperated look. "I've tried everything! I've ignored her. I've pleaded with her. I've meditated every day upon Marya's portrait, hoping to refresh the memories of the woman that this ghost only mocks."

"What is she saying?"

"She is incapable of speech. She says nothing because she is noth-ing!" This last phrase was plainly not directed at her.

"Tell me anyway."

Senlin cleared his throat and fidgeted with the rumpled, dirty cuffs of his shirt. He seemed to be reverting into the skittish, priggish man she'd first met. "If you must know, she's not saying anything at the moment. She is just sitting beside you and—she's getting paint in your hair. Stop it! Oh, that's enough. Now you've gotten it everywhere."

"Paint in my hair? Why is she doing that?"

"I don't know."

"Well, ask her."

"I would be conversing with myself!"

"Just ask!"

Senlin leaned forward and looked sharply at the empty air at Edith's side. "You! Yes, you. Stop touching her hair. It's rude, and she doesn't like it."

"That wasn't a question. Is that really how you'd speak to your wife?"

"That is not my wife!" Senlin pointed angrily at the unseen specter. "Will you please put on some clothes!"

"Oh," Edith said, a little shocked, which was itself a surprise: She'd thought her time with Captain Billy Lee had cured her of such sensibilities. It came as something of a relief to know she wasn't entirely debauched.

Rallying her composure, she said, "All right, let's pass over the fact that she's undressed and getting paint in my hair. Just calm down and ask her what she wants."

Senlin sawed back on the mattress. The blush that had stormed up his throat began to recede. He breathed himself steady, and when at last he spoke, his voice was almost level. "Madam apparition, why are you here? What do you want?"

And then he listened.

Edith watched the answer register in his expression. It seemed to untie some long-standing knot in the muscles of his face.

After a moment, she asked, "What did she say?"

"She—" He had to stop to clear his throat. "She said I needn't hurry. I needn't try so hard because she doesn't need to be found. She's not lost anymore. She said she hopes I can accept that." His head followed as the unseen vision moved across the room and to the door of their cell. "She's leaving. She's gone."

"Do you think that's the end of it?"

"I doubt it. She has a flair for the dramatic, my ghost."

Edith took a long breath, nodding her head with a rhythmic persistence. "What do you think she meant?"

"Well, she meant nothing, of course. I am conversing with my own insecurities. So, in many ways, the meaning is purely associative—"

"Tom," Edith said, and rolled her hand in the air to speed his prologue along.

"But I imagine that she expresses my private anxiety that I will never find my wife, and that perhaps she would prefer it if I don't. It has been a year since we parted, and the likelihood is that she has found, or perhaps has been coerced into, a new life. A woman of her talents and appearance would have no difficulty finding one. She was carried off by a nobleman, after all . . ."

"I know the Tower has been cruel to us," he continued, glancing at Edith's engine arm and then quickly down at his clasped hands. "But I have read accounts of urbane ringdoms filled with polite societies and immodest wealth. Surely not everyone is a thief, a rogue, or a tyrant . . . Maybe she basks in a better life. Ours spent together was so brief, it may have slipped her mind."

"You don't really believe that. You just feel guilty. But guilt is not a duty, Tom, no matter how devoted you are to it," she said. "Do you know why I insist you call me Mister Winters in front of the crew?"

"No, I don't. I think it's silly, honestly. You hate that man. You never speak of him. You want to divorce him, yet you make us call you by his name."

"My husband is a confirmed weasel who married me for my father's farm, and I will divorce him the minute I'm able. But until then, I keep his name to remind me of my commitments, not just to him, but to myself, and to you, and to the crew. I admire your devotion to your wife."

"But how long do I torment you and everyone else with that devotion?"

"You believe she is in Pelphia?"

"Yes, I do, though I have very little reason to."

"Then we must look. We must. That is all we need to decide for now."

He clapped his knees and turned up a brave face. "You're quite right, Mister Winters. Quite right. I'm letting my disappointment spoil my perspective. This is a setback. But it's not the first we've had. We will overcome it. We'll find another way into Pelphia."

"Hear, hear," she said, fluffing the small pillow at the head of her bed. "Now, if we are not going to escape this instant, I'd like to close my eyes. I just need a half hour's sleep."

"Of course. You rest, and I'll try to figure out whether we can talk our way out of this open-door prison, or if we have a bloody getaway to look forward to."

"You're not going to faint again?"

"I have never fainted in my life," he said, stretching his legs over the blankets on his bed.

"Well, you've taken some abrupt naps," Edith said through a yawn. "At least this cage is cozier than our last one."

He laughed dryly. "If it keeps going this way, eventually we'll land in a cage on a grassy hill somewhere in the country. We'll have four rooms and a pantry."

"I think that's just called a cottage, Tom," Edith said from under the blanket.

"A little jail on a hill," he said, his smile softening. "Edith?"

"Yes?"

"Thank you."

She yawned again. "You're welcome."

He crossed his ankles and folded his arms under his head. The light of the forest shone silvery through the golden bars. In the distance, a hammer struck upon an anvil, the sound rhythmic and incessant as the clacking of a train.

He awoke to the panicked realization that he had fallen asleep, and worse, they were no longer alone in the room.

A hunchbacked hod in a heavy cloak sat at the foot of his bed, his bald head backlit by the lamps of the atrium. Senlin bolted upright and prepared to throw himself at the intruder. His lunge was arrested by a familiar, goofy chuckle.

Voleta's wide eyes stared back at him. Her hair, her beautiful rolling hair, was shaved now as short as corduroy.

"Captain," she said while he was still marveling.

"Voleta?" Edith said, sitting up in her bed. Her clothes and hair held the dishevelment of sleep, but her eyes were quick to clear. "What are you doing here? What—what did you do to your hair?"

"I cut it. I'm a hod," she said.

"Not really?" Senlin asked, aghast.

"Of course not really. These people are insane. It's just a disguise."

"How did you find us?" Senlin asked.

"I've been exploring for, I don't know, an hour or two. This place is enormous. There are a lot of interesting things to look at. I saw a room full of guns."

"Yes, we saw it, too," Edith said, nodding at the adjacent cell.

"There's another one on the third floor. It was right next to a cell full of open vats and drying trays. It smelled awful, like an old latrine."

"They're making saltpeter," Edith said, and smiled a little when Senlin gave her a surprised look. "You learn a lot working on a farm. Urine reduces to potassium nitrate, which you need to make fertilizer. It's also one of the main ingredients of gunpowder."

With her cloak removed, they saw why Voleta had appeared hunchbacked at first: Great coils of rope hung about her neck and shoulders over her clothes. Senlin and Edith helped untangle her from the mass of rope. "They let you keep your swords? I'm surprised," Voleta said.

"I don't think they considered us much of a threat," Edith said.

"They never do. Captain, I found their pantry, too; it's enormous. I filled a sack with as much as I could carry and socked it away downstairs."

"Just for that, Voleta, I'll forgive you for leaving the ship," Senlin said.

"I was only following orders, sir. You told me to keep an eye on everyone. I was keeping an eye on you and Mister Winters."

"This is not a game," Edith said.

"I know it's not a game," she said, scrubbing a hand back and forth over the side of her shaved head. Her expression clouded at an ugly memory. "I saw the local guards kill a man. He didn't do anything to them. He was just a hod who wanted to go on. They told him that if he joined them, he'd be free. Then they killed him."

"These people are all tea and biscuits until you tell them, 'No, thank you,' and then the knives come out," Edith grumbled.

"At least we know we won't be talking our way out of here," Senlin said.

"I think they're getting worked up over something," Voleta said. "I can't understand a word they're saying, but it looks like they're forming an expedition. There's a line of empty wagons waiting at the gate."

"The ship," Senlin said. "That's why he's left us here. Marat knows we came on a ship. They're going to pick it clean. Adam, Iren—they don't know what they're in for."

"We have to get to the ship before them," Edith said. She began pulling up the bedding. "We'll disguise ourselves with these sheets."

"They'll spot you straight away," Voleta said. "That's why I brought the rope."

"What do you expect us to do with rope?"

"Squeeze through the bars and climb down."

"Don't be mad, Voleta. We're five, six stories up. Even if we climbed down, there'd be nothing but bars on one side of us and an open field on the other," Senlin said. "We'd be spotted in an instant."

"That's why I planned a diversion," Voleta said, shimmying back into her cloak. "You two will slip out the bars, and I'll meet you back at the ship."

"We're not going to leave you to bait a zoo full of armed hods. You'll come with us. We'll just have to be discreet."

"It won't work, Captain. Besides, if you're really worried about me, I'll be safer on my own. I'll be in the trees and halfway home before the fuse runs out."

Senlin blinked. "The fuse?"

Chapter Eleven

If living on a coast taught me anything, it was that every ship in the sea wants to sink. It is only the frenzy of the crew and the grit of the command that keeps a ship from foundering. The *Stone Cloud* is no different. If it soars, it is by dint of our will. It sinks as a matter of course.

—The *Stone Cloud*'s Logbook, Captain Tom Mudd

The *Stone Cloud* rose like an elephant coming up from its knees. Adam and Iren hurried to reposition sandbags of ballast about the deck to balance the ship. The new rigging bawled as it stretched. The umbilical crackled like burning sap as the heat from the furnace filled it for the first time. For all the complaints, nothing snapped, nothing caught fire. The ship was a shapeless, unsafe scrap of her former self, but Adam was confident she would fly. All they needed now was for the captain, Mister Winters, and Voleta to return.

As soon as the ship was level, they both collapsed. Iren, battered in sand and coal dust and sitting on her haunches, looked like a big toad. Adam lay sprawled across the forecastle steps, a delirious smile frozen on his face. The hard work of raising the umbilical and shoehorning the collar had distracted them from their hunger and exhaustion, but now as they relished their success, their discomfort returned.

Neither of them had mentioned the possibility that the crew might be delayed, or that they might come with no provisions, or that they might not come back at all. There was no point to speculating, though the temptation was strong.

"How are we going to get the ship out?" Iren asked. "The wind blew us in, but it's not going to blow us out again."

"I've been thinking about that," Adam said, rubbing the socket of his good eye, which only looked blearier when he was through. "I bet they used teams of horses to pull the ships out of port."

"Or autowagons," Iren said.

"Maybe." Really, it didn't matter how the airmen of the past had maneuvered their ships. He and Iren had no choice but to tow the ship down the long entryway themselves. He pictured them with bridles and blinders on. The thought made him laugh, though he wasn't sure it was particularly funny. "I think we're the horses."

"Quit talking about horses. I'm starving."

Adam had never really associated horses with dinner before, but he supposed another day of starvation might turn the entire world into a menu. "I wonder what spider-eater tastes like. I bet it—"

A deep *whump*, like a door being slammed in the far distance, interrupted him.

His exhaustion forgotten, Adam ran to the recently cobbled rail that faced the murky forest. "That was an explosion," he said, and then listened for more. More explosions would suggest resistance, retaliation, a battle, but what would one mean? A short struggle? An accident? An execution? The stillness of the skeletal woods seemed as menacing as the boom. "She's like a moth," he murmured. "Always flying into the fire."

Iren knew what he was thinking. "When she gets back, I bet she'll be ready to leave."

"Mmm." Adam slowly turned to her, his eye refocusing upon her grimy face. "Next time, we're going to make sure that she's the one who stays behind and worries."

"That's fair." Iren gathered a heavy rope around her arm. "Next time we'll be the moths." She held the line out to him. "Now, it's time to play the horse."

*   *   *

Waiting for the explosion did little to prepare them for it.

Voleta promised it was just a little keg of gunpowder. The little keg was sitting in a corner of a cell on the third floor, approximately across the atrium from them, but there was no need to worry because the keg was really quite small and the cell was empty, save for some books. Edith argued that Voleta had no experience measuring gunpowder, which was an exact science to anyone who liked having all their fingers. Voleta countered that she had helped Iren load the harpoon on several occasions and still had ten fingers to prove what a good job she'd done. This did nothing to assuage Edith's concern, and she pressed Voleta on the point of the fuse, which she could not possibly know a thing about. Voleta responded that she'd already lit the candle fuse, which was even then burning down toward an open bung in the barrel. When Senlin asked how much time they had left, Voleta replied with an evasive little shrug. "About an inch?"

Voleta had been gone for a quarter hour when the flash of light threw their shadows across the room.

A warm gust blew in a split second later, chased by a percussive boom. The bars of the cage chimed and rattled, and for a moment, Senlin believed that Voleta had killed them. But then the explosion crested, and the light turned to smoke. The singed pages of devastated books wafted in through the bars of their cell.

Cries rose over the explosion's echoing coda. They peered through their open door and saw hods on every level of the Zoo rushing about. Those already on the second floor hastened toward the fire that the explosion had ignited. The red curtains on either side of the bombed-out cell had turned to yellow flames. A bucket line quickly formed between the elevator banks and the water tanks below.

Senlin suspected that the hods would stifle the blaze soon enough, and then they would begin to wonder who had set it off.

"Quickly now," he said, nodding to the outer wall of their cell where Voleta's stolen rope lay coiled, one end already knotted to a bar. The poles of the cage were too narrowly spaced for them to slip through. Fortunately, they traveled with a dynamo that could easily bend soft metal.

Under the covering racket of the panic outside, Edith wedged the elbow of her engine between two bars and began to flex.

A gear buried deep inside the machine ground and screeched. The hairs on their necks rose, but the bars did not budge. The only sign that her arm was exerting any force was the appearance of eggshell cracks on the surface of the bars. Then the gold began to flake away.

Dark iron stood beneath the gilt.

The revelation was disastrous. It had not occurred to them that this ancient landmark of affluence might only be lacquered in gold. But perhaps that was the reason it had endured, why it had not been dismantled years ago and carried off by thieves: It was worthless.

Steam hissed from joints that had never vented before. Senlin wanted to tell her to stop, to spare her arm. But the fact was when the smoke of the explosion cleared, they would be the first people Marat looked to, their arrival being too conveniently timed with such an unexpected attack. Senlin did not doubt that Marat would be far less sanguine once he thought they were saboteurs.

But Edith needed no convincing, and she showed no sign of stopping. Either the cage would give, or her arm would. And for a moment, it seemed her arm would bend first. The plates at her elbow began to buckle under the pressure. A sound like cracking glass rang under the armor.

Then one of the bars creaked, giving a little ground, and a gap began to open.

A moment more, and the space was wide enough for them to slip through.

Senlin did not allow himself time to reflect upon the drop. He stepped through the gap, swung to the side, and clung to the face of the cage. He stared resolutely back into their cell rather than the direction they had to go. They wrapped their palms with bits of torn sheet, took the rope in hand, and began their descent without discussion. Senlin went first, ostensibly because he was their leader, but really because he was afraid he would lose his grip. He couldn't tolerate the possibility that his fall might carry Edith down with him.

They passed the levels of the Zoo quickly. Most were curtained off.

Those that were open stood empty. Voleta's distraction had worked. No one saw them slide past. Senlin's relief was tempered by the appearance of paint on the rope under his hands. Wet, colorful globs oozed from between his fingers. And though he was sure that the paint was not real, knowing this did not stop his grip from slipping. He burned his fingers breaking his descent, but no sooner had he stopped his fall than he lost his footing on the gilded bars. His legs swung beneath him, and that set him spinning. The blue light of the forest flashed by once, twice, and a third time, then he bounced against the bars on his shoulder hard enough to knock the rope from his hands.

He fell, and did not know from what height.

He struck the soft moss flat on his back. He'd only fallen a short distance, though it was sufficient to drive the wind from him.

Edith came down a moment later, landing deftly on her feet, one on either side of him. Straddling him, she helped him up. "Taking another abrupt nap, Captain?" she asked.

He replied in a proud croak: "Do try to keep up, Mister Winters." He unwrapped his hands and was relieved to see the paint had disappeared.

They crossed the clearing at a quick trot. A smaller secondary explosion clapped behind them and was answered by a renewed chorus of shouts. More hods emerged from the porcelain woods ahead, summoned by the blasts.

The haze of smoke, the dampened glow, and the general commotion helped to distract everyone from the two figures running the wrong way. Senlin's mind flew ahead to his ship. Would it be ready? Would Voleta be there? If they escaped, how long until they starved?

But his thoughts had wandered too far ahead of them. They were still a few strides shy of the cover of the woods when a hod, a woman with jowls and wiry eyebrows, pulled up short as they passed her. They did not turn to look even as she began to cry out like an operatic crow. They had been discovered.

There was no time for subtlety now, no time to look for a trail. They ducked their heads and ran behind the plowshare of Edith's raised arm. Senlin did his best to read his compass while the needle swung in sympathy to his pitching body. He nudged Edith one way then another until she felt like a rudder in a storm.

Senlin's coat tugged at him. He turned, expecting to find it snagged on a branch, but instead he found a hod holding him by the coattail. The hod appeared wraithlike in his rags. He drew the barrel of his pistol level with Senlin's forehead. Senlin kicked like a mule, catching the hod on the knee. The weapon discharged as the hod fell, his shot scattering the brittle timber above Senlin's head.

Incoherent shouts echoed behind them. The hods had recovered from their distraction and were coming for them now. They had no hope of escaping so long as they bored a hole through the woods. They had to find a clearing or a trail and try to conceal their progress. But there was nothing, nothing but rising voices, jabbing branches, and fleeing spiders.

Suddenly, the arachnids were everywhere, darkening the forest to their right, overwhelming the luminous wood with their numbers. Spiders rained from the trees, their fat abdomens pelting Edith's and Senlin's backs like hailstones. With an undulating curtain of spiders before them and a posse of armed hods closing behind them, they were trapped between two terrible fates.

Edith looked to Senlin for his preference, and he nodded grimly forward, and that was all the consultation she needed. She faced the arachnid host, and they breached the swarm.

Everything they touched in the enveloping darkness was alive. The branches moved under their hands, the ground crunched and shifted under their feet. Their skin tingled under the wash of ten thousand running legs. It felt as if they ran through a heavy rain. Senlin closed his eyes and, holding on to the laces of Edith's bodice, let himself believe they were running through the rain. Mercifully, the spiders seemed indifferent to the two giants flailing through their midst and took no time out of their furious trek to share their venom with them.

The storm ended abruptly, and the forest glowed again around them like snow under a full moon. They stood at the edge of a flat, sandy clearing. There was no pool, no benches, and no rusting beasts; there was only a haphazard arrangement of boulders that were swaddled in shaggy moss.

Taking advantage of the momentary respite, Senlin consulted his compass while Edith shook the gloamine dust and a lingering spider from her hair. "The ship's that way." He pointed past the boulders to the far side of the clearing. "Maybe a mile off. I'm not sure," he spoke in a whisper. They could still hear the chattering hods. Their pursuers seemed to have been detoured by the spiders, but they were quickly regrouping.

"These hods are disciplined." She touched the fresh dent in her arm.

"Come on," Senlin said. "We can't keep beating a path; we need to find a trail."

"What happened to your map?" she asked.

"I made Voleta take it. I have my compass; we'll be fine."

He led her at a sneaking pace across the glade. Both kept a close eye on the tree line for any sign of the hods. The air was thick with the rank odor of carrion—an odor they'd smelled before. It was the warm musk of spider-eaters. Senlin had no doubt the beasts had caused the spiders to swarm, which meant they must be nearby.

The revelation dawned on them both at once, and they froze amid the dark boulders. The stones about them swelled and shrank and swelled again. They breathed. They stank. What they'd taken for moss was quite clearly long, matted fur.

The spider-eater at Edith's elbow sighed in its sleep. Its short, muscular trunk stretched out from its bulk, quivered with a yawn, then curled in again. She allowed herself a brief cynical pout. This was the final indignation: to have escaped a zoo only to blunder upon wild animals.

Senlin put his finger to his lips in an entirely needless signal for quiet. Their only hope was to slip past the drowsing spider-eaters and back into the woods before the hods broke upon the scene and roused the beasts.

They recognized the hod who burst from the forest. He yelled in a voice that quavered with excitement, "Come and be free!" And then Koro fired his pistol at them.

The shot struck one of the sleeping boulders with a plunk. The spider-eater unfolded its long neck that winnowed to a small, toothless mouth. A crest of gray fur hung on its chest. Rearing up on its hind legs, the beast spread its shaggy arms to their full length. It raised a cry that was as forceful as a cannon and tuneful as a rusty hinge. Its fetid breath ran down Senlin's collar and over his curdling skin.

Edith and Senlin cringed as the four other beasts stood up beside their large brother, who appeared not at all hurt by the bullet that had pricked its hide. At the same moment, the woods began to produce hod after hod, each silent and severe. Their numbers continued to swell until a legion of armed men lurked at the clearing's edge.

The spider-eaters held their scarecrow pose, and the hods, seeing what they had stumbled upon, turned to stone.

Amid this terrible silence, they heard the approach of three distinct ascending squeaks. The notes played again and again like a music box harping upon a wretched song.

Chapter Twelve

I'm suspicious of men who think it better to revise an entire society than to reform their own manner of address. A constructive revolution is as impossible as an architectural fire.

—*Inaugurations of the Silk Gardens*, Salo

During his old life, Senlin had always enjoyed ringing the sturdy hand bell at the start of recess. At no other point in the day did he feel so absolutely in charge, so entirely the master, as when the students fled the schoolhouse. He stood in the doorway as they spilled under his arms into the yard and felt as placid as a king.

It is a fact, which students suspect but which teachers are loath to admit, that being the tallest in the room contributes more to one's authority than all the years at college. Why else have the children sit and the teacher stand? To make the small pay attention to the tall!

But how easily Senlin had forgotten what it was like to be a child: always underfoot, always looking up. How difficult it was to think at all while cowering at the hips of giants. Now, standing in the shadow of the spider-eaters, Senlin felt guilty for having been so insensitive toward his students.

The sickly fanfare of his rusty chair concluded with Luc Marat's appearance at the forest's edge. The king of the hods said nothing, but his beautiful face showed a cruelty that he had carefully concealed during their tea. He regarded them with the antipathy of an executioner.

Senlin expected a volley of gunfire to pin his organs to the air, but none came. The hod regiment stood ready, waiting for an order now that Marat had arrived. The hod king, sensing that the bloody work would be done just as well by the beasts looming over his wayward guests, gave his men no signal. He bowed his head slightly, first to Senlin then to Edith. And Senlin understood this smug gesture as Marat's way of saying, *See, this is the sort of fate that comes to those who haven't any friends in the Tower. This is the sort of thing I would have saved you from, if only you had been reasonable and joined me.*

Of course the hods wouldn't fire: It would only antagonize the spider-eaters into pouncing upon them rather than the two interlopers who had blundered upon their den. Senlin decided quite abruptly that his and Edith's only hope was to provoke the hods into shooting at the beasts. He had to draw Marat out.

The spider-eater at his back gave a second, more guttural bleat of warning. Senlin knew he hadn't much time. He made his final gamble.

He reached into his breast pocket, which shivered with the thrash of his heart, and extracted Ogier's painting. Senlin could only hope that Marat would believe he had been burgled and would fear that his prized forgery would be ruined by the spider-eaters if they were left to dismember the thieves.

Unfurling the scroll with unsteady fingers, Senlin turned the canvas toward Marat, offering the man an infuriating smirk of his own, an expression that said: *See, this is what happens to arrogant men who leave sticky-fingered thieves alone in their houses.*

The effect was immediate and gratifying: Marat flinched. Shock spoiled his pompous expression, and he struggled a moment to regain his composure.

"Get ready to drop," Senlin said to Edith from the corner of his mouth.

The signal Marat gave Koro was almost imperceptible, just a slice of his gaze, but the hod was quick to relay the order. Koro raised his arm high, then chopped the air.

Edith and Senlin went slack as one and fell to the sand. The crack of guns, the dull *whump* of shot striking hide, and the infuriated wails of the spider-eaters pierced their ears. Senlin could not lift his arms to shield himself before a dense, furry leg kicked him in the head. He tumbled forward into the scissoring limbs of the beasts and curled into a ball.

The churned sand befogged the scene, but through the frenzy Senlin watched the spider-eaters scoop up men with their long claws and toss them into the trees. The work of the beasts was quick and savage: They stamped on the fallen, and they cut down many hods before they could drop their pistols and draw their swords.

Still dazed and tucked against his knees, Senlin looked for Luc Marat amid the fray, but he saw no sign of the hod king or his musical chair. He had withdrawn as soon as the battle had begun, though apparently the esteem he held for his own life was not duplicated in the breasts of his men. They threw themselves at pricked Death with a thoughtless tenacity. The hods seemed never to tire of being gored and dashed and ground into the sand.

Yet, the powerful spider-eaters were not untouched by the efforts of Marat's hods. The hods nicked the beasts with their swords, and though the wounds were not mortal separately, together they turned gruesome. Dark blood stood in a sheen upon the spider-eaters' coats. The smallest of the beasts had been driven from its feet, and now lay on its side, kicking wildly as hod after hod leapt upon it and drove a sword between its ribs. The bleat it raised was of such a terrifying octave, Senlin felt a rush of pity for the dying animal.

All of this occurred in a span of seconds, and still when Edith grabbed him under his arms and pulled him to his feet, Senlin felt as if he had attended a play: a thing of scenes and acts and many hours. He was relieved and a little surprised to find that he had not lost hold of Ogier's canvas.

Edith's lip was bleeding, and she looked a little wild-eyed, but her voice was clear when she said, "We should run."

Before they had time to turn toward the uncongested end of the clearing, the largest spider-eater with the magnificent gray mantel reared back from the fight, marked them as deserving of its wrath, and charged.

The sand under them leapt with the force of its gallop. The beast was as imposing as a runaway carriage, and Senlin wondered if he'd be spry enough to leap from its path. But even as he crouched to spring away, he felt Edith plant her hand on his shoulder and leapfrog over him, shoving him aside in the act.

She seemed to hang in the air, her engine arm craned wide. The beast lowered its head to meet her. Brass fingers splayed, she brought the engine around. The blow landed on the side of the spider-eater's head, deflecting the beast's charge as effectively as a wall. Its stride broken, the big creature stumbled to the side, but rather than fall, it jogged on until it recovered its step and disappeared into the woods.

Senlin knew something was wrong when he saw Edith lurch back to the ground with uneven shoulders, her expression so pinched it seemed to have driven all the blood from her face.

The engine hung from her, a lifeless plummet.

Senlin took her hand, squeezed it, and pulled her toward the twilit forest.

Adam had hoped that towing the airship by foot would be no harder than walking with a balloon on a string. Only after he and Iren had lifted the tow bar and leaned their weight into it did he realize the difficulty of the chore. It was like trying to pull a fifty-foot kite.

Even against a light breeze, towing the ship required back-straining, toe-digging, blister-raising effort. Momentum helped a little, but when one of them slipped in the sand and brought them to a stop, it took all their strength to get the ship moving again. The tantalizing light at the end of the tunnel winked with the passage of clouds outside. They trudged past the shins of giants, and felt those kingly pillars snickering at their feeble work. And still they persisted, though the brink of the port seemed determined to shrink from them.

After an hour of enduring splinters from the tow bar and chafing from the sand, they were finally able to hook the aft anchor on the rocky lip of the port. They knew they would have to run the ship off the edge to get her underway, which would leave them dangling under the hull like two worms on a hook, but for the moment there was nothing else to be done. Until everyone returned, they had time to bask in the brisk air slanting across the mouth of the port and enjoy the sun that made them look vital again after the corpse tones of the gloamine. They sprawled on the broad stones at the threshold and enjoyed the inebriation of their fatigue.

"This is no time for lounging!" The familiar voice called down at them from the quarterdeck of the ship. Adam and Iren sat up in a daze, regarding the bald specter of Voleta leaning over the lashed-up rail at the battered rear of the ship. "The captain and Winters are coming, and I don't think they're coming alone."

"What happened to your hair?" Adam said, squinting at her stark shadow through the glare of sun. "Where have you been? We heard an explosion."

"That was me. Captain found the man he was looking for. Turned out to be the bad sort, and easily offended."

This stirred Iren's old vigilance, and she came to her feet with a stifled groan. "How many are coming?"

"More than you can handle." Voleta hoisted up a heavy sack for them to see. "I stole their breakfast!"

"Adam, take the pistols and defend the bow. Keep low and let them fire first; that'll tell you their distance."

"Can you move the ship on your own?" Adam asked.

She shook out her arms, the voluptuous bulbs of her muscles rolling then tightening into place. She wrapped the towline about her forearm and said, "With breakfast waiting, I could scoot the Tower."

Edith had never been able to explain, at least not to her brothers' satisfaction, the pleasure she took from labor. Her brothers, both elder, enjoyed their father's fortune but deplored the effort he'd exerted to acquire it. They found the business of agriculture boring and the act of farming tiresome. As far as they were concerned, work was the penalty of poverty, and they were not poor.

Edith's interest in the family enterprise was an absolute puzzle to them, especially considering the leisure afforded to her sex. When their father decorated and furnished the parlor, at no small expense, for the sole purpose of giving her a suitable arena for receiving gentleman callers, the brothers had been at first envious of the long days of loafing and flirting that awaited her, and then mystified when she refused to even sit in the room.

She married late—*very* late compared to her peers—partly because no suitor could ever catch up with her. She was always tromping through the fields, or checking the corn for wireworms, or mending fences, or learning to harness the draft horses, or a hundred other supposedly tedious things she was not required to do.

What her brothers failed to understand was that labor was not without reward. Underneath the caked mud and calluses, she had developed muscles and dexterous joints. The more she labored, the more confident she became, and she found this self-reliance deeply comforting. She believed that, unlike fortunes, which could be won and lost, the recompenses of hard work endured.

But that was before she'd ever laid eyes on the Tower.

Now, she was unable to even walk a straight line.

The dead weight of her arm swung from her shoulder, pitching her one way then another. Too stubborn to stop, she blundered along after Senlin for some time before a loss of balance sent her careening into a thicket of young porcelmores that shattered like fireworks around her. The bramble of saplings cut her like saw grass. She was only more infuriated when Senlin came back to pull her out.

"Quit fussing and run," Edith said, knocking his hand away as soon as she was upright. "Why are you taking off your belt?"

Without answering, Senlin cocked her engine arm up to her breast and hooped his belt around the articulated joint of the wrist. "Turn around," he said, and she did with a huff. He reached around her shoulders to grasp the belt. She moved her hair for him. She suffered a brief, pleasant shiver when his breath touched her nape. He buckled the ends of his belt together. With the simple sling complete, he turned her around again and said, "There. All done. I couldn't have you diving into the brambles at every turn."

"Thank you," she said, though he couldn't tell if she meant it.

Since they were already stopped, Senlin took a moment to check his compass. They were still on course, but their progress was slow without a trail. They couldn't go fifty feet without clambering up an artificial knoll or over an ornamental wall. The Silk Gardens had been built for dalliances, and so the going was like leaping between the back gardens of a crowded city block.

"Look, it's our old friend the emu," Senlin said, coming upon the rusted machine from the wooded side.

"Won't the paths be full of hods? I think we're better off here in the thick of it," Edith said, rolling her neck against the new weight that hung from it.

"I disagree. They're going to pass us, if they haven't already, and then they'll be standing between the ship and us. We haven't any choice but to take the trail. You lead. I'll fend off whatever runs up behind us." He struggled to draw his rapier in the cramped space between trees. He managed it, but inelegantly.

Senlin knew she would want to be the one to bring up the rear, the one to defend him, her captain. But the exhaustion of her engine had unbalanced her in more than one way, and they both knew it. Of course, this shared knowledge only made her more frustrated, more determined to prove she was capable.

She opened her mouth to argue, but Senlin cut her off. "It's an order, Mister Winters. If I have to give every order twice, it's going to take us forever to get anywhere. You can scowl at me on the boat. Now, off we go."

Edith drew her blade with a grace that seemed to make a point: even one-armed, she was the superior swordsman.

The trail was so twisted and clouded with the diffuse blue light they could see only a short distance in either direction. For the moment the way was empty. Perhaps the hods were still embroiled with the spider-eaters; perhaps the fight had broken them. Senlin and Edith didn't care which it was. With every blind turn and every revelation of safety, their pace quickened and their hearts leapt. They were nearly home.

The trail opened onto the beach and the voluminous theater of ship-wrecks. The sight of sunlight beaming through the port tunnel made them almost giddy with relief. There was a bright smell in the air; it was crisp and nothing like the cold, loamy odor of moss and stale water.

It was almost like the sharp perfume of cracked pepper. It was, Senlin finally identified, the smell of gunpowder.

Chapter Thirteen

Despite the evidence of my chosen profession, I am
far from comfortable with violence. Unfortunately,
the consequence of practice is mastery.
  —The *Stone Cloud*'s Logbook, Captain Tom Mudd

Creeping ahead of Edith through the deep shadow of a derelict,
Senlin heard a tumult of breathing, creaking leather thongs,
and the grating slide of ramrods inside of gun barrels. He
peered around the edge of the silk-wrapped hull and saw a platoon
standing at the start of the tunnel. Beyond them and down the long
channel, the *Stone Cloud* floated at the sunny mouth of the port.

He counted thirty hods. They looked a little haggard: Some of their
robes were singed, probably from the explosion Voleta had touched
off, and they were winded from running. Some looked half-dead on
their feet, victims of smoke poisoning. They leaned on their swords
staked in the sand and panted until they wheezed. Still, there were a
lot of them.

"I think they're going to charge the ship," Senlin whispered over
his shoulder to Edith. "They have to. There's hardly any cover. When
they start, we'll follow and pick them off one by one from behind. If
they drop a gun, take it. As soon as they start shooting at the *Cloud*,
we'll start firing at them."

"Two against thirty," Edith said. "Those are terrible odds."

"No, it's two fronts against thirty backs."

"How honorable." She reseated the engine that hung in a frozen salute at her breast.

"Look at this beach. Look at all these doomed ships, and look how organized and ready the hods are to plunder us and murder our crew. I suspect they've made a habit of victimizing castaways for years," Senlin said, buttoning his coat up to the neck to keep his collar from flapping.

"That does assuage my conscience. Thank you."

"Not at all." He put his hand on her shoulder to stop her from breaking cover just yet. "Wait a moment, Edith. I want to say something."

"Oh, don't start making your peace, Tom. The last thing we need right now is peace. A little disquiet is good for your courage."

"Perhaps so, but I must speak. I never said how much I regret having lied to you about my illness. It was wrong of me, and I handled your confrontation of my error poorly. I am sorry. You have been exceedingly patient and wonderful."

Edith didn't think she'd ever been described as patient before— and certainly never wonderful. She looked up to find him beaming with sincerity and appreciation, and she could not help but smile. "If I forgive you, are you just going to run out there and get shot?"

"If you're worried about me being too at peace, believe me, I have quite a ways to go."

This was not the platoon's first assault on a marooned vessel. The abandoned port attracted a reliable trickle of desperate airmen who coasted in upon coal fumes and glue patches, who chose the deserted Gardens over the Valley, where they were certain to be swarmed by pilgrims and tourists. The hods had learned to wait awhile until the vigilance of the stranded airmen had softened. They knew, too, that a long siege just wasted valuable shot and powder. It was better to lunge in quickly and with the advantage of surprise.

Today, the regiment was without its usual command, which had taken another platoon to pursue the villains who'd set off a bomb in their home. Fortunately, this was not the sort of work that required much supervision. And the ship looked on the verge of leaving the port, which was something Marat had absolutely forbidden. It took only a little consultation to agree that they would charge the ship before it escaped.

The platoon began an orderly trot into the vaulted tunnel, though the men who had swallowed too much smoke soon bent the formation. It mattered little. This was their terrain, and they knew it well. They regularly conducted drills in the shadow of the colossi, though none of the hods felt any reverence for those giants of the old aristocracy, and they expressed their contempt by using those stately heads as targets for their practice. They had pocked many chins and blunted many noses with the pecking of their rifles.

Knowing the crew of the ship would spot them soon, they made no attempt to disguise their advance. Experience had taught them the value of unnerving a foe, and so they raised an intimidating shout.

Their roar had the unintended effect of also covering the strangled cry of one of their own when a lanky pirate in a tricorne hat crowned him from behind. The hods began to fire their guns at two hundred yards out, and so did not notice as two more of their own collapsed after being shot in the back.

The hods, as a whole, felt very optimistic about the assault. The ship looked pinned and pasted together. There was no cannon on the forward bow—what remained of it. No crew amassed in the shadow of the ship, waiting to rebuff them, save for a lone figure who seemed to be single-handedly trying to launch the ship. The lone airman dropped to the ground and covered his head the moment they started firing. The hods' battle cry turned into a merry cheer.

They were a little disappointed when two crewmen aboard the ship began to fire pistols at them from the blunted prow. Comrades who'd been jogging happily along a moment before now fell to the sand clutching one bloody limb or another. The front line of their ranks began to fray. But these losses, the hods knew, were surmountable. They returned fire, though the barrage seemed more modest than before.

One of the hods at the fore looked back amid his stride to see if there was a fresh man with a loaded gun ready to replace him, but instead of being relieved, he was shot in the head. Those around him saw the corporeal eruption, saw him fall, and saw, quite clearly, that he had been shot by someone at the rear. This was disturbing, but sometimes amid the fog of war, a friend shoots a friend. Perhaps they would've investigated the error further if they weren't a mere fifty yards from their dangling prey, which now launched a fresh hail of shot at them. Four more fell.

They began, as a unit, to sense that they were dwindling. It's not wise amid a charge to stop and take stock of one's supporting presence, but out of the corner of their eyes, they recognized a paucity of bodies. Still, they were now under the umbrella of the ship's envelope and only twenty paces from leaping at the rope ladder and boarding the ship in a swarm.

Since they were fewer, and more timid now, their cheers turned into a chugging grunt like the breathing of a horse run nearly to death. Amid this, they heard the unlovely noises of men crying out in pain, crying out despite a lack of gunfire. Then the shooting resumed, again from behind, and each blast seemed doomed to strike friend rather than foe. The fog of war, it seemed, had become a soup.

The platoon finally came to a halt before the ladder of the ship, and they turned to see how many of them were left to claim their triumph. The breathless platoon was pained to discover that their numbers had been reduced to one.

The remaining hod looked in bewilderment back down the hall of grim, defaced kings. His brothers, some squirming, some motionless, littered the ground. While this was a terrible sight, worse were the two figures standing immediately before him with pistols leveled at his head.

Now that the shooting had stopped, Iren got to her feet and stole up behind the last, gawking hod. She hammered him on the head with a closed hand. He fell like a tree and landed on his ear.

"Iren! Is Voleta aboard?" Senlin asked, sheathing his sword with an arm that shook from use.

"She is."

"Is the ship airworthy?"

"She is."

"Then you have dispatched your duties wonderfully, and I thank you."

Iren looked the captain and first mate up and down, taking in Edith's split lip, the gory stains on her tattered scarf and the captain's shirt, the sling that pinned her mighty arm to her breast, the gash of blood on his forehead, the glowing dust that frosted them from hat to boot, and the strong smell of smoke wafting from their clothes.

"How was the zoo?" she asked.

Chapter Fourteen

There is little in the world more curative than a picnic. Some call for doctors and tonics when they fall ill. I call for friends and wine. "But," you say, "what if you are really dying?" Of course I am! We all are! The question is, gentle reader, in these uncertain times, would you rather be a patient or a picnicker?

—*Folkways and Right of Ways*
in the Silk Gardens, Anon.

They hadn't far to go before they found a tranquil bit of air near an unremarkable expanse of block. The ship clung to the spot as firmly as to an anchor. The afternoon shadow and the color of the Tower's masonry were favorable for concealing them from the other ships in the sky. For the moment, the *Stone Cloud* was as inconspicuous as a moth on a tree.

Breaking the long-standing tradition of crew and command dining separately, luncheon was served in the great cabin, which was still a rough mess, though Adam and Iren had managed to board up the old chart house and replace the captain's door. A leaf was added to the table and barrels were brought to fill out the seats, so they could all enjoy Voleta's pilfered feast together. There were loaves of millet bread, wild honey, clotted cream, boiled ham, turnips, green apples, limes, pickled cabbage, and jerky that some believed was venison and others most definitely bison. To this bounty, the captain contributed the last of his private stock of rum and real linen napkins. Iren proclaimed the napkins too fine to use, and so dined with hers draped over her shoulder to keep it from getting soiled.

They hummed around mouthfuls, clapped their pewter cups of diluted rum together, and scratched so furiously at the captain's china with knife and fork it was a wonder the plates didn't split in half.

The only person untouched by the high spirits was Edith. She ate as hungrily as the rest, but she seemed to relish neither the rare victuals nor the tart grog. At the start of the meal, she posed her forearm on the table so that it might appear more natural, with the fist standing and the wrist bent. The ruse was unnecessary; everyone knew when she had to be helped up the rope ladder that something was the matter with her arm. But she had said nothing of it, and the crew was too in awe of her to ask.

They were just beginning their second portions when the wrist of Edith's engine was jostled by a bump of the table. Her fist rolled against her mug, tipping it over. The resulting spill wetted the tablecloth and the conversation alike. Amid the difficult silence that followed, Edith pushed back her chair, picked up her arm to keep it from swinging against her hip, and exited to the main deck.

The crew turned to their captain for some sign of how to react.

He smiled reassuringly and said, "We all owe our first mate an enormous debt of patience. Let's see if we can't pay down our balance a little."

The crew stared at their empty plates with a mixture of drowsy pleasure and amazement. Senlin knew it wouldn't do any good to try to squeeze any more wakefulness out of them. They had to sleep.

He announced the suspension of watches for the day, and at that, the crew lurched to their feet and filed out the door, carrying dishes, cups, and cutlery in precarious stacks. It didn't matter that the evening was hours off. Iren, Voleta, and Adam were in their hammocks and asleep before Senlin had finished shaking out his tablecloth.

Senlin found Edith tying telltales to the rigging. Replacing the simple ribbons that helped them track the wind was not an especially pressing chore, but it had given the rest of the crew an excuse to go below without engaging the first mate, and more importantly, it had saved Edith from having to discuss her dead engine.

With only one hand and her teeth to help her, she struggled to knot the ribbons. Senlin offered his assistance, but she refused with a forced politeness that told him she would take any further insistence as an insult.

He wanted to broach the subject of where she would sleep since her room had been demolished. He had come with every intention of offering his bed. He could bunk with Adam, and she could have the great cabin to herself. But he thought better of the idea now. Sympathy, he suspected, would only make her feel pitiful, and that would make her angry. She would bunk with Iren and Voleta and probably feel better for being nearer her crew.

Senlin informed her of the suspended watch and left her gritting a red ribbon between her teeth.

In all honesty, he was relieved to keep his room and bed. He didn't feel well and hadn't since collapsing in the Golden Zoo, though he had a difficult time articulating, even to himself, what pained him. The closest he could come to describing the malady was to say it was like an itch that shifted between organs. One moment, it was in his brain, then his heart, and then his liver. The itch caused an anxiety so intense it made him nauseous. He'd assumed this was all a symptom of malnutrition, but the gluttonous meal he'd just indulged in, his first real meal in days, had not cured him.

Perhaps he was really ill.

The thought made him laugh. He'd been seeing ghosts for weeks, and only now did it occur to him that he might be genuinely unwell.

As soon as he was alone in his cabin, he felt an intense desire to meditate upon Ogier's portrait of Marya, to refresh his memory of his wife.

He put on a nightshirt and climbed into his cockeyed bed. He withdrew the painting from the cavity behind the headboard and pressed it to his forehead as if it were a holy relic. The faint odor of linseed and varnish had, over the months, begun to replace his memory of

Marya's natural fragrance. The brushwork of the painting had a tactile fingerprint that he took great comfort in tracing.

After only a moment's reflection, he began to feel better. His nausea faded; the itch turned into a warm, gentle pressure.

And to think, he'd left the portrait behind during his trek to the Zoo, knowing full well that Iren might have been forced to withdraw. How close had he come to losing this last glimpse of his wife? He resolved not to make the same mistake again. From then on, wherever he went, he would carry her portrait with him.

He was hardly surprised, given the sincere feelings that the painting revived, when the specter of Marya appeared in her nightgown under the quilts at his side.

"I'm glad we're talking again, Tom."

"I thought you were gone," he said, glancing to see if she was still made out of wet daubs of paint, but she had returned to her former, flesh-and-blood self.

"Why would you think that?"

"The last time I saw you, you told me to let you go."

"Don't be absurd. I only said that because that horrible woman was there, and you were telling her everything I said."

"She isn't horrible. She's a faithful friend who has saved my life more than—"

"A faithful friend!" Marya broke in with a punctuating scoff. "She's cut from the same cloth as the Red Hand, if you'll recall. For all you know, she's another assassin."

"Then she's made a terrible botch of it." Since the moment of quiet reflection was ruined, Senlin stowed the painting again. He turned to face the apparition in his bed. "What do you want?"

"Oh, that hurts, Tom. I just want to help you. I'm the little voice in your heart that keeps you on the right."

"You're my conscience, are you? I must be a terrible person."

Marya gave him a tart smile. "I'm only looking out for you. I'm tired of seeing you squander your advantage."

"What advantage? We're nearer to starving than not. We've grown so accustomed to tucking our tail and running away, we're in danger of making an art form of it."

"Yet, you have in your possession a thing that, time and again, has shown itself to be of great value to powerful men. It doesn't matter that you don't understand why it's valuable, Tom. What matters is that it is a boon! How long until you recognize that? How long until you take control and stop with the wait-and-sees and the wish-I-mays?"

"Oh, shut up!" he barked.

The knock at his cabin door was tentative but familiar: three swift taps. He sat up in bed, smoothing the quilts about his lap. When he looked around again, the specter of Marya had vanished.

He called for Edith to enter. The first mate wore what passed for pajamas on the ship: a shapeless tunic cinched at the waist with a rope. The outfit made her look like an altogether different person, not least of all because it hid her engine arm. Senlin fancied he could see her old country self peeking through.

"So, I guess she's back?" Edith said.

"I think we need a new knock," he said. "Maybe something like, hard, soft, hard." He rapped the pattern out upon his bedside table. "How does that sound?"

"Fine, but what is it for?"

"Well, it's just our way of saying all those awkward things we'd rather not say out loud. Things like, 'Don't mind me, I'm just shouting at ghosts.'"

"Oh, I see. Could it also say, 'I'm sorry I ruined lunch by storming out like a spoiled brat?'" She delivered the pattern on the table: hard, soft, hard.

"Absolutely," he said. "That is exactly the sort of thing it would say."

"Between the two of us, I think this knock will get a lot of use."

He pulled on a robe, a ridiculously colorful silk thing that had been Captain Lee's.

"No, you really don't have to get up," Edith said, trying vainly to wave him back to bed.

He ignored her protests and cinched the belt around his waist. "How's your lip?" he asked, pointing to the corner of his own mouth.

She touched the dark crack in her lower lip. "Fine, fine. How's your head?"

"Better, actually."

"I'm just hunting about for a blanket and a pillow. The blanket is for the draft; the pillow's for Iren's snoring."

"Of course. I have more than enough. Let's see." He dug through the tall wardrobe, gathering a bale of bedclothes. He helped her hook it all under her able arm. It took a little tucking and retucking of blanket corners before the mass would stay.

"You do realize that Lee didn't wear that robe? It was for his... guests," she said.

"It fits surprisingly well. He must've preferred tall women," Senlin said, plucking at the pattern of tropical birds.

"That he did."

The pause grew into a silence, yet she made no move to leave. He felt certain that she wanted to say something more and only needed a gentle prod to come out with it. He wanted to ask the question she had dodged many times before, so he tapped the rhythm upon the table: hard, soft, hard.

"Wearing it out already? All right. Let's have it," she said, hiking her chin at him, playfully daring him to speak his mind.

"Why won't you talk about what happened to you? Why won't you tell me about the Sphinx?"

She was smiling still, but sadly. "That's a big knock, Tom. But you've been patient. You've been very patient. I've avoided talking about it because you'd look at me differently if you knew. And I don't want to feel any less like myself than I already do."

"Well, that's not fair. I let you mediate between me and my ghost, knowing full well you'd look at me differently. But I did it anyway because you are my friend, and I needed your help." He squared his shoulders inside the flamboyant robe. "Trust me, Mister Winters, whatever you tell me, I will think no less of you."

She was struggling to keep the bedding in hand and so allowed Senlin to take it and set it upon the table. Though her gaze had been elusive at first, it now became direct and probing. "Before the Sphinx saved my life, he made me sign a contract. I knew I was dying. All I had to do to stop it was sign my name. How strange is that? To be resurrected by a pen? It was only later when the fever broke that I thought about what I had signed."

"What did you agree to?"

"To be a Wakeman. To watch over the Tower," she said, and stroked the elbow of her lifeless arm. "You have to understand: Most of what I know about the Wakemen I learned from Billy Lee, and there was a lot he didn't know. I think there are a couple hundred of us spread throughout the ringdoms. We're not too hard to spot."

"Like the Red Hand. He stood out in a crowd. He was a Wakeman, wasn't he? And that's why you couldn't kill him, not on purpose. The two of you serve the same master."

Edith nodded repeatedly, mechanically, as if she had to shake the word out of her head. "Yes," she said at last. "But I'm nothing like him." She laughed, but her expression was almost frightened.

"No, of course you aren't. But if the Red Hand was a Wakeman, why was he working for the commissioner?"

"The Sphinx contracted him out. I'm sure the commissioner paid a lot of money to have the Red Hand on his staff. And he isn't the only one. Armies, agencies, port guards: Everyone wants a Wakeman on his roll. We have our uses."

"Assassination, for one," he said. She gave him a pained look, and he rushed to reassure her. "You know I don't hold you responsible for anything that thug did. But I need to know: Did the Sphinx order the Red Hand to kill me? Does he want me dead?"

"I don't know, but I doubt it. It's more likely that Commissioner Pound ordered the Red Hand to do it. You did rob him, after all."

"But I don't understand: What is the purpose of the Wakemen? How can you be expected to keep the peace while conducting assassinations and public executions?"

"The Sphinx isn't really concerned with peace—or war, for that matter. He's interested in maintaining the Tower. Wars have come and gone. The Tower endures."

"So, it's about the distribution of power? The Sphinx places the Wakemen where he sees an unbalance of might?"

"I think so, but it's only a guess. He hasn't given me my orders yet. I had to get my strength back and grow into my arm before I'd be of any use to him. That's what I was doing on Lee's ship."

"What will the Sphinx do with you?"

"I don't know. And honestly, I'm afraid to find out. My plan was to avoid him for as long as I could. I always knew I'd have to go back for more fuel eventually, but I'd told myself it might be years. He could order me to do anything."

"Give me an example of anything."

"He could assign me to the Baths to replace the Red Hand."

"Would you go?"

"Would I climb aboard the *Ararat* and chase after my old crew? Of course not. But I don't know what the consequences of refusing would be. He could take his arm back, I suppose. Though I think it might kill me if he did. He didn't just strap the arm on. It's bolted to my bones," she said, and paled at the thought.

"Perhaps you could learn to live without his batteries. Look at Marat—"

"Are you really suggesting I follow his example? You want me to break my word? You want me to live as an invalid and a coward? Pride and honor aside, the Sphinx does not give up his toys easily, Tom. Short of surrounding myself with guns and slaves and living in a cage in a spider-infested hole, there's nowhere to hide."

"You could go home."

"To what? Assuming the arm of the Sphinx doesn't reach that far, which I wouldn't lay a wager to, have you forgotten what drove me to the Tower in the first place? The weasel used a little hay fever as an excuse to exclude me from my own affairs. What would my husband do with a one-armed wife? I'd be shut up in the attic so fast... No, I go home whole, or I don't go home at all."

Senlin's internal casting about for an answer was reflected in his shifting stance. He looked like a man trying to learn to waltz from figures in a book. Every plot that came to mind for how she might escape her contract or the Sphinx's reach seemed, even to him, impossible. After a few fits and starts, his agitation turned to resolution. "Then I suppose we have no choice."

"I have no choice. You do. You have to keep the crew, especially Adam, as far away from the Sphinx as possible."

"Why Adam in particular?"

"Because I don't want to pick up where Billy Lee left off. He was the Sphinx's headhunter. Lee scouted everywhere he went for maimed and desperate souls, souls like me. He was such a cruel opportunist, and still he was not half as bad as the Sphinx. The Sphinx has a predator's eye for injuries and insecurities. He can be very persuasive. I'm afraid he'd put a tin eye in Adam's head the minute we turned around."

"Did the Sphinx pay Lee to supply him with...recruits?"

"Handsomely."

"That means the Sphinx has use for money. Which is good for us, because I suspect we have something that's worth a lot of money. I used to think that Pound was on a foxhunt, that he was just chasing us for sport, and the painting and the theft were only an excuse for the outing. But after seeing those forgeries in the Zoo and Marat's response when he thought I'd stolen one, I'm beginning to think our painting is worth quite a lot."

Edith gave him a sidelong look, obviously mistrustful of the direction of his logic.

He went on. "Perhaps we've been going about this the wrong way. We've been on the defensive so long we've grown accustomed to thinking of ourselves as powerless, without resource. But what if we're not? What if I proposed a trade with the Sphinx? He repairs our ship and he gives me a letter of introduction that will get us past the port guards of Pelphia. I'm sure that wouldn't be any trouble for a man who has a finger in every ringdom."

"But what have you to trade?"

"I have Ogier's painting, which he can sell to the commissioner or Marat or whomever. I don't care. And we have information about Marat and his band of babblers. You said the Sphinx is concerned with maintaining the status quo. Don't you think the Sphinx would like to know about the revolutionaries hiding out in the old park?"

"That is an awful idea, Tom. Did you not listen to anything I said?"

"You're right! What am I thinking? First I must bargain for your freedom, for you to be released from your contract." He brightened, looking as proud as a rooster in his colorful robe, though he did not see his confidence reflected in her expression. "Why not face our bullies, Edith? Let's have no more of these wait-and-sees and wish-I-mays. Let's get on with it."

"You have no idea what you're stirring up," Edith said. "You should leave me at the nearest port and take the crew as far away as you can."

"Absolutely not. The crew stands behind me, Mister Winters, and I stand with you. We are going to see the Sphinx."

Part III
The Bottomless Library

Chapter One

It is common knowledge the Sphinx does not exist. This fact, however, has not diminished his fame.

—*The Myth of the Sphinx: A Historical Analysis* by Saavedra

No aeronaut worth his wind believed the Sphinx was real.

The Sphinx was a bugaboo that airmen blamed for inconvenient gusts, or stubborn fog, or morning frost on the privy seat. He was a shibboleth of the superstitious and the illiterate. When a scullery maid dropped a plate only to have it bounce but not burst upon the floor, she might exclaim, "Oh, thank the Sphinx!" When the carriage door snagged the footman's coattail, he might utter a curse and say, "There's the Sphinx, at it again."

Many enlightened citizens of the Tower believed the Sphinx was almost certainly a historical entity, though they disagreed on whether he had been a person or the brand of a now-defunct guild. Whichever it was, his blaze was everywhere—on the beer-me-go-rounds of the Basement, on the mechanical hippos of the Baths, on the belfry full of lightning in the heart of New Babel. His name graced plaques and plinths in every ringdom, and yet somehow his ubiquity had made him easier to overlook.

Some educated men and women believed the Sphinx was a poetic flourish, like Old Man Winter or Mother Moon. The Sphinx was the

Tower personified, and all the creations attributed to him—the brass-limbed half-skins, the autowagons, and sure-footed mechanical insects that crawled about the masonry making repairs—were not the fruits of an unseen genius, but were, in truth, products of the great houses of Babel: the Pells and Algezians, the Japhethites and the Thanes.

Being a relative newcomer, Senlin was unfamiliar with the associations the Sphinx conjured in the native mind. So, while it seemed not very remarkable to him that they should go knock on the man's front door, it came as something of a surprise to his crew when he announced that they were going to visit the mythical Sphinx. He might as well have proposed that they sail to the edge of the flat earth and fish for falling stars.

Hitherto, the crew of the *Stone Cloud* had not argued with the captain's orders, bizarre and reckless though they sometimes seemed. When he'd asked them to dress up as wounded damsels, lie prone upon the ship's deck, and wait to be boarded, they had done so without complaint. When he'd asked them to slip onto a hostile ship under the cover of a cyclone of seagulls, which were all furiously expectorating and eliminating half-digested fish, they had raised a hurrah and leapt to. They had grown accustomed to the creativity of his leadership, yet his present plan of action seemed a novel test.

It wasn't that Iren, Adam, and Voleta disbelieved that Mister Winters's recent past included some traumatic interlude during which an engine was added to her person. The evidence for that was plain enough. But must it really have been the Sphinx that did it? Could this not be an airman's yarn: a pleasant exaggeration to cover an unpleasant reality? Even she admitted to being feverish during the ordeal. Perhaps she had imagined it. Perhaps her reluctance to discuss the matter was an indication of her own uncertainty on the subject.

"It is a necessary detour," the captain assured them during the morning assembly on the main deck. Their little cove of quiet air still held them to the Tower's bosom, though the sun now threw their shadow upon the sandstone where it stood out like a wine stain on a shirtfront.

"Mister Winters's arm needs refueling, and the Sphinx is the only one who has the fuel. It will be a brief layover, but hopefully it will give us time to finish the essential repairs that Adam and Iren so valiantly began." Senlin glanced about, trying his best to smile at their work, though in the stark light of morning the ship looked as lovely and lasting as a bird's nest. "In fact, I doubt it will be necessary for us to disembark." It was a point Edith had insisted upon, and Senlin couldn't see any reason to argue with his mate. She was quite vocal about her concern for the crew's safety, especially Adam's. "I think it best that we all stay aboard the ship as long as we're in the Sphinx's dock."

Voleta tried to stop the dumb chuckle before it started, but she couldn't pinch it off in time. She wasn't laughing because she found the captain's speech amusing. She was laughing because Squit had chosen that inconvenient moment to discover that Voleta's navel was the same size as her furry nose, a discovery that tickled unbearably.

Mister Winters, who had been standing quietly beside the disemboweled console, her engine cinched to her breast in a black cotton sling, rolled her eyes around to Voleta, still strugling to stifle her laughter. "Captain, may I say a few words?"

"By all means." Senlin cordially waved his first mate forward.

Earlier that morning, Voleta had watched Iren dress Edith in their cabin belowdecks. The first mate had not asked for Iren's help, but neither had she refused it. The solemnity with which Iren guided Edith's engine through the sleeve of her blouse, and pulled the laces of her bodice, and tugged her bootstraps until her heels were snugly seated had made Voleta uncomfortable for reasons she could not enumerate. It was such an intimate and vulnerable act. She had wanted to run from the room.

In that moment, Voleta had wondered whether Mister Winters would lose some of her bearing with the loss of her arm. But now, as the first mate leaned into her and fixed her with a leaden gaze, Voleta knew the answer.

"I blame myself," Mister Winters said, though her expression suggested otherwise. "For months, I have overlooked your disregard for any order that did not amuse you. I let you run wild about the ship and through the harbors. I let your impertinence and rashness pass without rebuke. I am sorry. Forgive me. I will make amends."

Her parting words were delivered with such grim conviction it might have been enough to reform even an inveterate criminal. Unfortunately, Voleta struggled, even in the gust of Mister Winters's breath, to keep a straight face amid Squit's investigations.

"I can imagine what you're thinking," Edith continued at a deliberate clip. "You came to the assistance of the captain and me. You couldn't have done that if you'd followed orders. And that's true. But if you want to take credit for that, then you must also take responsibility for taunting the port official in Pelphia and for the cannons they fired at us. And don't forget our barring from the Windsock, which your thievery ensured. And you must take credit for failing to spot the *Ararat* until it was on top of us, a mistake which nearly brought down the ship."

Tickle or no, the mate's words doused the laughter in Voleta's expression.

"So, go ahead and take credit. You have a lot to take credit for." Edith cupped the back of Voleta's shorn head, pulling the young woman's pretty, heart-shaped face nearer her own. "But there is only room for crew aboard this ship. And the crew follows orders without question, without exception. If you would rather not be part of our crew, the captain will pay you the wages you are due, and we will drop you off on the nearest convenient ledge."

When the first mate stepped back, Voleta's mouth seemed to have come unhinged.

She turned her shocked expression toward her brother, expecting him to come blustering to her defense, or at least to look as if he were marshaling his anger at this rough handling of his sister. But what she saw was indifference. He only shrugged at her as if to say, *Don't look at me.*

Voleta found his response very interesting. Something had changed between them; something was different.

She swallowed and said to the waiting first mate, "Aye aye, sir."

Senlin returned to the fore. "Mister Winters emphasizes an important point. We are flying into dangerous currents. Captain Lee had a standing arrangement with the Sphinx, which included the delivery of wayward souls." A melancholy smirk lifted a corner of his mouth. "A cargo we are never wanting." He quickly sobered. "Lee's work is not ours, of course, but the Sphinx may try to take advantage of our circumstance. He may try to separate us, seduce us, appeal to our insecurities. It is essential, therefore, that we stick together."

"May I ask a question?" Iren said.

"Of course."

"What is the Sphinx like?"

"Dangerous," Edith said, quick as a spring. "Determined. Soon as he decides he wants something, he takes it. Manipulative. Unpredictable."

"I mean, what does he look like?" Iren said.

Edith frowned at the amazon. She understood what Iren was really asking. Iren was unconvinced the Sphinx existed. So Edith offered a most contrary answer: "He looks like a spoon."

"Like a spoon?"

"A spoon," Edith said with utter conviction.

Voleta laughed and immediately apologized.

Gesturing like a conductor trying to quiet his players, Senlin said, "It doesn't matter what he looks like. You won't see him. You'll be on the boat. Now, I've spent the morning reviewing Captain Lee's notes for navigating to the Sphinx's lair. It lies just beneath the summit, under the Collar of Heaven, on the southern face of the Tower. We haven't the ballast, the gas, or the coal to fly out and return at altitude, which is the only sensible course. We have no choice but to take the direct, insensible route. I've identified a suitable current that will deliver us in about an hour's time to the Sphinx's stoop.

"Unfortunately, the route will take us past quite a few ringdoms, which are heavily fortified and, it's safe to assume, leery of strangers. I doubt any one of them would have much trouble swatting us from the sky."

Edith watched the courage drain from the faces of her crew. Considering her recent reprimand of Voleta and the announcement that they would be rendezvousing with a dangerous myth, morale seemed to be taking quite a beating this morning. Now seemed a time for aspiration and reassurance. She interjected before Senlin could itemize the dangers any further. "But I'm sure you have a plan, Captain, that will deliver us safe and sound."

"Of course I have a plan," he said, clapping his hands. "We are going to die."

Chapter Two

The origin of a myth is like that of a river. It begins
in obscurity as a collection of tentative, unassociated
flows. It streams downhill along the path of least
resistance, seeking consensus. Other fables join it,
and the myth broadens and sets. We build cities on
the banks of myth.

—*The Myth of the Sphinx: A Historical
Analysis* by Saavedra

Edith lay on the quarterdeck, a rapier jutting from her bloody
back, her arms thrown out in an attitude of mortal surprise.
Black smoke streamed and scattered in the wind.

Tricorne askew on his head, Senlin slouched against the ship's console with his hands in his lap as if he were begging. Blood pooled in
his cupped palms.

A rifle slug gouged the board by Edith's hip.

The wind stroked her hair against her turned cheek.

She did not stir.

In months past, they had been careful to keep to the big, open theater of blue sky over the Valley of Babel. The traffic was thinner there,
the visibility wider, and the winds tamer. It was not safe to sail close to
the Tower, and it only grew more treacherous the higher one climbed.
Frigates flying under the colors of powerful ringdoms patrolled the

shipping lanes. Suspected pirates were not boarded and arrested; they were shot down. Airpower aside, the upper ports were so stoutly fortified, they resembled citadels, their guns so numerous, they stood together like the teeth of a comb.

And yet it was through these contentious lanes and past these menacing forts that the *Stone Cloud* now rose, unpiloted, undefended, turning like a cinder rising from a fire. The envelope was a whiffling malformation of rags. The hull was so ravaged it resembled a carved bird.

A shadow slipped across the deck. The passing galleon stirred the air with long, tapered wings that moved as languidly as oars. The handsome, three-decked warship was enrobed in gold leaf and green silk. Half of the thirty gun ports stood open. The noses of cannons protruded from the dark of the gun deck. A rifleman, bored by his commander's decision not to waste a barrage on a harmless ghost ship, reloaded his gun and took aim again at a corpse on the quarterdeck.

His second shot thudded into the wood by Edith's hand.

"Steady," Senlin murmured.

Edith opened one eye. The sword, which seemed to skewer her back, only pierced her shirt and the deck near her ribs. The black smoke came from oily rags burning in kitchen pots that they had placed surreptitiously about the ship. The blood had been Voleta's idea: juice from the beet jar. The smell of it was driving Edith mad. She'd been lying in pickle juice for half an hour, and still they weren't out of the woods.

They had passed a dozen forts and twice as many gunships, but this was the first that had bothered to fire on them. She wondered what sort of rogue shot at corpses. It took all of her self-restraint not to jump up and return fire.

At first, she hadn't particularly liked the idea of lying out in the open, but Senlin had made a good argument for it. A military mind might see an empty deck and imagine a galley full of armed brutes, waiting to leap out and take advantage of a careless commander. A battered derelict littered with corpses, however, would inspire little concern.

Iren, Voleta, and Adam finished off the tableau of corpses on the main deck. Voleta had taken particular delight in choosing her pose, and after experimenting with several positions, she had decided that dangling from the rigging like a tangled marionette would be the most dramatic. Adam, lacking any talent for the game, just sprawled out like a starfish.

"Is Iren snoring?" Voleta asked without lifting her chin from her chest.

Adam only shushed her, but he wanted to say that the old amazon could sleep for a week if she felt like it after the work she'd put in yesterday. And where had Voleta been during all that wearisome lifting and towing? Out swinging from the trees.

A moment more, and the shadow of the passing galleon slipped from the deck, and the bored rifleman lost his line of sight. The crew of the *Stone Cloud* shared a sigh, except for Iren, who snorted and rolled onto her side.

A new exotic view spooled by as the ship's lazing ascent continued. Senlin thought it a shame he could not savor these sights, but the pitch of the hull and his slanted view afforded him only tantalizing glances. He saw an onion dome tiled in lapis and turquoise that caught the sun like a gem; he saw a pillared coliseum, with tier upon tier of empty stands and cheery banners. He glimpsed the statue of a rearing horse that must've been a hundred feet tall. The top of the horse's head accommodated an observation deck. If it had been raised anywhere else, the monument would've been considered a wonder of the world, but here on the Tower of Babel, it was just another embellishment.

It never ceased to amaze him how densely built and varied the Tower was at these heights. Balconies and friezes, galleys and porticoes pressed together so tightly they became one great glittering mottle.

The view reminded him of a favorite classroom experiment. Once a school year, he took his students down to the beach for the purpose of collecting a little sand. It was always a struggle to keep them undistracted by the wonders the ocean spilled upon the land, but what a delightful problem to have! Back at their desks, they would spend some minutes studying and documenting their pocket dunes: the texture, color, and shape. When they were convinced there was nothing more to see or say, he had them come one by one to his desk to peer at their sand through his microscope. He showed each student how to turn the mirror until it illuminated the world under the lens. What had seemed dull grit a moment before was transformed into a beautiful collection of tiny shells, stones, and crystals—a trove of unrepeatable miracles.

The Tower was no different: uniform to the distant eye, unique to the near.

It seemed a shame that such thoughts should be wasted on a man who had no time for experiments and observations anymore, a man who was playing dead.

They were as high as the surrounding mountaintops when the character of the construction changed again. The fierce airships and august ports thinned and then disappeared altogether. The walls of the Tower turned barren and smooth as a salt lick. The cloud ceiling shifted from a distant haze into a defined bank, and so they knew the Collar of Heaven was at hand.

Satisfied that they were safe for the moment, the crew rose and stretched. Adam smothered the smoking pots with their lids. Their ascent having taken them into colder air, they had little choice but to break out their heavy clothing.

Belowdecks, Edith removed her pickle-scented shirt with Iren's help and shortly thereafter stuffed it into the furnace. Wearing her wool coat over her shoulders like a cape, she found Senlin on the foredeck, holding the captain's log.

She blew into her hand to warm it, then cinched her coat's collar to her neck. "I'm not going to be able to talk you out of this, am I?"

"I'm being decisive." He squinted at the book, shuffling between pages.

"I wish I'd been awake for this part last time," she said.

"You were too busy trying to survive. No one blames you for being confined to bed."

"Any luck finding the directions?"

"Lee was such a miser with words, wasn't he? I keep expecting there to be more. But this is all I could find. Here, see what you make of it," Senlin said, passing her the log with his thumb in a page. She recognized Lee's primitive handwriting, but the particular passage was unfamiliar. It read: "To find the Sphinx, rise to Collar edge at 210° from NW. Wind 5 to 10 knots. Gate is one thousand hands tall. Flash signal. Run at it hard. Come kissing close to death."

"Well, that's obscure," she said.

"What's this about a signal?"

"I don't know. Lee had an open contract with the Sphinx. He just showed up when he had a lost soul to sell. It makes sense that they would have a signal, but he never told me what it was. Maybe the Sphinx will recognize the ship."

"Would you?" Senlin asked, swapping the log for the compass in his deep coat pocket. He studied the dial. "I fear we may have ruined her figure."

Voleta climbed around the underbelly of the envelope, clinging to the rigging as confidently as her squirrel. As soon as she was in shouting distance, she called down, "We're right under the Collar, Captain. If we climb another fifty feet, we'll be in the soup."

"Thank you, Voleta," Senlin called back and then turned to Edith. "We're in the right place, but I don't see a port. Are we sure Lee's records are credible?"

"They're his personal notes. I can't imagine why he'd try to deceive himself."

"I agree," he said, closing the cover of his compass. "Which means the port must be there. Do you see that crack?" He drew a vertical line with his finger in the air. "I don't think it's part of the mortaring."

They were so close she could hardly detect the Tower's curvature anymore. The sandstone blocks were large and smooth, and amid this barren expanse, Edith could just make out a hair-thin fracture, straight as a beam, perhaps one thousand hands tall. Perhaps. "It might be a flaw."

"But a very straight one. It breaks the mason's pattern. See, it cuts right through those blocks."

"You think it's a door?"

"I do." Senlin tilted toward Edith in a friendly, confiding way. "You came down on Voleta rather firmly." Edith looked ready to argue, but

Senlin hurried to reassure her. "It was the thing to do. I was just... surprised. I suppose I'm more comfortable disciplining school children, and even then I never had what you would call a heavy hand."

"That was not a heavy hand, Tom. That was as gentle a spank as I know how to give. I'm used to barking at cutthroats. They were easy to command. There was no pretense of loyalty or friendship. I knew they didn't like me, and half of them would strangle me in my sleep if they had the chance. But I could always speak to their sense of self-preservation and greed. When I did, they'd fall into line. But Voleta doesn't give a fig about survival or reward. It's just one big lark to her." Edith paused, apparently to conclude the topic but ostensibly to keep from admitting that a part of her understood the girl's attitude. Theirs was often a tangled trajectory. "Have you had any visitors recently?"

Senlin smiled tartly. "Marya was playing jacks by your side through the entire ascent."

"Still doesn't care for me?"

"Oh, she's moderated a bit. Just the standard hair pulling and finger bending."

"You'd think she'd tire of it," she said, and Senlin understood what Edith was really saying: *When will it end?* When would the overdose run its course? How long until they would have to assume his condition was permanent? They studiously avoided voicing the alternative: that his ghost was not a specter of the Crumb, but was in reality a native of his subconscious, which only a violent expulsion of brain matter could hope to evict.

It was such a grim thought, Senlin felt compelled to confess to something lighter, though no less absurd. "I've taken to winking at her."

"Flirting with your ghost now, are you?"

"It seems preferable to the alternative. I can acknowledge her without looking like a lunatic. As long as I pay her some mind, she's relatively cordial."

Edith scrutinized his expression. "Do you enjoy her company, Tom?"

"Don't be absurd," he said with a buck of his head. "But what good does it do to be a martyr about it?"

"Captain," Adam called from the quarterdeck. "We're being blown into the Tower. We need to get out of this current."

Straightening his neck, Senlin cupped his hand to his mouth. "Stay the course!" Then in a more intimate tone: "I'll call it off if you think I'm wrong."

Edith pinched her lip. "If it's just a crack and we dash ourselves to pieces, then Lee will have had his revenge."

"Consider the alternative. If we vent any gas, we won't be able to climb again. This ferry only goes down from here. So, either we flinch and see what the ground makes of us, or we flash the signal, make a run at it, and come kissing close to death."

She exhaled a cloud and shook her head at the pitiful choice. "I suppose an uncertain wall is better than the certain ground. But we still don't know the signal."

"I suppose that would have to be you."

When the captain announced they were going to see the Sphinx, who lived just shy of the Collar of Heaven, Adam had felt that fortune was spoiling him. He'd only had a few moments to study the journal he'd pulled from the topsy-turvy shipwreck, but already he was utterly convinced that the ingot of gold and the account of its discovery were genuine. A great treasure lay swaddled in the clouds at the Tower's pinnacle. Before the captain's announcement, he had all but despaired of ever reaching something so remote. Now he was spitting distance from his prize.

The tale told by Joram Brahe, captain of the *Natchez King*, was compelling, not least of all because it showed a resilience and determination that Adam suspected he was capable of, though he wondered whether he had squandered too much of his resolve on a sister who did not need or want it.

The ascent had given him time to think, time to decide. He would slip away when the opportunity arose and go see for himself what hid behind the fog. He would climb the Tower, hand over hand if he had to, and he would bring the captain back a fine plum. He would change the course of their fate, and his old betrayals would be forgotten.

When the order came from the captain that they would hold their course and let the ship be driven into the Tower, Adam was not overly alarmed. For the moment, hope had anesthetized fear, and besides, it would not do to doubt the very man whose trust he wanted to win back. If the captain wanted to make a run at the sun, Adam would stoke the furnace.

Adam and Iren watched from the quarterdeck as the captain took the first mate's gauntlet in hand and raised the dead engine above their heads. The two held it as if in victory over what remained of the ship's prow.

Iren was not so cavalier about running out of sky. But she suspected that even if they opened the vents now, it was too late. Their momentum was too great. They would run afoul of the Tower and tumble from the roof of the world.

She felt the same bewildering regret she had while fleeing the spider-eater, and with that regret came a sudden and, she knew, unreasonable resentment of the captain. But hadn't he taught her dissatisfaction? He had taught her to read, and that had only revealed how little she knew and how much she had not experienced, and would never experience now. He had taken her away from her home, which though admittedly grim, afforded a few pleasures: She had been feared; she had been certain.

The captain had done what no man before him had managed: He had made her feel weak. And she didn't know what to do with this frustrating thought. They were moments away from crashing. The end was here. And after a lifetime of stoic readiness, she felt absolutely unprepared.

She gave a low, bawling shout that startled Adam so badly he screamed in sympathy.

The wind at their back freshened, and the ship surged at the slight fissure in the masonry. Iren and Adam gripped each other, bracing for the moment when the ship's envelope would bunch against the rock and be torn to shreds.

Then the fissure widened. The Tower began to crack.

Incredible as it was, the miracle was happening too slowly. The darkness behind the opening gates was not growing fast enough. The ship would be squeezed; their balloon would burst just shy of salvation.

Voleta scuttled down from the rigging, cheering with excitement, her cheeks aflame with fear and joy. At the fore, the captain and Mister Winters held her engine over their heads as if in offering. The Tower showed its unlit heart.

The ship's silks passed through the gates as narrowly as a cat darts through a cracked door. The wind perished at once, and before their eyes could adjust to the gloom or anyone could think to find a match, the gates closed again, snuffing out the living world like a coffin lid.

Chapter Three

Had the Sphinx not existed, surely the mothers of the Tower would have had to invent him. Who better to encourage children in their studies than a ghoul who riddles you and eats you if you answer wrong? "Why should you study, my son? Because you never know what the Sphinx might ask!"

—*The Myth of the Sphinx: A Historical Analysis* by Saavedra

One drizzly Saturday morning many years before, Senlin had bought a ticket and boarded a train without any luggage. He had felt buoyant and impatient. He stared out the window but did not see the pleasant countryside flit by because he was too busy squinting at the future.

Two hours later, he debarked upon a rural station, which was little more than a few planks laid over a cow pasture, and joined the crowd of townsmen tearing up the pasture with their boots.

Curiosity had called them all to the last stop on the main line to witness the excavation of a canal.

Senlin had seen canals before, of course, and while they were worthy feats of engineering, he had not been coaxed from his cozy armchair that dreary morning to watch the scarping of a ditch. No, he had made the trek, along with hundreds of kindred spirits, to catch a glimpse of something they had never seen before: a steam shovel.

The steam shovel looked a little like a child's stick-and-ball drawing of a dragon. It had an iron boom for a neck and a boiler for a belly. A stoker fed it coal with a shovel, and it breathed steam through a great nostril in its back. In place of a head, the beast had a horned bucket that ate the earth by the barrow load. Amid the hundreds of spectators who doffed their hats and stood on tiptoe, Senlin elbowed a little room to watch the man-made leviathan chew straight through a hill. It was mesmerizing.

Yet, there was something a little unsettling about the engine's inexhaustible strength. The stoker and driver had to be relieved, had to eat lunch and rest, but others took their place, and the steam shovel carried on.

By late afternoon, it had devoured three hills and five hundred yards of emerald grass.

He was surprised by the tumultuous feelings the machine inspired. On one hand, he couldn't look at such rapid industry without feeling optimistic for the future of human progress. On the other, he couldn't help but feel irrelevant to the effort. If one machine could do the work of so many men, what would be left for those men to do? In a thousand years, when the last human work was taken over by an automatic engine, would it conclude the liberation or the enslavement of the race?

These questions plagued him the whole ride home.

The machine that descended upon their ship under the cover of darkness dwarfed the steam shovel from Senlin's former life. The immense engine resembled a leech. Its body was black and serpentine, its movements undulant. It curled down from the rafters to the unsuspecting *Stone Cloud* with terrifying grace.

With a throat wide enough to swallow a carriage and have room left over for the horses, it reached for them. Its maw of jagged gears began to whirl all at once. The metallic din turned to a roar. When the mouth touched the ship's envelope, it locked upon it and siphoned off the gas in an instant. It sucked up the empty silks as if they were noodles in a bowl.

The leech severed the tethers and the umbilical, and the rigging rained down upon the crew, who stood stiff as belaying pins. They stared up at the furious mouth and its mill of teeth and waited to be devoured.

Then the grinder slowed, and the shrieking metal groaned into silence. Sagging with the exhaustion of a glutton, the iron leech left behind a quiet that was filled by the drumming of blood in their ears.

A tear of black oil splashed upon Senlin's cheek.

Wiping it away, he studied the dark sheen on his fingertips. His shocked mind foggily acknowledged two facts. First, despite being closed inside the Tower, he could suddenly see as clearly as if he were standing under the sun. And second, a metal-headed leviathan had gobbled up their balloon, and yet his ship had not fallen from the air.

The electric light from hundreds of polished hoods beamed down from girders overhead. The great doors they'd passed through, which from the outside resembled stone, were backed with steel plates, warted with rivets as big as a man's head.

They were inside some sort of hangar. A central trough connected a score of horseshoe berths, most of which held airships, hidden under immense white shrouds. The scene recalled a closed-up country manor: spacious and haunted with covered furniture.

The bays and catwalks about them crawled with engines, great and small. Some resembled hermit crabs, with conical shells of iron twisting over hooked legs. Others seemed to have been inspired by centipedes and beetles, each armored in brass and puffing steam from mandibles and joints. Their eyes and abdomens glowed with a familiar red light. And indeed, they were beautiful in the way Edith's arm was, and no less daunting.

Yet these scuttling machines, some large as coaches, were toys compared to the monstrous engine that held their ship aloft.

Craning over the rail to see what had kept them from falling, Senlin spied the iron feet of a colossus. The elephantine pads filled the floor of the channel. Its arms were as large as boxcars, and its monstrous hands cupped the hull of the *Stone Cloud* as if it were no more burdensome than a loaf of bread. The colossus's face was a blank, white dial, big and glowing as the clock of a city tower. Though it had no eyes with which to peer at him, Senlin was quite certain the giant was studying him and coming to some conclusion.

The colossus began to stride.

The ship rolled with its gait, flinging Senlin back into the arms of his crew. The *whump* of the giant's footfalls resounded through the hangar like a cannon fired again and again into a hillside. The slip-covered ships dashed by; the arc lamps above jerked and danced like drunken stars.

Then abruptly they reached the hangar's terminus, and the ship pitched violently beneath them. They were thrown from the deck like dice from a cup and sent tumbling over one another across a platform of unyielding steel.

Senlin looked up from the tangled heap of his crew to see the giant already turning and retreating, carrying the shell of his ship with it.

He asked whether anyone was injured and was relieved to hear no one was, though it seemed quite possible that they were all concussed and bleeding into their guts, and only the indignation of being bowled out of their boat was keeping them from dying on the spot.

"So much for staying on the ship," Voleta said as she squirmed her way out of the pile. Squit popped out the back of her shirt and ran around her neck twice before disappearing into her collar again.

Of the lot, Edith had the most trouble getting to her feet; her unslung arm upset her center of gravity. "Iren, would you please hold Voleta's hand?"

"You must be joking," Voleta said, and plainly saw the first mate was not. She took the amazon's offered hand without further argument, though it made her feel like an absolute child to have her hand swallowed up so completely.

"Is that the usual welcome?" Senlin asked Edith.

"No. We must've done something wrong."

"Already? That's quick even by our standards." Senlin helped Edith reset her arm in its sling. "The Sphinx has quite a doorman."

The short landing they stood upon offered a spectacular view of the hangar, the tantalizing and hidden armada, swarmed about with walking, crawling engines. Adam gaped at a copper-shelled crab firing a blinding spark from its mouth into a nearby joint. "Look, it's welding. I wonder if someone is guiding it, or if it has some sort of clockwork mind." Entranced, Adam edged nearer the automaton. Iren's firm grip drew him back abruptly.

"Don't," she said.

"Oh, come on, Iren. That's one of the most fantastic things I've ever seen."

"She's right, Adam," Senlin said. "Let's not go touching anything." Still off balance, he cupped one hand to his forehead and looked around. "Mister Winters, any of this jogging your memory?"

"Well, I definitely remember that." She pointed to the green copper door that waited at the end of the platform. It was as round as a coin and tall as a house. An elaborate frieze raised the face of it. Figures walked heel to toe all the way around the wheel, each carrying a brick on its shoulder, or in the basket of its arms, or balanced upon its head. The blocks were gilded and stood out from the oxidized scene. Center to their labor, set in proud relief, were the words, THE BRICK LAYER.

Even as they studied them, the words tilted, and the frozen figures began to move. The door was rolling away, and someone waited behind it.

He wore a crimson military uniform, piped in black, with bushy gold epaulets set upon his square shoulders. His hands were made of brass and yet appeared finer and nimbler than the hardy digits of Edith's arm. But none of this seemed remarkable given the nature of his head, which was not a man's. His was the head and neck of a stag.

The stag's antlers branched and curled elegantly over his broad, active ears. The creature's dark eyes were bright and probing and belied a startling intelligence.

"Byron." Edith spoke the name as if it were sour.

"Edith. You came back," the stag said without a hint of warmth. His voice was queer and creaking, like someone speaking beneath his range. The stag raised his arm, and though the sleeve of the gallant uniform concealed it, it moved with the too-perfect fluidity of a machine. "I see you broke the arm already. How surprising. Did you damage it while battering heads, or perhaps it was headboards?"

Voleta gasped.

"I had completely forgotten you, Byron. It was a wonderful time in my life."

"Yes, I hear that people who suffer from brain damage are quite happy. That's what I always wanted for you, Edith: for you to be happy, no matter how many blows to the head it takes."

"Excuse me, are you... are you the Sphinx?" Senlin said, stepping into the stag's line of sight.

"Oh, what a jolly idiot!" the stag said. "You just heard her call me *Byron* twice. Where's Captain Lee? At least he could follow a conversation."

"Dead," Edith said.

"Dead? Well. I'm sure his lice are utterly heartbroken."

"You're horrible!" Voleta's voice shook with laughter.

The stag raised the long, slender prow of his face in her direction and seemed to smile. He had such beautiful, curling eyelashes. "And you're a little scrub brush."

Senlin had been so surprised by the appearance of a talking woodland creature that he had momentarily been blinded to the environment. They stood before a cobbled street, fronted on either side by stone buildings. The facades and old slate shingles were wet from the persistent drip of plumbing overhead. Great jade-shelled snails clung to the pipes, their silvery trails visible everywhere under the shine of sooty streetlamps.

A red macaw, perched atop the arm of a pub sign, croaked, "Time to go! Time to go!"

It took Senlin a moment to realize he stood on the cusp of the Basement, or at least however much of it fit inside a single, modest chamber. Unlike the Basement that was overcrowded with beggars and pilgrims, this model was uninhabited. Behind the buildings, which appeared to have been cut in half, rose the wall of the room itself. Ahead of them, at the end of the cobbled street, was a white door.

"Why did he take our ship?" Edith asked.

"Did Henry take your ship? How peculiar. You used the signal, of course?"

"Not exactly. We didn't know what it was."

"Well, then you're lucky he opened the door at all."

"When can we expect to have it returned?" Senlin asked.

"I'm sorry; I think you've mistaken me for the valet." Byron clicked his boot heels together stiffly and undertook a quick march. "Come on, come on! You will have to explain all of this yourself. I'm not doing it."

The crew looked to their captain. Edith gave him a reassuring smile he felt he did not deserve. He had been cavalier; he had brushed her doubts aside. And still she smiled at him. What a marvelous gift.

Senlin spoke at a confident volume to his crew. "We have survived stranger things. Stick together. Follow my lead."

"Yes, please follow him following me," Byron said over his shoulder with a snort. "Follow on, fearless leader! Edith, really, I don't know where you found this donkey, but I miss the old rooster. Say what you want about Lee; at least his ears worked."

Byron's jibes continued even as he opened the white door.

Inside, cobblestones gave way to woolen rugs. Crown molding framed the room instead of mossy plumbing. Pelts, antique arms, and dusty heralds decorated the walls. Decanters and tumblers, lined upon a dark wood bar, glimmered in the firelight. A creature they all recognized loomed in a corner. One shaggy arm of the beast had been posed over its head like an eager student raising their hand.

"That spider-eater is posed wrong," Adam said. "You can tell whoever mounted it never saw one alive."

"I liked you better when you didn't talk," Byron said.

Senlin and Edith shared a different memory. With one step, they had returned to the Parlor and the start of everything. It made Edith feel wistful in a way she was unaccustomed to. Once, she had been a tourist; once, she had believed she could leave the Tower whenever she liked.

Another white door waited for them on the opposite side of the room, and they filed after Byron while he berated them for dawdling.

They stepped out upon a wrought iron bridge that clanged and shivered beneath them. Water flooded the floor, though it did not seem very deep. Low vents breathed upon the surface, raising ripples that were as fine as lace. Dangling from the ceiling, a ball of mirrors spun an ethereal knit upon their skin. A single mural spanned the four walls, depicting well-lit cafés and colorful changing stalls.

Senlin recalled his time in the Baths with a pang of embarrassment: He'd been such a naive and bumbling pawn, and yet, inexplicably, unfairly, he had escaped while Tarrou was made a hod and Ogier was assassinated. What an absurdity.

"Will you stop showing off, Byron. They're all very impressed, but nobody wants to tour the whole Tower."

"I would like to," Voleta piped up, but when Mister Winters lowered her brows at her, Voleta quickly recanted. "No, I wouldn't. I shouldn't like that at all."

"Is there a room done up for every ringdom?" Senlin asked.

"Yes. It's meant to make our guests feel more at home."

Iren frowned at the kitschy scene. "It isn't working."

"Well then, you must not be a guest."

"Why are we going this way, Byron?" Edith said.

Byron's big calla lily ears sagged, and his mouth tightened. "You do realize that most civilized callers find the model rooms enthralling and my tour scintillating?"

"Can we please take the corridor?"

"I wasn't going to take you through all the rooms," Byron continued. Senlin struggled to interpret their guide's pinched expression, but it looked as if the stag was pouting. "I just thought this way was more... *pleasant*."

"Is Ferdinand in the hall?"

"Of course Ferdinand is in the hall! If he could fit through the door, he'd be standing on my toes right now. He's such a monstrous stain! He follows me everywhere, and I can't get a minute's peace. He's gotten worse, Edith. Much worse."

"Who's Ferdinand?" Adam asked.

"Come on, come on," Byron said, turning right at the junction in the bridge and out another door.

Emerging from the minutely detailed model ringdoms, the corridor was a little astounding in its shabbiness. The floor, covered with layers of rugs that clashed and overlapped like wet autumn leaves, was spongy and smelled of must. Tears and scuffs marred the pink-and-white wallpaper. In between the parade of white doors, shallow alcoves were decorated with alabaster sconces and hazy paintings.

On the face of it, the hall was unremarkable, the sort of thing one might expect to see in an abandoned hotel or an unpopular resort. But they only had to glance up to understand what distinguished the Sphinx's corridor from those pedestrian tunnels, because just a few feet above their heads stood an exact repetition of their level, right down to the procession of doors and filmy paintings. Above that iteration was another, and above that, another. They stood at the bottom of a pink-papered canyon, nested with a thousand white doors, all inaccessible to anyone trying to get in, and presumably deadly to anyone wanting to get out. It was a dizzying sight.

And yet, this was not what presently captivated them. The mechanical giant charging down the corridor occupied the main of their attention.

It resembled the colossus that had carried their ship in, and though only a quarter as big as that mountainous doorman, it was still large enough to make Iren seem a child. Its shoulders were broad, its legs were stout, and its arms hung near the ground. It suggested, at least to Senlin's eye, the unlikely marriage of train locomotive and gorilla.

Running made it sound like an anchor chain unspooling from a winch. The blank, white dial, which stood in the stead of a face, made it difficult to tell whether it saw them standing in its way or not. It skidded to a halt just short of the unflinching Byron, who had apparently been yelling, though no one could hear him over the clamor.

"Don't run! Don't run! You're tearing up the carpets again. Bad! Naughty Ferdinand! Why did the master think it wise to give a two-hundred-and-ninety-ton train legs to run on and the brain of a fourteen-pound dog to think with?"

"You shouldn't say that about your brother," Edith said.

Byron stamped the ground at her, a gesture that seemed to suit his stag head more than his piped trousers. "If you ever call him that again I will gore you."

As they spoke, Ferdinand bent down to examine each of the crew separately. Adam could not resist touching the side of the giant's face. The feel of cold steel was almost surprising; the thing seemed so full of life.

"He's a genius," Adam said.

"I assure you, he's not," Byron said.

"I mean the Sphinx. These machines, you, all of it, it's like seeing the future," the young man said in a wondering way. The stag tossed his head in pleasure at the praise.

Like a dog inspecting houseguests, Ferdinand's movements were at once rapid and clumsy. The walking engine's glowing face illuminated theirs, which only spotlighted their alarm when he began tapping at their sidearms with a finger like a stovepipe.

"You're armed?" Byron said, touching his throat in a formal gesture of shock.

"Don't pretend you didn't notice," Edith said, unbuckling her sword belt amid Ferdinand's probing. "We were thrown off the boat before I could explain—Get off me, Ferdinand!"

"He's not going to let us go a step farther until you give them up. You know how protective he is."

Following the first mate's lead, captain and crew laid their pistols and sabers in Ferdinand's waiting hand. The walking locomotive stowed their weapons in a cupboard inside his chest with all the reckless zest of an underpaid porter. They cringed to hear their beloved pieces clang and rattle inside his cavity.

"And the chains, too," Byron said without looking at Iren.

"But they hold my pants up," Iren said, which was increasingly true. Their poor diet had taken its toll.

"Well, it's a good thing you have two hands then," Byron said.

"You want me to walk around holding my pants?" She attempted to loom over the stag, though he pointedly ignored her.

"Frankly, I think you're the best man for the job," Byron said. "But if you want, you can ask the scrub brush to do it for you." He nodded at Voleta.

Senlin knew Iren well enough to detect the subtle change in her stance, the squaring and opening of her feet. She was preparing to attack. Senlin stepped between them and craned his head about until Iren was unable to look past him. Only after securing her gaze with his own did he speak, and then in a most moderate tone. "We must read this situation carefully. This is a lot to absorb at once. We must think long and hard, must delay any confrontation until absolutely necessary. And we can only do that because of you. You are our courage, Iren. We don't look to you for your chains or your might; no, we look to you for your nerve. That is all we need now."

Iren was reminded why she liked the man, why she had decided to yoke her fate to his; for all his failings, he was at least appreciative of her and all the crew. She should never forget that Finn Goll had made a life for himself while taking hers for granted.

Even so, she was uncomfortable with their present lot. "I liked the Sphinx better when he didn't exist," she said, handing her chains over.

Satisfied that his duty was done, the colossus turned quite friendly, almost frolicsome. Byron continued to bark at the amiable wrecker as he approached a brass panel set into the wall. It contained three rows of numbered buttons, twenty-three in all. He depressed one, and the passageway began to rise.

It had occurred to none of them that the entire length of the corridor's floor was in fact an elevator and the means for approaching the white doors set so high on the pink paper cliff. The elevation made the door they had come by seem to shrink. Everything around them was falling into the floor. It was quite disorienting. A hum permeated the air, and the shiver of unseen machinery traveled through the pack of rugs. Otherwise, their ascent was quite placid.

Without further explanation, the irksome stag began a stiff march down the corridor. Traversing the hallway as it rose played a terrible trick on their equilibrium; it appeared as if they were climbing a hill, though the floor was perfectly level. With each step, they staggered like foals. Since he was accustomed to the phenomenon, Byron was pitiless in his pace.

"You might not guess it to look at it now, but once upon a time, the

Sphinx hosted hundreds of leaders, dignitaries, intellectuals, and artists. Since the Sphinx could not allow his guests free access to all his inventions and experiments, he constructed this hall to manage the flow of traffic."

"What happens if you open the door and the hall's not there?" Voleta asked, pulling at Iren's arm as she tried to keep pace with the marching stag.

"The doors won't open until the hall arrives."

"What if I broke it down?"

"You would fall into a hole, and no one would miss you."

Their ascent halted just as they arrived at the end of the hall. The doors before them looked as if they belonged on a bank vault. Byron turned to deliver some final insult, but his fraternal engine spoiled his act. Ferdinand pushed the doors open.

The Sphinx, what could only be the Sphinx, waited on the other side. And they saw Edith had been right. He did look like a spoon.

Chapter Four

The Sphinx could never reveal himself without losing his essential mystique. To be the Sphinx is to be unknown. If, however, he were a myth, he would be just as unknowable. We can only hope that one day he will emerge and prove once and for all that he does not exist.

—*The Myth of the Sphinx: A Historical Analysis* by Saavedra

Butterflies colored the air with bodies bright as a woman's brooch and wings as fine as vellum. Separately, they ticked like a pocket watch; together, the fluttering kaleidoscope raised a mechanical drone.

Their wings were painted to mimic domestic scenes: the blue-and-white pattern of a china plate; the gleaming grain of polished burl; the creamy porcelain of a sink; and the yellow blooms of a bouquet. The swarm gamboled inside the burnished-copper dome overhead, dazzling Senlin and his crew with their quaint camouflage.

A bolt of lightning shot up and, in an instant, transformed the butterflies into smoking, tumbling ash.

Voleta tried to catch one of the larger wafers, but the moment the black flake lighted upon her hand, it crumbled into soot. "What a waste! They were so pretty. Why did you do that?"

The Sphinx's voice sounded as if it were being blown through an old trumpet. "To keep their secrets, my dear," he said.

He was tall to the point of gauntness and showed not an inch of skin. His hood started in a crooked point at his crown and ran to the floor, where it formed a puddle of black velvet. He still held the device that had thrown the lightning; it resembled a tuning fork, but it seemed far too innocuous to be capable of striking such a spark. Under his cowl, he wore a concave mirror as a mask.

"I see the resemblance," Iren whispered to Edith, though the first mate was too on edge to respond. Iren had never seen Edith look so pale. She wished she hadn't given up her chain so quickly.

Senlin was not oblivious to the strain his friends were under. First, the essential bond of the ship had been taken from them, and now they stood in the presence of a myth. It was all a little much to digest at once. He knew they would look to him for composure. Whatever came, he had to hold himself together.

The room recalled a gentleman's study, albeit an opulent one. A vast desk dominated much of the lacquered floor, its top bearing the trappings of industry. Books and papers were stacked and strewn amid a variety of tools and equipment, from a jeweler's tweezers to a sewing machine, from a rack of test tubes to a ball-peen hammer. Engines lay in states of assembly or disassembly; it was impossible to tell which. Some of the machines resembled an animal's limb, and one, alarmingly, a humanoid head.

The shelves behind the desk banked enough books, artifacts, and pottery to stock a museum. The miscellany encompassed the room, rising up to the lip of the copper dome. Senlin noted the absence of a ladder or stairs, leaving him to wonder whether the display was for show, or if the Sphinx, when no one was looking, climbed his shelves like a spider monkey.

Marya waved to him from a high alcove where she sat swinging her legs. She plucked an emu's egg from a gold eggcup and began to bobble it playfully, pretending that she might drop it. Senlin winked at her.

Whatever came, he had to hold himself together.

"What have you done to my arm?" the Sphinx said.

Edith stiffened. It was all she could do to formulate a reply, though the Sphinx had crossed the room before she could finish. He moved strangely, gliding as easily as a dust mop across the glossy floor.

"Nothing. It's run out of fuel, and my stock was lost. The engine is fine." She had just gotten the arm out of its sling when the Sphinx glommed to it.

"Fine? Fine?" The Sphinx's gloved hands ran all about the arm, caressing it, peeling back its many panels like the petals of an artichoke. "Where did this dent come from? Is this rust? You've soaked it. And you haven't been oiling it, have you? Look at this: The radius is sheared. What have you done?"

The chastisement was so rapid and fierce Edith hadn't time to reply.

"Now, see here..." Senlin began valiantly.

"Ferdinand, if he speaks again, tighten his lips for me, please," the Sphinx said without interrupting his inspection of Edith's arm. "Where's Captain Lee?"

"Dead," Edith said.

"Did you kill him?"

"No."

"No, I'm sure the thought never crossed your mind." The Sphinx stepped back from the limb and emitted an unnerving, reverberating *tsk-tsk*. He produced an eggbeater drill from some recess of his robe and began unscrewing bolts in Edith's shoulder. "It'll take a few days to repair, and then maybe a few days more to decide whether you deserve to have it back or not. Now, tell me who you've brought me."

Though jostled and disturbed by it, Edith tried not to look as the Sphinx worked upon her arm. "These aren't recruits, sir. These are my captain and crew."

"A cyclops, an addict, a hod, and an old woman who seems to have lost her belt. Quite the crew."

Iren pulled and twisted the waist of her pants, wringing their hem rather than the Sphinx's neck. Voleta petted the amazon's arm to calm her.

"The boy seems like a fine candidate for an eye. I have just such a thing, a perfectly good ocular engine that was ejected by its last host."

"Ejected?" Adam said, surprised that the conversation had wheeled so quickly around to him.

"An infection pushed it from her head, but don't fret, my boy—the eye is in perfect condition."

"He's an inveterate coward and a thief," Edith said in a near bark. "He'd take your wonderful engine and pawn it without a second thought."

Adam looked as if he'd been skewered by the first mate's words. He understood what she was trying to do, but he wished she might've invented a flaw that was a little further from the truth.

"And yet you have him on your crew?"

"He's working off a debt," Edith said.

"What about the hod girl? Is she ill at all?"

"Absolutely healthy, except for her conscience, which was stillborn, I'm afraid. We nearly left her on a ledge this morning."

"Truly," the Sphinx said, amused.

"It's true." Voleta craned out her chin proudly. "But if you're giving out engines, I'd like an extra set of arms."

"Oh, you would? Whatever for?"

"So I could waltz with a man and punch him in the kidneys at the same time." She put a manic smirk on. "That'd be grand. He'd say, 'Oh, darling, someone is pummeling my guts!' And I'd say, 'I can't imagine who!' "

"See, she's ruthless," Edith said.

"Why are you being so defensive?" the Sphinx said, churning his drill into her arm. "You're obviously fond of them, Edith; you needn't pretend. You act as if my gifts would be a punishment. But you know I am nothing if not fair in my terms and explicit in my expectations."

Having loosened the final bolt, the Sphinx pulled the engine from her shoulder and handed it to Byron, whose demeanor had turned quite servile.

Pale faced and with brightened eyes, Edith touched her shoulder where the scarred and purpled skin puckered about four empty bores. She had not believed, had not wanted to believe, that her arm would be so summarily removed. It was too essential a thing to be just

unscrewed and walked away with. There wasn't even blood to mark
the loss, just a sense of unbalance and a terrible lightness.

Byron carried her crooked, lifeless arm to the Sphinx's desk and
laid it down as reverently as a mourner sets flowers on a grave.

"You are very disappointing." Senlin's voice, clear and loud, startled them all. Remembering his charge, Ferdinand clomped over to
Senlin, who was barreling on. "I've walked through your Tower and
seen your mighty works. But I never dreamed that their fruits would
be squandered upon such vanity!" He shouted the final word into
the milky glass of Ferdinand's face. The walking locomotive's hands
parted on either side of Senlin's head as it prepared to applaud the
man's brains out.

Only after Ferdinand had begun to drive its hands together did the
Sphinx intervene with a small signal. The palms of the machine, each
broad as a washboard, stopped within a whisper of Senlin's ears. "It is
not my Tower. But, please, do go on," the Sphinx said.

"The Tower is an electrical generator. The Basement pulls the
water, the Parlor fires it, the Baths move the steam, and the turbine
of New Babel turns out the current. I'm sure other ringdoms contribute to the process. Your machines make this possible, but much of the
work is done by men and women, some of them slaves, some of them
free but throwing all their health and wealth at this useless industry.
Because what becomes of the electric current? Why, it drains out upon
your doorstep. All those lamps burning away in your corridor, burning away in empty rooms—is that how you spend their sacrifice? How
noble. How worthwhile."

"I agree," the Sphinx said.

"With what part?" Senlin asked.

"The agreeable part."

Ducking past the looming engine, Senlin approached the Sphinx.
Byron raised huffing objections, but Senlin was undeterred. "You
have these machines, these powerful, autonomous locomotives capable, I'm sure, of incredible feats of strength." Narrowing the gap, his
own upside-down reflection grew in the Sphinx's mocking bowl of a
face. "Take that colossus in your port, for example. I bet he and a few

more like him could replace all the hods in the Tower. You could free men from their drudgery if you just released your valets."

"Oh, please, let's not pretend," the Sphinx said and leaned down, drawing so close that Senlin observed his upside-down face swell, twist into ribbons, and then coalesce again, enlarged and right-side up. It was strange to be menaced by his reflection. "You don't care. Not about the hods or the masses pedaling for beer and stoking for a show. You don't care about anyone really, not even this supposed crew of yours."

"Really?" Senlin said, and refused to look away from the shaking saucers of his own eyes.

"Of course not. I'll prove it to you." The Sphinx's buzzing voice lifted with merriment. "But why don't we continue our conversation in a more comfortable environment?"

The Sphinx led them through a brief vestibule where Senlin found time to whisper in Edith's ear, "We will get it back."

Her dazed stare flitted to his and seemed to find a little relief.

They entered what was in many ways a traditional music room, complete with portrait chairs, a cheerful fire in a glazed-brick hearth, and hanging tapestries depicting scenes of musicians playing instruments. But where one might reasonably expect to see a piano, there stood instead a wizened tree.

The hill of soil that held the tree lay upon the floor like the sweepings of a broom. A fishbowl lens in the ceiling cast a pale, orange light. Almond-shaped leaves adorned the bowers and dried upon the tile floor all about the twisted trunk. Most curiously of all, a scattering of piano keys erupted like mushrooms from the soil.

Voleta ventured over to pluck one from the dirt. "It's a piano tree?"

Byron took the key back with a deft little snatch and returned it to its socket in the earth. "It's a type of ash. It was given to the Brick Layer by one of his masons." The stag clapped the dirt from his hands, ringing them like finger cymbals. "Originally, it was just a sprig in a pot that lived upon the Brick Layer's piano. But after several months, the piano began to lose its tone. When the Brick Layer tried to open the instrument, he found the sapling's roots had broken through the lid and grown all about the strings. The Brick Layer couldn't bear to cut them out, so he decided to sacrifice the instrument, which he continued to play until the last note was silenced by the tree."

"That's quite enough, Byron," the Sphinx said. "You make us sound like museum pieces, the way you talk. Please, everyone have a seat."

Iren sat gingerly upon the lip of her chair, partly because she distrusted the antique with her full weight, but also because she wanted to be ready to spring up should the need for action arise. She hadn't taken her eyes off the trudging engine since it had demanded her chains and now was forced to crane her neck uncomfortably to one side to keep Ferdinand in view. And all of this was done while still holding on to Voleta's hand.

Seeing that their host did not intend to sit, Senlin remained standing, though he migrated to the mantel over the fire, a spot he found quite comfortable. The Sphinx tracked his movement but raised no argument.

"Now, I was about to prove to you that you don't care about the hods, your fellow tourists, or even your crew."

"Yes, please, enlighten me."

"Your name is Thomas Senlin."

"It is," Senlin said, refusing to give the Sphinx the satisfaction of appearing surprised. "We shared a mutual friend in the Red Hand, I believe. I'm sorry to report he's passed on."

"Oh, has he?" The light of the fire threw a fiery eclipse on the edge of the Sphinx's mask.

A single leaf fell from the ash behind them. It pirouetted in the windless room and landed with an audible tick on the tile.

"I know where Marya is," the Sphinx said.

Senlin repressed a gasp. Though this was exactly what he'd hoped to discover from the Sphinx's company, he found a complex, almost fearful sense of doubt well inside him at the announcement. "I don't believe you."

"She still has the red sun helmet. She keeps it hidden inside a wardrobe and only pulls it out occasionally at night when she thinks no one is watching. But my eyes are everywhere."

"Where is she?"

"You could be at her side by this time tomorrow."

"I know she's in Pelphia," Senlin insisted.

"Very good. I will provide you a salary and a ship—a new, superior ship—and you can fly to Marya this very evening. You can hire a crew, find yourself a hardy bunch of airmen, and after your reunion with Marya, you may resume Billy Lee's work and live quite well by it. Once or twice a year, I require a few new recruits, which you will provide, but the rest of the time, the ship is yours to fly as you please. When you tire of the life, you may return the ship and go about your business."

Senlin released the mantel he had begun to grip, his knuckles white. Ferdinand's bulk shifted warily, but Senlin moved away from their enigmatic host. He strode calmly to the leaf that lay upon the polished marble. Pinching it by the stem, he returned with the fragile green eye to the fireside. "What about my crew?" he asked with his back to them.

"They will remain here with me," the Sphinx said. "You will have Marya, and they will be given all the improvements and opportunities they could ever want. The only thing that will be lost is this charade of an adventure you all seem to have agreed to."

Senlin held the leaf out to the fire, inspected its tender skeleton. "I'm sorry, Edith," he said. "I hope you can forgive me."

Chapter Five

Some scholars believe the Sphinx must be a supreme mesmerist to bring so many to ruin. He spellbinds his victims into self-destruction. Other students of the Sphinx, however, contend that, rather than hypnosis, he practices the black art of legal contracts.

—*The Myth of the Sphinx: A Historical Analysis* by Saavedra

I n some ways, Edith expected the betrayal.

A part of her even suspected she deserved it. Not as a criminal deserves to be punished, but in the way that a longtime houseguest, who has strained all convention and hospitality, deserves to be asked at last by an embarrassed host to leave.

She had dabbled in a better life and with better company than she had any right to. And though they had helped her forget the base existence she'd grown accustomed to under Billy Lee's command, though they had let her pretend she might be deserving of admiration and perhaps even affection, Senlin's betrayal brought the ruse to an end.

Though was it fair to call it a betrayal? Was it reasonable to expect a devoted and determined husband to forgo a reunion with his wife in deference to a friend whom fate had thrust upon him?

Because she understood his choice so well, she was quick to put on a brave face when he looked her way, his strong features sharpened by the intensity of his expression.

He said, "I'm sorry I didn't pay you better mind when you told me the Sphinx was conniving and manipulative. You were right; he is monstrous."

She could not help but beam with relief when he turned to the Sphinx and continued hotly, "What a tepid seduction! You offer a false choice and then behave as if you've graced me with the keys to the Tower. My reunion with my wife has no bearing on your ability to torment us. Don't pretend that I have any say in the matter. I will not be complicit in your villainy. Even if I were to accept your ludicrous condition and abandon my friends to be with my wife, she would find me a heartless, dishonorable stranger. If this is how you treat your guests, then please show us the door."

The Sphinx did not hurry to reply. At Senlin's warming back, the garrulous fire chattered and whistled. Ferdinand expelled a long breath of steam from vents on either side of his lunar face.

When at last the Sphinx spoke, it was prefaced by brittle laughter. "No, you're not like Lee at all. Do you have *The Brick Layer's Granddaughter* with you?"

Senlin's indignation turned to confusion. "I beg your pardon?"

"Ogier's painting; do you have it, or did you leave it on your ship?" The Sphinx began to ferry back and forth across the floor. His restlessness was exhausting to their nerves but fascinating to observe. Senlin supposed the Sphinx had miniature feet or else took mincing steps; such was the sleekness of his gait.

"*Girl with a Paper Boat*, you mean? Yes, I have it," Senlin said.

"You should find a number discreetly painted in the bottom right corner."

Doubtful that he would have missed such a detail, Senlin unfurled the work and scrutinized the spot in question. To his chagrin, he found a digit hiding among the brushwork. "Look at that. I believe it's a three. What does it signify?"

"Its place in the series. There are sixty-four versions. One for every ringdom. A gift from the Brick Layer."

Senlin could recall a time when the number of ringdoms seemed the greatest mystery of all. Now he absorbed the news with only the dimmest interest. "Who is the Brick Layer? The Tower's architect? The builder?"

"He would never have said so. Hods built most of what lies beneath. As for architects, there were thousands, and tens of thousands of artisans and tradesmen besides. The Brick Layer thought of himself as a foreman." The Sphinx stopped under the canopy of the wizened ash tree; the light from the lens, strained by leaves into many points, fell upon his black robe in a galactic sprawl.

An inquisition's worth of questions occurred to Senlin concerning the Brick Layer's vision and his reason for stacking humanity so tenuously high, but he was quite certain the Sphinx's patience was not inexhaustible, and there were more concrete questions he needed answers to. "Why are so many people determined to forge this painting?"

"What do you mean?"

"I saw five copies locked up in a cell inside the Golden Zoo. Then there was Ogier, or the imposter claiming to be Ogier, who drove himself mad trying to re-create this work from memory and sketches."

"Five, five, five," the Sphinx muttered. "Five already."

"Perhaps the imposter painted the copies for him," Senlin offered in a speculative tone. He found it interesting the Sphinx was so upset by the number of copies in Marat's possession. This at least confirmed Senlin's suspicion that he had information the Sphinx might be willing to bargain for.

"No, I'm sure they're not forgeries. They're not copies either. Though very similar, they are quite unique; they are part of the series." The Sphinx emerged from the tree's starry light and returned to the fireside.

"And they're all of the girl? Seems a tad obsessive. And I don't understand why anyone would care so deeply about them. Surely there are greater works to squabble over," Senlin said, making room for the hatch mark of a man at the mantel.

"They cared because they agreed to care. At first, the Brick Layer tried to see everyone who came to visit him, to hear every complaint and request—he was quite a social fellow, especially in his dotage—but it just wasn't feasible. There were too many people to let the doors hang open. Even then, there were those who would harm him if they could. Hence the paintings. The Brick Layer gave one to each ringdom with the understanding that only those who carried the painting would be admitted. It was like a token."

"And the paintings couldn't be forged?"

"No, that was Ogier's genius, and the genius of the series. They are absolutely irreplaceable and unrepeatable."

"Well, I'm surprised he didn't foresee the consequence of doling out so few passes to so much political influence and technological wizardry. Of course people like Commissioner Pound snapped up the paintings. Didn't the Brick Layer realize he was legitimizing, if not necessitating, the rule of tyrants?"

"You can't hold the Brick Layer responsible for the injustices committed by governments he did not form. He was an engineer, not a politician. He never wanted anything to do with politics."

"So he is no longer among us?"

"No, no, no." The Sphinx's mirrored face threw a slowly turning pan of light upon the wall. "He's long deceased. I try to carry on his work as best I can, though there are many ringdoms who've forgotten about him and his granddaughter and the pledges they once made."

"Since you are continuing his work, it stands to reason that you might consider my proposal. I bear his token after all." Senlin wagged the painting he'd rolled again before returning it to his breast pocket.

"It's more than a token, Mr. Senlin," the Sphinx said. "But yes, let us for the sake of argument pretend that you are entitled to my ear—what would you like to propose?"

"I have reason to believe there is a revolution afoot that may, if it takes hold, upset the balance of things. I have, in fact we all have, firsthand knowledge of this plot, which I think would be of some interest to you."

"You're talking about Luc Marat."

"Yes. I know how many men he has under him, how many weapons.

I know that he has virtually taken over an entire ringdom and broken open the black trail. I have conversed with him and heard his philosophy. I have looked him in the eye and gauged his resolve."

"Well, go on. Tell me."

Senlin resisted the urge to smile, though he felt he had the Sphinx hooked upon a line. "No, not until we come to an agreement. I will tell you what I know, but first, you must consider our humble requests. Our ship is in need of repair—"

The Sphinx interrupted with a slice of his gloved hand. "Let's not understate the facts. Your ship is in need of a eulogy."

"It was airworthy before your iron leech ate our sails."

"Is that all?"

"Second, I request a letter of introduction on our behalf that will guarantee a favorable reception in Pelphia, and any information that you have about the exact whereabouts of Marya. And finally, I ask that you give Mister Winters back her arm, along with a stock of fuel, as soon as it is repaired."

"That seems quite an expensive trade for information I likely already possess. Rebuilding your ship alone will cost a small fortune."

"Our financial situation is not especially robust at the moment," Senlin said, though the subtext was clear: They were broke. "We are between windfalls, you might say." And they weren't especially good pirates, either. "I would entertain a counteroffer."

"Ah, wonderful. The details. My favorite part." The Sphinx clapped his hands and held them together as if he'd just caught a fly. "Byron, fetch your desk."

The stag left the room very briefly and returned with a shallow box suspended from his neck by a strap. He would have resembled a girl selling oranges if it weren't for his attitude, which was as reverent as a footman carrying in the crown. The hanging desk supported a black typewriter and two wings: one held blank paper, the other waited to be filled. Byron threaded a sheet into the roller, raised his long, almost willowy fingers over the keys, and waited for the dictation to begin.

The Sphinx spoke quickly, and Byron transposed his words into a rhythm so rapid it made the air ring.

Senlin did not let the Sphinx's conditions go by without comment. He interjected his own conditions, which the Sphinx laid new stipulations to, which required Senlin to counter and the Sphinx to reply. In this way, the contract was bickered into existence.

The Sphinx insisted that he be allowed to interrogate each member of the crew, separately, independently, and at his leisure, until he was satisfied that he had heard all pertinent information regarding the supposedly fomenting revolution.

Granted, but only if no attempt be made during these interviews to coerce the interviewees into surgical or mechanical augmentation of any kind whatsoever.

Granted, with the understanding that the aeronauts of the *Stone Cloud* might, of their own free will, decide to investigate the gifts of the Sphinx without objection or interference from their captain or first mate.

Granted, under the condition that the captain or first mate be allowed to review any resulting contracts before they were signed.

Granted, but...

At first, Senlin felt relatively clever. He was holding his own against a superior intellect who was obviously more experienced with legal documents. He was definitely holding his own, though he couldn't imagine a court that could possibly claim any jurisdiction over the Sphinx. The man had an army of mechanical beasts at his beck and call for heaven's sake! But it didn't matter, because for the moment Senlin was holding his own.

Almost certainly.

Of course, there would have to be compromises. Only the possession of the painting gave him any credibility, and he was in no position to resist if the Sphinx decided to take it back. Ferdinand would settle any argument in a moment.

So Senlin conceded that the ship was in need of extensive repair, and that it would be quite expensive, and wouldn't it only be reasonable for him and his crew to do the Sphinx a favor in return. Senlin couldn't say no. It was very clear to him that this man was no heavenward philanthropist. The Sphinx was a businessman.

Edith watched Senlin's position erode with alarm and a little anger. She had tried to warn him, but Tom was too busy being gallant to listen. And how do you argue with a man when the ghost of his wife is standing behind him?

When Senlin abruptly agreed that he, while joyfully seeking a reunion with his wife, would do a bit of spying for the Sphinx, Edith could not contain an audible groan.

Byron's fevered pecking stopped. The Sphinx and Senlin looked at her in silence, presuming she would speak. And she did indeed want to say something, but she wasn't sure exactly what. She didn't want to be the one who spoiled Senlin's chance of finding his wife.

Edith was still thinking when the two men resumed their negotiations, speaking almost over each other, their words tangling as Senlin conceded, protested, and conceded again, until at last it was done, and the papers presented in a tidy stack and the pages signed, every one.

It was over.

Edith could hardly believe it and wondered if Senlin understood exactly what had happened. They were all working for the Sphinx now. And it was her fault. She had brought them here. She could have refused. Instead, she had finished Lee's dirty work for him. She had conscripted her friends.

Through it all, Voleta was having a wonderful time. First, she watched Byron, beating his typewriter like a drum. What haughty conviction! Voleta caught his eye once, and the poor thing started and then wouldn't look at her again. She wanted very much to inspect the walking engine, but it was standing off behind her, and she didn't dare crane around in her chair while Iren was holding her hand. *Still* holding her hand. It was absolutely ridiculous, and as soon as she could get in a word, which might be some time the way the captain and Sphinx were going at it, she would lodge a vigorous protest either by blowing a raspberry or throwing a shoe. *This was not on.*

It was in this black moment that Voleta decided to climb the tree. It was a pretty tree, a good lounging tree with leaves thick as hairs on her head.

No, that wasn't really true. It was an old tree, an august tree. The leaves were thin, and the knots stood out. She shouldn't climb it. She might hurt it. Better to let it rot alone in peace. Though it occurred to her that the tree had spent its entire life watching wood burn in the fireplace. Oh, what torture that must have been for the tree!

Perhaps it was not just alone; perhaps it was lonely. Mightn't the tree prefer to risk some scuffed bark, a lost leaf or two, for the opportunity to be enjoyed and loved by a very good climber? Surely, the tree would like to be climbed. Yes, a climb would be good for the tree.

Voleta looked over at the amazon and smiled like she had just caught a flower in her teeth.

Iren frowned.

Then the Sphinx got all of their attention by saying very loudly, "So, what are we going to do about your addiction to White Chrom, Captain Thomas Mudd Senlin?"

"Pardon?" Senlin said.

Adam had been thinking about Captain Joram Brahe's journal. He found that he often thought of it now. After the big meal on the ship, he had dreamed of rivers of silver and bowers of gold.

But then the Sphinx had announced that Captain Thomas Senlin was on Crumb and suddenly the room had all of Adam's attention.

He had not cared for the Crumb addicts he knew in New Babel. They were such a helpless, defeated sort. Finn Goll never had any problem hiring addicts because they could always be relied upon to be desperate for pay. They didn't ask questions. They didn't stand up for themselves. The Crumb made them dreamy, absentminded, and strange. That did not sound like the captain to Adam.

Perhaps it did a little.

Adam was relieved to see the captain defending his name against "the spurious accusations of a featureless paranoid" that he was presently intoxicated. He was not. He was as straight as the Tower. But the Sphinx wasn't satisfied by Senlin's protests. He brought Senlin's attention to page fourteen, section three of their pact, which stipulated that he "dispatch all contractual obligations with absolute and uncontested sobriety." The captain immediately agreed to any test of his clearheadedness.

"Wonderful," the Sphinx said. "I would appreciate it if you would fetch a book from my library."

"Certainly. I always enjoy perusing another man's books. They say so much about him."

Edith groaned a second time and couldn't stop herself from exclaiming, "It's bottomless, Tom! It's a bottomless library."

"Bottomless, eh? Well, be that as it may, I have agreed to fetch the book, and by my word, I will fetch the book," Senlin said, turning his face back to the Sphinx. "But we never resolved the question of Mister Winters's contract. Since I am doing you a favor, perhaps you could do one for me in return and release Edith from the exploitive contract you coerced her into signing while she was struggling for her very life."

The Sphinx tapped the pages of their contract square on the mantel and said, "No."

Chapter Six

It is by studying the Sphinx that we realize all wonder is seasoned with dread, all courage is tinctured with fear, all wisdom is the fermentation of folly.

—*The Myth of the Sphinx: A Historical Analysis* by Saavedra

The fact that the librarian was a cat came as something of a surprise. The orange-and-white tabby was not an amalgam of animal and engine like Byron; he was entirely feline, from whisker to paw. He neither spoke nor was he arrayed in any finery. The pattern of his fur suggested a map, though not of any particular nation. He seemed, as with many of his kin, to embody a self-contained dignity that could neither be questioned nor explained.

Though at first, Senlin wondered if he wasn't stuffed.

The librarian lay in the valley of an open dictionary with all the vigor of a bookmark. It was several moments before the cat turned his head and resolved once and for all the question of whether it was alive.

Senlin thought it ridiculous. What possible qualifications in the archival arts could a cat hold? Perhaps this was some sort of joke. Perhaps it was a test of his patience or his sense. He wondered whether he should say something.

They had ridden the elevating hallway deep into the canyon of hotel doors to reach the library, and all had sunk into their own thoughts along the way. Senlin spent the silent journey watching Marya stand before him as if she were the subject and he the painter. She winked at him and he at her until the Sphinx took notice and asked if he had something in his eye.

He would not admit that he did, and quite a stubborn mote at that.

When they first entered the Bottomless Library through an unremarkable white door, Senlin was pleasantly surprised by the absence of a pit ringed around with books. He had half expected to be set upon a narrow, spiraling path that plunged downward into a provocative gloom, but here was a cheery atrium with shelves rising on either side and stacks branching off to other well-lit sections. It was a vision that hardly commanded the terror implied by the term *bottomless*. Senlin found the smell of the books as enthralling as a woman's perfume. Bradded leather chairs capped the aisles, and there were sofas, reading lamps, and gurgling fountains besides. It seemed the absolute antithesis of an abyss.

Senlin realized late that Byron was speaking to him while he had been busy gawking. Senlin had to squint to beam his attention at the quarrelsome stag. "...Has been the librarian for over fifteen years. In that time, how many books do you suppose he has failed to locate? Not one. All I have to do is tell the librarian the title I'd like to retrieve and then follow him to the spot," Byron explained.

"Wouldn't he be a more practical librarian if he could carry a book?" Senlin said.

"Now you've hurt his feelings!" Byron said, lifting his brass hand to his lip in a coy gesture of shock. "Maybe he'll decide to lead you through the traps. I wouldn't blame him."

"Traps? In a library? Whatever for?"

"Books are traps," the Sphinx said in a private, musing way.

"I suppose," Senlin said without much enthusiasm. The Sphinx had turned aloof as soon as the documents were signed. Senlin wished he would just go away and let him deal with Byron, who was not at all mysterious, having an absolute inability to hold his tongue.

Byron presented him with a canvas pack that was bulging and lumpy and, Senlin discovered, quite heavy.

"What is this?"

"Your pack, and here is the title of the book the librarian will guide you to." The stag handed Senlin a little scroll of paper, like something his students had once passed between rows during class.

Senlin unrolled it and read the neatly written title aloud, "*Zoetropes and Magic Lanterns: An Introduction to Moving Stills.*" Senlin turned to the Sphinx, and using his best beseeching and reasonable tone, said, "I can't help but notice this title begins with a *Z*. I sincerely hope you haven't just chosen an inconvenient book to test my patience." The Sphinx made no reply. Senlin wished that the man would remove his mask so that he might see whether the Sphinx was smiling, glaring, or falling asleep.

Byron patted the top of the pack in Senlin's arms to bring the captain's attention back around. "Just follow the librarian, and you'll get there soon enough. Now, I am saddened to have to say this to a grown man, but I feel it is quite necessary given your history of crippling intoxication. You must not eat the cat food."

"I'm sorry?"

"No matter how chafed you get while wriggling down from your noxious high, you mustn't eat the cat food. There are plenty of biscuits for you. The fish is for the librarian. Every twelve hours."

The cat hissed.

"Every twelve hours," Byron reiterated. "Here's a pocket watch so you don't lose track of time. I'd very much like to see it returned."

"This pack is quite heavy," Senlin said. "How many tins of fish are in here?"

"Yes, I suppose I shouldn't have expected you to be able to count so high. There are twenty-eight tins. That's two weeks' worth."

"Two *weeks*?"

"It's a bit like talking to a parrot, isn't it, Edith?" Byron said.

"Ignore him," Edith said to Senlin as she helped feed his shock-stiffened arms through the straps of his pack. She turned him about and adjusted the buckles at his shoulders. "You should always take more than you need. Captain Lee told me about how he fetched a book once. He was gone no longer than a few days, a week at most." She straightened his shirtfront, her touch soothing him. "You're sure you want to keep your coat on? There'll be no one to see you. You could even leave your shirttail out, if you like."

"Madness." Senlin smiled.

"Would you please empty your pockets?" the Sphinx said, gliding across the polished marble. "You should keep *The Brick Layer's Granddaughter* with you, but give everything else to me."

Even without seeing the man's face, Senlin understood the insinuation well enough. "You think I'm carrying Crumb?"

The Sphinx seemed taller now. Senlin had to look up to see his own face boiling and twisting back at him. Other than a button in one pocket and a bit of string in another, the only things on him at the moment were the two paintings. "I have a memento I would very much like to carry with me."

"Show me," the Sphinx said. Senlin slipped the painted board from his coat pocket. The Sphinx's gloved hands snatched it away before he could properly present it.

"It's of my wife." Once, Senlin would've felt the need to justify her appearance, but no longer.

The Sphinx turned the nude all about inside the focal of his sunken mirror, scrutinizing the painting like a banker might a suspicious note. His face beamed the sacred image back at Senlin, the curved reflection perverting it, making it ugly and unfamiliar.

"This board is tainted," the Sphinx announced. "White Chrom has seeped into the grain and bonded to the paint. Did you pack it in Crumb and then expose it to water?"

"Snow," Senlin said.

"You called it a memento. I imagine you handled it regularly?"

"Yes."

"Yes, and every time you did, every time you caressed this totem of your wife, you stirred a little Crumb into the air and then breathed it in. You dosed yourself. To look at you, I imagine it was a daily affair."

Turning to his crew, Senlin was met by a uniform expression of shock: wide eyes and rounded mouths. The friends who had followed him with such reckless devotion, who had faced spider-eaters, warships, and even the banality of starvation without blanching, gaped at him now as if he were an imposter. It was heartbreaking.

And, he had to admit, it was also a great relief. Because at least it meant he wasn't insane. He was only poisoned.

"I didn't know," he told them with soft conviction. He cleared his throat, and said it again, more resolutely. "I didn't know."

"You mean you suffered no symptoms of mood or of vision?"

"I—" he began, and then turned to Edith for strength, but she was looking inward in bewilderment. "I just thought I was...insane," he said, though he immediately saw how this confession would not improve his crew's impression. He had not thought himself an addict, only a lunatic, and he had hidden it from them. In one stroke, he had revealed his narcotic dependence, his own doubts about his mental rectitude, and his willingness to deceive his friends for the sake of his command, his search, and his pride.

"Why didn't you tell us you were sick?" Adam said. The young man's thoughts had not cleared enough for disappointment or anger to set in, but the sense of betrayal was immediate.

The question was so simple it jogged an unguarded answer from Senlin. "Because I wanted you to trust me."

"Ah, the inverse logic of the addled mind," the Sphinx said, secreting the Crumb-tainted painting into the folds of his robes. "But not to worry. Nothing clears a man's head so well as perusing a library."

Byron had begun to shoo Senlin's crew ahead of him as he worked his way back out the door. Adam, Iren, and Voleta were too confused to resist. They left without looking back. The Sphinx followed at their heels.

Byron held the door, his long muzzle raised in smug salute. Only Edith lingered, though with her back to him. Amid the vault of books, the weight of knowledge, Senlin seemed as thin and inconsequential as a periodical. A moment before, she had been fussing intimately with his collar; now she stood off like a stranger.

"I'm so sorry, Edith," Senlin said.

She began to reply, stopped, and then left in a rush. Byron slammed the door behind them, the muffled sound echoing through the library like a pail dropped down a well.

Alarmed by his abrupt severance from his friends, Senlin ran to the door. His boots slid under him, and he bounced against a jamb, which was crypt-like in its fixedness. He wrenched the knob, found it completely resistant, and before he could stop himself, began to thump upon the door with the heels of his fists.

They couldn't really mean to lock him in here, to leave him alone with his ghosts and his guilt for days and days on end. What if he fell ill? What if he was afflicted by the delirium tremens? What if the cat held a grudge and there really were traps? What if he never found the bottom of the library, or himself, or the Tower, and just went tumbling down forever?

Hands stinging, he broke off his useless flailing and set his head upon the door. Had his ear not been resting so close, he might've missed the sound, a noise that the thick, impassive wood blunted. And yet he heard it: three distinct knocks. Hard, soft, hard.

He returned Edith's knock, and it came back again, so he played it once more. He rolled his cheek upon the cool door, feeling a surge of gratitude. Though this was just their way of saying nothing, of admitting the existence of things unsaid, it told him at least that their friendship could survive this test as it had survived so many others before it.

And so he had no choice but to survive it, too.

Mister Edith Winters &
Master Adamos Boreas

Chapter Seven

Routine is rather like the egg whites in a batter: It imparts little flavor, but it holds everything together.
—*The Wifely Way* by the Duchess K. A. Pell

A dam was trying hard not to be bored. Boredom was his sister's weakness, and he thought himself above it. As long as he had work to do, he had never been discontent.

Yet, one week after they'd shut the door on the captain, Adam had become intimately acquainted with the tedious phenomenon of *leisure*.

Part of the problem was the Sphinx's refusal to let him work on the *Stone Cloud*. Somewhere beyond the frowsy wallpaper and the incongruous rooms, inside a cavernous dock full of windup porters, their ship was being repaired without him. The fact was quite galling, but since the materials, the tools, and the slip all belonged to the Sphinx, Adam wasn't in much of a position to argue. Who would oversee the work and who would carry it out, the Sphinx had refused to say.

Not that the Sphinx had divulged much of anything to them. After all the bickering over a contract that guaranteed him unrestricted access to the crew of the *Stone Cloud*, the Sphinx had proved to be in no hurry to interview them. In fact, since showing them to their accommodations the evening after the captain's cloistering, the Sphinx had not returned, though he sent his stag-headed lackey to look in on them from time to time.

At least the Sphinx had furnished them with a proper suite. It was not at all like the flophouse "suites" of New Babel, which were scarcely distinguishable from a dog crate. This was proper, albeit a little tattered, luxury.

The Sphinx's apartment was well furnished, with high-flung ceilings. Beside their own private rooms, the crew shared a dining table, a fireside, and a fully stocked kitchen, complete with the miracles of a gas stove and a tap that ran an apparently endless supply of hot and cold water. The open layout and the exotic equipment made cooking something of a spectator sport. If they discovered a deficiency in their pantry stores, they only had to ask Byron to fill the order, though doing so necessitated at least one quarter hour of moaning that was so eloquent it verged upon soliloquy.

The fireplace and mantel were weathered but stately; the velvet upholstery of the club chairs had gone bald at the arms, but the cushions still held their shape. They had two lavatories to share between the four of them, and each of these tiled shrines of cleanliness included an enamel altar in the shape of a claw-foot tub. Adam's first soaking had tinted the water so noticeably, he felt like a tea bag.

Meanwhile, the captain was off chasing a cat in a purportedly bottomless library in an attempt to prove to the Sphinx he was, or at least would soon be, sober.

They hadn't really talked much about that, though their silence hadn't stopped them from churning on the subject privately. For his part, Adam's desire to win back the captain's confidence was a good deal more complicated now. In addition to that riddle, Adam no longer knew what to say to his sister; having relieved himself of the duty to scold and smother her, he now found himself at a general loss for what to say to her.

But materially, practically, he wanted for nothing.

Except for excitement or work or the swift passage of time.

As first mate, Mister Winters was responsible for restocking the tedium whenever it ran in short supply. She established and enforced a routine that Adam found pitilessly dull. Worse, she rarely let him out of her sight because she was convinced the Sphinx had plans for his eye and could whisk him away without a word of notice. Edith took the bedroom adjoining his while Iren and Voleta occupied the two rooms opposite. Adam suspected that Mister Winters had sat guard outside his door on the occasions when worry kept her from falling asleep.

The general tedium only nurtured his obsession with the ill-fated Captain Joram Brahe. At night, Adam reread Brahe's diary, puzzling over the lost captain's accounts of "sparking men" and "monstrous nostrils" that never ceased snoring, and "a city under an unbreakable bell jar." The journal was full of fantastic hints of the riches that waited just overhead. He wondered if there mightn't be a stairway or an elevator, concealed somewhere in the canyon of doors inside the Sphinx's lair, which could deliver him directly to the pinnacle. Though it hardly mattered if there wasn't; he was resolved to scale the Tower by hand if he had to.

Edith, meanwhile, considered the routine entirely satisfactory. In fact, she found herself clinging to the very thought of it during the dispiriting hours of the night—that aimless, elastic expanse of time that seemed incapable of sustaining a forward march. Like a fog about a ship, the wee hours robbed her of all sense of progress, speed, and direction. She passed the night rolling back and forth across her downy mattress, alternating between fretful dreams and wakeful anxiety. She worried for the safety of her crew and whether she would be able to keep the Sphinx from getting his hooks in them. She wondered whether the Sphinx would make good on his threat to keep her engine, and what it would mean for her independence if he did.

Then there was Tom. Poor, luckless Tom. He'd spent the past months poisoning himself with a portrait of his wife, terrified that his faculties were degenerating, a fear that he could hardly admit to himself, much less the crew. But the fact that he was just inebriated and in denial seemed so banal! How could they hope to succeed in the face of such towering indifference and pitiful odds if something as petty as powder on a board could come so close to undoing all that they had worked for? Perhaps they had struck against the limitation of hope, which adds nothing to ability and even less to luck. If all went well, he would reemerge in a few days, cured of his habit. But what then? Would he pretend all error lay with the Crumb? Would the crew embrace or shun him? Would he make an effort to win back their trust, or would he allow his embarrassment to ice over the corpses of the past?

Ah, but the sweet respite of routine! Routine provided an authoritative, if temporary, answer to that most troubling of questions: *What shall we do now?*

Voleta and Iren were in charge of breakfast, which, depending on their mood, ranged from burnt toast to buckwheat pancakes (also burnt). Blackened or not, they ate everything that crossed the table, gorging themselves like camels at a desert oasis.

After breakfast, they pushed the sitting room furniture to the walls and Edith led them in morning calisthenics: push-ups, sit-ups, lunges, and jacks. She had learned these "athletic forms" as a young woman by watching schoolboys exercise in the county schoolyard. At fifteen years of age, she had lain on her stomach in the grassy ditch across the lane from the school pitch and watched the boys jump as one, bend as one, and hike themselves uniformly into the air under the critical eye of the master of athletics, a stocky man with the voice and manner of a timber wolf.

Edith practiced what she'd learned in the privacy of her room at home until her jumping jacks rattled the ceiling of the study below and brought her father to her door. When she confessed where she had learned the aerobic forms, he jumped to the apparently uncontestable conclusion that she had gone to gawk at the boys.

Which meant it was high time they started planning her future.

If she was old enough to be curious, then she was old enough to wed, and quickly, before someone caught her lying in a ditch and ogling the county's sons.

Her father had always known she would marry young and then, straightaway, begin to fill a house with children. So convinced was he of her family aspirations, he spent the ensuing weeks making mortifying statements like, "Oh, how quickly nature calls forth the mother from the maid!"

Of course, her father was wrong on every count.

But then he had not seen those rows of young men, close and exact as paper dolls, militantly shattering the morning dew, too frightened of the master of athletics to stop. Even past the point of physical exhaustion, they leapt to his bark.

If her father had seen the spectacle himself, he might've understood what she found so compelling. It was not the red-faced boys, gritting and sweating their way through the morning flagellation. It was the command, the presence, of the master of athletics that had seized her imagination.

Adam found the tempo of her morning calisthenics and her enthusiasm for them exasperating. But when she fell to the floor and began to do push-ups upon her only arm, what could he do but join her?

Adam cooked the midday meal, and they were surprised to discover he had a talent for it. He could make a pudding from scratch; he could stuff, truss, and carve a bird; and he could make lima beans that were so silky and sweet even Iren ate them without complaint.

After lunch, Edith took them for what she called "the daily outing," though it was more of a short shuffle. First, they shuffled three doors down the elevating corridor to the game room, and then three hours later, they shuffled four doors back again to the reading room, which offered a hodgepodge of outdated popular books, all of which seemed better suited to fledgling socialites and children than a troop of marooned pirates.

They couldn't roam freely because Ferdinand was always in the hall. No sooner did they emerge from their apartment than he would thunder down after them, volcanic steam piling against the pink walls, the floor quivering and the carpets shredding under his titanic feet. It was terrifying. Ferdinand was never overtly hostile toward them, but they were under no illusions about why he was there.

Whether out of boredom or genuine contrition, Voleta had been uncharacteristically docile all week. She seemed to prefer nothing so much as napping in her bathrobe, which she had adopted from her room's wardrobe. She dozed on the chaise lounges of the game room while Adam and Edith shot billiards and Iren threw darts; she nodded off in the reading room while Edith scowled at etiquette manuals, Adam thumbed through cookbooks, and Iren toiled through the patronizing lessons of primers written and illustrated for children. And it seemed every time Adam turned around, Voleta had found a new surface to sleep upon. He wondered if she weren't suffering from a late growth spurt.

Edith cooked dinner, and it was easily the nadir of her day. Something always seemed to go wrong with her meals. Not obviously wrong, as it did when Voleta and Iren smelted breakfast, but subtly bad. There would be lumps in the sauce or bones in the fish. It made her furious, but she had to hide her agitation to preserve the peace. It was exhausting. There were just so many ways to ruin a meal.

She would've liked to blame this inability on her missing limb, but the irritating truth was that enduring one glaring lack had not cured her of a hundred unrelated inabilities. Her lost arm was not the cause of all her shortcomings. Which was comforting in a way. Not blaming everything upon her arm lessened the sense of loss, and that seemed especially important given the impoundment of her engine.

That night, after Edith had reconciled herself to the fact that the pork was undoubtedly overcooked, prompting her to ask Iren to saw her cutlet into manageable morsels, Byron burst into their suite like a figurine from a clock, come to hammer the bell.

"Any word on the captain?" Edith said without looking up from her plate. She asked the question procedurally and with scant anticipation. She had admitted to the crew soon after they had locked Senlin in the library that his errand could conceivably take longer than a few days. She had not been so blunt with him because he had already been confronted with a number of shocks, and telling him that he might need all of his rations seemed a cruel piling on.

"Must you ask that every time?" the stag said, pulling his white gloves off by the fingers. "Can't you just presume that I will bring you news if there is any? Better yet, why not assume that the moment the library coughs out that clog of a man, I will bring him to you, that you may pester him for the sake of variety and leave me in peace."

"I wish you were better acquainted with the words *yes* and *no*, Byron," Edith said. "You're dressed to receive orders, but apparently you're incapable of answering a simple question with anything less than a paragraph."

They had all continued to eat in his presence. Like he was some sort of butler. It was outrageous. To show his displeasure, he sidled up next to Edith in her dining chair and loomed over her so narrowly he could've spit in her food. "At least I don't pretend to be a free spirit while walking about on a leash."

Edith stood up so abruptly she nearly caught the stag under the chin. Even with one sleeve of her blouse tied up, she cut an imposing figure. Byron's dark eyes glistened with alarm.

"We're out of coconut oil," Voleta said, distracting Byron long enough for Iren to reach up, take Edith's hand, and gently pull her down. Iren did this without pausing the circuit of her fork between the mountain of mashed potatoes on her plate and her closely placed mouth.

Embarrassed, Byron snapped at Voleta to console himself. "If you don't stop drinking it, or ladling it about, or whatever it is you're doing with my blasted coconut oil, I shan't bring you any more," Byron said.

"We'll see," Voleta said.

Byron felt he had taken quite enough abuse. Here he was attempting to be hospitable, and they were ganging up on him.

Twisting his cuff's gold buttons, which were as plump as blueberries, he said, "The Sphinx wishes to inform you that the interviews commence tomorrow. He begins with Adam. I'll fetch you at eleven in the morning. Be ready."

He stamped from the room as if he were trying to knock mud from his heels.

Chapter Eight

A short list of potent stuffs for sparing use: cloves, especially in mulled wine but also in baked goods; perfume, which should be undetectable to you and elusive to everyone else; and frank conversation in every instance.

—*The Wifely Way* by the Duchess K. A. Pell

Adam lay awake listening to the incessant thrum of the Sphinx's home.

They had discussed the noise at breakfast as a crew and had agreed that the grumble sounded like a subterranean railroad or the deep rasping of a glacier carving out a valley. Though they all heard the same tone, they experienced its effects quite differently. Iren said the sound helped her sleep but gave her funny dreams. Voleta said she found the hum profoundly hypnotic, and perhaps this explained her recent lethargy. As for Adam, he could not stop imagining what sort of machine was behind such a suffusing groan.

Since he could not sleep for it, he turned inward.

He wished he could convince Mister Winters that he didn't find the Sphinx's gifts at all tempting. He had come to terms with the loss of his eye long ago and now considered his monocular vision as essential to his character as his short stature or the patchy, shapeless beard he had no choice but to regularly shave. These were his imperfections, and having mastered them, he would not trade them for the world.

What he did find tempting, however, was the thought of sneaking back to the soaring hangar. He felt certain that the horde of crawling engines came and went by some more surreptitious means than the big, main gate. If he could see his way back to the port, he could follow an automaton out.

A few provisions would be required for the climb, but even with a minimum of gear, he felt sure—he felt *reasonably* sure—he could make the ascent under his own steam. In fact, having read Captain Brahe's harrowing account of attempting to moor the *Natchez King* to the golden summit, where "sparking men" had violently rebuffed him and turned a number of his crew to piles of ash, climbing seemed a more sensible manner of approach.

He was so preoccupied by the thought of it that he nearly missed the tapping at his door.

Rising from the dressing table, which he had repurposed as his workbench, he went to the door, fully expecting to find Voleta, come at last to admit she was bored. He was mentally preparing to entertain his sister (perhaps he could show her the lamp he was disassembling), only to find a fully dressed Mister Winters standing outside his room.

The disappointment he felt was brief but pointed: It would be a while before he was accustomed to Voleta's independence. Or his own, for that matter.

"It's the middle of the night," he said.

"And you look wide awake." She shouldered into his room, and he saw she carried a pack with her. She shut the door gently. "I don't want to wake Iren."

"Why not?"

"We need to talk."

Frankly, he was glad for the company, unexpected as it was, but he had no interest in rehashing her recent obsession with his eye. He decided to clear the air and spare them both. "I don't want a new eye. I wouldn't take it if the Sphinx wrapped it in a bow and got down on one knee."

"Well. That's good. I'm glad to hear it," she said, trying not to show that he had caught her off guard. She surveyed his room to give herself a moment to revise her speech.

Their rooms were all the same, and like the corridor, were decorated in the tradition of a grand hotel, albeit one long neglected. But, unlike her room, which was littered with clothing, one or two empty tea-cups, and open books, Adam's room was impeccably tidy. The ancient doilies, thin as cobwebs and brittle as meringue, lay smoothed and squared upon the tops of the chest of drawers and the nightstands. The bed was made, the sheets tightly cornered about the mattress. Adam was usually neat enough, but this struck her as obsessive.

But then they were all under some strain, and the lavishness of their accommodations, while appreciated, had proved quite ineffective at curing anxiety.

"I've always appreciated your levelheadedness," she said at last. "You're sensible, and you listen to reason."

"Thank you very much for the compliment, but what are you talking about?"

"You have to understand; the Sphinx doesn't do anyone any favors. He doesn't ask. He insists."

Adam ironed a minor rumple from the bedspread. "Well, then I'll just remind him what a scoundrel I am and see if that doesn't put him off." The sting of how Edith had described him to the Sphinx was still fresh in his mind.

After a lengthy exhalation, Edith said, "I made a mistake."

Adam looked a little pleased to hear the first mate make such a grand concession, but he felt no less confused. "A mistake? What do you mean?"

"I should never have brought you here," she said, and he frowned because he knew she had been against it. If visiting the Sphinx was a mistake, it was not hers. "You can't say no, Adam. You can say yes quick or you can say it slow, but the Sphinx will have his yes."

"Then why lose sleep over it?"

"Because he is going to place a powerful and probably unstable machine *inside your head*." She punctuated the words with a tap of her temple. "He is going to conscript you into an ill-defined, yet probably endless struggle, and then behave as if you should be grateful to him. Though it hardly matters if you are, because he does not care if you are fulfilled or ruined by his gifts, just so long as you do his work."

Adam had unconsciously begun to touch the old injury, the leather of his patch soft and nearly as familiar as his own skin. The moment he realized what he was doing, he broke off with a rueful laugh. "That's quite a pep talk, Mister Winters."

She said, "I think you should leave." The shaded lamp at his bedside enlarged her shadow upon the wall, exaggerating her lopsided figure. "Tonight would be best."

"Are you serious? You know a way out? Why didn't you tell us? I thought we were prisoners."

"Because what I'm proposing is dangerous. I was hoping the captain would find his way back before the Sphinx decided to have a better look at you. This is a desperate act, Adam. I don't want to misportray it. But our back is against it, and I don't think we have a better choice. I've packed some food and a bedroll. You should probably travel light, but you might want to take something to read."

"You *are* serious." He shifted uncomfortably. This was, of course, exactly the opportunity he'd been hoping for, but now that the moment was upon him, he found the idea a little surreal: He was going to leave.

"It won't be for long. Just a few days, a week at most," Edith said. "All we have to do is find a ledge or a hollow in the facade to strand you on."

"You want me to camp on the Tower?"

"Camping! That's the perfect word for it. You're going camping! We'll pick you up the minute we leave." Edith set her hand on his shoulder as if she meant to build a bridge between them. "You should go for your sister's sake, if nothing else."

The mention of his sister reinvigorated his faded sense of duty, if just for a moment. "Is she in any danger?"

Edith frowned at the carpet. "Honestly, no. Voleta is too immature and undependable. The Sphinx is looking for reliable, improvable souls."

"Improvable souls." Adam grimaced at the phrase. "That doesn't sound like her." He began pulling on his boots, the process somehow more difficult with an audience. He hopped and quivered on one foot, trying to feed his other foot into the elusive mouth of the boot. He had to sit down on the rug to get his heel in.

He smiled at himself for being so flustered and was surprised to find tears standing in his eyes. He cleared his closing throat. "There's nothing wrong with Voleta." Adam got to his feet, brushing off his knees. "She's reliable enough, and certainly good-hearted, and sometimes helpful. I suppose I'd like some reassurance that you won't put her out on a ledge somewhere."

"Of course. Never."

"Not even when she irks you."

"She is part of my crew, Adam, and I am responsible for her." Edith didn't like the direction the conversation had taken, but she knew he was only being reasonable. Any parting in the Tower, no matter how minor or well planned, came with an element of risk. It was impossible to guarantee a reunion. "You're just going camping. Everything will be fine. We will see you again. But just in case, perhaps you ought to say goodbye to her."

"No," he said, looking uncomfortable. "I would never be able to convince her to let me go while she stayed here. Let's call it what it is. I'm going on a little adventure, Mister Winters. And my sister is not."

"No, I agree. If you both went, the Sphinx would suspect a conspiracy, and he might send the engines after you. If it's just you, I can claim that you snuck away on your own—the hubris of youth, and all that—and hopefully convince him that you're not worth pursuing."

"I do have an idea about where I would like to go."

"Now you're getting ahead of yourself, airman. First, we have to get past Ferdinand."

He gathered his personal effects, including the only book he owned, and followed Edith into the sitting room, which was dark but for one reading lamp.

Neither wanted to wake Voleta, which would not be hard, or Iren, which would be quite a challenge, so they proceeded through the apartment on tiptoe.

Reaching the front door, Edith pressed the white call button beside the jamb. A distant, almost inaudible rumble began. The elevating hall was coming.

"Won't that stir Ferdinand up?"

"I don't think he can tell who calls the elevator," Edith said. "So long as we slip into the hall without drawing attention to ourselves, we should be all right. He is a little nearsighted."

"That's consoling."

"He does have excellent hearing, though."

"Well, I guess he wouldn't be much of a guard if he was blind *and* deaf. How will we get past him?"

"Do not laugh."

"No, sir," Adam said.

"We crawl under the carpets."

Adam didn't laugh. He pictured squirming under a rug while a locomotive ran freely up and down the halls like an excited dog. If Ferdinand stepped on them, they'd be squished into meat pies.

"We only have to go as far as the rug with the big blue medallion," she said. "Maybe a dozen doors to the right."

The corridor announced its arrival outside with the clicking of their lock. "Where are we going?" he whispered.

"To the stable." She touched the doorknob lightly, deliberately, as if she were trying to slip the bait from a loaded trap.

Chapter Nine

Ferdinand could not speak, but he could whistle. Not songs. Not tunes. Just a single, toneless blat. For him, whistling was a reflex, a signal the master had built into him. The master had compared it to an egg timer, though Ferdinand didn't know what eggs were or why they needed timing. All Ferdinand knew was that whenever he completed a task, something inside of him whistled, and he liked it.

He wished he could sing. Music was so wonderful. A song could sound surprised, no matter how many times you played it. It could be always happy or always sad.

The generous master had known somehow about Ferdinand's fondness for music, knew that it gave him pleasure, and so, the master had installed a music player inside the great locker of Ferdinand's chest. It played songs off copper drums full of little nubs that plucked the teeth of a steel comb. The songs echoed inside of him, throbbing along with the plumbing of his heart. Ferdinand could change the songs whenever he liked. All he had to do was open up his chest and swap out the drums. He had three songs. He loved them all. One was sad, one glad, and one was for chasing things.

Tonight he was listening to the chasing song.

It excited him. He wanted to run down the hall and back again, but he knew he shouldn't. Running in the hall was wrong: It tore up the carpets and shook bolts out of the elevator, and most of all, it annoyed Byron.

But the music was building inside of him like steam inside a boiler. It said, *The chase is on!* It posed the eternal question, *How fast can you run?* It sang like a chorus, *Byron isn't here to tell you no!*

Mister Winters didn't seem overly concerned that the walking loco-motive had begun to emanate plinking, jaunty music, though it struck Adam as a bit eerie. Ferdinand stood far enough off, near the end of the hall, and though his great disc of a face was pointed in their direc-tion, the automaton gave no sign that he had seen them.

Adam looked up the face of the canyon, papered in peeling sheets of pink, the white doors as numerous as the nooks of a curio cabinet. He tried to imagine what the Sphinx's home had been like when it was new, vital and full of noblemen trying to impress their host. It was a difficult thing to conjure amid the tattered evidence of the present.

Before ducking under the carpet that butted against the threshold of their apartment, Mister Winters looked at him, pressed flat against the jamb. She took a deep breath and plunged under the dusty rug that was as worn as a hound's elbow.

He watched her lump begin to move away. What could he do but go after her? He got on his stomach and wormed into the wrinkle she had left behind.

It only took a moment for him to feel smothered and disoriented. He tried to keep her boot heels in reach, but when he momentarily lost track of them, he made the dreadful mistake of opening his eye. Centuries of dust and grit, disturbed by their activity, blinded him. The weave of the rug above him, rough as a bull's tongue, scratched his skin and snagged his hair. The rug beneath him reeked of abuse: stains, rot, and vermin. It was like they had crawled into an ancient burrow, inhabited by generations of badgers and foxes. He dreamed of retreat even as the fetid tunnel collapsed behind him. It no longer reminded him of an animal's den; it reminded him of a filled-in grave.

Adam wondered why Edith had begun to tap on the floor. Was she trying to get his attention? How did she expect him to reply without choking on the dust? And hadn't she warned him about Ferdinand's remarkable hearing? Surely a light tap would be sufficient; she didn't have to knock upon the floor so firmly. The beat was increasing, too, becoming insistent, like a derrick pounding the earth.

He understood at last: It wasn't Edith signaling him. Ferdinand had begun to run in the hall.

Whether they had been spotted hardly mattered. The giant was coming, and they had to get out from underfoot.

Edith threw off the rugs, the bulk falling back on Adam, hampering his escape. Seeing there wasn't time to extract him, she stood and waved her arm like a railroad signalman and cried, "Stop! No running in the hall!"

The engine charged them like a bull, and Edith wondered, even if it wanted to, whether it could stop in time. Dust plumed amid an ecstatic shriek of joints. The rugs curled up like shavings from a pencil sharpener. Eyes squeezed so painfully tight they filled her head with fireworks, Edith threw herself over Adam and waited for the end to come.

And then waited a moment more.

A music box raised its voice amid the abrupt calm.

Looking up from Adam's shoulder, Edith found the moon-faced giant stooped over them, its kettle chest plinking with a frantic, childish melody. Ferdinand squatted to her level, the light of his face paling enough for her to see the machinery behind the lens, the whirling, turning mind of the giant. It was a disturbing and exhilarating view.

Their dignity slowly returning, she and Adam rose under the sentinel's scrutiny. Edith said, "Thank you, Ferdinand. Now, please back up. There's no need to crowd us."

The engine took a wobbling step backward, his limbs apparently unaccustomed to retreating. He placed a steadying hand on the wall, shattering the plaster beneath the rosy wallpaper.

"He listened to you," Adam said, his face pale with dust. "Why did he listen to you?"

Raking down her dark, hackled hair, Edith said, "I don't know. Maybe he listens to anyone who barks at him."

"All right. I'll try it," Adam said, straightening his chin at the looming iron figure. "Ferdinand, turn off that music!"

Ferdinand's face glowed a little more brightly, but he was otherwise unmoved.

Adam nodded at Edith to try. She delivered the same command, and the walking locomotive opened a drawer in its chest and plucked the cylinder from the player.

"Why is that?" Adam said.

"Maybe it's because I'm employed by the Sphinx," she said. "It might think I'm its superior."

"I thought we were all employees of the Sphinx now."

"True enough, but I'm a Wakeman."

"A what-man?"

Edith quickly explained a Wakeman's role as enforcer of the peace— a sort of marshal who was expected to represent the Sphinx's interests, which were generally benevolent, as were the Wakemen. Generally.

"So you're something like a constable?"

"I don't think it's quite so grand as that. I'm more of a hired brute."

"I have never met a Wakeman in my life," Adam said.

"I'm not surprised. The Wakemen really only concern themselves with the powerful and elite. The Sphinx doesn't give a fig about the doings of port workers and pirates," Edith said.

"No offense," Adam said, his voice shaking with unhappy laughter.

"None intended. I've been a pirate, too."

"*Are*," Adam corrected. "You are a pirate, too."

"Well, until the Sphinx says otherwise. That's the thing, Adam. That's the thing I'm trying to protect you from. I don't have any control over what happens next. He could put me to work in any port, any court, any position he chooses."

"Are you saying you might leave? What about Voleta? What about the captain? Can you imagine them without you? You're the rudder of the ship! You can't leave." He sounded indignant.

Edith smiled at the compliment. "I promised to look after my crew, and I will. I hope that means keeping Voleta with me. But there are many things beyond my control, Adam, and the day may come when it's safer for all of you to be as far away from me as possible."

A doleful little nocturne began to play. They looked up at the colossus. Ferdinand still had his hand in his chest, hovering over the turning barrel. Though they wouldn't have thought a locomotive was capable of looking ashamed, Ferdinand was making a pretty good show of it.

"We should go before someone calls the corridor to another floor," Edith said, and led Adam a short distance to a rug emblazoned with a blue medallion.

Edith turned to Ferdinand, who had followed them, and said, "Thank you for escorting us. Please don't feel like you have to stay." When Ferdinand failed to shift, she shooed him with her hand. The giant turned awkwardly, seeming pinched by the narrowness of the hall, and sulked off while the music continued to weep inside his chest.

The thought of horses living here boggled Adam's mind. They'd be impossible to care for and feed, especially so high above everything natural and necessary to a horse. Did the Sphinx trot his steeds up and down the elevating causeway? Did they graze upon the carpets? It seemed absurd.

Yet, when Edith opened the door, he saw hay strewn upon the plank floor of a very convincing stable. He plucked up a straw, cracked it, and inhaled the piquant aroma. A vision of the grasslands, of the plains of his youth, overwhelmed him. He smiled and showed his delight to Edith; she seemed just as charmed by it.

"How did you find this place?"

"Lee showed me."

"Captain Lee? I'm surprised the Sphinx let him roam about."

"It was just a little excursion. Nothing sanctioned by the master of the house."

The main aisle was lined on either side by rows of box stalls of rough wood. Glancing left and right as they walked, Adam was disappointed to find the stalls bare and devoid of any sign of horses: There were no bridles, nor feed, nor droppings, nor the tools for removing them, and no brushes, blankets, or pails. Outside of the sprinkling of hay, the stable was an apparent sham. Which only made sense. What good was a horse here? He could hardly ride a hack up the face of the Tower. Still, he couldn't help but feel a little cheated.

Then he saw that the last stall was occupied, and by the queerest steed he had ever laid eyes on.

The mount had six legs, arranged in two rows of three, no head, and a bench affixed to its flat back. The articulated legs ended in toes that curled and split like the claw of a hammer. The steel and brass machine, apparently dead, was silted with a layer of dust.

Adam asked what it was, and Edith explained that it was a wall-walker, the last wall-walker as far as she knew, which had been built by the Sphinx ages ago for the purpose of ferrying passengers up and down the Tower. There had been thousands of them, once.

"Does it work?"

"It certainly did last time I was here."

Edith circled the engine, stroking it and making reassuring utterances as if she were gentling a horse. The mount was broad and squat as a farm wagon, and except for a few smutty fenders, the machinery was quite unmasked. She opened a hatch at the rear of the machine and extricated a long glass cylinder, which was a little more than half-way filled with a red, glowing ooze.

"Battery's all right." She locked the battery back in place.

"How are we going to get past the big doorman, the one who walked off with the *Cloud*?"

"You mean Henry? We'll bypass the dock. There's a whole network of service tunnels, and some of them go to the surface."

Having circled to the passenger side of the bench, Adam saw there was something in the footwell—several somethings, in fact. He removed an empty wine bottle and a wadded-up length of brightly colored silk. When he lifted it, the robe unfurled.

He gave Edith a quizzical look, and she seemed to suddenly have trouble swallowing.

"Won't need those," she said after a hard gulp.

"No, I guess not." He set them on the floor beside the cart, still trying to decide what to make of this funny discovery.

She set a boot on one of the walker's bent knees and hiked herself up onto the bench. "Come on," she said. "I've got to take you out and come back before everyone wakes up."

Adam joined her on the high-backed bench and accepted the end of the rope that she handed him. This had all begun to feel a little dreamy to him. What was one of Lee's bathrobes doing in the footwell of the last wall-walker? Edith pointed at the other end hanging off his side. "Use a good knot," she said. Adam knotted the ropes over their legs.

Edith straightened her posture, exposing the long-buried lessons of her horse-riding days, and stamped her heel upon the floorboard. A throttle sprung up between them. In the same instant the engine rattled, seized, and then revived again.

"Try not to fall out," she said, putting her hand to the throttle.

The ride was somewhat like a horse and somewhat like a train, though it combined the worst qualities of each: It bounced like a horse but clamored like a train. Adam gripped the dash rail. Edith looked a little insulted.

"She's just cold," she shouted, her voice shaking in sympathy with the vibrations.

"You've driven before?" The question seemed particularly relevant given the solid wall they were presently charging.

"Ridden, yes. Driven, no," Edith said. "I have the gist."

She pushed the throttle further, and their odd steed stamped smartly over the corner between the floor and the wall, and kept right on going.

Adam felt gravity shift to his back and was grateful for the tall bench and the knotted rope in his lap. The two sides of the stable's roof opened before them like a gate, exposing dim runners of electric light veining a stone chimney.

The wall-walker dug its grapnels in and began a rattling ascent.

Chapter Ten

Outings are essential to the health of a wife's self-esteem. How else can she learn if her things are in fashion, or if she has become the subject of gossip? As a rule, never air your linens more often than yourself.

—*The Wifely Way* by the Duchess K. A. Pell

They were like ants in a nest. The shaft before them split and converged, then forked again. Red cells beamed from the heads and engines of other machines, laboring through the gloom. Sallow bulbs illuminated the irregularities of the tunnels, the pockmarks left by chiseling arms, the evidence of an ancient industry.

Adam had no sense of place, no sense of what direction the surface lay or how distant it was, and yet he felt neither confined nor confused. He felt as one floating on a river, a thing carried without effort or attention. He was a contented part of this rattling, plodding accord.

In the darker distance ahead of their rocking steed, a star appeared. The star seemed to double and divide, black filaments of space growing between each new point of light. The celestial zygote swelled and spilled into the dark. A crisp draft of air touched his face, distinguishing every pore, every hair, every crease of skin, until he could feel his expression as distinctly as if he were seeing it in a mirror, and he was smiling with exhilaration.

The wall-walker squeezed through the opening in the Tower face so abruptly, Adam felt as if he had been thrown into the night sky. Then the engine crested the rocky sill and began to climb.

Adam let out an exuberant whoop that made Mister Winters laugh.

It was such a novel view he could hardly stop himself from craning all about. He looked over the back of the bench, downward at the foreshortened face of the Tower, and out at the gaudy crescent of the Market, that great morass of aspirations, shining with the light of campfires, torches, and helpless vigils. Beyond that, the cosmos dazzled like a new pitch roof over the gables of the mountain range. When he could stand it no longer, Adam turned his beaming face to Edith. She looked more content than he'd seen her in weeks.

"Incredible," he said. "We should've done this ages ago."

"The strange thing about driving up a wall is that it starts to feel normal very quickly. If you just look straight ahead, it seems like we're riding a wagon across a big, fallow field."

"Yes, but while lying on our backs and depending on six legs."

"As long as we keep three feet planted at all times, we never have to worry."

"What happens if we get down to two?"

"Two is as good as none." Wishing to keep her hand on the stick, Edith pointed ahead of them with a thrust of her chin. "There's the Collar."

It was strange to consider the cloudbank from this angle and range; from here, it seemed a common fog rather than the Tower's perpetual cowl. When newcomers first saw the Tower, the fact that it had no discernable pinnacle made a profound, though conflicted impression upon them. The Collar of Heaven seemed to suggest that either the Tower soared without end, or conversely that it had, in its great ambition, knocked upon some natural limit, like a houseplant grown to the ceiling. Because the truth was uncertain, it was left to the individual's imagination to either cap the Tower or build it ever on. Both beliefs had the odd effect of making observers feel as though they had contributed in some way to the raising of the monolith, and that gave them the confidence necessary to approach the Tower and be absorbed by it.

Both Edith and Adam felt they had outgrown such amateur ideas, though in fact neither was as enlightened as they liked to believe.

"I forgot how flat this area was. We may have to wander a bit to find a nook for you."

"What if we just continued on to the summit?"

"You mean drive through the fog?"

"Why not? We don't have to gallop. And if I have to be outside, I wouldn't mind having a little room to move about."

"The summit?" Edith repeated, the frozen smile on her face thawing into something like misgiving.

"Have you ever been?" he asked.

"No, and I don't know how far it is either."

"It can't be that far. It seems obvious the Brick Layer, or the Sphinx, or whoever our host is, claimed the penthouse for himself. I mean, we could spend the next few hours circling about, hoping to stumble upon a shelf, trying not to get noticed by the doorman, or we could just make a beeline toward level ground. Unless you're one of those who thinks the Tower goes on and on forever?"

"Don't be stupid," she said with a withering look.

"Then why not? We've come this far already."

As they spoke, the wall-walker continued its pitching approach of the cottony air, and the closer they came to it, the more navigable it seemed: The mist churned and parted and showed a little ground. It was navigable, if not a touch foreboding.

"All right," she said, depressing a switch by her foot. Twin headlamps came on at the engine's fore. "We'll go to the top."

The fog was warm as rising dough. And though its density and presence vacillated, little more than the immediate ground was ever visible. The sandstone glistened like a tide line in the wall-walker's lamps. The low thrum that permeated the Sphinx's lair could be heard here, too, though more mutedly.

There is no stranger privacy than the one supplied by a cloud. It is as containing as a room and as open as the sky. A cloud is intimate and exposed at once. A cloud puts a soul in a confiding mood, which is why old aeronauts stand apart when their ship hits a cloud: to keep from spilling their secrets.

After some moments of marching into the murk and thinking, Adam asked, "Were you joyriding out here with Captain Lee?"

Edith squinted into the fog and adjusted her grip on the shivering throttle. "It's really none of your business, airman."

"No, of course not. I'm sorry." He said nothing more for a moment and then, "What if we exchanged secrets? I'll tell you about my plans, and you tell me what went on with Lee."

"Just like that? Swap secrets like two diners at a table: white meat for dark, butter for jam, that sort of thing?" She didn't add that he had nothing to trade, regardless. The secret he was so gleefully keeping from her would inevitably include rivers of gold and trees of silver. Or was it the other way around? She had heard both. Many times. There was only one reason anyone ever wanted to go to the top of the Tower.

But she felt sorry for him, sorry for the disappointment they were hurrying toward even now, so she decided to give him part of an answer he wasn't owed. "I'll say this: The experience left me suspicious of the kindness of strangers."

The bench jostled beneath them as the walker got down to three anchored feet in the midst of stepping over a crack in the edifice. They held their breath as the engine beneath them began to pull away from the wall. Then the fourth foot caught again, and cinched them back to the bosom of the Tower.

"I learned that lesson, too," Adam said, loosening his grip of the rail. "I learned it so well, I taught everyone I met to be distrustful of strangers. And I was very convincing, that is, at least until the captain came along." He mulled over the memory. "That's the trouble. I still owe the man. His flaws don't absolve me of my debt." Snapping his mouth closed, his jaw began to work as if he were sucking the stone of a fruit. Edith could see he was trying to force himself to say more. "But it's hard to have absolute faith in a man who has given in to Crumb. I am"—he searched for the most diplomatic word—"*concerned*."

The internal hum of the Tower, which had been little more than a muffled thrum a moment before, was discernably louder. Soon, it drowned out the rattle of the engine beneath them. The air, warm before, was now nearly steaming. Into the sphere of their frail lamplight came a new feature, a vertical curb. Edith steered a little nearer, and they saw the iron slats of an immense vent. They could only guess its size by the torrent of hot air and the roar it made. It seemed a vast gill in the neck of the Tower.

They climbed a little farther, and the curb disappeared. The roar receded into a bark and then a grumble. They, seasoned airmen that they were, practiced a steadfast dispassion, devoid of amazement, as if a lack of surprise, a superiority to awe, could protect them from the unknown.

Edith returned to his last statement as if some minutes had not passed. "It's perfectly reasonable to be concerned. If you find you can't have faith in the captain right now, then have faith in me. I am determined to help and support the man, but if it becomes apparent that his responsibilities are making things worse for him, then I'll help and support him by intervening. And that's all we're going to say on that subject."

"Aye, sir. Thank you," he said, feeling satisfied for the moment.

"Now, do you want to tell me about your treasure map or not?"

"You've been going through my things!"

"No, I haven't," she said, rolling her head in exasperation. "And that was far too easy, Adam. If someone asks you about your treasure map, the only answer is 'what treasure map?'"

"It's a diary, not a map," he said sulkily. "And how did you know?"

"No one wants to just have a gander around the roof. As for the map, I've seen dozens of them, and diaries, and divining rods, special goggles that sooth a hidden path, even an astrolabe that funnels the wisdom of the stars and points the way to gold. Wherever there are aging air wolves trying to stuff their brains into a bottle, there are treasure maps for sale. Everyone has heard of the treasure atop the Tower."

"Well, if it's so famous, why hasn't anyone claimed it?"

"Because it's not there! The summit is just a roof, shrouded in an inconvenient cloud. That's the real culprit of the ill-fated crews: They ran afoul of the fog. They were dashed to bits."

"But have you never heard of the sparking men?"

"You mean lightning?"

He gave a frustrated grunt. "But the trees of silver—"

"—and the rivers of gold," she finished. "Adam, I don't enjoy ruining your plans, but there is absolutely nothing there."

Unconvinced, he turned under the rope a little so he could more directly address the mate. "All right, say those ships did crash into the Tower. That won't happen to us. Isn't it possible that we'll be the first to surmount the Tower? Unless you went there with Lee?"

"No, of course not," Edith said. She saw no point in arguing. Adam would have to see the summit for himself before he would be convinced. And since they were more or less near it now, what harm was there in indulging him? "Perhaps I have it wrong. You'll have plenty of time to scout about and tell me what you find."

"You admit to the possibility, then. Which means there's at least a chance that I will encounter some danger. I might never see you or my sister or anyone ever again."

"Granted. If there isn't peril, then it isn't an adventure."

"Exactly. So, it's not unreasonable for me, as your crewman and your friend, to make a last request."

"Go on."

"I'm very curious to know, did you have a romance with Captain Lee?"

"This is your parting favor? To stick your nose into my business?" Edith huffed but privately felt a little flattered by the young man's curiosity. Still, she wasn't prepared to indulge his cheek. "I can't believe you don't have a message for your sister. That's what you're supposed to ask for with a last request. 'Tell my family I love them,' that sort of thing."

"Oh, she wouldn't believe that," he said with a dismissive swat of his hand. "Besides, you have to understand, part of the reason I'm so happy to be out here in the fresh air is that I don't have to try to figure out what to say to her. We never had a thing in common. That's the truth. We rarely talk. She doesn't know who I am." He paused to consider, feeling surprise at the admission. "And I'm not sure I know either. But I do know that I'm tired of being a nag. I'm tired of being the unneeded mother. I think she's tired of running away from me, though I can't really blame her anymore. So now I just think maybe it's my turn."

When he looked up, Edith could see how battered by guilt and exhausted he was. And like a flush runs up the neck and floods the head, she recalled how it felt to be his age, what it was like to live for ill-fitting obligations.

She took a deep breath.

"After the Sphinx gave me my arm, while I was recovering, Lee started paying a little attention to me," she said with some difficulty. "You have to understand, it had been a long few weeks."

"Were you in love with him?"

"That is the most repulsive word you could have chosen for it, Adam. No. It wasn't a romance; it wasn't love. That's the captain rubbing off on you. I was—" She stumbled on the word, and that sent her eyes rolling at her own awkwardness. "I was recently disfigured and feeling unattractive. No, that's not the word. I was feeling ruined. I wondered who was ever going to see past this." She nodded at her empty sleeve. "Lee just had good timing. And Tom"—her voice cracked—"the captain had been so kind to me in the Parlor, it made me think there might be other kind men in the Tower. And perhaps there are. Lee wasn't one."

"Did he hurt you?"

"No, no, nothing like that. I enjoyed myself. It was restorative. And then we left here, and it was finished. It turns out, as far as he was concerned, I was the only skirt in port, and he had made do. Which was only fair, because I thought I was making do."

She felt a little rewarded by how shocked Adam looked.

"Was that worse than you guessed?" Edith said.

"No, so much better. It makes me like you more," he said, smiling. "It gives me hope to think—"

Edith jerked back on the stick. The engine staggered for footing in the pocked and weathered stone, and then fell quiet when she released the throttle. The walker stood upon a sheer edge.

They had run out of Tower to climb.

Chapter Eleven

When introductions are made, never be first in the reception line. "First to curtsy, first forgot," or so the saying goes.

—*The Wifely Way* by the Duchess K. A. Pell

Edith would later recount to captain and crew her initial impressions of the oft-speculated about and seldom seen summit of the Tower of Babel, and in so doing, she would discover just how firmly the scene had been embossed upon her memory. *How did the air smell?* Like geraniums and metal. *What was the hour?* It was just before sunrise, and the fog purpled with the light. *You stole a mount, but why not any weapons?* Because there was no need! There wasn't any danger. It was just a barren roof.

Far from it, though the pinnacle did not reveal all its wonders at once. Had there been no fog, Edith would never have agreed to a quick look around. Had there been no fog, surely they would have fled.

She had to give Adam credit: He took his illusions seriously. To avoid detection, he insisted that they proceed on foot, despite how easily they would have been able to survey the summit from the bench of the wall-walker. He further insisted that the machine be parked below the lip of the edge, to disguise their means of arrival. This necessitated that they stand upon the bench back, scrabble over the grate of the engine, and pull themselves onto the rocky verge, a process that the spectacular height and one missing arm made quite harrowing.

Edith agreed to all of this and bit down on her impulse to patronize the youth for his exuberance. Why couldn't she just enjoy his anticipation? Why must he suffer for her disillusionment? Reality would confront him soon enough, and it would be absolutely shameful of her to anticipate his disappointment with anything but remorse. She decided whatever happened, she would be supportive.

It would prove a difficult resolution to keep.

Beyond a narrow perimeter of unremarkable stone, the ground turned to metal plates that were fitted together as tightly as a weld. The metal resembled polished, toughened silver, but its luster was unfamiliar to Edith. Whatever the material, it apparently resisted the formation of rust, and perhaps the accumulation of spots. And dust. The ground was perfectly clean.

It was this inconsequential detail that tied the first knot in her gut. Shouldn't there be a buildup of dust, bird droppings, and the silt left by rain? There was none.

She pondered this as they walked deeper into the clouds, their progress shuffling and tentative. Edith had begun to itemize all of the types of natural phenomenon that might clean a roof when the silver tree emerged from the fog.

It was as tall as a tulip poplar, the trunk perfectly round, and the branches few and high and half-veiled by the clouds. The wind shifted subtly, and the top of the tree came into clear view.

The blades of the turbine did not turn in the wind. In fact, the windmill they had taken for a tree did not stir at all.

Hurrying to its base, Adam grabbed the mirage before it could disappear. It was real. The pole was silver, recently polished, and perfectly reflective. He ran his hands over it, his heart shaking his chest. Amid his joyful scrutiny, a second gleaming surface at his foot caught his eye.

He looked down to discover that he stood upon a vein of gold, flat as a plank, but wandering as a stream. It forked with tributaries that split and switched across the steely floor.

At his side now, Edith gaped with him at the gilded sinews running into the fog and nearer the shrouded hub of the summit.

"I'll be hanged," Edith said, touching the silver post.

Adam, already on his hands and knees, felt for seams around the vein of gold. If he could just get his fingers under the lip of it, perhaps he could pull it up. Of course, that presumed the gold was plated or tiled rather than fused. "Help me," Adam said. "How much weight can the walker carry?"

"No," Edith murmured. "This is not good." She peered into the fog.

"Why? How is this not the very definition of good?" Finding his fingernails too weak, he began rifling through his pack for some more useful tool. Why had he not thought to bring a chisel or a hammer? What good were an old book and a bedroll now?

"Because if the gold is real, that means—"

"Your hair is standing up," Adam said, squinting up at her.

"We should get back on the rock." She felt a tingling in her ears. "Now, Adam." She pulled at him and was frustrated by how heavy he was. How she wished for her arm!

The plates beneath them began to knell softly, like a doorbell rung in an adjoining house. They froze, harkening to it.

"Sounds like marching," Adam said.

"Run," she whispered.

There are several disadvantages to fleeing through a mist near the edge of a cliff. One is that you're never exactly certain where the edge is, and so it is difficult to convince your limbs to move with any alacrity. Another disadvantage is the effect that looking over your shoulder has on the internal compass: The more you look back, the more you get turned around.

So, they were all but immobilized by their disorientation when the first seething, blue bolt flew overhead. The lightning seemed to snag upon the fog and went fraying into sparks. Their skin tingled almost to burning, and Edith's dark hair stood out like a lion's mane.

Gripping each other with the grim conviction of drowning souls, they lurched helplessly under a second and third salvo of jagged light.

The men came at them directly, unflustered by the cloud. They wore uniforms of black rubber and red copper. Their shining conical helmets were slit at the mouth, the line curling up on one end in a stylized smirk. The lenses over their eyes stood out like a chameleon's. Black galoshes and heavy aprons protected them from the electricity that still crackled from the tips of the wands in their hands. The thick wands were tethered to ornate packs on their backs, and these emitted a constant, dispassionate hum.

Attempting to shield Adam from the squad of eight, Edith put up her hand and said, "We are not armed. Don't fire! Don't fire!" even as the sparkling light at the tips of their wands began to bloom.

Adam pressed around to her side, determined not to be struck down while cowering, and said, "We haven't taken anything. We just made a wrong turn. We're lost."

One of the sparking men stepped forward, and the coil around the barrel of his wand brightened with a fatal charge.

The foremost figure extended a glove-fattened hand and turned down his compatriot's weapon. This apparent leader hung his own wand from a hook at his belt, put his hands to his head, and twisted the helmet free of its collar.

He was not much older than Adam but was his opposite in nearly every other way. His eyes were a light blue; his complexion was as pale as glue. His long hair and full beard were the color of fresh straw.

"Adam?" the handsome soldier said.

In the realm of pirates, no good ever came from being recognized publicly. Indeed, there were few sounds less pleasing to a pirate's ear than his own name emerging from a stranger's mouth. Still, Adam could think of no benefit to denying the fact.

"How do you know my name? Is this some sort of trick?"

"A trick?" the officer scoffed, tucking his helmet under his arm. The others in his troop began loosening their own helmets, their vigilance softening. "I was wondering the same thing."

"Do you recognize me?" Edith asked, trying to discern the meaning of all this.

The blond officer surveyed her face briefly. "No. Perhaps you're part of the later story."

"Later story?" Adam said, but received no answer.

Now out of their helmets, the troop had begun an animated

argument over what they should do with these trespassers. They seemed as surprised to have found Adam Boreas during their rounds as he was surprised to be recognized. Perhaps Adam and the one-armed woman were the bait of a sinister trap, which was already sprung. Perhaps there were more of them coming even now. Perhaps they should raise the general alarm. Perhaps they should shoot them both or jog one of them off the side to stir a confession from the other.

All the participants in this argument, both male and female, were similarly young and blond, and it was difficult for Adam and Edith to follow exactly who was on their side and who was arguing for their summary execution.

At last, the bearded officer, clearly the leader, had heard enough deliberation, and pronounced his decision. "We'll take Adam back with us and put the woman down."

" 'Put the woman down?' " Edith said with a murderous scowl. She took one step toward the blond sergeant. "Give me a sword, and I'll show you how I put the woman down, you peach-faced toddler!"

"She's very exciting," the officer said to Adam with an unusual familiarity.

A young woman with silk-flat hair raised her wand again at Adam and said, "How do you know it's him? How do you know it's not an imposter?"

"A valid point. How about a test? Adam, what is your sister's name?"

"Voleta. How did you know I have a sister?"

"Anyone could know that," the young woman argued. "Ask him something only Adam would know."

"All right." The sergeant pondered this for a moment, then said, "What did your mother serve for your twelfth birthday?"

"Pheasant," Adam said archly, though apparently his humor was wasted on the attending. The silk-haired woman sighted him with her wand. "Wait, wait, it was a joke."

"Adam doesn't tell jokes," the same woman said. Adam thought her pretty, in a chilly sort of way. He wondered if everyone here was so aloof.

"It was a long time ago. I need a minute to think." He pinched his lower lip and closed his eye.

"Oxtail soup," he said, opening his eye as if he were emerging from a trance. "I remember, because the soup was bad or the meat was, and it upset my mother. She was a proud cook. She fumed the whole afternoon. And the next day she made the soup again, and made it perfectly."

"That is correct," the young woman said, dropping her weapon to her side.

"I know it's correct. I was there. I am Adam Boreas," he said, thumping his chest. It seemed a little absurd to be shouting his own name.

"There are some people who are going to want to meet you," the officer said.

Adam was sure this was all a trick. They must've overheard Edith and him talking in the fog, or perhaps they knew the Sphinx and had availed themselves of his intelligence. It really didn't matter how they knew what they did. The more pressing question was why were they pretending to know him? They must want something. He tried to think what qualities he possessed that they might lack. Finn Goll had recruited him because he had a trustworthy face and a flexible conscience, not to mention the leverage of his sister. Perhaps these lightning knights needed a ringer, or a foreigner to do some unsavory work they did not want to be associated with. Off the top of his head, he could imagine half a dozen scenarios where he, an outsider, might be of service to these odd natives.

The fact that they wanted something from him meant one thing for certain: He had a modicum of power in the relationship.

The same rubber suit that had made them appear large and imposing before, now, with the helmet removed, cast them as children who had gotten into their parents' wardrobe. Adam felt unreasonably encouraged.

"You have to let my friend go," Adam said. "I'll come with you, but she goes free."

The bearded officer, whose resting expression was apparently one of mild amusement, said, "We have to destroy your ship."

"We didn't come on a ship. We climbed."

The sergeant directed one of his men to look for himself, and the fellow donned his helmet and scoured the fog with his telescopic eyes. He soon proclaimed the sky empty.

"Then she may go," the sergeant said, but quickly raised a finger in condition. "With the understanding that if she ever comes back, she will be shot on sight."

"Agreed. Could I have a moment to say goodbye?"

"Absolutely."

"In private?"

"Absolutely not."

Adam scowled but thought it too soon to be making strict demands. He turned to Edith. She had the wild, disbelieving expression of a soaked cat. "It's really just as well," he said. "I wanted an adventure, and now I've got one."

"This isn't an adventure, Adam. This is an arrest," she said unhappily. She wanted to say more, to say that these people were obviously unbalanced and might be capable of any sort of dreadful thing. But it didn't seem prudent. Still, there was one thing she felt she had to know. "What do you want me to tell her? I have to tell her something."

When Edith later recounted the adventure, she would revise this portion of the story to spare the feelings she imagined Voleta would have. She would report Adam's parting words to his sister as being, "I hope with all my heart that we see each other again in this life. I love you. Be good."

What Adam actually said was, "Tell the little owl not to forget my birthday."

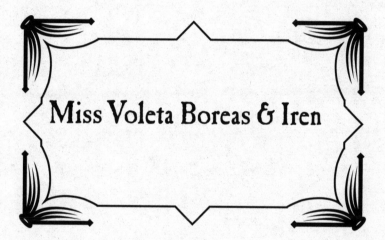

Miss Voleta Boreas & Iren

Chapter Twelve

C is for cheeky, coquettish, and coy, such as the girl who treats hearts as a toy.

—The Unlikable Alphabet, a Primer for Children by Anon.

Voleta owed her freedom to the intrepid Squit, though it took a little coaxing to remind the creature of her bravery.

In the early days of their time with the Sphinx, when they were still anesthetized by the shock of their captain's abrupt detention and trying to decide whether they themselves were prisoners or guests, the poor squirrel had been so traumatized she wouldn't come out of Voleta's bedclothes. She cowered anew at every strange sound, which were regularly supplied by unseen machines buried in the Sphinx's cavernous and apparently unpopulated hotel. Squit seemed to dislike both the fusty smell of the rugs and the unwinking glare of the electric lamps. Voleta could hardly blame the poor dear: The accommodations were a queasy mixture of luxury and decay.

Determined to cure her pet, Voleta undertook a campaign of pampering. She nursed Squit with treats from the kitchen. She piled her bedding into a nest and played with her under the quilts. Voleta stroked her fat cheeks and rubbed the bridge of her nose until the wide-eyed squirrel at last emerged from her hiding place.

The moment she recovered her spirits, Squit hopped down from the lofty four-post bed and bolted through a low vent in the wall.

Groaning at the ingratitude of her patient, Voleta prized the grate from the mouth of the duct, got onto her knees and then her stomach, and elbowed her way into the duct.

She was pressed on all sides and so had to squirm through the darkness that was only intermittently rayed with light from vents in other rooms. When she came to a branch in the duct, she listened until she heard the distant scratch of fugitive paws and then contorted herself around the mercilessly sharp bend. The seams in the metal shielding nicked her elbows and knees, and, not for the first time, she was glad to be free of her long hair, which would doubtless have snagged on every rivet in the chute.

She caught a whiff of wood smoke. A light wobbled in the dark ahead of her. She reached for it, and in the same instant, realized the glimmer was a reflection of light shining up from a sudden drop in the floor. But it was too late to catch herself; she had already begun to fall. Not fall, exactly, but slide down a precipitous angle.

She got her hands up just in time to keep from dashing her teeth out on the iron grate and popped from the vent like a cork from a bottle.

She landed in a heap on a soft verge of soil.

The great lens over the ash tree skinned everything in moonlight; the scattered, half-buried piano keys seemed to glow by it. The fire in the fireplace had burned down to an angry, orange core. The musicians inside the tapestries seemed to have stopped playing their instruments so that they could better and more fixedly stare at this clumsy intruder.

The Sphinx towered by the mantel, a thin and solemn mast. Voleta wondered what he had been looking at before she had shot out of the wall. Now, he was very obviously gazing at her.

"There's a squirrel in my tree," the Sphinx said, his metallic caw amplified by the quiet of the room.

Voleta got to her feet. Her long nightdress, now tattered about the hem, hung off one shoulder. She collected it. She knew she really should try to restrain herself. The Sphinx was dangerous. But she felt overcharged with a teeming, gleeful energy that would not be constrained and expressed itself in the form of a chuckle.

"You're in luck!" she said. "I'm a squirrel catcher."

The Sphinx closed upon her, the concave mirror of his face as black as pitch. As he approached, the Sphinx shrank nearly a foot, though he still loomed over Voleta.

Squit, no larger than a pear, sat on a low branch, looking very pleased with herself. Voleta held open the sleeve of her nightshirt and called Squit to her. The squirrel leapt from the tree, flattened her body into a wing, and glided through the air.

She landed snugly inside Voleta's sleeve.

The Sphinx clapped, the sound softened by his gloves. He seemed to grow a little taller. "Bravo, bravo," he said admiringly. "What a wonderful creature. You'll have to let me play with her sometime."

She thought the statement sinister but played it off lightly. "You must be joking. An untrained squirrel handler like you would be eaten alive by a squirrel like this."

"I like you, Voleta," the Sphinx said.

"Well, I'm not sure about you yet," she said. "Everyone says you're bad luck."

"Bad luck? Everyone says? Do you mean the trollops of the Steam Pipe?"

"Them most of all. Terrible gossips." She spoke quickly to hide her surprise.

"I saw your show once."

"I very much doubt that. I think you would've made an impression sitting in the crowd."

"I said that I saw it, not that I was in attendance. I have eyes in many places."

"Good for you."

"Your performance was quite pleasant."

"Oh, don't do that. That's so transparent. Rodion used to do that. He'd pay you a tepid compliment that was supposed to make you want to please him." Voleta didn't add that the girls who tried never lasted long.

"No, I'm absolutely sincere. Your act was pleasant, almost artful, but not particularly daring."

Now Voleta was offended. "If you really did see the show, then you know the tricks weren't the main draw. I had to waste half my effort mugging for the crowd: tossing my hair and kicking my legs. The brutes didn't come to see daring; they came to ogle a girl in a leotard. Like you, I suppose."

The laugh—Voleta assumed it was a laugh—that emerged from the Sphinx's curtained middle sounded like crackling static. "Well, you haven't any hair to distract you now, nor onlookers to please, nor a leotard to slink inside. Or do you have other excuses for being such an unremarkable acrobat?"

"You want a demonstration? Fine. I'll show you daring, you mean old spoon."

"Please," the Sphinx said, waving a small, satin hand at the crooked-armed tree.

Some friendships develop like flowers in a garden: They are conscientiously planted and nurtured. The ground about them is kept clear of competition. Then, after some weeks and months of incremental growth and laborious pruning, a flower blooms. Such cultivated friendships are agreeable and convenient, if not enduring.

Other friendships seem to arise spontaneously, like an egg in a nest or a freckle upon an arm, and these are often mystifying, as both parties are left to wonder how exactly this unexpected affection took hold.

So it was with Voleta and the Sphinx.

After that first evening, which Voleta spent traipsing in the treetop while the Sphinx applauded and goaded her ever higher, ever farther out on winnowing branches, the two were fast friends.

Theirs was a combative, often prickly amity, but it resembled a traditional friendship in one aspect: They were ever eager to be in each other's company. Every evening after pretending to retire for the night, Voleta slithered from her bedroom, through the walls, and into the Sphinx's music room.

Why Voleta liked the Sphinx was plain enough: He was determined to entertain her. The Sphinx's appetite for novelty appeared to almost outpace her own. Together, they explored his maze of suites and chambers, filled with a thus-far inexhaustible assortment of decorations, experiments, and wonders. They talked freely but exhibited a resolute disinterest in pleasantries. Mostly, they bickered.

The Sphinx was both a peerless tour guide and an acerbic wit. If Voleta played dumb or coy, the Sphinx pounced upon the pretense with merciless mockery. And yet, he allowed, even encouraged, Voleta's curiosity and her insatiable appetite for play.

Why the Sphinx liked *her* was a more difficult question.

On this particular night, the fourth since their arrival, the Sphinx led her on a roundabout trek through the rooms that had been staged to resemble the ringdoms below, if the Sphinx was to be believed. None were familiar to her. One ringdom-room was built entirely of glass. The houses all resembled overturned punch bowls. Not a single opaque door or curtain hung anywhere inside these crystal igloos. The only untransparent things were the people: painted figures, caught in various states of repose and repast.

Not a one wore a stitch of clothing. Voleta giggled the whole walk through.

The adjoining model was floored with loose, white sand that formed small dunes and valleys. All the structures therein were made of sand cemented with nothing more than water, according to the Sphinx. When Voleta brushed the frame of a standing arch, half of it collapsed and rained down upon her shoulders.

She shook herself off and told the amused Sphinx that she would like to speak to the builders about their shoddy work.

The next chamber was nearly stuffed, floor to ceiling, with a single engine that threw out pistons and flywheels in an endless frenzy of motion and drooling oil. It resembled a brass beetle turned on its back, with a tank for a thorax and plumbing for legs. Instrument dials, clustered like the eyes of an arachnid, shook their needles over a foggy porthole, which would not give up its secrets no matter how Voleta craned and peered at it.

The purpose of the machine, the Sphinx explained, was to hold an individual in a sort of permanent state of dreaming. Voleta proclaimed this an obscene way to while one's life away. The Sphinx did not disagree.

Voleta would've been happy to build sandcastles or crack open the dream engine and have a peek inside at its terrible industry, but the Sphinx promised he had something of greater interest to show her and said they would have to hurry if she wanted to be back in bed before breakfast.

They had never expressly agreed to keep their outings secret, and yet it seemed the thing to do. If her nocturnal explorations ever came out, she was sure a stern scolding would shortly follow, delivered either by Edith or her brother, though he had grown more distant of late. Voleta wondered if she hadn't something to do with that.

Though perhaps Adam was just upset by the revelation of the captain's habit. Her brother's veneration of the captain seemed to invite disappointment, if not hurry it along. Voleta liked the captain, but she also understood that the urge to escape sometimes takes asocial forms. Who was she to say her escapades were superior to his narcotic retreats? Yes, it was tragic and chancy, but so was sitting on your hands and wishing for a long life.

Still, so long as Mister Winters and Adam didn't know about her excursions, they would have no reason to fret, and she would have no reason to die of boredom.

The Sphinx stood before a white-paneled door, indistinguishable from all the other ordinary doors inside his impossible hotel. His black robes parted just enough for him to produce a little golden key. "You are about to see something no one else has seen in a hundred years."

"I don't like presents."

"No, of course not. Presents are just bait, aren't they? They're the cheese in the trap," he said in his now familiar, tinny rumble. "I'd never insult you with a gift."

"Wait," Voleta said, raising her hands. "I want to make sure we understand each other."

"I understand you completely."

"Then you know I am going to disappoint you." Voleta tried to confess it blithely so it wouldn't come off as a threat.

"How is that?"

Squit wriggled out of Voleta's nightgown collar and settled on her shoulder. The squirrel received her petting with closed-eyed satisfaction. "You have something in mind for me, some role to play or something for me to do."

"Perhaps," the Sphinx said.

"And you think because we are friends, I'll do what you ask."

"Perhaps."

"But my affection has little to do with my loyalty, and my loyalty has less to do with my behavior. Just ask my brother. Or Mister Winters. Or anyone. Whether I mean to or not, I'm bound to disappoint you."

The Sphinx said nothing to this but gave a small, permissive bow that allowed Voleta to hope, if not believe, she had been understood.

The Sphinx unlocked the door to his centurial secret.

The room was dramatically dim and theatrically vaulted. Other than a wooden scaffold isolated in the center of the room, the chamber was bare. The walls, ceiling, and floor had all been painted black. It reminded her of a backstage.

Inside the scaffolding stood a glass tank of admittedly impressive size. As far as it went, it was absolutely the biggest pickle jar Voleta had ever seen.

"It's great," she said with suspicious enthusiasm.

The Sphinx was undeceived. "What is it?"

Voleta laughed. "It's your jar. You should know. It looks like it's full of mud."

"Mud?" the Sphinx said, voice cracking with disgust. "That, my dear, is a distillation of more than two hundred ingredients, all painstakingly gathered and measured—"

"You mean, it's a soup?" Voleta interjected. She crossed the room, and the cistern seemed to swell in size. The glass wall of the reservoir towered over her, but even on narrow inspection, the liquid that filled it was a bland and colorless murk.

"No, it's not a soup, or a pudding, or a gravy. Don't pretend to be so stupid. I know you had to pretend while you were pinned up in the

Steam Pipe, but you don't have to pretend anymore. Believe me, I'm not going to be intimidated by the intellect of an eighteen-year-old. Now look at it! That is a chemically engineered medium that is able to hold an electric charge."

"Is that what Mister Winters needs for her arm?"

"Yes, it is." From under his robes, the Sphinx produced the same silver tuning fork he had used to transform the swarm of butterflies into a rain of ashes. He touched the fork to the hardy spigot at the base of the vat; a bright spark cracked the air. The medium lit up where the current had crossed into it, the red light undulating and flowing outward like an agitated cloud. The glow weakened the further it spread until it paled into nothing at all. "Obviously this is only a reservoir. The medium still must be charged in the electric crèche."

"The electric crèche? What is that?"

"That's where lightning is born."

"Have you ever been struck?"

"By lightning? Of course! How do you wake up in the morning? Shocks are good for the heart."

"I would very much like to see that," she said.

Voleta turned to find the Sphinx had taken off her mask.

Chapter Thirteen

In her bedroom, which was by far the most luxurious, ridiculous
room she'd ever slept in, Iren lay on her back in the middle of the
floor.

She hadn't always been on the bedroom floor. It only felt that way.
It had probably been no more than an hour. She could hear the clock
in the room, but she couldn't see it. She tried not to think about the
ticking because when she did, she ground her teeth.

Part of her wanted to blame the bed. It was soft to the point of
numbness. A hammock had a reliable bottom to it. This bed was a
white linen pit.

But it wasn't the bed that had put her on the floor. Not directly. It
was the dream.

In the dream, she had been ancient and feeble. She lived in a hovel
with holes in the roof. She seemed to have shrunk. The chains she had
once worn as casually as jewelry were now too heavy for her to lift. She
had no work, no friends. At night, she could hear men move outside her
hut. They peeked in through the holes in her roof. The only reason they
left her alone, she knew, was because she had nothing left to steal.

She woke trembling with frustration.

Her intent had been to tire herself out with a little exercise. Sit-ups were a good, quiet exercise, and she could do hundreds. Or, at least, *usually* she could do hundreds. Tonight, she got as far as fifty-three when a sudden pain in her back speared her to the ground.

It hurt less if she lay perfectly still. It was only a cramp, and cramps were nothing new. But this one lingered. She sincerely hoped her mushy bed was the culprit. Otherwise she would have to blame something worse, something inevitable.

She decided she would give the cramp until morning to go away, and then she would get up if it killed her. No one was ever going to find her lying on the floor of a frilly bedroom, unable to rise. Not Iren, the cracker of hulls, the mule of ships, the hurler of chains. Never.

But one can only lie on the ground seething for so long before the mind begins to wander, and hers wandered to Mister Winters. What would Edith do without her arm if the Sphinx never gave it back? She was resilient enough and brave and would probably lead a sufficient life, perhaps even a happy one.

But her engine had been so much more than *sufficient*. It was the perfect arm. It was tough and strong, and it would never grow any weaker, nor slower, nor subject to pain. If it broke, you replaced it.

If it broke, you replaced it.

Iren didn't notice when she began to grind her teeth again.

That beneath the shroud and mirrored mask the Sphinx was an aged woman was only the second most surprising thing about the revelation.

The foremost surprise, as far as Voleta was concerned, was the hovering tea tray upon which the Sphinx sat, cross-legged and smiling, it must be said, a little smugly. The floating silver tray stained the hollow inside of the black robe and the floor with a sanguine light. This explained the Sphinx's gliding gate and his inconsistent height. *Her.* Her inconsistent height.

A box hung around her neck, the grill of a speaker on the face of it. A voice pipe curved toward her sunken mouth, where a cone caught her words. This contraption, Voleta surmised, was how she disguised and amplified her voice.

The Sphinx's face was a patch quilt of leathery skin and metal plates. One cheek was copper, the other was a sagging jowl. One eye was a twisting brass loupe. One ear was real and bore that fleshy voluptuousness unique to the ears of the aged, but the other was a perfect golden shell. Her teeth, which she bared in a great smile, were all made of jewels: diamonds, sapphires, emeralds, and rubies. This shriveled woman, with hair as white and thin as steam, chewed her food with a king's ransom.

Yet, for all her patches, Voleta clearly saw the character of the woman, and in this, she perceived a kindred spirit.

"You look like you've led an interesting life," Voleta said.

The Sphinx turned the voice pipe away from her mouth. "Several," she said. Her natural voice was quavering but sharp.

"Can I take a ride on your tea tray?"

"If you'll answer a question first," the Sphinx said.

"I was wondering when you'd get around to that. All right. Go on. Do your worst."

"Is Thomas Senlin conspiring with the hods?"

"Conspiring? The captain? I shouldn't think so. Marat locked them up, and they had to fight their way out."

"A cover perhaps? Were you there when he spoke to Luc Marat?"

"No, I never saw him."

"Then you don't know what was said. Did you see him imprisoned?"

"I found them in a cell," she said, and then after a short deliberation added, "It wasn't locked at the time."

"You don't find that suspicious?"

"I know the captain. He has scruples. They can be quite irritating at times."

"A scrupulous pirate who has a taste for Crumb?" The Sphinx scoffed.

"I didn't say he was perfect. Why are you so suspicious? He's the single most harmless man—"

"Harmless? Lee is killed. The *Stone Cloud* is ruined. My engine is damaged and all the batteries lost, leaving Edith no alternative but to come here, to my home, with him in tow. It all seems a tad convenient."

"*Convenient* is the last word any of us would use to describe it. You are paranoid." Voleta blew her breath on the glass wall of the murky vat and drew a face in the fog.

"I am experienced. You say your captain has principles? Those are easily appealed to and plied. It doesn't take much of an imagination to guess what Marat might've said to convince your captain that his cause was just. And didn't he reproach me for my lack of charity toward the hods? Perhaps your captain was converted." The words came out with a sneer, showing the gleam of a ruby tooth.

"If you mean, has he been affected by the pitiful states of humanity we've seen along the way, then yes. Probably. We all have. We've been flying along on threads and coal dust, eating pigeons like they were ambrosia and dreaming of a safe place to alight. And here you are, sitting on a flying tea tray like it's not the most miraculous thing."

"Every piece of technology I have ever released to the world has been immediately adopted by the murderers and warmongers. Look at how good they have gotten at killing each other with balloons! Imagine what they would do with my tea trays and titans. Now, I would be the first to admit there is trouble and inequity in the world, but freeing the hods is not going to set the Tower aright."

"I don't think the hods need liberating."

"What do you mean?" The Sphinx's loupe twisted to a more narrow focus.

"They take off their collars and trade their shackles. I can't imagine why."

"What else did you see?"

"I saw some of the babblers kill a hod to get at his cargo."

"What was he carrying?"

"Black powder, about twenty pounds' worth."

"You're very observant."

"I am. And I never saw one thing to make me think the captain is conspiring with anyone. The only plot he's interested in is the one that takes him back to his wife." Voleta turned her head to kiss Squit, who sat preening on her shoulder.

"And yet, here you all are," the Sphinx said.

"Here we all are. Now, what about my ride on your tea tray?"

It was seventeen minutes after five o'clock in the morning when the bitter muscle in Iren's back relaxed at last. She rolled onto her stomach, afraid to breathe too deeply, and very gingerly pushed herself up to her knees. Rising without bending her back was a challenge, but she managed it, if not gracefully.

She knew it was precisely seventeen minutes after five because she looked the gaudy granddaughter clock in the face when she picked it up with a strangling grip and dashed it upon the floor.

The moment of pique passed, and Iren groaned at the shambles she'd made. She wondered if her temper had always been so short. She was sure she had just woken everyone. Voleta, a light sleeper, was no doubt running to see what all the excitement was about. She always ran toward crashes and bangs, never away.

Iren looked at the door expectantly.

A moment passed and brought no visitors. She began to breathe again.

Since she was completely awake, she decided that she might as well start breakfast.

As a matter of principle, she refused to wear the bathrobe that had come with the room. It was a little small, but very soft and very white. It looked like a bright flag of surrender, a signal to the world that the wearer had chosen to break in their funeral shroud in preparation for its eventual debut. Voleta had seemed to be just as leery of the mummy wrapper the first night she saw it. But the next morning she had come to breakfast in the bathrobe, and she had hardly taken it off since. Which was exactly what Iren was afraid of.

Dressing for the day, Iren cautiously tested her back and was satisfied with the present limits of her flexibility. It ached, but at least it wasn't petrified.

She snuck into the sitting room, dark except for a sole reading lamp, expecting to have the space to herself.

But Voleta was already in the kitchen, wearing her bathrobe and eating sugar straight from the sugar bowl.

"What are you doing?" Iren said.

"Eating sugar." She spoke around the spoon in her mouth.

"Didn't you hear a noise a few minutes ago?"

"No, I just got back... from bed."

Iren squinted at her. "Back from bed?"

"I mean *out* of bed. I just got out of bed. Why are we having a morning inquisition? You singe the coffee! I'll burn the toast!" She stamped the spoon upon the counter and threw open the pantry doors.

Chapter Fourteen

L is for liar, lip server, and lout, such as the boy who has more than one mouth.

—The Unlikable Alphabet, a Primer
for Children by Anon.

Voleta had not gotten her ride upon the Sphinx's tea tray, and she felt a little cheated by it. There had been time of course for the Sphinx to ask her questions, but the minute it was her turn, the Sphinx declared the hour too late to start another adventure and sent Voleta off to bed.

Tonight, Voleta would make sure there was time for the Sphinx to keep her promise.

She retired early, ostensibly to read, but actually to begin the somewhat tender process of dousing herself with the coconut oil she had taken from the kitchen. The oil made it much easier to squeeze through the ducts, and much less likely that she would be peeled like a potato in the process. The oil had the added effect of soothing the cuts, gouges, and scrapes she had acquired on previous outings.

By the time she was ready, the sitting room outside her door was dark, and all the rooms were quiet. She put on her vagabond nightgown, which was filthy and ragged from crawling through the walls, and wriggled her way through the open vent.

She hadn't gotten very far when she heard voices. Adam and Edith were talking, their conversation carried by the ductwork as effectively as the speaking tubes of a ship. Voleta turned her head nearer the shaft that led to her brother's room and listened. She caught her brother's words first.

"Is she in any danger?" She knew at once he was talking about her. He always had that earnest, weary tone of voice whenever she was the subject.

"Honestly, no; Voleta is too immature and undependable. The Sphinx is looking for reliable, improvable souls."

"Improvable souls. That doesn't sound like her."

It was strange to hear her brother and someone she considered a friend speak so candidly about her. What's more, Voleta didn't really identify with the person they were describing. She thought she was generally very dependable, and only immature in her refusal to parrot the ludicrous and sanctimonious behaviors of adults, many of whom were spoiled children at heart. She wasn't immature; she was self-possessed, for heaven's sake, and not afraid to tell the bullies off. The fact that she did was evidence that she was improving; she was growing and learning things and pressing against the boundaries of her courage. And the fact that her brother, her own flesh and blood, could not recognize this—well, it hurt her feelings in a way she hadn't known they could be hurt.

She had already begun to turn away, her ears ringing and her jaw in a knot, when her brother's voice sounded again.

"There's nothing wrong with Voleta. She's reliable enough, and certainly good-hearted, and sometimes helpful. I suppose I'd like some reassurance that you won't put her out on a ledge somewhere."

"Of course. Never."

"Not even when she irks you," her brother said.

"She is part of my crew, Adam, and I am responsible for her."

Voleta felt like an absolute cad. Not only was she guilty of eavesdropping, but she'd also begun drawing unfounded conclusions about the people who loved her with hardly a moment's hesitation. Was she really so insecure? Their differences notwithstanding, Adam had always been a faithful brother. She must never take him for granted.

She crawled on, and soon the familiar voices thinned and melded with the eternal hum of the Sphinx's home.

The Sphinx waited for her under the piano tree. Voleta was a little surprised to see she had dispensed with the shroud and mirror. Though of course she had. What would've been the point of resuming the disguise? Still, it would be a while before the picture of the Sphinx she held in her head matched the reality.

"Before you even say it, my dear, I had Byron put out a tea tray just for you." The Sphinx swept her arm toward a silver platter propped in one of the fireside chairs.

Approaching it, Voleta was disappointed to discover the tea tray was exactly that, right down to the braided handles and dainty filigree. "How am I supposed to fly on this?"

"I was wondering the same thing," the Sphinx said and wrung her hands with artificial concern. She showed Voleta the jewelry of her smile.

"I wanted a ride on your—"

"—on my levitator? Don't be absurd."

"Oh, don't look so pleased with yourself. You knew what I meant."

"I did. And no, you may not ride on my tea tray."

"You're going to play it that way, eh?" Voleta set her fists on her hips and cocked her head. "All right. May I see the lightning?"

"Yes, you may," the Sphinx said, and her levitator dipped forward to affect a bow.

Voleta liked to think she had a good sense of direction. But the Sphinx's lair was such a baffling collection of chambers, passages, and elevators, she had long since despaired of finding her way back. If the Sphinx ever left her, she'd be helplessly lost.

At least, that was what she wanted the Sphinx to believe.

Voleta had developed a reasonably clear picture of where the major attractions lay in reference to one another. There was some rhyme to the arrangement. The ringdom models were relegated to two levels. Another floor, the one with their apartment, was mostly accommodations, including a most depressing stable. The Sphinx's experiments and private dwellings were kept on the three floors underneath that, and so on.

Tonight, they were in a new area, which she believed was two levels under the piano tree and fifteen—no sixteen—doors off from the elevating corridor.

"I can hear you counting under your breath," the Sphinx said, turning on her disc so she could catch Voleta's eye. Voleta, who'd been murmuring so quietly she could hardly hear herself, was impressed by the acuity of the Sphinx's golden ear. "Are you planning an escape or some sort of burglary, perhaps?"

Without flinching, Voleta replied, "You would prefer it if I was?"

"Don't be silly."

"Yes, I'm counting doors. I don't like being lost or led around by the nose. Do you? Do you like being lost?"

"No, but I don't like people muttering behind my back either."

Voleta threw up her hands. "If you insist." She pointed at the next door they passed. "Seventeen! I don't understand your paranoia in the least. You live in an impregnable, secret fortress that's guarded by an army of obedient machines. According to you, you have an eye in every window and a man in every port. Eighteen! You're sitting on the tippy-top of the mountain. Everybody beneath you either doesn't think you exist or is terrified to think that you do. What could I or the captain or anyone possibly do to hurt you? Nineteen!"

"I preferred the muttering. I must make a stop before we get to the crèche," she said, hovering quickly on.

"I'll be very cross if I don't see any lightning tonight!" Voleta called after her.

The hall narrowed, the ceiling huddled nearer their heads, and the general hotel aspect of the decor, marked by humble paintings in noble frames, alabaster sconces, and the ubiquitous pink wrapper, turned abruptly domestic. Silhouettes in oval frames hung upon a wood-paneled wall. The profiles were typical enough: children with bulbous foreheads and shallow chins, sharp-nosed women, and whiskered men. Only the last in line distinguished itself, and that was due to the inclusion of antlers. Envelopes, a few brushes, and a pretty oil can sat upon an accent table outside a door, which the Sphinx entered without a knock.

It was evident at once they stood in Byron's private quarters. The room was warm and welcoming enough, though in a decidedly bachelor sort of way. A card table stood by a potbellied stove. A red jacket hung upon a chair set before a three-legged easel. A painter's palette lay on the seat, globs of paint shining like a jeweler's tray of unset gems. Model ships filled a shelf, paper sails plumping in an imagined wind. The air smelled of brewing tea. Someone was humming.

Byron came into the room with a wet muzzle and the straps of his suspenders hanging off his shoulders. He stopped humming at once and froze, his round eyes bulging from his head.

"Oh, dear," the Sphinx said. "I didn't mean to freeze you, Byron."

The stag shook off his paralysis and began to stammer before finally blurting out, "What is *she* doing here?"

"Don't be rude."

"Rude? How can I be accused of rudeness when I'm undressed in my own room?"

Feeling a little bashful but nevertheless excited, Voleta crept about to the front of the easel to have a look at the stag's work. Four sets of butterfly wings were pinned to a sheet of cork, and like those beautiful creatures the Sphinx had incinerated, these wings were painted to resemble domestic surfaces: white tile, a rainbow of book spines, the paisley of a carpet, and terracotta shingles. The detail was quite good.

"I brought her here," the Sphinx said with soothing aplomb, "so she could see what we do with the bottled lightning." The Sphinx crossed to a cigar box on the table and removed a vial of glowing, red fluid.

"You can't be serious!" Byron said, laying a hand on his shirtfront.

"Would you rather run down?" the Sphinx said, hovering to him. "Don't be a prig. Unbutton your shirt."

His nimble hands moved with a fluidity that seemed at odds with his long mouth, which trembled with indignation. Beneath his crisp, white shirt was a sleek, masculine chest of steel and brass. The stag looked steadfastly away as the Sphinx opened a little hatch where his heart should be.

"You should be nicer to her, Byron," the Sphinx said, plucking a nearly empty vial from the stag's chest. "She's a sharp one."

His body now unpowered, only Byron's head remained animate. "You can't adopt every stray that comes across our door."

"Stray?" Voleta said.

The Sphinx fitted the full battery into the cavity. "Don't forget where you came from, Byron. We're all strays here."

Byron, seeming a little chastised, looked at Voleta and attempted a smile. He said, "My apologies."

"Why do you hate Mister Winters so much?" Voleta said.

Buttoning his shirt again, the stag scowled at the floor. "She took advantage of my innocence."

"She did what?"

"She and Captain Lee plied me with alcohol one evening so that they could sneak away for a tryst."

Voleta's mouth fell open and then slowly ascended again, settling into a broad smile. "That is the most fantastic thing I have ever heard in my life."

"I hardly consider poisoning a compatriot with rotgut to be—" Byron blustered.

"No, not that part. The Mister Winters having a tryst part. I didn't think she had it in her."

"Oh, she had it in her, all right," Byron said. "And I was sick in bed for two days after. I haven't drunk so much as a drop of wine since."

"If you two are quite finished gossiping, it's time to go." The Sphinx floated into the hall. "When the wings are dry enough to move, please put them on my desk, Byron."

Before following, Voleta ran up to the stag, took his delicate clockwork hands in her own, and squeezed them appreciatively. "I'm so sorry we barged in on you. Thank you for telling me this wonderful secret. I'm going to have such fun with it."

Flummoxed by this unexpected expression of gratitude, Byron said, "You're welcome," as if some real good had been done.

Exploring the Sphinx's home would forever ruin Voleta for unassuming doors. Someday in the far future, she would stand before an ordinary door in an ordinary hotel and feel an unwarranted thrill of anticipation. And after opening that plain door that promised so much, only to find a broom closet or a sterile bedroom, she would think back to these nights when the Sphinx had spoiled her with surprises.

Before they saw the lightning, the Sphinx insisted she change her shoes. A pair of rubber galoshes, which were approximately her size, had been set out for her in the hall. Squit, the Sphinx told her, would have to stay here for her own safety. If she was afraid her pet would run off, the Sphinx suggested she could shut the animal in a bureau drawer. The suggestion so horrified Voleta she would not continue until the Sphinx had promised to never shut any living creature in a bureau drawer ever, for any reason. If Squit wanted to run away, that was her prerogative, just as it was Voleta's prerogative to chase her.

Voleta set Squit down beside her still-warm slippers, and the squirrel immediately climbed into the nearest one and curled up inside the toe.

The name *electric crèche* didn't exactly conjure a coherent expectation in Voleta's mind. She pictured something like a nursery full of cribs, only instead of infants, the bassinets contained piles of glowing batteries. Which admittedly didn't make much sense. But neither did the name.

Despite her efforts to prepare, she was a little disarmed when the Sphinx's ordinary door opened upon a black pit.

A narrow bridge extended from the well-lit, pleasant hallway into the ominous dark. At the conclusion of the gangplank, a small island stood suspended over the abyss. The floor, coated in black rubber, squeaked and gripped her galoshes and narrowly distinguished itself in color and luster from the endless dark waiting on either side. Even the usually sure-footed Voleta paid particular attention to where she trod. Once the Sphinx shut the door, the only light came from the meager glow of red vials that stood in tiered racks all along the perimeter of the island.

As interesting as all of this was, Voleta could not help but note the complete absence of lightning.

"It comes in bursts," the Sphinx said. "The next is due in thirty-three seconds."

Voleta peered over the racks of shining batteries down at the abysmal gloom. "Do you have a clock in your head?"

"Several," the Sphinx said, and settled her hovering tray in the middle of the rubber island. "I wouldn't stand too close."

And even as Voleta stared down, a distant flash of light revealed their dizzying height. The naked electricity leapt back and forth between the walls of the tube, revealing their metal shielding, the lightning tangling and arcing ever higher. The air took on a metallic taste. The short follicles of her hair felt like pins in her scalp. Her body tingled, and she huddled to the Sphinx's side just as the lightning broke all around them.

It felt like someone had fired a cannon inside her head.

Half-blind, she looked up in time to see the electricity break upon the ceiling of the shaft where a great coil received the energy like a sponge receives water.

The batteries all about them glowed more brightly now, bathing her and the Sphinx in a bloody light.

"I would like to see that again." She rubbed her ears in a useless effort to dislodge the ringing. "I closed my eyes for a moment."

"It's difficult not to," the Sphinx said. "Now you have seen what I'm afraid to lose, what I cannot afford to lose."

"The lightning? You think someone might steal your lightning?"

"It's very plausible," the Sphinx said, and patted the rubber beside her tray. "Come sit."

Voleta crouched alongside the Sphinx, her galoshes creaking beneath her. The Sphinx peered at her with her one human eye, which was the color of a cloudy sky. "I'm afraid I must ask a favor of you."

"I'd rather you didn't."

"I need you to replace my battery." The Sphinx began to untangle the dark skirts that covered her crossed legs. Voleta leaned away, more frightened of this than the lightning; she didn't want to see the woman's legs, demolished by age. But she was spared the discomfort; the Sphinx had no legs. Her torso ended in a trapezoidal base that more closely resembled a jewelry cabinet, with its cluster of small drawers, than any human appendage. Voleta was a little surprised to see how much of her friend was mechanical.

Opening one of the drawers, the Sphinx revealed a slot occupied by an all-but-extinguished battery.

"I'm trusting you, my dear. If you feel compelled to disappoint me, that is your privilege, but I will die."

"You can't be serious," Voleta said with nervous laughter. "Why in the world would you trust me with such a thing?"

"Because I want to, and you want to be trusted," the Sphinx said.

"I'll get Byron." Voleta was about to rise, her galoshes already chirping with the movement, when the Sphinx clutched her sleeve and pulled her down. Rather than argue about it any further, the Sphinx looked Voleta squarely in the eye and plucked the battery from its socket.

Voleta felt the Sphinx's lifelessness first in her arm, which was dragged down by the Sphinx's grip. Her neck, banded to her jaw in gold, slackened, and her head fell heavily to one side. The spent battery bounced upon the rubber floor, rolling to and then past the edge. The Sphinx slumped inward, downward, her breath running from her in a terrible hiss.

Only her human eye continued to rove, searching for Voleta, searching for some indication that the girl would not leave her here to die. And when that restless eye settled upon Voleta's round, frightened eyes, it blinked and teared with expectation.

Voleta tried to stand, but was dragged down again by the anchor of the Sphinx's arm. She wrested free of its grasp, which only made the old woman slump further, and faced the banks of glowing vials. She snapped one from its cradle and carried it in a rush to the Sphinx. Her hands trembled. The distant cackle of lightning made them shake all the more. Then she saw that the Sphinx's eye had closed, and she dropped the vial upon the lip of the levitator where it shattered and bled uselessly everywhere.

She went back for a second battery just as the climbing electricity seared everything in white. She snatched the vial free before the lightning could course into her and nearly fell upon the Sphinx in her leaping retreat.

A moment more, and the lightning had splashed upon the terminal coil. Voleta slid the battery into the base and snapped the drawer shut.

The Sphinx straightened like one startled out of sleep and gasped several times. Still catching her breath, she saw the spilled serum pooling about her tray. "Oh my, oh my, oh my," she murmured. "All my clocks stopped. What did I miss?"

Voleta, to her extreme consternation, burst into tears.

Chapter Fifteen

S is for snooper, snake, and for sneak, such as the boy who takes just a peek.

—The Unlikable Alphabet, a Primer for Children by Anon.

Crewmates, especially those who bunk together, do not respect one another's privacy so much as insist upon it. In the dark jungle of hammocks and among the narrows belowdecks, all the noisy evidence of life is present in vivid detail, and yet no one sees it. All involved agree not to.

Iren's inclination was to leave the girl alone.

But technically, Mister Winters had never rescinded the order to "hold Voleta's hand." Iren understood that the order had been what the captain would call a *metaphor*, which, as far as she could tell, was anything that said one thing and meant another. She wasn't meant to literally grip Voleta by the fingers for the rest of their natural lives. No, Iren understood that "hold Voleta's hand" meant that she was now responsible for the girl's welfare and safety. For the foreseeable future, if not longer, Voleta was her charge.

This fact was made particularly troubling by the discovery that Voleta was crawling around in the walls at night.

Iren had not gone snooping, not purposefully, but the evidence had come and found her. That night while Iren lay in bed, waiting for sleep to come and claim her, she heard someone cough. At first she thought someone was in her room, and she picked up a coatrack to greet them with. But finding herself quite alone, the amazon followed the sound to a low vent in her wall, through which she could quite clearly hear the girl scrabbling about and whispering to her pet.

She thought to call Voleta out, but that seemed exactly the sort of thing that would shoo her away. The duct was far too small for Iren to fit into, and so she couldn't follow the girl to see where she went. This at least explained why Voleta had turned so lethargic during the day: She was exhausted from roving through the walls all night.

Iren believed that Adam's mistake had been his smothering concern for his sister, which Voleta mistook for distrust. Adam had said as much himself: The more he chased her, the farther and faster she fled. The only course of action, Iren concluded, was no action at all. As long as Voleta was in the kitchen in time to make breakfast every morning, she would presume the girl was all right. She would not intervene. Nor snitch.

Given the generosity of this resolution, it seemed a particularly cruel coincidence that the very next morning Voleta would fail to appear for the making of breakfast.

In a state of denial that verged upon shock, Iren began the morning ritual without her. She cracked the eggs and whipped them with their shells. She strangled the juice from several oranges into the cream pitcher, catching not a single seed in the process. She put the kettle on without any water in it at all, and didn't notice until the iron sides began to glow red. She tortured herself, and the kitchen, for a half hour before finally giving in to the urge to check Voleta's room.

Though she knew she would find it empty.

She would never forgive herself for having been so indulgent of the girl.

When Iren burst into Voleta's bedroom without the thought of a knock, she found Voleta squirming out of an open vent in the wall. Her nightgown was soaking wet.

"I'm going to have to ask that you please not mention this to anybody," Voleta said in a high, peeping voice as she pulled her hips through.

She didn't appear injured as she sprang up and ran around Iren to shut the door.

The click of the latch made Iren feel as if she was already colluding with Voleta, though she had agreed to nothing. And she had still agreed to nothing when Voleta entreated her to sit down for a moment. She should sit and talk, just talk, the two of them, without anybody else.

Iren sat on the vanity bench, its turned legs creaking beneath her, seemingly in alarm.

"Why are you wet?"

"I went swimming to clear my head." Voleta wrung her hair out on the floor.

Iren grimaced at the puddle but reminded herself she was not the girl's mother. If Voleta wanted puddles on her floor, it was none of Iren's business. "Where?"

"In one of the pools. I've seen three. Only swam in one." She omitted the fact that it had been the Sphinx's idea to visit the pool. The Sphinx had been trying to cheer her up. It had worked wonderfully. "You really mustn't tell anybody."

"What am I not telling them?"

"I suppose it's only fair since I'm asking you to keep my secret that I at least tell you what it is," Voleta said, walking behind the changing screen in the corner. She slapped her sodden clothes over the top of the three-paneled screen, obscuring the top edge of the scene emblazoned upon the triptych, which depicted three sailors standing in a long boat, lancing a whale with grapples and harpoons. The unfortunate beast foamed and bled into the frothing sea. Voleta's wet head peeked momentarily around the edge. "I've been exploring."

"Where?"

"Everywhere. Anywhere I can get into. I've seen some strange things, Iren."

"Have you found a way out?"

"No, but why would you want to leave? This place is fantastic. And the captain's here, and the ship, too."

"Have you seen the Sphinx?"

"No," Voleta said very quickly. Iren wished she could've seen her face when she said it, but the morbid whale blocked her view. Voleta went on before Iren could decide if she was suspicious. "If I ever hear anything coming, I run the other way. Believe me, I was trying not to get caught. That's half the fun."

"Are you going to stop?"

Voleta came out from behind the screen and the men killing the gentle-eyed behemoth. She was dressed in her day clothes for a change, though she pulled at them and winced and walked stiffly about. "Those airshafts are brutal. I'm covered in nicks, but I was starting to feel like an invalid in that bathrobe."

"You aren't going to stop," Iren said.

"I really don't want to."

"All right." The bench gave a great squeak of relief when Iren stood. "Let's go make breakfast."

"Is that it?" Voleta said. " 'Let's go make breakfast?' "

"I smell something burning," Iren said, as if that answered Voleta's question.

Breakfast, being an unredeemable ruin, had to be begun again. It took them nearly an hour to make pancakes, a process that at times seemed like alchemy rather than the preparation of a staple since the adding of flour required the adding of milk, and then of eggs, and then flour again. In the end, they produced a baker's legion of lumpy, leaden pancakes.

They spoke little throughout the ordeal, Voleta for wondering whether Iren would stay silent on her explorations, and Iren because she was steadfastly refusing to interrogate the girl. Let them be friends, at least until Iren had a chance to decide whether she would tie the girl to bed at night.

It was only after they sat down to the table that either of them noticed they were apparently alone in the apartment. They checked Adam's and Mister Winters's rooms to be certain, but found no trace of either of them.

"Here I was feeling guilty for nipping out!" Voleta said, her hands on her hips. "I wonder if they decided to take a holiday." She hummed to herself as she returned to the table and began shifting pancakes from the common plate into a private stack. "I know exactly what happened. Adam got bored. Isn't that fantastic? My reliable, dependable, brooding brother went stir crazy without the ship to work on or the captain to follow, and he went looking for some excitement of his own. You know what this means, Iren?" She poured syrup on her pancakes, whistling as the amber stream stretched and then broke. "There is hope for us all!"

Meanwhile, Iren had lost the ability to sit still. She paced around the furniture and between rooms. She wished she had her chains, or a sword, or a pistol. She went to the kitchen and tested the carving knife on her thumb. It was as dull as a doorknob.

She was furious with herself. What had caused this utter collapse of vigilance and judgment? Edith and Adam might have been whisked away in the middle of the night, right out from under her nose. At that very moment, the Sphinx might be torturing them, or wheedling an eye into Adam's head, or who knew what else.

But somehow, it was Voleta's alternative that seemed the more frightening. They had not been kidnapped but had crept off in the night. They had left her to look after Voleta and Senlin and the missing ship all on her own. Iren snapped the knife in two and threw the pieces into an open drawer.

"You seem upset," Voleta said around a mouthful of food.

The front door flew open, and Mister Winters entered the apartment backward, calling into the hall, "Leave it, Ferdinand. Leave it! No, you're making it worse. Put the carpet down." The mate closed the door, obviously exhausted, and was still leaning there when the amazon stormed across the room and turned her roughly around.

She smelled like fresh air. Iren knew it the moment she put her hands on the mate's shoulder and felt the cold on her clothes. She had been outside.

"You cannot leave me alone with this mess!" Iren said, gripping Mister Winters, her arms shivering with her barely constrained frustration. Iren resisted the powerful urge to shake the mate when she couldn't even bring herself to look her in the eye.

Voleta leapt up from the table, emitting a little symphony of soothing sounds, and flew to Iren's side. She stroked and patted the amazon's trembling arms as firmly as she would a horse. And by degrees, Iren released Edith and took a halting step back.

"Sir," the amazon said. That was as much of an apology as she could manage at the moment.

Edith seemed unaffected by the confrontation, which was itself a worrying sign. She looked on the verge of collapse, but there was something else, something heavier hanging over her, something that was keeping her from meeting their eyes.

Voleta frowned at the shut door and asked, "Where's Adam?"

Relaying the ordeal took some time, long enough for them to work their way through the doughy plateau of pancakes, which they devoured as a crew, united, and with a solemnity appropriate to the subject at hand. For the rest of her life, Edith would associate pancakes with grief and sadness, and would endeavor never to eat them again.

Once it became apparent to Iren that the mate's story was not going to have a happy ending, she carried a bottle of rum to the table.

"I don't understand," Iren said, late into Edith's account. "How did they know him?"

"They didn't of course. How could they? The question is: Why were they pretending to know him?" Voleta said.

"That's what I wonder, too," Edith said.

"But it's hopeful, I think, that these sparkling men—"

"*Sparking* men," Edith corrected.

"I like my name better. Perhaps they are pretending. Which means they need him for something," Voleta said, pouring the mate another teacup of rum.

Edith downed half the pour in one gulp. "The worst part is, I don't know how we'll ever rescue him. I've never seen such terrifying weapons, and they all have spyglasses that can see through the fog. And I have no idea where they took him, or what those fortifications look like, but judging by how they talked, I imagine there are a considerable number of them." She skewered the last pieces of pancake onto her fork, and before stuffing the unwanted morsel into her mouth, said, "We will of course still try."

"Don't be ridiculous," Voleta said quickly. "Is there any reason to throw our lives away just to prove to my brother, who might never find out, exactly how much we all liked him?" Voleta looked to Iren for an answer, and the amazon shook her head minutely. "Whose idea was it that he go with them?"

"His. I was ready to make a fight of it."

"Then it's a good thing he was there." Voleta had begun to balance her chair on the edge of the back legs. She sawed on the edge absentmindedly. Still, this was as serious as any of them had ever seen her, and it made Edith uneasy, or rather it made her fully conscious of how terribly she had failed her friends.

The mate wiped her mouth and looked Voleta dead in the eye. "I just want to be clear. I realize that your brother traded his freedom for my life, and I will do everything in my power to be worthy of his sacrifice."

"Please don't torture yourself over it. He's old enough to make his own decisions. And think of us, Mister Winters. We don't want a first mate who's all martyred up. You said you had to get him away from the Sphinx. I don't think that was a bad idea. The rest is just the unforeseen consequence of doing the prudent thing." Privately, Voleta was thinking what a gift it was that though they had not had a chance to say goodbye, the last words she heard her brother speak were kindly and full of praise for her. Still, she suspected that he had said something more, something in those final minutes, something that Edith was omitting out of embarrassment or oversight. "Did he say anything else?" She tried to present the question as casually as she could.

"Yes. He did. He said..." Edith cleared her throat and recited the words she'd decided on during the long ride back without him.

The feet of Voleta's chair came down with a bang. "He said he loved me?" She stared so incredulously that Edith had to look away. "Mister Winters, I believe you. But I want you to know that you're not going to hurt my feelings. Did he say anything else, anything at all?"

Edith looked unhappy, though she was very appreciative of Voleta's diplomacy. "He said, 'Tell the little owl not to forget my birthday.'"

Voleta rolled her eyes in relief. "Oh, he's fine."

The Steam Pipe had all but gagged them. Rodion, the rogue organist and unabashed pimp of the Pipe, seldom missed an opportunity to gloat over their debt. He especially enjoyed leering at Voleta in front of Adam, knowing there was nothing the boy could do to stop it. Adam had no illusions that this lecherous display was done to bait him, but knowing this did little to lessen his rage. Voleta grew quite accustomed to seeing her brother red-faced and shaking with the exercise of self-control.

If ever Adam were foolish enough to plead for a moment of privacy with his sister, Rodion would straightaway reply: "Privacy is available at an hourly rate."

Complicating matters further, the backstage was constantly congested with stagehands, porters, and the troupe of unfortunate women in Rodion's employ. Voleta had once made the mistake of referring to Adam as *big brother* in front of one of the girls in the chorus line, and before the day was out, all the girls were calling their johns *big brother*. The fad lasted for weeks.

In this way, they were trained to always be on guard and to never exchange anything more than the blandest of pleasantries.

Except for the night of the fire.

It was wholly coincidence that Adam was at the Steam Pipe the night it happened. Finn Goll had sent him to deliver sixty bottles of sparkling wine to Rodion's cellar, and it was only by chance that Adam arrived with the cargo between performances when Voleta wasn't up on her swing.

Adam had just finished moving the crates of wine and was in the process of offering his sister some stiff salutation, when a boy sweeping the trodden-on bills and peanut shells from the bleachers spoke the magic word *fire* and a panic was born.

Rodion's cape was heroically enlivened by his dash for the exit. He was the first out, but chorus and crew followed close behind. Only Adam and Voleta lingered, pressing into the stage curtains for cover and peering about for any sign of the fire's progress. For the moment, there was only a little smoke.

Taking his sister by her arms, Adam wasted no time telling her what he had learned from his pickpocket expeditions. "If I don't make it back, you have to know when to look for me. It isn't enough to have a place; we have to have a time as well. Otherwise one of us might end up sitting around for the rest of our lives, waiting for the other."

"You're not coming back?" Her stage makeup embellished the widening of her eyes.

"I will. I will, of course," he quickly reassured her, sawing their arms between them. Men shouted in the auditorium beyond the curtain, calling for water and sand and all able hands. "But if I can't come back, if I'm waylaid or stopped at the border, look for me on my birthday, August twenty-third. You remember where?"

"Owl Gate," she said, the place they had long ago agreed to meet should they ever be separated. She realized what this meant. "You think I'll escape?"

"If anyone can, it's you. It may take a few years, a few tries; you might even have to change address—"

"Don't say that."

"I have a plan," he said, and was about to say more when they heard a soft chime behind them.

Neither of them had heard the anvil-faced amazon sneak up on them, but she had, and she stood now very close indeed, a pail of sand hanging from either hand. Voleta bleated with surprise, and the giantess, girded with her piles of chains, sucked in a great gust of air, and bellowed in their faces: "Fire!"

Voleta and Adam ran for the door like a pair of startled cats.

"It's funny," Voleta said as Iren rose and began to clear the dishes to the galley. "It was easier to get along when we couldn't talk to each other."

"Was there a fire?" Edith asked, and valiantly stifled a yawn. Her lack of sleep was catching up with her at last. She dosed her cold coffee with a spot of rum.

"Smoke mostly," Iren said, dropping the plates heavily into the sink. "Someone dropped a cigar on a rug."

"What was his plan?" Edith asked.

"He never had a chance to tell me, but it wasn't long after that he came home wearing the patch. I told him I didn't want to hear any more plans after that. He got a little more conservative then."

Scouring the dishes, Iren could not stop picturing herself as Voleta had described her. She had been an ogre. A terror. Not a person, but a presence. But look at her now: She was washing dishes like a regular person. With hands warming in the sudsy water, she marveled at her new life. It was a miracle they had brought her, a miracle they had forgiven her, a miracle that they liked her. She mustn't forget how fortunate she was.

She turned around, her arms covered in bubbles to the elbows, and said to the table, "I'm sorry for all of that. And for this last time, and for the next time I get angry." Then she went back to the wash. Edith and Voleta shared a shrug, both confused but not unpleasantly so.

Voleta carried the last evidence of breakfast to the kitchen, her feet splashing in the puddle of soapy water Iren had driven from the sink. "My point is, I think his talking about birthdays again means he has something in mind for those Tower sitters. Maybe he means to rob them. I don't know. I'll have to ask him on his birthday."

"So, you think he will escape?"

"If anyone can," Voleta said.

Edith was amazed by Voleta's calm acceptance, and the pragmatic part of her wanted to argue for what an unlikely scenario that was. Did Voleta really expect her brother to slip away from his captors, somehow descend the entire length of the Tower, and appear at Owl Gate in time for his birthday? While not impossible, it seemed a slender chance. But then, what good were clear eyes in the face of bad odds? And who was she to throw cold water on a young woman's hope?

"Voleta, as long as we're together, I promise we'll spend Adam's birthday at the gate. And I'm very sure he will do everything in his power to keep the appointment." Edith stood, her exhaustion making the simple act laborious. "Now, if no one minds, I need a nap."

"It's eleven o'clock. Don't you remember?" Voleta said with an expression of surprise.

"We'll dispense with the calisthenics this morning," Edith said, leaning upon the open doorway of her bedroom. The rum that had first warmed her limbs now filled them with a pleasant weight. From where she stood, she could see her bed: the too-plump mattress, the tufted headboard, fortified with half a dozen pillows, and the sheets as soft as clover.

A single, sharp rap at the apartment door heralded the entrance of the red-breasted stag. Byron quick-marched into their living area, his epaulets neatly combed, his gloves in hand, and his nose in the air.

"All right," Byron said, surveying the room. "The master is waiting. Where's Adam?"

Chapter Sixteen

F is for fawning, false, and for fake, who lives to be
liked by those that he hates.
—*The Unlikable Alphabet, a Primer*
for Children by Anon.

B yron held his gloves lightly, not choked up in a fist, but pinched
precisely between thumb and forefinger as a reader might hold
a book or a doorman the brim of his cap. He'd learned the man-
nerism from a powerful man, an admiral from some ambitious ringdom, who'd once visited the Sphinx to beg for a military advantage he
would not receive. The admiral punctuated his arguments by slapping
his gloves into his palm, and then, in a fit of frustration, the side of his
leg. It was quite a display of authority and disdain, which was only a
little diminished by his summary expulsion.

The trouble was, Byron never knew what to do with his hands. Or
his feet, for that matter. Or any of it. Especially at first. It had taken
him two humiliating months to learn to walk. That was when he could
still remember what it was like to bound along on four strong legs.
While acclimating to his new man-shaped shell, he'd been so terribly
awkward that every visitor felt obliged to point it out. The way he
moved, stiffly, lurchingly, swinging his arms too wide or holding them
too firmly to his sides, was apparently the very pinnacle of comedic
entertainment.

Making a concerted effort to improve, he began to collect a repertoire of mannerisms for an array of occasions.

This morning, he had hoped to project authority, self-possession, and the sort of fatalistic stoicism unique to men in uniform. Instead, before he'd even had a chance to snap his gloves upon his hand, Edith had announced that Adam was gone.

"What do you mean, *gone*?"

"Escaped. Run away. Scarpered off," Edith said. "He has departed the premises." She realized she was feeling a little punchy.

Byron squinted at her. She looked terrible, even by her marginal standards. Her slate-colored hair only needed a pair of birds to make it a perfect nest. Her eyes were raw and underscored with bruises. Her broad lips were chapped; her blouse, knotted at one sleeve, was in desperate need of a launderer at the least and an arsonist at the most. It seemed a shame to him, because he suspected she could be attractive, even striking, if she would just make a little effort on her appearance.

"Have you been drinking?" he asked in a tone of delight, though his expression was aghast.

"I had stopped, actually, but if you insist." Edith tilted the stone jug over her teacup. "I can pour you a snort while I'm at it. Or, if you'd rather save time, I can just throw it on the floor for you. You won't even have to get it on your costume."

"You helped him escape," Byron said, hands now behind his back, an ideal pose for correction and disappointment, though Edith looked resolutely unimpressed. "You took advantage of the master's hospitality, his trust, to take your sailor out for a little canoodling."

Edith rallied her self-restraint and set the teacup down to keep from throwing it at the stag's head. "I won't have you slandering my crew."

"It's not slander, Edith. It's an accusation based on the evidence at hand. Either Adam took advantage of your dalliance to assist his escape, or you willfully abetted the enemy."

"The *enemy*?" Voleta inserted herself into the conversation with a diplomatic laugh. "He's my brother, Byron. Come now. There's no need to blow this out of—"

"Miss Voleta," Byron said, turning to her with a staid and distant expression, one meant to discourage any memory of having seen him with his suspenders off. "You're appealing to the wrong person. I'm merely a forecaster. You'll have to make your case to the Sphinx yourself during your next visit."

Forking her hands into her hair, Edith collected the strays and shaped the rest as best she could. "All right, I'm ready," she said. "Take me to him."

If you looked at it, if you really inspected it, the pink wallpaper had a pattern as fine as a fingerprint. Edith had never noticed it before. But marching with Byron ahead of her and the jangling Ferdinand at her back, the corridor took on a merciless clarity. The tattered rugs revealed their frantic mazes, the congested growls and clanks of the elevating hall and the juggernaut seemed to compose a song. She felt the pleasant pressure of a breath, the heart-like throb in her fingertips, all vivid symptoms of a mortal dread. She felt as one marching to the gallows.

She thought of Tom, wandering through the recesses of the Bottomless Library. She and the crew had a routine to distract them, beds to console them, and a stocked kitchen to spoil themselves with. What did he have? A backpack full of cat food? His ghost? His habit? His memories? She recalled the moment he had grabbed her hand inside the Golden Zoo's elevator, recalled the tense look she had given him, which probably seemed aloof or horrified or otherwise discouraging, though she hadn't meant it to be. She had only been surprised. He'd done it so naturally.

Byron stumbled ahead of her.

The toe of his boot caught upon a hole in a rug, and he only had time to voice a single startled noise before he crashed onto his knees.

Edith rushed to him without thinking, knelt beside him, and got his arm over her shoulder before he could disagree. They stood together and quickly disentangled.

Byron couldn't look at her when he thanked her in an emphatic whisper. He pulled on the points of his jacket and continued as before.

But Edith couldn't stand the silence any longer. Not now. Not so close to the end. "I'm sorry I got you drunk."

Byron turned his head a fraction. "And for Captain Lee?"

"I thought you liked Lee."

"Awful man," Byron said. "I shudder to think of the two of you petting each other over my inebriated sprawl."

"We absolutely did not do that. I fully admit to pouring the rum, but I wasn't trying to poison you. How was I to know mechanical stags are allergic to liquor?"

"I thought we were friends," Byron said in a voice that shivered with emotion. "I thought we were sharing a drink. I was flattered. I didn't know I was in the way. You could've just asked me to leave, to look the other way. Instead you had to humiliate me."

Edith was flabbergasted. In those early days of her recuperation from the loss of one arm and the addition of another, the stag had never, not once, shown her the slightest shred of kindness. In fact, every time she saw him, they bickered. He called her names, she called him names—back and forth like a pair of cooped-up children. She hadn't thought anything of it. It was just banter to stave off boredom. But Byron, apparently, had thought they were becoming friends.

"Wait," Edith said, stopping, forcing Ferdinand to come to a clomping halt behind her. Byron paused but did not turn around. "Why would you ever want me as a friend?"

"It's nice to be talked to," he said over his shoulder, adding after a moment, "And you're not the worst person in the world." He hurried on before she could imagine what she should say.

It was a room Edith had never been in before, which, in itself, was not very remarkable; the Sphinx's home was mostly mysterious to her. And yet this chamber seemed especially odd.

The main of it was occupied by a long, brass tank that resembled a silo lain on its side. Quivering, ticking plumbing curled between it and the ceiling. The floor, tiled in white and fitted with drains, would not have been out of place inside an abattoir. The air was warm and thick as a spring mist. It beaded upon the cluster of dials set over the porthole where the Sphinx stood, turning a large socket key as if he were winding up a toy.

Byron seemed to be fighting the animal urge to run.

Edith refused to be afraid. No matter how terribly the Sphinx scolded her, no matter what punishments he threatened, she would be contrite. In the end, she could only hope that he would not deprive himself of a useful subordinate just to begrudge her a second chance. She would have her arm back, Senlin would come home and be captain, and all of this would be put to right.

What else could she believe?

"You look proud of yourself," the Sphinx said. He moved the key to another bolt in the porthole. Edith realized he was opening it. She was close enough now to feel the warmth of the tank, to see the condensation on the window, the gold light within.

"No, I am horribly ashamed," Edith said. "I betrayed my oath, I—"

"No, please, Edith, spare me; spare us both. Let's not carry on like strangers. I know why you did it. You were being sentimental. All you could think was, save the boy! Save the boy! Save him from what? Save him from me." The Sphinx's metallic voice squawked like a crow.

"Yes," Edith said, lifting her chin. She was not ashamed of what she had done—disappointed at the result, perhaps, but not ashamed.

"See, there. Honesty suits you. And I'll forgive you the boy. The girl is more than enough."

"I'm sorry?" Edith said.

"The girl. I have taken her under my wing."

"Voleta?" She felt light-headed. She couldn't tell whether it was from the closeness of the room or the thought that while she had been busily shielding Adam, his sister had fallen prey to the Sphinx.

"Why are you surprised? Because she is young? Because she is small? Because she is willful? Edith, for someone so . . . *untraditional*, you certainly are judgmental." The Sphinx shifted the socket key to a new bolt.

"I have you to thank for that."

"Haven't you outgrown that story yet? Do you honestly believe I did this to you, that I turned the world against you? I did not maim you, my good woman; I made you whole."

Feeling chastened and drained of her optimism, Edith's voice sounded thin even to her own ears. "Will you put her in harm's way?"

"In a heartbeat," the Sphinx said, pulling the last bolt free of the steel ring. "She wouldn't love me if I didn't."

"Could you pick someone else?"

"No."

Edith was starting to feel as if she were drowning.

"I'd like to show you something. Come here, Edith. Come look."

As Edith left his side, Byron pawed one boot on the tiled ground in agitation. The black Sphinx loomed before her, tall as a charmed snake. He opened the porthole and a great hiss of steam fogged the mirror of his face. Edith felt as if she were moving automatically. She set her foot upon the rail that encircled the tank and pulled her face level with the window. Inside, there lay a man, his loins swaddled, his limbs posed in the formal attitude of a corpse. His veins were visible beneath his pale, white skin, and they glowed red as an ember.

The man's eyes fluttered, struggled open, and then moved to find her. The Red Hand smiled.

Edith's foot slipped, or her knee unlocked, or the Tower shook beneath her. Whatever the cause, she fell as if bucked from a horse.

Chapter Seventeen

P is for prankster, picador, and peeve, or the young lad who keeps tricks up his sleeve.

> —*The Unlikable Alphabet, a Primer for Children* by Anon.

Iren and Voleta had agreed the moment they set eyes on the felt-topped monstrosity, with its fussy braided pockets and big claw feet, that billiards was furniture masquerading as sport. It was absurd. Iren found the cue sticks impossibly fragile, and Voleta couldn't understand the game's obsession with knocking the pretty candy-colored balls into the pockets, as if that was the only interesting thing to be done with them. Wasn't it more fun to watch them ricochet about, pop over the rails, and roll across the floor? Why was juggling not allowed?

It felt odd to be in the billiard room without Mister Winters and Adam, who both liked the game and had spent afternoons racking and cracking the balls. Edith proved to be as good a shot with one arm as Adam was with two. She rested the cue stick on the bumper and struck the ball with more finesse than force. Adam liked to play for a shekel a game, though neither of them had any money to gamble with. They ran a tab that they agreed would be settled next time they were paid. Presently, Mister Winters was ahead by three shekels. Voleta couldn't help but wonder how long the debt would stand.

They had come to the room because it was on the schedule, and neither of them was quite sure what else to do. They were nervous, and so to give their hands some activity, they began rolling a ball back and forth to each other. After a few minutes, Voleta said she was going to try to carom the ball past Iren and back to herself. It was like keep away, she said. Iren did not disagree, but neither did she try very hard to catch the girl's volleys. Her thoughts seemed to wander.

"Come on, Iren. That was an easy one!"

" 'On your next visit,' " Iren said.

"What?" Voleta rolled the white ball again.

Iren watched the cue ball bounce between her hands and return to Voleta. "Byron said, 'on your next visit.' You've been seeing the Sphinx. Why didn't you tell me?"

Voleta rolled the ball again, with more feeling. "Because I don't like being told what to do."

Iren put her hands on the corners of the table to signal she had quit the game. "I don't tell you what to do. I'm not your mother."

"You're sort of like my mother."

"What do you mean? Big?"

Voleta laughed. "No, my mother was really quite small. But you keep an eye out for me. And I often confide in you. And I know you worry. Doesn't that sound like a mother? You seem the sort of friend who will be generally suspicious of young men when they start to come around."

"They'll have to come through me first," Iren said.

"See, there you are. If mothers were elected, I would vote for you."

Iren's expression seemed more appropriate to a toothache than a compliment. "How can you say that? I used to scare you out the door."

"In New Babel, you mean? Oh, none of us were ourselves there. That's the trouble with prisons; they're full of prisoners, people who have forgotten or surrendered their character. I don't think of who I was with any pride, and I certainly don't blame you for being scary. I would've loved to be scary. Besides, you're so reliable now. I depend upon you. You know that."

Iren did know it, and it only made her more certain that she could not afford to ignore the injury that plagued her: the anxiety, the dreams, the great vacillations of her temper and courage. Something inside of her was broken. Something needed replacement, and she owed it to Voleta to take care of it.

"Do you consider the Sphinx a friend?" Iren asked.

Voleta blinked like a cold wind had struck her face. Confused by the abrupt change in subject, she said, "I do."

"Would you ask him to come see me?"

"Come see you? Why?"

"I have a favor to ask."

Now Voleta was very curious. She held the cue ball on one palm and squinted at it like a fortune-teller. "What sort of favor?"

"The private sort."

"I know what you're thinking," the Sphinx said, bolting the pane back in place. Edith, still humbled upon the floor, stared back in slack-jawed shock. "How in the world did he survive the fall? The succinct answer is, *barely*. He was quite broken and drained by the time my engines found him and brought him to me. But he had just enough of the battery medium in his veins to preserve him. He's made remarkable progress in recent months."

Byron helped Edith to her feet, and as he did, he whispered in her ear, "Don't be afraid. He's paralyzed."

"Yes, he's paralyzed," the Sphinx's voice chimed against the tile of the room. He finished his work on the final bolt. "And it's rude to whisper behind people's backs, Byron."

"Forgive me," the stag said with a stiff bow.

"I think what you did is very interesting," the Sphinx said, turning his attention again to Edith.

"What I did?" Edith asked.

"Trying to kill the Red Hand, not by action but by inaction. You waited for my engine to run out of power and let gravity do the murdering for you."

"He told you that?" Edith raised her chin to make swallowing easier. Swallowing had never been so difficult. "That's not how I remember it."

"Stop it. How can I trust you if you insist upon lying to me? Do you want me to put you somewhere awful? Somewhere far from your friends? Yes, Tom, too. Really, Edith, did you think I could make a Wakeman out of him? Out of that?"

"That's not what I thought at all."

"Because it's absurd. He's another lost soul on a hopeless errand, which, if he ever sees the end of it, will just be replaced by another hopeless errand, and on and on till the end. But you—you are not like him. You have a litigious mind. You broke your contract in spirit, but not in letter. That's very clever. You get to keep your word and still do what you want.

"No, don't interrupt, Edith. Listen. I can improve a lot of things. I can replace lost limbs. I can give a body more might. But I cannot improve upon a mind. Believe me, I have tried. Any fiddling around in here"—the Sphinx pointed at his shrouded head—"and the lights do not come back on."

Edith cringed at the thought of having the Sphinx rummage about inside her head.

"The trouble is, the Wakemen need to be clever. They must be," the Sphinx said, vanishing the wrench key in the recesses of his robes. "Can you imagine giving an imbecile a tool such as your arm? It would be a nightmare. The trouble with intelligent people is that they always think they could do a better job if they were in charge. But intelligence is not the same thing as vision or shrewdness. What a prime example your captain is. Privately clever, perhaps even smart, but give him a smidgen of power, and his incompetence is revealed.

"I cannot trust the Wakemen for similar reasons. They're generally obedient but not truly loyal. They might try to overthrow me if they thought they could do it. Who do you think Ferdinand and all my engines are protecting me from? It is you, Edith. It is your kind. Among others.

"But I want to trust you. Do you know why? It's very simple: because you let me take my arm back."

"I was just afraid."

"You were not afraid. Don't say that. You were being true to your word. You may be litigious, but you are not dishonest. You are the first honest person I have met in years, decades. Think about that."

"I've been lying to you since I got here."

"Only to protect your friends. So, you are smart, honest, and loyal," the Sphinx said, counting the qualities on his gloved fingers. "I need someone like you. Now, it doesn't have to be you. Feel free to say no, my dear. I can always put my favor elsewhere."

"What are you proposing?"

"You become more than a Wakeman, more than a counterweight to keep the Tower from leaning toward one power or another. I want you to become my arm, Edith. Not just wear it, but become it. Because I think I am about to need a very strong and loyal arm."

"I would like it back," she said in a dazed voice.

"Of course you would, but how long do you want to keep it? How long do you want it to work? How long would you like access to fresh batteries?"

"A long time." This was not the direction she had thought the conversation would go. She realized with some despair she was a little drunk. She wondered how long it would be before he started talking about contracts.

"Yes, Edith, for quite a long time. But think about what would happen if someone were to get in here, someone with poor intentions. They could knock the Tower down."

"Impossible," she murmured.

"Don't contradict me. Not only is it possible, it's simple. I could tip us on our ear just by fiddling with the plumbing. The ringdoms are all so busy squabbling with one another, they've lost sight of what they were meant to protect: the system! The system! The Tower is susceptible to sabotage. If some rogue, someone like Luc Marat, were to begin to coordinate an attack on a few vital joints, the whole Tower might be brought down. Millions would die; the world would lose its lighthouse. Civilization would degenerate and an epoch of darkness would dawn. What do I need to say to you to get you to understand? I am not the villain. I am trying to keep this swaying pile of humanity upright!"

"But what do you want me to do?"

"The age of subtlety and diplomacy has passed. The Tower is infested, and you will intervene on my account. You will dispel the myths and remind the ringdoms of my power and their responsibilities. You will confront the threat of the hods. I have removed from your contract the restriction regarding other Wakemen."

"You're saying I can kill my kin?"

"I'm saying you will probably have to. One Wakeman in particular. But don't fret, my dear, I am going to make you the most formidable proponent of my will. I am going to give you the sky." The Sphinx raised a finger at the stag, standing nervously by the chamber door. "Get your typewriter, Byron. I think we are ready to begin."

Despite her absence, Voleta and Iren dutifully followed Mister Winters's schedule. They languished in the billiard room until the lunch hour, though Adam wasn't there to prepare it. Neither of them had an appetite anyway, so they shifted to the reading room and resumed languishing until dinner. They were convinced she would be back. She would not miss dinner. Not if she could help it.

They found Ferdinand in the elevating corridor. He waited outside their apartment door, steaming softly and playing sad music. He hardly looked at them as they squeezed past the iron trusses of his legs to their door. Hoping his presence heralded Edith's return, they entered in a rush, Voleta already calling to her, boasting about how good they'd been while she was away.

Byron sat at their table in front of a teapot and three teacups. "Let's all sit down and have some tea," the stag said.

"Where's Winters?" Iren asked.

"Sleeping." Byron nodded at the closed bedroom door.

"Is she all right?" Voleta felt her throat constrict.

"Actually, in some ways, she's much better; in other ways, worse. She had a bit of a shock." The stag poured the tea with perfect grace, the stream steady and true. Voleta started after the first mate's door, but Byron called her back. "No, no, no, she really must sleep. She's had the procedure."

Voleta stopped. The stag opened the sugar bowl with his lithe, polished hands, and using the set of delicate silver tongs, extracted a cube.

"One lump or two?"

"Four," she said, returning to the table. She slid into her chair without taking her eyes off of Byron. "What do you mean, the procedure?"

"Perhaps it would save time if I just poured a little tea into the sugar bowl," Byron said archly.

"Tell us what happened." Iren laid her hands on the table and leaned into him.

Byron dutifully deposited four cubes into Voleta's cup. "The Sphinx has replaced her arm."

"That's wonderful news!" Voleta said, coaxing Iren toward a chair in an effort to get her to sit. "But why call that a procedure? It only took a minute to remove. How long could it take to put it back?"

"The Sphinx had to amend some of the internal supports in her shoulder."

"Internal supports?"

"Some of her bone had chipped away."

"Oh, that's so awful," Voleta said in a hush. "Is she in pain?"

"Not at the moment; the Sphinx has seen to that. Though when she wakes up, she will be sore for a time." He took a sip of tea, a practiced routine that was silent and kept his muzzle dry. He might stumble on occasion, but he was very confident in his tea-sipping skills. "It's not the same arm as before."

"He changed her arm? Just like that? Does she like it?" Voleta asked.

"You'll have to ask her when she wakes up." His expression straightened again, and he set down his teacup. "Though that's not why I'm here. I want to tell you something that she won't, though you need to hear it. This is not coming from the master. This is coming from me."

"I won't keep any secrets," Iren said. "I don't like lying to my friends." She gave Voleta a pointed look. The girl squirmed in her seat.

"Well, flog it if you have to: I'm still going to speak my mind. Do you know who the Red Hand is?"

"Of course," Voleta said. "He's the lunatic that tried to kill the captain. He turned on the commissioner like a rabid dog. I'd never seen such mad violence. Three cheers for Mister Winters for tossing that monster off the Tower."

"Don't say that to the Sphinx. He considers the Red Hand one of his greatest feats: He is the man with lightning in his veins."

"Is? *Was*, surely," Voleta said.

"He's very much alive."

"How is that possible?"

"As I said, he is the Sphinx's greatest feat. Although, at present he is an invalid. The Sphinx has him shut inside a tank where he does nothing but sleep and mend. He's been in there for months. Every time I see him, he looks stronger."

"Why are you telling us this?" Iren asked, not bothering to conceal her distrust.

"Because it isn't clear whether the Red Hand will hold a grudge. I'm saying that if you like Mister Winters and you don't want to see 'mad violence' done to her, you should be...watchful."

"Why would the Sphinx want to revive him?" Voleta was horrified to think her friend could be so callous. It was one thing to create him—the Sphinx couldn't know how he would turn out—but now that she knew very well he was a monster, why bring him back from the dead?

Byron made another production of sipping his tea, and after reseating the cup on the saucer without ringing the porcelain, he said, "Because the Sphinx is preparing for war, and he needs all the help he can get."

Senlin & the Librarian

Chapter Eighteen

All glory goes to the man who is willing to hurl himself, hat and boot, over the brink just to hear in his dramatic exit a smattering of applause.

—*A Beginner's Guide to the Game of Oops*

Day 2

It doesn't matter *what* I write, only that I write *something*. I must keep my head down, must keep my thoughts in line.

What I need are a few of the old morning drills. They were always good for shouting the mind straight. *Six times seven is forty-two! Six times eight is forty-eight! Six times nine is fifty-four!* Class, what is our mnemonic for remembering the taxonomy of animals? *Dan Kicked Penny's Cactus. Ouch! For Goodness Sake.* And what does that stand for? *Domain, Kingdom, Phylum, Class, Order, Family, Genus, Species.* Ha!

I am writing this account on a flyleaf that I tore from a book at random. I know a flyleaf is a sacred thing: It is where lovers express their affection and authors, their awkward gratitude. I am ashamed to admit that I have forgotten the title of the book I defaced. I believe it was something related to the maintenance of barns. This is what I have come to: rank vandalism. I suspect that a society might endure for ten thousand years and still fall apart in the span of one day. How flimsy is the veil of civility!

But I needed the paper. I need to write. My mind feels like a key turning endlessly inside a broken lock.

This pen is a small marvel. I found it on one of the desks. It has a reservoir of ink built into it. No dipping required! It is heavy and a little ungainly, but the strain upon my fingers is a small price to pay for the ability to write uninterrupted. What a blessing.

The librarian is resting now. Sometimes he sits and licks his paws and looks at me with his great green eyes, and sometimes he slinks off with hardly a sound. I'm terrified he will leave. But then, I have his food—his ghastly fish. I can't even share the same air when he eats because his dinner stinks so savagely. Why in the world would Byron think I'd be tempted by such a thing?

I should look to see if the librarian is still there.

I should not have looked.

The librarian is there. But I should not have looked at who is petting him. Eye contact seems only to embolden it. Oh, it's huffing in my ear now. It's turning my spine to ice.

I will attempt to record from memory the names of my last class roll. Hugh Brice, Nara Doughtry, Penelope Doughtry, Stuart Greenwood, Gerald Kaufman, who once distinguished himself by falling so heavily asleep in the school's outhouse that Mr. Brice, upon discovering his friend, announced to the class that poor Gerry was dead.

No, this sort of rambling won't do. Eventually, I'll read this and find either encouragement or discouragement, sanity or its opposite.

The question is: What would I like to say to myself?

An observation. This is not a library.

The tradition among libraries of boasting about the number of volumes in their collection is well established, but surely, it is not *aggregation* that makes a library; it is *dissemination*. Perhaps libraries should bang on about how many volumes are on loan, are presently off crowding nightstands, and circulating through piles on the mantel, and weighing down purses. Yes, it is somewhat vexing to thread through the stacks of a library, only to discover an absence rather than the sought-after volume, but once the ire subsides, doesn't one feel a sense of community? The gaps in a library are like footprints in the sand: They show us where others have gone before; they assure us we are not alone.

But here, in the Bottomless Library, I have not seen a single break in the procession of spines. The books are so numerous they spill onto the floor. Volumes crowd the benches and overload the lecterns. Fat reference books stand together against the wall as snug as molars. They occupy the stairs that spiral between floors; they lie under the water fountains, those dribbling gargoyles that mark the water closets, which are themselves full of books.

The Sphinx's athenaeum distinguishes itself from a proper library in another, more essential way. None of the books are numbered. There are no subject plaques, nor, as far as I can tell, any order to the shelves, not even alphabetical. The catalog is a shuffled deck. Which means that if the librarian turns out to be just a house cat out on an aimless trot, I will never find the Sphinx's book.

And if we keep making turns, I won't be able to find my way back either.

The air is redolent of parchment, glue, leather, and must. It is a soothing perfume. I wonder why. What is the appeal of this pulp and board technology? Books are seldom more than an author elaborating upon their obsession with the grammar of self-doubt. How superior are books to authors! Nothing believes in itself so much as a book; nothing is less bothered by history or propriety. "Begin in my middle," the book says. "Rifle straight to my end." What difference does it make? The book comes out of white, empty flyleaves and goes into the same oblivion. And the book is never afraid.

Day 3

Well, I did go on yesterday. Hiding under desks, scribbling like a madman. Not my finest hour.

I can't imagine what the librarian thinks of me. I hesitate to even continue this record. There is nothing quite like sleeping on a pile of books in a bottomless library to make one question the need for one more written account.

Be that as it may.

Since this errand will apparently take several days to complete, I think an inventory is in order.

Tins of cured fish (22)
Hardtack biscuits (53)
Dry sausage (2 links)
Chocolate (1 square)

The small, foil-wrapped square of chocolate was a particularly dastardly addition, and I can't help but suspect Byron was behind it. The chocolate pops into my mind much more often than I would like during the daily march. I could eat it, of course, but then there would be no chocolate, and having it around makes me feel things are not so desperate.

Perhaps I should explain why I was so agitated yesterday.

The first twelve hours I spent shut in with this fantastic collection were cordial enough. The librarian kept a brisk but not unreasonable pace; the pack was heavy but not insufferable. Marya kept me company, and without an audience to horrify, I engaged her in some lighthearted banter: those winsome observations and silly jokes that only a spouse can tolerate and enjoy.

I am quite sure this indulgence only made my subsequent descent into terror more dreadful.

I do not mean to suggest that my physical environment is unattractive. The chambers are full of carved wood and the loveliest fixtures. Wonderful frescoes span the ceilings, depicting scenes of robed philosophers gathering to debate, ecstatic battles between mounted armies, and glades overrun with sheep, grazing under the sleepy watch of barefoot shepherds. I gawked up so often and for so long that my neck developed a crick.

Oh, the profusion of books: the encyclopedias and dissertations, the plays and poems! During those first hours, whenever I entered a new chamber I would snatch up the first interesting title I encountered and begin reading like mad. I absorbed as much as I could during the cat's lazy transit of the room, until his disappearance into the next wing of the library forced me to shelve the book and run after him.

I can hardly imagine a more exhausting way to travel. Or read.

But as the hours slipped by and the presence of the Crumb dwindled in my blood, Marya, who had been an amiable companion before, began to change. She knocked books off shelves. When I asked her not to, she hurled them at me. Her appearance changed, too. No more the red helmet; no more the white blouse. Her skin turned to paint as it had in the Golden Zoo, showing a hundred hues of flesh, all shining and wet.

She left prints and streaks everywhere she went, walking with her hand out, drawing it over the shelves like a brush. It made me very anxious. I pleaded with her to stop.

I was having this argument with myself, of course, and yet somehow I still managed to lose.

Soon, the colors ran from her like muddy water, and beneath that fatuous skin, stood a machine.

The machine was nothing like the crude steam shovel I'd once stood in the mud to see. This machine was elegant and voluptuous; it was beautiful as all of the Sphinx's machines are. But its eyes were empty of that spark of life one expects to see. The last vestiges of my wife were gone, and I was left in the company of a dead-eyed doll.

It followed me everywhere I went, lashing out at the rooms like a snared animal. Oh, the wonders it tore! Miracles of thought, which perhaps survived here and nowhere else in the world, ripped up like wrapping paper.

The faster I marched, chasing the librarian ahead of me, him hissing in protest, the more violent the doll became. It reduced a room to splinters around me. It could not speak—its mouth was like the drain of a sink—but it could scream. And did as I ran.

I would've preferred a tiger. There is little more dreadful than resemblance.

The only thing that tamed it, I discovered out of pure exhaustion, was stillness. If I sat still, it calmed and waited. If I stirred, it stirred. If I ran, it screamed.

So, I began to write in self-defense.

When I woke this morning, all evidence of the mechanical doll was gone.

My bones ache, and I'm sure I have a fever, but I am so relieved to be free of the shrieking drudge I will suffer these symptoms without complaint.

(It occurs to me that I have felt this way before. When I fainted in the Golden Zoo, I hadn't caught a chill during our unanticipated bath, I was suffering the effects of withdrawal. It had been too many hours since I'd handled Marya's portrait.)

Yesterday, when I was running from that terror, I felt like such a victim. After all, I didn't ask for the Crumb; I did not seek out this habit. How could I deserve such a punishment as this? But now I wonder if I am so innocent. I wonder if I knew, if only on a subconscious level, what I was doing. I clung to that painting. And between the comfort it brought and the vivid visions of Marya, I felt less alone and, if I am honest, less responsible.

I am still having trouble deciphering my thoughts. They perform like an orchestra of soloists, each musician playing a different composition. How easy it is to hide from the truth amid such a constant din.

Nevertheless, there are realities I must begin to face.

The librarian was very cross when I gave him his breakfast. I can hardly blame him. He couldn't see what I believed was pursuing me. As far as he is concerned, I spent yesterday chasing him in a wild-eyed state. What would I have done if he had decided to leave me? This place is a maze; there are wings upon wings, rows on rows. I am lost.

I apologized profusely. I even offered him some of my sausage, but he has spent the past half hour with his nose in the corner. I suppose this is my punishment.

Oh, now he's yawning. Now he's stretching his back. Now it's time to go.

Chapter Nineteen

A bad painter only worries about how his barn looks.
He doesn't work his brush into the nooks and shadows. His barn is handsome enough from the road. But
when a wet spring comes, the eaves fall off. Do not
neglect inconvenient corners.

—*The Art of Painting a Barn* by Mr. B. Ritter

Day 4

I have eaten the chocolate. To the future me that reads this: I am sorry.
It was delicious.

And entirely deserved.

When Byron said there were traps, I didn't believe him. This place
is so attractive and congenial. I thought the stag was trying to provoke
me the way he does Edith. Unfortunately for me, he was in earnest.
The Sphinx is a trapper of men.

The absurdity of this is not lost on me. Snares in a library? What
next? Bears in the schools? Vipers in the hospitals?

The librarian knows where the traps are, I am convinced, and so
the going is absolutely safe so long as I never stray from his shadow.

Again. So long as I never do it again.

We'd had such an agreeable walk, and though I felt a little achy and
ill, I was in good spirits. How could I not be? My hallucinations had

ceased. For the first time in months, I was free of ghosts, and my head was beginning to clear.

The librarian was just tucking into his dinner, and I was sitting upwind at the opposite end of an atrium that seemed a sort of crossroads. Aisle after aisle broke off from the central courtyard. Some aisles sloped downward into shadow; others canted up toward light. Some turned sharply in a new direction and so seemed to dead-end. One aisle ran straight toward a point that was so distant all the shelves appeared to merge into one.

What an architectural onion this library is! I cannot imagine how it was built or filled.

I had just cleared a stack of brittle newspapers from a warm leather chair and was preparing to dive into a particularly interesting book I'd found about a Pelphian pastime called the Game of Oops, when my ears pricked to the distant sound of someone crying.

No, not crying: It was a low, consternated weeping.

I had heard this sort of sob before. In that old life of mine, a student would occasionally wander from the schoolyard during recess. I'd chase after them to turn them around and lecture them of the dangers of truancy. Unless I found them crying. Then I would walk with them in a wide circuit around the yard, careful to keep the school and the other children at a comfortable distance. I'd wait until their frustration began to wane, and then I would undertake the most egregious small talk. I'd say things like, "Oh, aren't the roses pretty this year!" Or, "Did you hear that Mr. Hardy caught a four-foot flounder?" Or that most miserable saw of polite conversation: "Do you think it will rain?" And so on, until the student, now dry-eyed and desperate to get away, would ask to be excused.

Oh, those were the little rescues of which I was so proud!

I followed the voice into a dim, narrow aisle. The space was so tight I had to turn to the side to enter it. More than once, I was forced to duck under or step over a volume that protruded into the lane. I felt like a leaf pressed in a book. I wanted to reverse course, to escape that strangled feeling, but the sobbing grew more distinct. I was sure it was a child.

The alley came to a corner, which I barely wedged around, and then opened upon a high, wide rotunda.

There were no furnishings there, and for the first time in days, I saw not a single book. Fat pillars of greenstone stood in a circle under a flawless, egg-white dome. It seemed the perfect place for giving speeches. The open floor before me was inset with a round, copper plate some thirty feet across. It resembled the Brick Layer's front door, right down to the embossed figures walking in a circle, though they were subtly changed. Rather than passing their bricks and sharing the load with smiles stamped upon their faces, these miserable figures struck at one another's backs with daggers and with spears.

A man lay on the floor at the precise center of the big coin. He—I presumed it was a he—was dressed in heavy leathers and curled nearly into a ball. His helmet, an old-fashioned iron morion, obscured his face.

The sobbing seemed to be coming from him.

From the brink of the medallion, I called, "Sir, madam, are you all right?"

There was no reply.

Without further deliberation, I rushed to the man's side. He lay curled, a little protectively it seemed, around a drain in the floor. A child's pale hand reached up through the iron grating, like a prisoner in a foul oubliette. The sobbing emerged from that bleak recess.

"I'm here," I said, leaning over the curled man. I grasped the child's hand.

Then everything went very oddly.

I realized the child's hand was made of wood an instant before I felt the click of a switch travel up through it. A heavy clang shuddered the floor.

I stepped away from the grate, and the room tilted. The ground ahead of me began to descend. Teetering onto my toes, I glimpsed the darkness hiding under the floor.

I fell backward over the leathered body, and the great medallion leveled again.

My fall jogged the helmet from the man's head. The skull behind it was as brown as a raisin. I scooted away in revulsion, and the floor sank under me. I threw myself upon the skeleton again, and the ground righted. I tried another direction and was thwarted by the same result.

Whichever way I stepped, the whole, heavy plate of the medallion tilted and chased me back into the arms of the corpse.

I was sitting on a plate balanced upon a point, and beneath me was a yawning gulf, a nothing, a bottomless pit.

I was trapped.

(The librarian is asleep, and I am exhausted. I'll finish this account in the morning, unless some horror befalls me in my sleep. In which case, there will be no point to bragging about the time I cheated death.)

Day 5

(I survived the night! Books make terrible bedding. The librarian is eating breakfast. I think I will endure the stink of it this morning. Somehow, the thought of sitting off on my own has lost its appeal.)

It was quite something to realize I'd been caught in another man's trap. I had laid so many of my own, I suppose I thought myself immune. Worse, it was an obvious trap: an empty room, a funny floor, an unresponsive body, and the sound of a bawling child. Really, what else could it have been?

But what sort of paranoid and conscienceless person puts a trap in a library? The Sphinx wishes to distinguish himself from Marat, who seems bent on destroying the records of our race for reasons I cannot fathom but which I presume are ignoble and shortsighted. Yet is it any better to preserve the canon of human thought by making it inaccessible and unfriendly to all? One man destroys; the other man hides. The difference seems academic.

I do wonder how the Sphinx managed to capture and replay a human voice. His technology is so advanced it hardly makes sense; it just seems a sort of casual magic. It's bizarre to think that right now Madame Bhata is likely sitting in her web of yarn, sewing a crude record of the day's events in hieroglyphs and hatch marks. Meanwhile, the Sphinx has divined a method for bottling voices!

How different would the world be if such wonders were to get out?

But, back to the trap.

The grate with the protruding lever of a hand wouldn't come off, no matter how I pried. The sobbing stopped once the trap was sprung, which was a small mercy. It was one thing to rot in stoic silence; it was quite another to be serenaded to death by a bawling child.

Since I had no choice but to sit so close, I could not help but scrutinize my companion. I came to the conclusion that he had been some sort of errant knight. The antiquated helmet, the leather armor, and the brocaded tabard, balled like a pillow under his head—it all suggested nobility. He had perished coming to the aid of what he thought was a child in distress. Whoever he was, we were kindred at least in this.

I wondered how long he lasted before succumbing to dehydration. On closer inspection, I made the grim discovery that much of his leather jerkin had been systematically chewed.

The thought crossed my mind that the librarian might come to my rescue, and I spent perhaps a quarter of an hour shouting for him. But the more I cried for the cat to come (a bankrupt prospect from the start), the more I wondered what exactly I expected him to do. Fetch a rescue party? It hardly seemed likely. And what had Byron said: Once the librarian went looking for a book, nothing turned his head?

I wish to spare myself the embarrassment of recording all the troubled thoughts that spooled through my head while I sat in the lap of the dead knight. But who would I be hiding the truth from? The oblivion of a shelf? The possibility of another trap, another pit I shan't escape? Or perhaps I wish to hide the truth from myself?

The trouble is, I did not dwell upon the subjects I should have. Faced with a slow death, I should have reflected upon my life with Marya, both the one that we shared and the one we anticipated, a life cut short by my arrogance and prudishness.

But I did not meditate on such regrets.

Instead, I thought of how diligently I had deceived myself in the months since our separation. First, I hid my doubt, then my despair, and then my fear. It seems a conspicuous litany of flaws to blame upon the Crumb. I can't in good conscience do it.

I recalled my impression of the old woman I saw long ago at the foot of the Tower, scouring the Lost and Found with a determination, which, at the start of my own ordeal, seemed far from noble. I thought her weak and neurotic. And I believed I was superior to such a trap. Hope. What is its dimension? How long is it? Where does it lead? When does it become habitual, automatic, the answer not only to doubt, but also to action, and redemption, and living?

Again and again, I thought not of Marya, but of Edith: her patience, her resilience, her poise, and her sound advice amid all of my bad. I thought of the coincidental embraces we shared, all the occasions when fate put us in each other's arms, an innocent thing, but not unaware. Not without feeling. And I wanted to survive, because if I did, I knew I would see her again.

Is that wrong? Is it wrong to miss what is attainable?

I spent perhaps an hour in a state of absolute turmoil before concluding that I would rather die trying to escape than die chewing up my clothes.

The proud headmaster in me resurged, and I thought, *This is the sort of thing I can puzzle my way out of.* Which may seem a completely asinine thing to think. But I have learned a little arrogance in the face of death is not the worst approach.

I studied the copper floor, the green pillars, which marked the shoreline I would eventually have to leap for, and the unblemished dome above. While craning about, I stumbled again and again over my companion. It began to seem a sort of clowning routine. I tried not to think about him because I knew he had stared at this room for hours, days, until he withered away. He had pondered himself to death. Which didn't bode well for me.

What did I have that he didn't?

I began to wonder how well the trap would work if a dozen men were standing on the plate when it was sprung. The more men, the more likely it seemed that the unbalance would be sudden and fatal. Even if by some miracle the men were evenly distributed, they would all have to leap clear at once, or most of them would end up in the hole.

Probably, the only hopeful scenario was one in which two level-headed and similarly weighted individuals were standing together on the fulcrum at the moment when the trap was activated. If they had any presence of mind, it would not be too difficult for them to pace in exactly opposing directions, using each other's weight as a counterbalance, until they both had traversed safely back to solid ground.

And in this lay the revelation: What did I have that my poor stranded companion did not? I had a counterbalance. I had *him*.

The trouble, of course, was getting a dead man to walk.

But he didn't have to walk. He could slide.

I spread out his tabard and rolled him upon it, hoping that the length of felt would be as good as a sled. I did not allow myself to dwell on what I planned to do; I suspected on this occasion consideration was the enemy of courage.

I set my heel on the corpse's side and pushed him away.

I won't pretend the production went smoothly. I overestimated the skeleton's weight and almost slid off at once. The slope brought him coasting after me, and I had to leap over him as he flew past. One of us got off center, and the plate tilted in a new direction. I tried to correct it, but sent the gallant knight sliding back to center instead.

After all that hopping and sliding, we were back where we began.

My second attempt was more considered. By degrees, I managed to shift the knight toward the opposite shore of the plate. I shuffled forward, and he retreated; I shuffled backward, and he stopped. Our telescopic dance went on for what seemed hours, but which could scarcely have been more than a few minutes.

When at last I had backed my way to the edge of the trap, it occurred to me that the moment I stepped off the plate, the knight would be unceremoniously dumped into the void. It seemed an unkind way to handle the man who had saved my life, but there was no helping it.

Stepping from the coin, I glimpsed the abyss beneath and the spire upon which the plate balanced. Then the floor fell again, and the knight was gone.

I returned to the crossroads where I had left the librarian and found him curled upon my backpack, sleeping on his tins of food like a dragon on its hoard.

Chapter Twenty

The lion's share of blunders occur in the final hour of a job. Pails are kicked, hinges painted over, and brushes lost in the lime. When the end is in sight, mind how you go.

—*The Art of Painting a Barn* by Mr. B. Ritter

Day 6

I've been monstrously ill all day. I'm rattled by chills and hobbled by vertigo. What I wouldn't give for a bed, a bed warmer, and a bowl of broth. I'd rather eat a sand dollar than another cracker.

I had hoped my recovery would follow some reliable upward trajectory. Instead, it has felt as if I am surveying the peaks and valleys of a strange hinterland. Down I go into troughs of absolute dread and discomfort, only to ascend some moments later into clarity and calm, which endure just long enough to sharpen the next decline.

When will it end?

I have been repeatedly forced to halt our progress to catch my breath, an event that the librarian, that orange opportunist, uses to beg for food. He has allowed me to doze once or twice, though each time I have awoken from the most appalling nightmares. If my condition worsens, I wonder if I'll be able to go on. But what choice do I have? What choice did the Sphinx give me? I can almost understand how a man like Marat would come to loathe such a cold-blooded master.

For the first time since beginning this terrible errand, I am glad to be alone. I would not want to be seen like this. Dignity is entirely ephemeral; it is like the dust of a butterfly's wing. Once shed, it is impossible to recover. Besides, I do not wish to extort any more kindness from my friends. They have already lavished enough patience upon me.

Despite my delirium, I think I detect a change in my environment. I don't trust my senses well enough at the moment to be sure of it, but I suspect I have entered a new hemisphere of the athenaeum.

I still hear plaintive calls and sobs come from the dark rows of the stacks, but I have no difficulty ignoring them now. I have learned my lesson. Though the voices make me feel quite alone.

The librarian must suspect I am ill. Quite uncharacteristically, the furry academic has just spent the past half hour curled upon my lap. I did not dare pet him, but I appreciated the warmth and the company.

Tomorrow will be the seventh day of our journey. I choose to believe it will be the day that I lay my hands on the Sphinx's book on zoetropes, the day we turn around and start the walk home.

Home. What a funny word to use for all that lies behind me.

Day 7

I am halfway through my food, and still there is no end in sight. (What a stupid phrase to use while wandering through a maze. Of course the end isn't in sight! That's the entire enterprise of a labyrinth!) Tomorrow I will begin to ration the biscuits. Somehow, I doubt the librarian will submit to such an injustice.

What on earth am I going to say to Edith?

Obviously, a proper apology is required. These are not sentiments one can rap through a door. I have been making too much of myself. I am not a man of destiny. The Tower is not punishing me. I am one of millions, and my troubles are really quite usual.

The question I keep returning to is this: When does chasing after lost love turn into self-loathing? Can a soul be loved quite sincerely and just as sincerely be lost? The disciplinarian in me wants to believe that punishment is redemptive, but if whipping were any good at reforming a man, would I not be a saint by now?

I must forgive myself. I must beg the pardons that I owe. And I must decide to make my life more than a tribute to past failures.

I have committed to go as far as Pelphia, and I am resolved to do so, though in all honesty, I do not expect to find Marya there. I am sure the Sphinx is clever enough to discover a few details of my rather public life to bait me with. All he had to do was say *red helmet*, and I happily signed my ship away. What a fool. I can't afford to continue to be so desperate, so naive. I imperil my friends!

If Marya is not there, I will not carry the search any further. It has been almost a year since I wandered away from her and she from me, almost a year since I began turning in this maze, expecting to see the end appear around every new corner.

This must end in Pelphia. One way or another, it must end.

Day 8

I woke up this morning thinking about what I had written last night, which is never a good sign.

Ah, this is the devil of writing in ink! A pencil allows one to speculate and retract, to play a card and then renege. But ink immortalizes gestures and moods and muttered truths. If pencils were all we had, I suspect there would be far fewer books.

I did briefly consider scratching out a line or two of what I wrote, but the specter of Luc Marat's black library does not linger far from my thoughts.

And the truth is, I don't want to take it back. I stand by what I have written, and I want to add a further taboo to the record.

I think Edith Winters is an attractive woman.

There.

I haven't the formal training to elaborate upon this point. That is the domain of poets. They know how to organize an ode, how to polish a woman's features separately, then arrange them like pieces of fruit in a bowl. They are adept at making astute observations about the troubled quality of beauty; they do not struggle to produce sensitive metaphors. They have the courage to speak.

If there were some form of verse composed only of ellipses, interjections, and parentheses, I would be a bard!

There can be no doubt about it now: The rooms are shrinking, and they have been for days.

At first, I thought I was suffering from claustrophobia, a condition that sometimes afflicted me in my youth. Claustrophobia is such a useless and intense feeling. I know very well the tricks it plays upon the senses: Space constricts, the body tightens, and the world seems to inhale forever and ever.

I knew I could not afford to give in to claustrophobia, and indeed, my renunciation of the panic was so firm that it persisted even after I began to bang my head on doorways and stir ceiling lamps with my shoulders. When I realized at last that I was walking with my nose down, like a hen chasing a tick, I had no choice but to admit it was not my imagination. The rooms were really growing smaller.

Not only smaller, but less distinct, too. The corners of the rooms, softening at first, have now completely vanished. The white plaster has flaked away, revealing the chiseled stone underneath. All evidence of chambers has ended. If the passage constricts any more, I will be forced to crawl along on my hands and knees. I will have to live as a mole.

All the pretty vestiges of the library, the frescoes and gargoyles and flowering capitals, have surrendered to the pinching of space. Except the books—they linger still, though without any shelves. They line the floor at my elbows, lying in the dust, their corners balding in the grit, their pages sagging like fat between the bones of their bindings.

One might reasonably expect these books to be the most worthy, the most valuable and occult of the collection. Why else stow them in such an inconvenient shaft? But they appear to be common novels, fairy tales, and quaint family manuscripts. These works are the very soul of mediocrity. It seems appropriate that I squirm among them.

I feel as if I have wandered into a mine shaft, but rather than coal or minerals, books are the ore, the ceiling, and the floor. If I rolled onto my back and plucked a volume from one of the tightly packed ribs above, I believe I would be crushed by the ensuing collapse. What seemed a pleasant perfume in the library, here tastes like depleted air; it is as if these books have breathed all the sweetness in and exhaled a thin and sour gas.

The librarian slinks before me, his tail raised nearly to the limit of our tunnel. He leads me like a color guard. When he looks back to see if I am still with him, his eyes shine like chartreuse stars. I make no qualms about petting him now when we take our rest. I feel quite fortunate to have him with me.

What did the Sphinx say? *Books are traps.* But how are they so, and whom do they trap: the author or the reader? Perhaps they are just the boasts of vainglorious minds, and what we hold up as literature is in fact a cult of unlikable characters. I hate to think they are like a fishing weir to the swimming mind, a trap easily swum into but rarely escaped: a neurosis, a dogma, a dream.

No, no, I must not be so cynical! If books are traps, then let them be like terrariums: sealed-up and still-living miniatures of the world.

Light bulbs run upon an electric vine. I have to take care not to crush them as I writhe along. The bulbs cast such a feeble light I can hardly see these letters as I write them.

I have tried to recollect everything I know about zoetropes, since that is the subject of my errand. As I recall, a zoetrope is a cylindrical device that contains a series of subtly different images, which, when spun before a candle and observed from the right angle, give the impression of movement. A zoetrope is the sort of trifle that adults show off at parties.

I don't believe the Sphinx honestly needs the book. This has all been an outing to clear my head. I won't pretend it was unwarranted or ill conceived. But now that my head is clear, I am left to wonder, when does the exercise end? When will we turn around?

Day 9 (or thereabouts)

I think it's the ninth day. It may still be the eighth, or perhaps it's the tenth, or eleventh. I let Byron's pocket watch run down. What a silly thing. The librarian can't be relied upon to tell me when it's dinnertime. He would eat at any hour, even beyond appetite and good health, and I do not wish to be stuck in a tunnel with a sick cat.

My knees are ready to come off; my trousers are frayed half to rags. I can hardly force myself to crawl anymore. The librarian could have the decency to look concerned, but he seems not at all worried. I wonder if he knows how much food he has. Perhaps he would be willing to share. Surely his tinned fish can't be so different from pickled herring, which I have often enjoyed. Come to think of it, the two aromas are not so different. Perhaps spread upon a cracker...

Byron was right. I want to eat the cat's food. I must think of something else.

It's awfully uncomfortable to write while lying on one's stomach. So, I will get to the point of my present thoughts: I know I do not deserve it, but I would greatly appreciate a rescue. If Edith were to come crawling the other way just now, a fate I would not wish on her of course, I would weep with joy.

I have encountered a cave-in. The way is blocked by a great jumble of books.

I spent the past half hour trying to convince the librarian to turn around. Either we are lost or we have been thwarted by a structural failure, and regardless of which it is, pawing and scratching at the pile won't change the fact that we *cannot go on.*

I'm not sure whether there is enough room to turn around, or if I will have to undertake a backward crawl for some distance. If I try to turn about and get stuck, I will die here. I am going to die here. I don't want to write anymore. What is this for? Who is this for?

The cat has just batted me twice on the nose. It was necessary, if humiliating. At least I feel more composed.

The librarian is convinced we must go forward, so I will undertake an excavation. The odds seem fair enough that I will only weaken the structure further and bring the library down on my head. I can only hope the Sphinx's book on zoetropes is near the front of this cave-in.

And since this may very well be my final word, I would just like to say, I have no regrets about coming down here. I feel much better, actually. I loved my wife. I loved my friends. Goodbye.

Chapter Twenty-One

The essential lesson of the zoetrope is this: Movement, indeed all progress, even the passage of time, is an illusion. Life is the repetition of stillness.

—*Zoetropes and Magic Lanterns: An Introduction to Moving Stills*

Senlin's excavation became a worming, and the worming became a burial as the tunnel buckled and collapsed.

It had never occurred to him how unforgiving books were until he lay at the bottom of a great pile of them. They were all hard corners and rough cloth. The saw teeth of fore edges slit his hands as he searched for air amid the folios, finding none. Every breath he surrendered returned shorter and tighter. Yet incredibly, he suffered no panic within the crushing dark, just a broad regret that he would die so far from his friends, so far from anyone, in fact, that he might never be found and so be forced to share an eternity with the unremarkable and the unread.

The pressure abated all at once, and he found himself sledding down a metal chute. He tumbled amid a shower of books and landed with a bump upon a plain, plank floor.

Volumes continued to dribble out, pelting him upon the back and shoulders, until at last the librarian leapt down from the open vent and concluded the little avalanche. The cat looked perfectly composed.

Senlin imagined he'd had the good sense to stand well clear of the collapse.

"Perhaps I should hire you on as a chimney sweep," the Sphinx said, looming over him, his mask a shadowy cavity. Senlin gave a startled yelp. "Oh, don't be so dramatic," the Sphinx said, leaning away. "Stand up, stand up."

Senlin attempted to compose himself, but the hours he'd spent on first his knees and then his stomach had rubberized his legs. With some effort, he got his feet under him and straightened his back. A bolt of pleasurable lightning ran up his spine. It was only then that his environment came into relief. He had fallen out the bottom of the Bottomless Library into someone's private quarters.

A pair of leather boots, bent at the ankle and ashen with age, lay at the foot of a rotting field cot. A dented canteen on a strap hung on the back of the only door. Six or seven small volumes, insufficient to justify a shelf, lay upon a petite writing desk, which was attended by a spindly stool. Other than an oil portrait upon the wall, the room was quite austere. It reminded him of a neglected wing in a museum, and he would not have been surprised to see labels pinned beneath the humble relics.

"Is this your room?" he asked.

"Don't be absurd. You will never see my room. Do you have my book?"

Senlin voiced an "ah" that stretched into a musical phrase. He looked about for the librarian, not to blame him, but in the scant hope that the cat would come to his defense.

He found the big tabby sitting with his white paws perched upon one of the volumes that had followed them down. Senlin retrieved it and read the title. "*Zoetropes and Magic Lanterns: An Introduction to Moving Stills*. My word. You found it," Senlin said with unvarnished awe. The tabby blinked at him affectionately.

"He really is a wonderful librarian," the Sphinx said, taking the volume from Senlin's suspended hand.

His amazement shifted from the cat to this unlikely reunion. "How did you get here?"

"By elevator, of course," the Sphinx said, stowing the book inside his cloak. "I'm not the one who needed a walk, Tom. I'm not the one who needed to clear his head. But don't let your thoughts run back to your friends just yet. You'll see them soon enough. There are one or two things we must discuss first."

It felt unfair to have someone so enigmatic call him by his first name, though Senlin could hardly protest. "If it's about the Crumb, I am cured of it. The visions have stopped."

"Bravo. But, no, that's not what I've come to talk to you about. I want to—" The Sphinx saw Senlin's gaze flit to the portrait behind him. "Do you like it?"

"Yes, I think so. There's something unusual about it."

"What I wouldn't give to see it for the first time. Familiarity is such a cataract. I can't see past my stale impression of it anymore." The Sphinx moved to stand at Senlin's elbow so they could regard the painting together. "Please, tell me what you see."

The portrait was formal in style but rustic in subject: A plainly dressed man sat upon a stool before a great, golden haystack, framed narrowly by an untroubled sky. At first glance, it was a common pastoral scene: the country laborer romanticized for the urban landlord. But the more Senlin looked at it, the more complex the humble character became.

"He has one of the strongest brows I've ever seen. It's incredible, almost a turtle shell." Senlin cupped his mouth and drew his hand down to his chin. It all felt a little surreal. A moment before he had been grappling with his mortality; now he was playing the art critic. Somehow it was easier to feign composure than to express his lingering distress. "I suppose he's about sixty years old, though it's difficult to tell. There's nothing ostentatious about him: His collar, shirt, and boots are all quite practical. He looks the sort of fellow who would trim his own hair." Senlin leaned nearer, studying the undertones of the skin. "I recognize the style. Is it an Ogier?"

"It is." Senlin could feel the Sphinx watching him closely.

"The mustache is a departure. It's so thin and dapper," Senlin said, absently scratching the whiskers on his cheek. "It seems like a vestige of a former life, like the aging madam who still paints on a beauty mark every morning." The Sphinx sniffed at this, and Senlin could not tell if it was in stifled amusement or irritation. "His complexion is a little inscrutable. I would hazard to guess he's either a native of the south, or he's from the pale east and spent his days outdoors under the sun."

"Very good," the Sphinx said, and Senlin clearly heard pleasure in his tone.

"A laborer, I should think, or a craftsman. Look how knotty his hands are." Senlin sketched the air over the painting with a finger. "Look how he displays them on his knees. He's proud of his hands."

"That is one of the most accurate descriptions of the Brick Layer I have ever heard."

"That's the Brick Layer?" Senlin looked again and tried to reconcile this relatively unassuming man with the grandeur of the Tower. It was impossible.

"Don't you recognize the stool?" the Sphinx said, touching the modest seat that stood by the desk. Senlin saw veneration in the act. This was not a museum after all; it was a shrine. "He was always moving. That's why he had so few things. Everything he owned, everything you see here could be packed on a mule at a moment's notice. He slept where the hods slept, and since their beds rose with the work, his did as well."

"He toted around a portrait of himself?" Senlin said with a touch of levity, though he saw at once it was not appreciated.

"Don't be crass. I hung it there. He was not at all a vain man, though he had every reason to be. You said he looked sixty. When he sat for this, he was one hundred and nine years old."

"That's incredible," Senlin said as charitably as he could.

The Sphinx was not fooled. "You don't think it's possible? Believe me, it is."

"Are you speaking from experience?"

"Well, aren't you fearless."

"Sir, I have spent the past ten days being terrorized by hallucinations, fever, and lethal traps. A few minutes ago, I penned my goodbyes because I thought I was going to die. Anything you do to me will seem a reprieve."

"Wonderful!" The Sphinx laughed. "Now I see what Marya saw in you."

Despite his profession of invulnerability, Senlin could not help but be upset. "Surely I have proven my character by now. I have signed your contract; I have delivered your book. Would you please tell me what you know about my wife?"

The Sphinx emitted a sigh that pitched and scraped like a braking train. "Not everything. I know she resides in Pelphia. I know she has some connection to Wilhelm Horace Pell, who is a powerful duke, though I'm not sure about the nature of her association with him. She may be on his staff; she may be his guest. It has been several months since I last had my eyes on her, but I have seen no evidence that her situation has changed."

"How many months?"

"Ten months. It was early October, I believe."

"October!" Senlin meant to scoff, but the sound stuck in his throat and came out as a strangled groan. It was already July. How many lives had he lived since October? He'd been a bookkeeper, a pirate captain, and now a spy. And how many lives would Marya have lived? He felt horribly cheated. "How can you claim to know anything with any certainty? Ten months!"

"I beg your pardon. I know a great deal," the Sphinx said with sharper inflection. "My eyes inside Pelphia haven't been very reliable of late, but nothing passes into or out of the port without my knowledge. I would know if she had left."

Senlin couldn't stop shaking his head. "Even if it were by the black trail? Even if it were by funeral pyre?"

"Perhaps not. But I presume she is generally well and looked after."

"Why would you assume such a thing? Everyone I have met here has either become a hod, an outcast, or a corpse. Assuming anyone is well and looked after is just delusional!"

The Sphinx rose up until he seemed to stand en pointe. The silver tuning fork he'd once used to smite a swarm of butterflies appeared in his hand. "Do not bark at me, Thomas Senlin. I will stop your heart."

Senlin raised his hands at once and retreated a step. "I'm sorry. I meant no offense. I was only a little surprised."

The sparking wand vanished again into his sleeve. "I assume she is safe because the alternative would discourage you, and we both know that you must see this through. Your life will remain a quagmire till you do. I need your eyes in Pelphia; you need my assistance to get there. *That* is why you will assume Marya is healthy and whole and waiting to be found."

Senlin absorbed the Sphinx's words with a dry, difficult swallow. The Sphinx was right in one respect at least: He had to see this through. "Thank you for telling me," he said hoarsely.

"You're welcome." The Sphinx turned to the room's only exit. "Now, there's something I would like you to see. I think it might cheer you up."

The adjoining room seemed the very antithesis of cheerful. Dimly lit, low of ceiling, and stale of air, the room was dominated by a structure that resembled a boarded-up gazebo.

"What is it?" Senlin said, peering through one of the slits between staves. He saw nothing in the dark recesses of the installation.

"It is a device for animating still images."

"A zoetrope? It's enormous. I thought they were toys."

"As far as you're concerned, they probably are. Technology tends to degenerate the further it flows from its source. That's no conspiracy. It's just the natural process of users modifying a machine to their level of understanding. The wise man's tool becomes the simpleton's toy."

"Simpleton!" Senlin said with a crow of offense.

"Don't be so sensitive, Tom. Enjoy the moment. Before you stands a wonder of the world: Ogier's Zoetrope. You cannot fathom the kind of genius required to create such a thing. Sixty-four painted panels on which every touch of the brush, every tint of paint is exactly tuned to the next image in the sequence."

Senlin's face tightened as he tried to imagine such a thing. "May I see it spin?"

"First, we must install your panel. May I have your Ogier?"

Senlin produced the rolled-up canvas. It had bent inside his breast pocket and was beginning to fray at the edges. He felt a little ashamed to have handled such a valuable artifact so roughly.

An iron band divided the zoetrope into two hemispheres: The top half was slatted like a fence; the bottom contained a succession of cabinet doors, each emblazoned with a number plate, one to sixty-four. The Sphinx turned the wheel by hand until the number three stood before him. He opened the cabinet, extracted an empty wooden frame, and began the delicate work of mounting the masterpiece.

"If there's even a single crease, it will spoil the effect," the Sphinx said as he tightened the stretcher.

"How many paintings do you have?"

"Patience, Tom." The Sphinx reseated the now-filled frame inside the cabinet. "We must take our seats. This is only the projection room. You didn't honestly think the Brick Layer meant to squeeze sixty-four dignitaries, plus their husbands, wives, and retinues, inside this closet, did you? That's no way to premiere a miracle. Come on."

The Sphinx skirted the zoetrope, opening a door secluded in the shadows. Senlin followed him into a swinging forest of black curtains.

The Sphinx seemed to vanish, and for a disturbing moment Senlin thought he had somehow wandered under the Sphinx's robes. He cast about while the heavy drapes caressed him with unwanted familiarity.

Shuddering with revulsion, he broke upon a well-lit and echoing stage.

The bright auditorium before him rose so steeply it seemed a sheer bluff. Hundreds, perhaps thousands of white, velvet seats packed the slope and the balcony above. The plaster ceiling resembled a vast nautilus shell, split in half, its chambers spiraling toward a colossal chandelier, the likes of which he had never seen before. It resembled a great branching frond of transparent seaweed. The flat leaves mingled with milky globes of electric light. It was breathtaking.

Not waiting for Senlin to take it all in, the Sphinx descended from the shallow stage and began to mount the steep flights between rows. Closing his mouth, Senlin hurried after the black gash of a figure, taking the stairs two at a time and never gaining any ground on the tireless Sphinx. Breathing heavily, Senlin sidled out to where the Sphinx sat, centered upon the snowy bank, his stark robes piled about him like the melted skirt of a candle.

Before them, squared under the black proscenium, was a perfectly white backdrop.

The Sphinx said, "I'm going to turn the lights down. Don't be afraid." The shining orbs above them dimmed until they were no brighter than twilight stars.

"I'm not scared of the dark," Senlin said, sinking into the plush seatback.

The Sphinx leaned over their shared armrest and said in a chorusing whisper, "Not the dark, you silly man. The light."

Color burst upon the auditorium, fierce as morning sun upon a sleeper's face. Senlin flinched and blinked at the assault but refused to look away.

He gaped at the rippling reservoir of the Bath that beamed at him. Light scattered over the water in shimmering scales, fine and dense as the mail of a fish. The girl, now a giantess, was no longer frozen. Her ankles stirred her shadow in the water; her braids swayed over the back of her bathing dress. The folded boat in her hand, firmly pinched at first, loosened and began to slip from her grasp. Then the scene restarted with a jarring burst of white, and the boat appeared cinched between her fingers again.

This final flare was not the only of its kind: The scene strobed like a cloud overflowing with lightning. The repetition was hypnotic. Tears welled in his eyes.

"How is this possible?" he whispered.

"Do you know what a camera obscura is?"

"No."

"Mirrors, my boy. And a trick or two more."

Senlin made an effort to time the sequence and decided it was no longer than five seconds. Five seconds! He wondered how many years of Ogier's life it had taken to create these five seconds of absolute sublimity.

"The flashes are from the empty frames," the Sphinx said. "Out of the original sixty-four, twenty-eight paintings are still in circulation."

"But isn't that where they are supposed to be?"

The Sphinx changed the subject. "Tell me what you see. Describe it as you did the Brick Layer. Refresh my impression."

Senlin frowned at the feint but dutifully answered the request. "I see the Baths. The reservoir. I've been there. It's like the ocean with the fury poured off. He's captured the light and the gauzy quality of the air perfectly."

"What about the girl?"

"I have wondered about her. It's always struck me as a melancholy choice to have posed her facing away. I wonder why Ogier did it. She's obviously just a child, and yet look how world-weary she seems. There's something—*bereft* about her, isn't there? Of course, I could be completely wrong. One thing I know about children: They're more pensive than adults give them credit for. We often misread them badly."

"True."

Senlin closed his eyes for a moment and savored the respite from the glaring light. "Who is she?"

"You've covered the setting and the girl, but you've missed something quite significant. Look at the water under the boat," the Sphinx said.

Senlin studied the spot beneath the dangling paper boat. After a moment, he glimpsed something, a cursive-like movement of light. The effect reminded him of using an ember to draw in the night air. The ghostly trail lingered just long enough for his mind to distinguish a shape before a flash of white consumed it.

"Was that a number? Was that a nineteen?"

"It was."

"Why are there numbers?

"It's part of the combination."

"To what?"

"To the heavens, of course," the Sphinx said. The animation stopped abruptly, and the lights came up. Senlin felt disoriented by the reappearance of the pale slope of empty seats about them. "Come, I'll show you."

In his former life, there had been little in the world Senlin loathed more than a theater lobby. The charmless corrals were filled with patrons who came and went with all the poise of a general panic. And though everyone was too busy elbowing one another into stanchions to pay anyone else's appearance the slightest attention, this never stopped one and all from flaunting their station in life through the display of canes, cravats, brooches, décolletages, muffs, watch chains, perfumes, and professionally coached accents.

So it was strange for him to stand in a lobby and feel so at ease.

There were no red rope mazes, no underpaid ushers in imperious uniforms. The low chandeliers were no brighter than a candle on a bedside. Sofas and upholstered chairs encircled attractive rugs. Beyond this comfortable lounge, a row of elevators stood open, their interiors glowing with a warm, yellow light. The only interruption to the procession of inviting exits was a shut steel door. It seemed the sort of thing one might find in a bank. Senlin was disappointed but not surprised when the Sphinx marched straight to it.

Naturally, the vault door included a tumbler, which stood out like an illuminated eye. The tumbler was marked with a hundred digits, which seemed a tad excessive to Senlin, though he was no expert in such matters. A relatively discreet plaque beside the vault was embossed with the curious phrase, THE BRIDGE OF BABEL.

"What's in there?" Senlin asked.

"I don't know."

Senlin was surprised by the Sphinx's frankness. "I thought all of this was your home."

"Inherited home, yes, but this vault was installed by the Brick Layer before my time. I do not have the combination."

"What's this about a bridge?"

The Sphinx laid his hand on Senlin's shoulder. The contact made him shiver. Senlin turned to stare into his own distorted reflection. He could hear the Sphinx's raspy breathing behind the mirror. "Tom, I am going to ask you to entertain an alternative view of the world. First, you'll find it funny; then it will make you angry; then you'll be frightened. It's all perfectly natural. It is the feeling of discovery, and it grows more unsettling the older we get. I want you to persevere."

Senlin squared his shoulders. "All right. Enlighten me."

"What if I told you that this floor and everything beneath it, this ceiling and everything above it, all the brick and mortar that surrounds us, is not part of a tower?"

"It's not a tower? Well, it certainly is an elaborate decoy."

"It is in fact a bridge. An unfinished bridge."

"A bridge? To what? The moon?" He couldn't help but smile at the thought.

"Yes. The moon, the planets, the stars, and everything else. It is a bridge to the heavens."

"That's preposterous. You can't build a bridge to the air. If you build to the air, it is called a tower. You're playing some sort of semantic game."

"I am not. It is a bridge. Not to the air, but to the edge of our world's influence. The whole universe waits to be explored. And we're stuck here, squabbling in the mud."

For the first time, it occurred to him that the Sphinx might be utterly mad. If not mad, then at least obsessed. And Senlin had signed a contract with him. He had rejected Marat's hopeless crusade only to join a man who was jousting with the stars.

"If you remember nothing else of what I say, remember this: When humanity ceases to aspire, it begins to decline. Do you know why the status quo is so tyrannical and nauseating? Because it does not exist! There is no stasis in the world, and certainly not where humans are involved. The status quo is just a pleasing synonym for decay. You've seen what the Tower inspires: cruelty, apathy, casual violence, self-destruction, and empty gratification. Those are the fruits of the Tower."

Senlin rubbed the furrow in his brow. "I won't argue with that characterization."

"You cannot. It was not meant to be a tower, a stratum of senseless competition and oppression, a structure that requires war to renew it like a forest needs fire to prosper. What a barbaric thing! The Brick Layer aspired to better. He knew harmony was not a symptom of plenty, or political climate, or even that crushing stalemate your kings call *peace*. Harmony is the result of purpose. So the bridge was imagined, and construction begun."

"But what happened? If this is truly a bridge, why didn't he finish it?"

The Sphinx turned his face away. "He came to the limit of his day's technology. He came to the limit of his life. He realized that years—decades—would be required to develop the understanding, the expertise, necessary to continue the work. The halt was supposed to be temporary, a time of invention, research, and preparation. Instead, men took the opportunity to lay their stakes, to shore up their power, and to demean the hod. Thus, the unfinished bridge became a finished but unworthy tower."

Senlin bit his tongue, but he wanted to say it didn't matter what the Brick Layer had envisioned; it only mattered what he had built. And that was the Tower: the very thing the Sphinx blamed but refused to take responsibility for.

He felt a stirring at his feet. He looked down to find the librarian butting his head upon his pant leg. The cat looked up, then rubbed his chin on the same spot. Senlin bent and scratched the librarian behind his ears.

"Inside this vault there is the means to restart the work. A catalyst. A plan. The way forward, the way upward. Our redemption lies behind that door."

"How do you know?"

"I know it as I know many things I cannot begin to explain to you," the Sphinx snapped. "The Brick Layer built the zoetrope and distributed the paintings so each ringdom would hold a piece of the vision. He insisted upon cooperation, and to ensure it, he embedded the combination in the animation of the frames. The vault can only be opened when all the panels are present."

"If cooperation is so important, why have you begun to collect the panels on your own?"

"Generations of war and turmoil have dimmed the memories of many men. The ringdoms have forgotten their promise. For years, I have watched carefully, and I have only intervened when a panel was threatened by obscurity or neglect."

"Then you would open the vault yourself? Whatever is in there, whatever the catalyst is, you would unbox it on your own?"

"If I must. You have to understand, I am fighting for the future of our race, and there are those who would see all come to ruin."

"You mean Marat," Senlin said.

"You may think you know him, but you do not. He means to lock us out, to keep the work from continuing. This rebellion he stirs is not for the good of the hod. He doesn't care about them, not really. He is a cynic who would rather preside over ruin than see our race ascend."

"He doesn't think much better of you."

"But what do you think of him? Were you charmed?"

"I sympathize with some of his sentiments, but his methods are wicked. He tried to kill my friends; he tried to kill me. He appointed himself judge and jury of the hods and apparently hasn't any conscience against capital punishment. He's trained his followers to systematically blot out perfectly good books, for heaven's sake. No, I wasn't charmed!"

"He calls it meditation, all that scribbling. Back to front so they never accidentally read a word, until after a while, the words start to lose their meaning; they become abstract shapes. He wants his followers to unlearn the act of reading and thought."

"Reprehensible," Senlin said with genuine disgust, though his loathing of Marat's mission did not make him like the Sphinx's theories about the Tower any more.

"I cannot afford to be a myth any longer. I must reassert my influence. We must act. We must aspire. The time has come for you to go to Pelphia and infiltrate the ranks of the hods."

"But why me? You think me an incompetent dupe."

"You might not be the smartest or bravest person I have ever met, but you are astute, and you have a knack for getting out of trouble. You're quite the slippery fellow, Tom. And I think you'll make an excellent spy."

Chapter Twenty-Two

Do not allow small people to make large impressions. Do not fritter your beauty upon mirrors. Do not make wishes, for wishes only curse the life you have. Never forget, you stand at the end of a long line of short lives.

—*The Wifely Way* by the Duchess K. A. Pell

Edith felt like a new moon slowly filling up with light.

At some point during the waxing of her thoughts, she became aware there were others in the room with her. Their faces were familiar, though she could not quite place them. They were taking excellent care of her; she understood that much. The younger nurse's hair was cut like a military recruit's. She had an expressive face and luminous, lavender eyes; she was talkative and restless. The older nurse said next to nothing and was so large she shook the floor when she walked.

Why was she in bed? She couldn't remember. She wasn't exactly sure where she was, though the question did not bother her a great deal. Nothing bothered her, in fact. Nothing at all.

The young nurse fed her warm milk mixed with oats and dabbed her chin. The big nurse brushed her hair, a little roughly but not unkindly. Edith let her head be pulled by the brush. She liked the rocking sensation. She closed her eyes for a moment, and when she opened them again, the room was quiet and the lamps were turned down low.

It felt like someone was sitting on her arm. It wasn't painful, exactly. It was more of a constant pressure. Each time she tried to shift to a new position, her limbs resisted. She wondered if she wasn't paralyzed, but she didn't feel numb. She only felt a supreme indifference.

Hours passed before it occurred to her that she should look to see who was sitting on her arm and tell them to get off because it was starting to hurt. She turned her head.

A third nurse, dressed in a tidy, starched uniform, sat on her shoulder as if it were a sidesaddle. Humming a mindless tune, the nurse lifted a cattle brand from a pail of red coals. She stuck out her tongue and touched the pink tip to the glowing iron. Steam hissed, and the nurse pulled back, chortling and popping her dry lips.

Edith wondered whether the nurse knew she was awake. She tried to ask her why she was sitting on her, but the noise she made was only sufficient to draw the nurse's attention. The nurse smiled and patted her hand. Edith didn't like her. She could feel the hairs rise on her skin, could feel the blood throb in her fingers. She could feel the whole sensitive bulk of the limb, and for a reason she could not exactly recall, the sensation filled her with sorrow.

"To the count of three," the nurse said, and then pressed the brand into the soft skin of her arm.

The pain was like a buttonhole into which she narrowly fit.

Edith came awake with a terrific gasp.

Voleta was at her side in a moment, clasping her hand and reassuring her that she was in no danger. She was in her bed and resting, and the worst was over now.

Edith began reassembling her dignity at once. She sat up, politely declining any assistance. Her shoulder was throbbing, but she felt otherwise able-bodied.

"What time is it?"

"A little before midnight. You've been drifting in and out for two days. I don't know what the Sphinx dosed you with, but it was stronger than rum."

Edith rubbed her face. "Is the captain back?"

"No," Voleta said, coming off the bedside. It suddenly seemed awkward to be sitting so close to the first mate. "You really haven't missed much. Byron has been coming around every few hours to look in on you."

"Byron's been examining me?" Edith grimaced at the thought.

"Under supervision, of course. He just took your temperature and pulled back your eyelids and held your wrist for a bit. Once he brought a little dropper of something from the Sphinx because you were moaning in your sleep. We poured it into your mouth, and it seemed to help. He's been quite wonderful, actually. I think you should be nicer to him."

Edith was too dazed to roll her eyes. "Where's Iren?"

"She went to bed a few hours ago. We've been taking turns watching you. Are you hungry?"

"No." She turned her legs out of bed. The air felt suddenly thin. For a moment, she thought she might faint, and to stave off the light-headedness, she took several deep breaths. Feeling a little restored, she pulled herself out of bed by the bedpost and adopted a shaky, broad stance.

Voleta watched the mate's dizzy stagger across the room with concern, and was relieved when Edith reached the bench of her dressing table without collapsing.

Examining herself in the mirror, Edith felt disassociated from what she saw. Her new arm was as drab as a washtub. All the finery and flourishes were gone, replaced by bulky plates and a pauldron that would never fit in a sleeve. It was larger than her previous engine almost by half.

"It's different, isn't it?" Voleta said, her image appearing in the mirror behind Edith.

"He said my old arm was built for diplomacy and only light bludgeoning. It wasn't designed for the constant abuse I put it through. This is more of a field model," she said, knocking at the arm. It rang softly and deeply like a cast iron pan. "I've never once in my life looked forward to wearing a dress, so it's nothing I'll miss. But I wonder if anyone will ever look me in the eye again, or if they'll be too busy gawking at this—*tractor*."

"Nonsense. It's nothing a nice scarf can't fix." The girl tugged at the mate's nightshirt, adjusting the collar. One sleeve of the shirt had been cut off to make room for the engine, and it made the rest of the gown hang lopsided about her neck and chest. "Perhaps you can ask the Sphinx to update your wardrobe."

"He told me about taking you under his wing. You don't have to pretend." The young woman was still looking at Edith's reflection, particularly her hair, which she lifted and piled, examining the effect with a pout of concentration. "I don't understand why you did it. I wasn't trying to deprive you of anything. I just wanted to protect you."

"I did it because we can't keep making enemies of everyone we meet, sir. That's not going to turn out well for us. Besides, I was feeling like a prisoner, and I don't enjoy that feeling."

"Why do you keep calling me *sir* if you aren't going to do anything that I ask?"

Voleta shifted her gaze from the mate's hair to her face in the mirror. "I know it's a conflict of interest, but I think we've handled it very well so far. You're a superb first mate, and I look forward to following most of your orders for a very long time."

"One day I'd like to take you back to my home and introduce you to my father. Just so he can see I was not the most precocious young woman in the world."

A soft tap at the bedroom door was followed shortly by the appearance of antlers. The stag had his eyes closed. "Are you awake and decent?" he whispered.

"Just," Edith said, turning on the bench. "Come in, Byron."

Sticking his head in a little farther, the stag politely gazed at a corner of the ceiling rather than the women in their nightclothes. "I'm glad to see you're up and about."

"Yes, you can go tell the Sphinx he hasn't killed me yet."

"That's not why I'm here. The Sphinx went to collect Senlin. He'll be on an elevator shortly. I anticipate you will have your captain back within the hour."

Edith closed her eyes to better enjoy the swelling sense of relief.

"Oh, for heaven's sake. He would have to come back in the middle of the night," Voleta said, setting her fists to her hips. "Byron, would you please make some tea? I'll try to wake Iren. Mister Winters, it's not my place to say, sir, but perhaps there's time for a bath?"

Edith sniffed her hair, made a dour face, and then with some of her old spirit said, "All right, everyone out."

Iren had not gone to sleep, though she had briefly collapsed on top of the bedding. She hadn't even the energy to take off her clothes.

Caring for the sedated first mate had turned out to be rather easy; it was Voleta's version of nervous pacing that had really tired Iren out. The girl chased her squirrel about the room incessantly. She climbed the mantel and walked it like a beam. She performed the most ambitious tumbles, to the peril of every lamp, vase, and mirror in the room.

After two days of this, Iren nearly regretted discouraging Voleta from taking her exercise with the Sphinx. At least she knew the girl was safe.

Iren had just nodded off when she was awoken by the certainty that someone else was in her room. Calm as an early riser, she sat up and switched on the lamp at her bedside.

The Sphinx stood by the chamber door: a long shadow under a little spur of reflected light. "What do you want?" The Sphinx's voice was a tinny whisper.

"What do I want?" Iren said, standing.

"I heard you tell Voleta you wanted to speak to me. Here I am. What do you want?" The Sphinx moved across the ancient rug, his long robe dragging like a brush full of ink.

Iren did her utmost to appear neither imposing nor unhappy, which was difficult given the preference of her features. The resulting expression was not quite civil, but it was as close as she would ever come. "Something's wrong with me. I'd like you to fix it."

"Sit down on the bed, please." The amazon complied, and the Sphinx stood so close his cloak brushed her knees. "Now," he continued, feeling the glands under her jaw. Iren found the hands disturbing. They were too small, almost childish, and yet hard as rock. "Tell me what needs *fixing*, as you say."

Iren squinted at her own face stretched across the mirror mask. "Are you a doctor?"

The Sphinx paused a moment. "No, I'm much better than that. Are you sleeping well?"

Iren decided at once that she would answer the Sphinx's questions without any deliberation. She wanted to be honest; she wanted to seem honest. "Sometimes. I have bad dreams."

"Do you find that you flush more often, or do you ever wake in a sweat?"

"Yes."

"How old are you?"

"Fifty-five, I think. I don't know."

"That's all right. Birthdays are dreadful things. I haven't celebrated one in a century at least." The Sphinx turned the amazon's head and peered into her ear. "What else?"

"I can't control my temper. I get furious, and then very sad."

"Are you usually an emotional person?" The Sphinx pulled down one of her eyelids and inspected the vascular web.

Iren sniffed. "No."

The Sphinx stood back. "Open your mouth. Stick out your tongue. Good. Now, say 'ah.' Excellent. Excellent. Let me ask you, when did you start to feel this way? Was it when you left the Port of Goll, perhaps?"

Iren tilted her head. "I think so."

"Before that, did you have many friends? Did you socialize regularly or have any strong family ties?"

"I played with Finn Goll's children."

"Often? Whenever you wanted?"

"No. Just when he let me. Just once in a while."

"As if it were a reward? That doesn't sound very friendly. Was there no one else?"

"Not until Senlin started to tutor me."

"Do you still like him? Even now? Even knowing about the weakness he hid from you?"

Iren's expression narrowed, her thin eyes all but disappearing. "We all have weaknesses. Not everyone has strengths."

"I suppose. All right, I have a diagnosis for you. This is not like a stab wound: a local injury with radiating effects. It is almost the opposite of that, in fact. I think you are experiencing the onset of the cessation."

Iren blinked, thinking for a moment that the Sphinx had said *assassination*, but that wasn't what he had said. "What's that?"

The Sphinx slid back, his shadow shrinking upon the papered wall. He looked almost approachable. "The cessation is what happens at the end of your child-bearing years. For some, it affects their moods. It can interrupt the cycle of sleep or result in sudden changes in body temperature. It's all quite natural, though often unpleasant."

"But I keep losing my nerve. I never lost my nerve before. Is that the . . . cessation?"

"No, I think it's shock, my dear. When you worked for Goll, you were an enforcer, were you not? You were Goll's personal hammer, which is physically taxing but doesn't require a lot of consideration of others, or deliberation over consequences, or emotional attachment. Things are different now. You have friends. Not borrowed friends, but friends of your own. And as wonderful as that is, it's terribly complicating. For the first time, you are confronted by feelings you can neither grasp nor throttle. You finally have something to lose, and it frightens you."

"No, something else is wrong," Iren said in deep frustration. She wanted to strangle this shadow of a man, to flatten him against the wall. "I feel different. I can't explain it. I pulled a muscle in my back doing sit-ups."

The Sphinx laughed, the sound like a jailor jangling his keys. He patted Iren's scarred cheek, and she scowled. "You're just getting older, my dear. There really is nothing to be done about that."

"What do you mean nothing? I'll take a new spine! I'll take a new arm! Give me a foot. Give me a thumb. I'll take anything!"

The great oval of the Sphinx's face rotated through a ponderous shake. "There's nothing wrong with you. Physically, you're in fine shape. You may even have another decade of brutish behavior to look forward to, if that's what you want. Now, you'll have to excuse me. I have to look in on your captain."

Iren hung her head. She could not recall a time when she had felt more dejected.

"Chin up, Iren. You have a part to play, yet, and it's going to be quite an interesting challenge for you. Less hammer, more heart."

Voleta found Iren sitting on the edge of her bed, her elbows on her knees, her face pointed at the carpet. She looked as still and pensive as a statue in a park.

"You're awake. Mister Winters is up. Byron says the captain is coming home. Everything is going to be fine." When Iren did not raise her head or show any sign to acknowledge this good news, Voleta's gaiety shifted to concern. "Are you feeling all right?"

"Do you know what the cessation is?"

Voleta crossed the room nearly on tiptoe, as if she could somehow make the moment less delicate. "I do."

"I didn't," Iren said in a hush. She looked up, her face bereft of emotion. "I won't have anyone. I'll be alone."

"Oh, no, Iren. No, please don't say that. You poor thing." Voleta put her arms around Iren's mountainous shoulders. "I love you. The captain loves you, Winters loves you, and you know how much Adam admired you. He followed you around like a puppy. I'm sure he's going to miss you terribly. But I promise you, I'm not going anywhere. Me and you are as thick as thieves."

The amazon took a breath so deep it carried Voleta from her feet. She exhaled in a long, weakening stream and said, "I love you, too."

Chapter Twenty-Three

Myth is the story of what we do not understand in ourselves.

—*The Myth of the Sphinx: A Historical*
Analysis by Saavedra

There was no way around it. The reunion would be awkward. For one thing, the event would take place in the pink canyon, amid its agoraphobic sprawl and numbing repetitions, which was not an especially warm or auspicious spot. For another, Byron and the crew arrived several minutes before the captain's car arrived. They waited uncomfortably before a door that opened upon a closed elevator.

They had not, as a crew, really broached the subject of the captain's habit or whether he was fit to lead, and now it seemed they never would unless he broke the uneasy silence. They hoped this would be the case, but of course, it all depended upon what version of the man emerged from the bowels of the Sphinx's library.

The captain's state of mind was not their only worry. Edith found the idea of having to explain where Adam was absolutely nauseating. Never mind the fact that the Sphinx was keeping the Red Hand alive. Never mind her monstrous arm, which had already torn one shirt and gouged two doorways. She half expected the elevator doors to open and for Tom to shriek at the sight of her.

Though she knew he wouldn't. As much as she dreaded the inevitable conversations, she was looking forward to seeing him. Befuddled or not, he had always been on her side.

By the time the elevator pinged and the doors slid back, they were all huddled in and staring like a family of owls.

To their relief, the captain was smiling and demonstrative, embracing each of them in turn, even the scandalized stag, whom Senlin shook by the shoulders and told, "Thank you for the chocolate!"

He looked like a castaway: His trousers were shredded, his coat was in tatters, and his chin and cheeks were buried under half an inch of whiskers. He seemed thinner, almost gaunt, but his spirits were high and his eyes were clear and bright.

Their joy was only half expressed before he asked where Adam was. His shock at the answer was tempered by Voleta's assurance that Adam was, even as they spoke, conning the cloudy men right out of their cloudy houses. When Senlin raised the question of a rescue, Edith shook her head and stammered negatives. He retracted the idea at once, saying he was sure there was more to the story and there would be time enough for full explanations later. For now, he was just pleased to see them and to know Adam was safe, at least to the satisfaction of his sister.

Senlin of course noticed Edith's new arm at once, but he saw in her bearing, the way she held it a little apart from her side, that she did not like it, and so he only briefly remarked that it was good to see her whole again. She looked, he said, very well, indeed.

As they waited for the elevating hall to carry them back to the apartment, Voleta boasted that she'd been playing with the Sphinx at night, which surprised Senlin, though the news did not seem to alarm anyone else.

It dawned upon him that as transformative as the past ten days had been for him, their experience had been no less exciting and fraught. How much had changed in less than a fortnight! He wondered what a year's separation would do to two people.

It was a lot to absorb, but all of it was suffused with the glow of their company, which Senlin said, again and again, was what he had missed the most during his days in the library.

He recounted a few parts of his own adventure over tea in their apartment: the dead knight caught in a terrible trap, the unstable tunnel of books, and the abysmal biscuits. Voleta served him a plate of cold chicken, which he declared the most delicious bird he'd ever tasted. She gave the librarian a bit of lamb to work upon, a display that she found delightful and worthy of narration.

"I am not the man I was," Senlin said abruptly, as if he were afraid to delay the confession any longer. His friends around the table looked to him expectantly. This would be the apology then, and knowing Senlin it would be long-winded, roundabout, and obscure. They collectively braced themselves for the oration. "I tried to be my old self while living the life of the new, this life with you. I tried to be there and here, then and now, a headmaster and a captain. I fear I failed on all counts. I am sorry I have been so—ambitiously dishonest. I hope you can forgive me. I would very much appreciate another chance to earn your confidence, your faith. You are all such dear, dear friends."

He looked them each in the eye, held their gaze for a second, and then finding nothing further to say, picked up a chicken leg and took to it like a horse takes the bit.

Voleta and Edith were caught off guard by the relative brevity of the speech, but Iren was not. She knew exactly what the captain meant. She raised her teacup and said, "To the life of the new."

Senlin set down the chicken leg to return the toast, as did Edith, Voleta, and Byron, one by one, until they were all sure the moment had been pressed into their memories like a seal into wax.

Then Byron announced that the hour was very late and advised them that it was time for bed. The Sphinx, Byron said, would be paying them all a visit in the morning to make an announcement about the ship. Carrying the librarian in his arms, the stag bid them all good night.

Iren needed no further encouragement to go to bed, and her snoring could be heard through the door of her room within minutes of her having closed it. Voleta followed shortly thereafter, though not before telling the captain that she was very glad to see him, but she didn't particularly care for his beard, a confession which Senlin took in good humor.

No sooner was he alone with Edith than Senlin became acutely aware of how bedraggled he looked. He was filthy, especially compared to her. She was as scrubbed and combed as he'd ever seen her; her skin shone in pretty contrast with the wide collar of her blue blouse, which just minutes before his arrival had been relieved of one of its sleeves.

Embarrassed by his state, he expressed his keen interest in continuing their conversation but asked if they might not do so in the morning. She graciously agreed, and he retired to what had lately been Adam's room.

There, he addressed all the tedious rituals of hygiene that no man is superior to, including the eradication of his whiskers, which were, to his annoyance, not free of gray. He selected a shirt and pair of trousers from the room's stocked wardrobe, and though neither fit very well, he was satisfied they were at least recently laundered.

At some point in his ablutions he realized he did not intend to go directly to bed. For one thing, he wasn't the least bit sleepy. For another, he was still feeling very clearheaded, and he wanted to speak to Edith before he lost this feeling.

Yet, when he found himself standing outside her bedroom with his hair slicked down and the too-few buttons on his too-blousy shirt done up, he did wonder what it was he intended to say. The apartment was still. Shadows rayed from the furniture like the petals of a black flower. The golden stamen of a lamp glowed in the dark. He felt safe and happy and at home.

He knocked, and there was a long pause before Edith appeared, clutching the collar of her blouse closed. "I can't button it on my own. These new fingers are so fat and difficult..."

She stopped, recognizing the expression on his face. It was the alert gaze of a man who had spent the past ten days locked up with his thoughts and a taciturn cat. She had seen the look before. He had come without a clear purpose in mind, which was an errand in itself. She did not believe in idle visits to the pantry, or idle walks down the lane, or idle appearances outside doors in the wee hours of the night. These were not idle things. They were urges too inconvenient or unseemly to admit: They were hunger, they were frustration, they were yearning.

But understanding his urge did not spare her from experiencing her own. She had suffered so much indignity while he was away, so much self-doubt, yet here he was, looking at her as if she hadn't got a rainspout for an arm, as if she were not the Sphinx's worst lackey, as if they were not standing on the cusp of an adventure that would almost certainly tear them apart. They were like the daily crockery of a public house: They'd been broken and glued back together so many times it was a miracle they retained their shape, a miracle they could still be filled and hold anything inside of them.

They embraced and shared an impassioned kiss.

It seemed an ecstatic prelude, like the choral gasp that precedes the first note of an opera. As much as they felt not quite themselves, they seemed a perfect match for each other.

Separating, they saw in each other's expression the terror and splendor of what they had done.

He said good night, and she shut the door.

Neither saw the butterfly flattened to her dressing screen, its wings painted to blend into the heathered silk.

Early the next morning, Byron rapped like a woodpecker on their bedroom doors, rousing them from various states of insufficient sleep. Insisting there was no time for breakfast, not even a cup of tea, the stag all but chased them from their apartment into the elevating corridor.

Ferdinand startled them further by sounding his train whistle, apparently out of an excess of excitement. He romped at their heels, unaffected by Byron's protests. Though when Edith told him to stop, Ferdinand complied at once, to the stag's great annoyance. Byron recommended that Edith not grow accustomed to the locomotive listening to her because it was surely just a phase.

Voleta noticed that the captain and Mister Winters had said good morning to each other twice in the first minute of their walk, both times in a different tone and with a changed expression, as if the words were capable of communicating more than a ho-hum hello, as if they were speaking in some code. She thought it funny and so told Iren good morning several times, raising her eyebrows higher with each repetition. The captain and first mate looked scolded by the joke and developed a sudden interest in the loamy tatter of carpet underfoot.

They paraded back through the great medallion of a front door, where green copper figures walked in a harmonious wheel, and onto the platform they had once been bowled across. The Sphinx waited for them there, standing at the rail over the central trough of the hangar with an air of absolute pride.

It wasn't difficult to guess what their host was feeling boastful about. The airship filling the central vein of the hangar behind him was nothing short of spectacular.

There was not an exposed plank of wood anywhere on her; every side and rail was plated or piped in polished steel. The hull was shaped like the head of a splitting maul: The stem was a sharp wedge, the stern, a blunt hammerhead. Two rows of cannons protruded from the portside that faced them. Sleek parallel lines like a musical stave decorated the mirror-bright broadside and accentuated a pair of stout fins. The long, pristine envelope was rigged to the hull by a perfect matrix of cables and a pair of silver umbilical stacks. It was as imposing as the *Ararat* but infinitely more graceful and lovely of line.

"This was once the most respected vessel in all of Babel. The Brick Layer used it to ferry his favorite guests to and fro. It is unconquerable and luxurious, and you don't at all deserve her. This is the *State of Art*."

"It's marvelous. Stunning. But where's our ship?" Senlin said.

"Your 'ship,' as you generously refer to it, won't be ready for some time. My errand cannot wait. There are changes afoot in Pelphia, and the time for us to move is nigh. I am loaning you my ship so that you may fulfill your end of the agreement."

"I'm flattered that you would trust me with such a vessel."

"Ah, well, that's the thing, Thomas. Since it is my ship, I choose its captain. Which would be you." The Sphinx pointed at Edith. She flinched as if she'd been thumped on the nose.

She saw at once that the announcement was meant to humiliate Senlin, to dispel what was left of his authority. She did not understand her employer's plan for the lapsed headmaster, but she knew it was not as Lee's successor. The Sphinx understood that Senlin would never become a harvester of souls, though that hardly excused this rough treatment of him. Yes, his efforts as captain had been imperfect, but he deserved the courtesy of being informed of the loss of his command in private rather than surprised in front of his crew. There was also a very good chance that if he resisted, Voleta and Iren would rally to his side. That would not only poison her command, it would put them all in immediate danger because for all his haggling, the Sphinx was not really negotiating terms; he was toying with them. He would have his way, even if it required the shedding of a little blood.

Edith looked to see if Senlin understood.

"That's not fair," he said, attempting to look self-possessed in his borrowed clothes.

His words pulled the plug from the bottom of her heart, and the blood drained from her face.

Senlin, however, was not upset. In fact, he was having difficulty containing his elation. For months, he had not allowed himself to dwell upon the weight of his command or how ill suited he was to carry the burden, because ultimately it did not matter whether he was the right man for the job; he had asked for and accepted the responsibility. His duty to his crew had always been sincere, and he had not wavered in his commitment to them. Yet given the chance to step aside, albeit without much grace, he felt an abrupt urge to smile and laugh, to embrace them with the same gratitude he'd felt upon emerging from the Bottomless Library. He felt free.

He knew the announcement was not without casualty. Edith had made no bones about her disinterest in being captain. Senlin did not understand the cause of her hesitance, especially considering her talents and her past. Hadn't she been the Generaless of her father's gardens? But the Sphinx was insensitive to her reservations and now forced her to confront the source of her insecurity. It was a delicate moment, one requiring composure.

Senlin squared himself before Iren and Voleta. The amazon's neck was thicker, the veins more distinct. She held her head low like a taunted bull. Voleta was glaring at the Sphinx with a puckered smirk.

Senlin raised his hands to gather their attention. "It is not fair to tell a crew their captain has been replaced. One must ask for their support."

"Their support doesn't matter," the Sphinx said, a draft twisting his dark robes like candle smoke.

"It does to the captain," Senlin insisted. He turned to Edith. "I have every confidence in you, Captain Winters. I look forward to voyaging on your ship and serving under your command." He gave her a very deliberate if not entirely competent salute.

Her bleak expression softened with affection. She wanted to embrace him again, though such a thing was even more impossible and ill advised now than it had been before. Though hadn't he been captain when he came to her door? Would a reversal of their roles make such a difference? She hoped at once it wouldn't, but she suspected that it would.

"Now let the others speak for themselves," Senlin said.

Iren heaved a sigh that drove a little tension from her shoulders. "I don't have a problem with you, Winters. I'll follow you." She pointed at the Sphinx. "But you, I don't care for. I've known men like you before. No respect. No trust. No courage. It doesn't end well for the likes of you."

The Sphinx swayed a bit but seemed neither surprised nor impressed by the amazon's anger.

Voleta rolled her eyes and said to the Sphinx, "You do make it so very difficult to be your friend." She turned to Edith. "Captain Winters, it's not your fault how the trap was sprung. I think you'll do a fine job, and it's a pretty enough ship. I look forward to following your orders most of the time."

Edith stuck out her chest and raised her chin. She had just begun to say, "As your cap—" when the Sphinx broke in.

"Well, that sounds like a consensus. Which doesn't matter at all. I expect you to keep your word, do my work, and take care of my ship. If you lose her, I will use you for spare parts." The Sphinx raised his finger. "That absolutely must be added to your contracts. Byron, please fetch your desk."

As the stag's heels clicked across the platform, Voleta wedged her hand into Iren's dangling fist. Squit wriggled from her sleeve and ran up the amazon's thick arm and onto the silver crown of her head where it surveyed the hangar like a lord. Senlin smiled at them and then at Edith, staring out at her ship, glistening like mercury.

He wondered if he wasn't overlooking what he was looking for.

The mechanical butterflies with painted wings congregated in the Sphinx's workshop inside the copper dome. They came and went through ducts in the walls, sentient enough to go where they were told, clever enough not to be caught, though no one would know what to do with them if they were.

The Sphinx was out of her cowl and hovering before her desk, where several butterflies lay, their wings moving on occasion, indolent as a lover's blink.

She picked one up and pulled its thorax from its abdomen. The heathered wings began to beat more quickly, and when the Sphinx raised her hand, the disembodied butterfly rose to join the others flitting mindlessly about the dome.

The butterfly's thorax was black-lacquered tin interrupted near the middle by a crystal lens.

The Sphinx turned on the projector standing at the corner of her desk; it whirred to life and cast a circle of white light upon a blank portion of the wall. Opening the side of the projector, she slid the thorax into a chamber as one might insert a shell into a rifle. The porthole of light changed to an image, somewhat bleary and warped at the edges. The ghostly animation was accompanied by the thin sound of movement, a rustle of clothing, the tinny drone of someone breathing.

The recording was of Edith's bedroom. She sat at her vanity, working her new arm, staring at it directly and then reflected in the glass.

A knock on the Sphinx's door did not distract her from the scene. She called for Byron to enter. As soon as the stag saw the scene playing upon the wall, he looked away, clenching his dark eyes in shame.

"Oh, don't look so guilty. You were just doing what you were told," the Sphinx said.

It hardly made him feel any better. He had gone to Edith's room with a doctor's bag the day before, supposedly to help mitigate her pain with a dose of opiates, though that had not been his primary goal. He had set the open bag on the floor at her bedside, and while he administered the medicine, the Sphinx's spy had crawled out. He had betrayed Edith scant hours after rekindling their friendship.

"I checked the music room. As you anticipated, Voleta was not there. I believe she's in bed," Byron said, resisting the urge to look at the colorful flames dancing upon the wall. Edith sighed heavily, and the sound made him suffer.

"The girl is pouting," the Sphinx said. "She'll forgive me."

"The librarian found Senlin's diary, or whatever it is," the stag said, pulling from his red jacket a short stack of uneven papers. "You were right; he dropped it in the shaft." Byron placed the papers on his master's desk near the painted board the Sphinx had confiscated from Senlin at the mouth of the library. Something about the nude woman's expression unsettled him: the lack of shame, the forward stare. Or perhaps it was the knowledge that the image was responsible for the near-ruin of a man. He shifted the papers to cover her. The Sphinx seemed not to notice or did not care if she did.

There was the sound of knocking, and they both looked to the projection in time to see Edith fuss with her shirt and touch her hair. She opened the door, and over her shoulder, they saw Thomas Senlin, looking ardent. Edith apologized for her appearance, and then they just stood there, staring at each other.

"My goodness," the Sphinx said. "What do you suppose——" The kiss interrupted her. Byron could not stop himself from stamping his foot once upon the floor. They watched in silence until the two separated, reluctantly, haltingly. Edith shut the door a moment later and turned to face what she thought was an empty room. At first she looked troubled, and then she began to smile.

The Sphinx ejected the butterfly's body from the projector and held it up with a gemstone grin. "Ah, youth!" she said with a short cackle. "Byron, you should pack your things. I think I'll need you aboard the *State of Art*. I'm not sure how focused Edith really is."

"You want me to go outside?" Byron said, touching his breast with the fine tips of his fingers. His eyes were wide with wonder and fear.

The Sphinx opened a small, ornate chest on her desk, revealing racks full of thoraxes. She added the recorded kiss to her collection of private scenes and extracted another cartridge from the box. "Byron, you mustn't care so much what others think. Now, leave me alone. I have work to do."

The stag gave a stiff bow and retreated from the high, round room.

Alone, the Sphinx inserted the thorax into her projector, and again the white circle was filled with a foreign interior.

A woman with rolling auburn hair was humming, almost singing, inside a pretty yellow room. The furniture was uniform but artisanal, and bespoke great wealth. A golden-haired doll in a frilly bonnet sat atop a perfectly weighted bureau.

The humming woman parted the crinoline curtain that encircled a bassinet and lifted out an infant swaddled in white. The infant made fussing noises, its pink face still clenched from the horror of being born.

A man in dark navy entered the picture and joined the woman holding the babe. He put his arm around her waist. She seemed reluctant to look at him, but when she did, her expression was full of nervous searching.

"Doctor said you should be in bed," the man said, turning enough to show his handsome profile.

"I just wanted to see her, to make sure she's all right," the woman said, though she was already returning the child to the bassinet, her movement guided by the arms that wrapped around her.

"That is what the nurses are for."

"You won't blame her? You promise you won't?" She could not stop herself from looking back at the veiled crib.

"Yes, yes. I promise," he said in the singsong tone of a settled argument. "Come, come, Marya. Back to bed."

The Sphinx shut her one wet and hooded eye as the recording ended and said to no one, "Ah, youth."

The story continues in . . .

THE HOD KING

Book Three of the Books of Babel

extras

orbit

meet the author

Photo Credit: Kim Bricker

JOSIAH BANCROFT started writing novels when he was twelve, and by the time he finished his first, he was an addict. Eventually, the writing of *Senlin Ascends* began, a fantasy adventure, not so unlike the stories that got him addicted to words in the first place. He wanted to do for others what his favorite writers had done for him: namely, to pick them up and to carry them to a wonderful and perilous world that is spinning very fast. If he's done that with this book, then he's happy.

Josiah lives in Philadelphia with his wife, Sharon, and their two rabbits, Mabel and Chaplin.

if you enjoyed

ARM OF THE SPHINX

look out for

THE HOD KING

The Books of Babel: Book Three

by

Josiah Bancroft

Chapter One

Some men seem to think that temperance is preservative, that moderation somehow pickles the soul. They would place their beating hearts inside jam jars if they could. Which begs the question: What on earth are they saving themselves for?

—Oren Robinson of the *Daily Reverie*

The sun clacked along an iron track among the gaslight stars high above the white city of Pelphia. Ringed in flames and stamped with a broad smiling face, the clockwork sun drew a line of soot across the sky-blue dome. Below, the natives flowed like blood through the narrow streets, clotting about cafés, theaters, and burlesque parlor windows, where sheer curtains turned complicated persons into simple shapes. The happy hordes littered the streets of Pelphia with programs, bills, handkerchiefs, dance cards, the feeble heels of ambitious shoes, the delicate frills of collars, and a thousand assorted tokens of foreshortened affection.

Early every morning, hundreds of hods emerged from their alley shacks with brooms and brushes to scrub the streets. They came with pots of whitewash to paint over lip rouge graffiti, vomit, and lamp soot, blanching the ringdom from port to piazza, where the spine of the Tower rose over the city like a tent pole.

The ringdom's three most ancient institutions stood in the shadow of its spine: the Maze of Court, a sprawling, winding hedge of silk and wire; the Vivant Music Hall, a cathedral that seemed as frail as a bleached reef; and the Colosseum. Once, the Colosseum had been a university, and its tall columns and carved gables still bore the evidence of that former use: Scenes of robed philosophers and bearded poets decorated the lintels over immense windows, built to invite light and air and wonder.

And yet, in recent years the windows had been bricked up with red blocks that stood out like scabs against the pale masonry. The venerable figures in the lower friezes had been torn from their stony offices, leaving great pockmarks behind in the mortar. The colonnade entrance, once as wide as an avenue, had been shrunk by the addition of iron bars and a cage door that was never unguarded.

Inside the Colosseum, a keening crowd watched two half-naked men fight like dogs.

The warring hods shoved each other about the red clay ring, iron collars clanging as they grappled. Winded, they staggered apart and wiped ruddy sweat from their eyes. In the bleachers about them, men in unpolished shoes and last season's fashion shouted themselves crimson.

The older of the two twisted behind his rival and hooked him about the neck. Muscles standing out like an overbred bull, the elder hoisted the younger hod from his feet. Cheeks purpling, the youth gasped and clawed at the elder's arm. The crowd pealed toward a higher octave. And like a shepherd yokes a lamb, the old hod grabbed his rival by the thigh and hoisted him onto his shoulders.

A lavish balcony haloed the bleachers. The balcony rail, sparsely attended a moment before, began to fill with noblemen, summoned by the louder cheers. They peered down at the brawl, sipping Chartreuse from crystal glasses and smoking black cigarettes that stank like wet bedclothes. Only members of the Coterie and their guests were allowed on the balcony.

Shaking from the exertion, the old hod lifted the youth over his head. He turned in a slow circle, showing every seat his defeated rival, who had not ten minutes before strutted out of the tunnel like a rooster. The mob bayed. Above, the nobles drew on their cigarillos. The old hod drove the youth to the ground, where he bounced once and settled in a prostrate sprawl.

Every man in the arena—save one—made thunder with his hands. The victorious hod paraded with his arms up, his expression as inscrutable as an executioner's hood.

A team of groomers emerged from the tunnels that ran under the stands. Some raked the clay; others dragged the moaning youth underground. The victor was gathered last, his iron collar hooked to a pair of poles, by which he was escorted from the floor amid a shower of losing tickets.

The man who refused to clap scanned the balcony railing, studying the faces of the noblemen in military and dining jackets. They did not pay him the compliment of acknowledgment.

As a wanted man, Senlin found the snub amusing. But the same realities that had frustrated his own search for Marya now befuddled the ringdom's search for him. The Tower overwrote the obsessions and longings of men and women with an indifference so intense it almost seemed purposeful. One did not have to hide long nor change much to disappear inside the churning mass. Thomas Senlin had slipped again into the camouflage of the crowd. It didn't hurt his anonymity that the published bounty for the Pirate Tom Mudd included a sketch of a much fiercer-looking man, with an anvil chin, cannonball cheeks, and a gaze like a crucible full of slag. Perhaps Commissioner Pound had been too embarrassed to describe the man who'd robbed and eluded him more honestly as a thin man with sharp features, kindly eyes, and a nose like a rudder, turned slightly starboard.

The crowd funneled from the bleachers to the lobby, a great vaulted room that not so much echoed as it roared with voices and commotion. A rowdy queue formed at the concessionary, where cloudy beer was being poured and splashed upon the floor. Another line grew about the betting cages, where guards in severe black-and-gold uniforms watched the room for men who were overly drunk or overly distraught. Finding any such show of excess, the guards offered a first warning by rifle butt and a second warning by bayonet. One man who was waving a mismarked ticket left with hands clutched over his bloody stomach.

Caught for the moment in the human vortex, Senlin engaged in some idle eavesdropping. Most of what he heard just concerned the last fight or the next, but one conversation distinguished itself from the rest.

"I heard they're recalling Commissioner Pound," a man in a plum-colored vest said.

"It wasn't in the *Reverie* this morning," his companion complained.

"It will be tomorrow, I'd wager. Commissioner Pound: outwitted by a man named Mudd!"

"Wasn't he a pirate, though? They're sly enough."

"But Pound was supposed to be a terror! All he's done lately is get robbed, beaten, and outfoxed by a bandit. I can't wait to see General Eigengrau drag him over the coals."

"How quick the wind turns!"

Senlin resisted the urge to pull up his collar.

Wedging through, he splashed across a growing lagoon of beer and made his way to the balcony entrance.

A pair of sharp-chinned guards stood at the base of the balcony stairs. Senlin tried not to look at the swords that hung on their hips as he smiled and said, "Hello!"

One of the guards shifted his forward gaze just long enough to size Senlin up. And seeing nothing deserving further conversation, he looked away.

Senlin reached into his coat pocket, a movement that inspired both men to show him several inches of their swords. With the slow care of a surgeon navigating a wound, Senlin removed his billfold. He drew out a stiff white card and a five-mina banknote, an amount which once would've been enough to feed his crew for a month or more. He folded the money so that it was all but hidden by his card, and presented both to the guard who'd blessed him with a glance. "Perhaps you could give my card to the club manager." The nearest guard took the money and card. "With my warmest regards."

The guard ripped the card and the bank note in half, turned it and tore again, then dropped the mess at Senlin's feet. Even as he looked down at his destroyed offering, the guard gripped one sleeve of his coat and ripped it half from his shoulder, a treatment he repeated on the other sleeve.

Senlin was still gaping at the torn seams of his coat when he was brusquely elbowed aside by the arrival of several men in suits that were as black and sleek as hot pitch. Both guards saluted, and the one who'd ripped Senlin's bribe and coat said, "Good afternoon, Duke Wilhelm."

Ignoring the guard, the duke continued his cheerful conversation with his friends, all of whom were completely oblivious to the man in gray watching them with a gaze reddened by the boiling of his heart. Senlin tried to discern from a sliver of profile, the trim cut of his blond hair, and his tailored clothes what sort of man had made off with Marya.

He thought to grab for the guard's sidearm, cock, raise, and fire it before he was stopped. He pictured the shot striking the duke squarely, pictured him crying out as he clutched at his back and tumbled down to land at Senlin's feet in a lifeless knot.

He resisted the urge, not out of a lack of courage, but because he foresaw the consequence of such a rash act. Doubtless, he would be dead a moment after the duke, and that would leave Marya twice-widowed and only half-rescued. And that assumed she wished to be rescued. It was a question only she could answer, and a question he could not ask.

Senlin had the Sphinx to thank for this absurd state of affairs.

A week prior, the Sphinx had wasted no time introducing Senlin to his role as contracted spy. Mere hours after he unveiled

Edith's astonishing new command, the *State of Art*, the Sphinx, in ghoulish shroud and mirror mask, led Senlin down the rose-colored canyon of his home, through one of a hundred indistinguishable doors, into a queer and cramped dressing room.

Sizing charts hung upon the walls. A seamstress's dummy stood in one corner, wire ribs rusting through cotton skin. Much of the room was dominated by an immense wardrobe. It quivered and rumbled like a boiling pot. Brass tumblers and dials consumed one of the wardrobe's doors. Byron, the Sphinx's stag-headed footman, attended these controls, making minute adjustments and muttering to himself.

Senlin hardly glanced at the odd piece of furniture that seemed part closet, part engine. His sense of wonder had been depleted by the Bottomless Library, where he had been forcibly nursed off the Crumb with the assistance of nightmares, booby traps, and a feline librarian. He hadn't yet had time to fully absorb the mysterious vault the Sphinx had shown him, the so-called "Bridge," which the Brick Layer had built to hold an untold something and sealed for reasons unknown. And that was to say nothing of the loss of his former command, nor his ill-advised visit to Edith's room and the kiss they'd shared with the sort of starved passion one expects of the young. It all left him feeling out of sorts.

And then Byron told him to strip to his underclothes.

He reluctantly did, and Byron assaulted him—throat, shoulder, waist, and inseam—with a tailor's tape he pulled from his pocket. Every new measurement sent Byron back to the wardrobe to turn one tumbler or another.

Senlin was so distracted by the process that he was slow to absorb the Sphinx's announcement that he would not be traveling with his old crewmates aboard the *State of Art*, and would instead go on ahead to Pelphia early and alone.

Senlin's voice rose with his alarm: "But why? We're all going to the same place, aren't we? What possible reason could you have for dividing us?"

"Will you stop fidgeting!" Byron said, cinching his tape about Senlin's chest.

"You mean breathing? Am I being fitted for a casket?"

"Not yet!" Byron said.

"Stop it, both of you." The Sphinx's voice buzzed and crackled over the humming of the wardrobe. "Senlin, please reassure me that you're not an absolute fool. Tell me, why would it be a mistake for all of you to march, arm in arm, into Pelphia together?"

Ignoring Byron's probing as best he could, Senlin said, "I suppose it would make us easier to recognize. We are a rather... memorable troop."

"Ah! It's good to see the Crumb didn't cook your brains entirely."

The stag bleated unhappily. "You'd think your ears were on your hips, the way you twist about!"

Senlin was too dazed to offer a quip. "So, I'm to go alone?"

"Don't be so dramatic! You'll have my moths to keep you company. Byron will intercept your missives from the *State of Art*, pass on any pertinent information to the crew, and then send them on to me. You'll only be alone in body. In spirit, we'll be as close as needle and thread."

"Splendid," he murmured.

"Now, I know you will be tempted to look for your wife, especially when you start to feel lonely. But, listen to me: You will make no effort to contact your wife when you—"

"If!" Senlin gripped the carpet with his bare toes. "*If* she is there." He had been poisoned by hope once already and was determined not to let it happen again.

"Byron, would you fetch the paper I gave you?" the Sphinx asked.

Byron threw the tape measure over his shoulder with a snort and began to rummage through his leather satchel. After a moment, he produced a folded newspaper and handed it to Senlin, who opened it, as Byron bid a quick retreat back to the wheezing wardrobe.

Senlin read the headline aloud in a dwindling voice: "Duke Wilhelm Horace Pell to Wed the Mermaid, Marya of Isaugh." He looked to the date at the top, which he found under the paper's herald: *The Daily Reverie*. The paper was almost seven months old. He wished to read on, but his arms failed him, taken by a sudden weakness. The paper fell like a curtain.

It was a fact now, and yet his mind was slow to accept it. The feeling reminded him of that nauseating confusion he had felt when, as a boy, he had been told that his grandfather had died in the night. He *believed* it was true at once because his mother had told him, and she would never lie about such a thing. But that evening, when he was shown his grandfather's body, washed, and dressed, and laid out for the wake, it had become true in a different way. Believing was not the same as knowing.

"She married the count," he murmured, his throat closing about the words.

"Duke, actually," the Sphinx said.

A cry like a swooping bird interrupted them, the sound rising from a murmur into a muffled shriek. It seemed to come from the wardrobe, which rattled more and more frantically, its hinges chattering like teeth.

Neither the Sphinx nor Byron seemed very concerned. When the shaking abruptly stopped, Byron pulled the latch on the wardrobe and opened the doors.

Inside, Voleta hung from a wooden coat hanger as if it were a trapeze. Pink-cheeked and with scarves and stockings tangled about her neck, she leapt into the dressing room. "That was absolutely terrifying!" she blurted. "It goes so blasted fast! I've never gone so fast! Can I ride again?"

"I told you, it's not a ride. It's the Fardrobe," Byron said. "And you're supposed to be waiting your turn to be fitted, not running amok in my storehouse."

Voleta, apparently oblivious to Senlin's state of undress, began speaking to him in an exhilarated rush: "It goes to a vault full of gowns and suits and socks, all hanging like bats from the ceiling. There's hardly any light, and there are these lithe mechanical arms that reach out and snatch the hangers and then whiz all around through the walls!" As she spoke, she peeled the loose garments from her and passed them to the Sphinx's very disgruntled footman. "I promise you, one go-around and that frown will be blown right off your face." Voleta reached into the back of her blouse and pulled a black velvet disc from the collar. She flipped it about, rapped it with a knuckle, and the disc popped open. Voleta put the top hat on. It sank over her ears at once.

Still in a daze, Senlin handed her the newspaper and said, "I found her."

Voleta took the paper, her expression blooming with excitement and then wilting as she read. Feeling foolish, she pulled the hat from her head. "A duke? She married a duke? I can't believe it. I thought she...I'm so sorry, Captain."

"Not *captain* anymore," the Sphinx said, as if searching for a bottom to Senlin's humiliation.

Senlin turned back to the Sphinx and said, "Did she *want* to marry him or was she coerced?"

"Eavesdroppers and newspapers can only tell so much. I don't know whether Marya said, 'I do,' or if the duke said, 'You will.' What was whispered, what lies in the heart—those are things that require a closer ear." The Sphinx shrank as he spoke, his black robes pooling upon the floor. He put his face, large as a silver platter, level with Senlin's. Slow breathing rasped behind the mask.

"Then I must ask her," Senlin said, resolute in his undershirt.

"Is your memory really so short? I just told you, you are not to speak to your wife. You won't write her letters. You won't spy on her from the bushes. You won't go near her, her husband, or their home."

What had begun as cold, numb sorrow now warmed Senlin from core to extremity. "How can you be so cold? Is there no humanity in you? You act as if she is a fancy, an errand. She is not! She is a woman whose life I ruined! Ruined with my pride, my inability, my selfishness. I *will* find her. I *will* offer my help if she needs it, my heart if she wants it, my head, even if she would see it on a stake. And you, with your plots and contracts, you with your cowardly mask and tick-tock heart, you cannot stop me!"

Voleta and Byron stood frozen in the silence that followed. They waited to see whether Tom would survive his outburst, or if the Sphinx would spark the life from him.

At last, the Sphinx sighed, the sound like coins rattling down a drain. Reaching up, the Sphinx twisted the mirror. It fell away even as the black shroud piled upon the floor. Senlin gasped. Her face was a quilt of metal and flesh that was as tan and creased as a walnut. Plates of precious alloys crowded about an eyepiece that would've been better suited to a microscope than the face of an ancient woman. Perhaps strangest of all, she did not stand, but sat cross-legged upon a floating platter. Senlin passed a hand near the red glow that emanated from the bottom of the floating platform. The air there was vaguely warm and unsettled, as if possessed by static, but it did not burn him.

He looked to Voleta to share his amazement. When she caught him looking, she blurted out a not particularly convincing, "Oh, my word! She's a floating monster!"

"Really, Voleta," the Sphinx said, moving the brass horn that distorted her voice away from her mouth. Her unfiltered voice was creaking and reedy but otherwise ordinary. "The only living persons who have seen my face are standing in this room. You see, Thomas, a business contract is just a sort of artificial trust. But we four are beyond that now."

"But I don't...Why me?" he asked. "And why Voleta?"

The Sphinx pulled thoughtfully at the thick lobe of one ear. "Perhaps because you are capable of remorse. There is nothing in the world so inspiring of trust as regret. And I trust Voleta because she reminds me so much of myself—"

"We're veritable twins," Voleta piped up.

"—right down to that pert mouth of hers."

"But if you have such faith in me," Senlin said, his confusion verging upon ire, "if you understand me so well, why would you forbid me to speak to Marya? Surely, you must know remorse is not enough. If amends can be made, they must be."

"Just because I trust you, Thomas, doesn't mean you're not sometimes a fool." Before Senlin could balk, the unveiled Sphinx pressed on, her tray pacing the carpet before him. "Let's think this through; let's think how your attempt to see your wife would probably go. Let's say that you defy my counsel, my orders, your contract, and our friendship, and go in search of Marya. Let's say you actually manage to meet her, which is no small feat because she is married to a popular and very powerful duke. How do you think she will react when her husband of old suddenly materializes?" The Sphinx stopped shifting about, as if to give Senlin a chance to reply, though as soon as he drew a breath, she carried on for him. "Perhaps she'll be happy! Perhaps she'll say, 'Oh, Tom! My love has returned! I am saved! Carry me home!'" The Sphinx clapped her still-gloved hands together in a mockery of joy. "But perhaps she'll be angry. Perhaps she'll say, 'You! You ruined my life, you miserable worm!'" The Sphinx shook a fist at him.

"Whichever it is, whatever her feelings are, will she not be surprised to see you? And what do people do when they are *actually* surprised?" The Sphinx cut her gaze toward Voleta. "What if she blurts your name or gasps or faints or screams? It won't really matter whether it's done out of delight or fright if the duke overhears it. Do you really think he will be pleased to see you, his absent rival? If you are lucky, he will take his displeasure out on you. But, if he is an unreasonable or jealous man, if he is cruel, might he not take that displeasure out on her as well?"

Senlin scowled at the Sphinx's logic because he could not think of how to argue against it. At least, not yet. "What do you propose?"

"Voleta will speak to Marya on your behalf." The Sphinx swept an arm toward the young woman. "Voleta can wear a dress. She can curtsy her way into court. She can, I think, get invited to the sort of parties the duke and duchess go to. She can wait for the right moment, and when it arrives, she can make a discreet inquiry."

"I don't want Voleta doing my dirty—" Senlin began, but Voleta interrupted him.

"I'll do it."

"Is it dangerous?" Senlin asked.

"Of course, it's dangerous!" The Sphinx laughed. "Most things worth doing are. But she won't be alone. I'm sending the amazon with her."

Senlin had no doubt that Iren would protect Voleta with her life, but she was still only one person. What could she do if the duke or the navy or the whole ringdom turned against them? "I can't put their necks on the block for my mistakes. We'll have to think of something—"

"You aren't captain anymore," Voleta said. She did not say it meanly, yet even so, the words stung. "You can't give orders any longer, Mister Tom. So. I want to go to Pelphia."

"The parties are glorious!" Byron said with a happy shake of his antlers. He helped Senlin slide his arms into a newly delivered white-collared shirt. "The people are dreadful, but the parties are sublime. I've read a hundred stories: the waltzes, the music, the hors d'oeuvres, the wits—"

"I'm not going for any of that!" Voleta said. "I don't care about waltzes and minces and how-do-you-dos! I'm going because he saved my life. He saved my brother's life. So, it's my turn to be…good? Or whatever it is we are." She turned to Senlin. "I promise, I'll bring her home."

"That's so incredibly brave and generous and…thank you." Senlin knew her too well to think she would be dissuaded once she had decided upon a course. "All I ask is that you are honest with her. Tell her everything. Tell her about the thievery and the piracy. The bloodshed. Tell her about the starving, and the Crumb addiction, and…all of it."

"*All* of it?" Voleta said, squeezing the hat flat again. "What am I supposed to say, 'Hullo! You don't know me, but your old husband sent me to tell you what an awful person he is now. A real rotter! But he wants you back. Oh, yes he does! Wait, madam, where are you going?'" She popped the hat out with her fist. "That's a hard sale, Mister Tom."

Senlin pushed his arms into the jacket Byron held out for him. It fit perfectly. It felt strange to wear a new, tailored suit again. He looked at his scarred and weathered hands, protruding from the pristine cuffs. He felt like two different people stitched together.

"Marya should know what she's signing up for." He tried to put his hands in his pockets but found them sewn shut. "I won't trick her. I won't pretend I am the man she married. I don't think I'm completely ruined, or at least not beyond redemption, and perhaps there will be a homecoming for us, but if she is happy in her new life, I would not pluck her from it."

Not knowing what to say to this sincere declaration, Voleta attempted a curtsy. She bent both knees, threw her head downward and popped up again like a spring.

Byron brayed in horror and said, "What on earth was that? Are you bobbing for apples?"

"There'll be enough time for practicing curtsies later," the Sphinx intervened before Voleta could retort. "Now that your business has been settled for the moment, I'd like to discuss mine."

"I imagine it has something to do with Luc Marat," Senlin said.

"I suspect it does. Someone is destroying my spies. Specifically, someone inside the Colosseum. That's where the natives pit hods against one another and gamble on the result."

"They sound like lovely people," Voleta said.

"It's just the sort of injustice that rallies hods to Marat's cause. It's not that he's against bloodshed; he'd just prefer it to be spilled on his own account. Whether he's involved or not, one thing seems certain: Someone doesn't want me to know what's going on inside the Colosseum."

"But what would those nobles want to hide?"

"Ah! Now you're asking the right questions. I knew you'd make a fine spy. There is one other thing you should probably know. The Colosseum is run by the Coterie, which you may know Duke Wilhelm is a member of. So, your investigation might place you near his orbit. Just do your best to avoid him."

"For such a large place, the Tower seems awfully small sometimes," Senlin said with a dour smile.

The Sphinx cleared her throat. " 'Small,' he says. This is the trouble with heroes; every offer of help is taken as a stroke of fate." The wand she gripped began to spark like a green log on a fire. Her voice quickly rose to a shout. "If you'd prefer, I can dispatch you to the ringdom of Thane, where five hundred rifles have disappeared, despite being locked inside the armory. Or I can ship you to Japhet, where a street recently collapsed, apparently the result of mysterious tunneling. Or I could send you to Banner-Wick, where the citizens have begun to lynch hods in the streets and the hods have begun to fight back. The gasworks in Morick have been blocked; last week the library was burnt to the ground in Andara Nur; and three ringdoms in three days have confessed that they've misplaced the paintings I loaned them." Her voice recovered its composure, and her wand fizzled into silence. "I chose to send you to Pelphia because we share a common interest there. But do not confuse my charity with some comic contrivance. Only a small man would say the Tower is small."

Feeling sufficiently chastised, Senlin said, "I apologize. I didn't mean to sound so vain."

The Sphinx pulled what seemed a small ball bearing from the sleeve of one glove. She presented the copper pellet to Senlin, who was horrified to see it sprout eight legs and run a little circle about her open palm. The Sphinx tut-tutted and tapped the mechanical arachnid with her finger. The spider balled up again. "Swallow this."

"You can't be serious," Senlin said.

"It's perfectly harmless. It will only help us find you if you get lost. Consider it a safety line, like the airmen wear." The Sphinx again presented him with the balled-up spider. "If you'd rather, I can have Ferdinand assist you?"

Senlin took the pill, placed it on his tongue, and swallowed with a small shudder.

"That wasn't so bad." The Sphinx took a long leather billfold from her tray and handed it to him. Opening it, Senlin found a thick stack of twenty-mina banknotes. "You will be posing as a Boskop tourist; an accountant by the name of Ceril Pinfield."

"Ceril!" Voleta guffawed.

"We'll have to work on that laugh of yours, too," Byron said.

"Is it genuine?" Senlin asked.

"Of course it is. But that's not pocket money. I expect most of it will go to the hotel bill and bribes. If you run low, let Byron know. We can always print more."

"Genuine!" Senlin scoffed, closing the billfold and securing it in his inner breast pocket.

"You should be safe enough if you avoid any unnecessary socializing and limit your exposure. There are a lot of people looking for you, but very few who can recognize you on sight. Still, don't roam about. Stick to the Colosseum and your room."

"And what will E—Captain Winters—be doing while I'm off spying?"

"After she has acquainted everyone with the *State of Art*, she will deliver Voleta and Iren to the king's court. Then she will recover the ringdom's copy of *The Brick Layer's Granddaughter*. I want it back before Luc Marat gets his hands on it. Assuming he hasn't already. Now, as soon as you're packed, Byron will take you to the stables so you can be on your way."

"Stables? What, I'm leaving tonight?"

"Today. As soon as possible."

Senlin smoothed his graying temples. "I suppose I'll say my goodbyes, then," Senlin said.

"There's no time. I promise you Marat does not let sentiment slow the pace of his efforts. Besides, you will all see one another again soon enough."

"But what possible harm could it do to say goodbye to—"

The Sphinx cut in, showing the jewelry of her smile, "I think you've seen enough of Edith Winters, don't you, Tom?"

Feeling suddenly transparent, Senlin shut his mouth.

if you enjoyed
ARM OF THE SPHINX

look out for

WAKE OF VULTURES

Book One of the Shadow

by

Lila Bowen

*Nettie Lonesome dreams of a greater life than toiling
as a slave in the sandy desert. But when a stranger
attacks her, Nettie wins more than the fight.*

*Now she's got friends, a good horse, and a better gun.
But if she can't kill the thing haunting her nightmares and
stealing children across the prairie, she'll lose it all—and
never find out what happened to her real family.*

Wake of Vultures *is the first novel of the Shadow series
featuring the fearless Nettie Lonesome.*

1

Nettie Lonesome had two things in the world that were worth a sweet goddamn: her old boots and her one-eyed mule, Blue. Neither item actually belonged to her. But then again, nothing did. Not even the whisper-thin blanket she lay under, pretending to be asleep and wishing the black mare would get out of the water trough before things went south.

The last fourteen years of Nettie's life had passed in a shriveled corner of Durango territory under the leaking roof of this wind-chapped lean-to with Pap and Mam, not quite a slave and nowhere close to something like a daughter. Their faces, white and wobbling as new butter under a smear of prairie dirt, held no kindness. The boots and the mule had belonged to Pap, right up until the day he'd exhausted their use, a sentiment he threatened to apply to her every time she was just a little too slow with the porridge.

"Nettie! Girl, you take care of that wild filly, or I'll put one in her goddamn skull!"

Pap got in a lather when he'd been drinking, which was pretty much always. At least this time his anger was aimed at a critter instead of Nettie. When the witch-hearted black filly had first shown up on the farm, Pap had laid claim and pronounced her a fine chunk of flesh and a sign of the Creator's good graces. If Nettie broke her and sold her for a decent price, she'd be closer to paying back Pap for taking her in as a baby when nobody else had wanted her but the hungry, circling vultures. The value Pap placed on feeding and housing a half-Injun, half-black orphan girl always seemed to go up instead of down, no matter that Nettie did most of the work around the homestead these days. Maybe that was why she'd not been taught her sums: Then she'd know her own damn worth, to the penny.

But the dainty black mare outside wouldn't be roped, much less saddled and gentled, and Nettie had failed to sell her to the cowpokes at the Double TK Ranch next door. Her idol, Monty, was a top hand and always had a kind word. But even he had put a boot on Pap's poorly kept fence, laughed through his mustache, and hollered that a horse that couldn't be caught couldn't be sold. No matter how many times Pap drove the filly away with poorly thrown bottles, stones, and bullets, the critter crept back under cover of night to ruin the water by dancing a jig in the trough, which meant another blistering trip to the creek with a leaky bucket for Nettie.

Splash, splash. Whinny.

Could a horse laugh? Nettie figured this one could.

Pap, however, was a humorless bastard who didn't get a joke that didn't involve bruises.

"Unless you wanna go live in the flats, eatin' bugs, you'd best get on, girl."

Nettie rolled off her worn-out straw tick, hoping there weren't any scorpions or centipedes on the dusty dirt floor. By the moon's scant light she shook out Pap's old boots and shoved her bare feet into into the cracked leather.

Splash, splash.

The shotgun cocked loud enough to be heard across the border, and Nettie dove into Mam's old wool cloak and ran toward the stockyard with her long, thick braids slapping against her back. Mam said nothing, just rocked in her chair by the window, a bottle cradled in her arm like a baby's corpse. Grabbing the rawhide whip from its nail by the warped door,

Nettie hurried past Pap on the porch and stumbled across the yard, around two mostly roofless barns, and toward the wet black shape taunting her in the moonlight against a backdrop of stars.

"Get on, mare. Go!"

A monster in a flapping jacket with a waving whip would send any horse with sense wheeling in the opposite direction, but this horse had apparently been dancing in the creek on the day sense was handed out. The mare stood in the water trough and stared at Nettie like she was a damn strange bird, her dark eyes blinking with moonlight and her lips pulled back over long, white teeth.

Nettie slowed. She wasn't one to quirt a horse, but if the mare kept causing a ruckus, Pap would shoot her without a second or even a first thought—and he wasn't so deep in his bottle that he was sure to miss. Getting smacked with rawhide had to be better than getting shot in the head, so Nettie doubled up her shouting and prepared herself for the heartache that would accompany the smack of a whip on unmarred hide. She didn't even own the horse, much less the right to beat it. Nettie had grown up trying to be the opposite of Pap, and hurting something that didn't come with claws and a stinger went against her grain.

"Shoo, fool, or I'll have to whip you," she said, creeping closer. The horse didn't budge, and for the millionth time, Nettie swung the whip around the horse's neck like a rope, all gentle-like. But, as ever, the mare tossed her head at exactly the right moment, and the braided leather snickered against the wooden water trough instead.

"Godamighty, why won't you move on? Ain't nobody wants you, if you won't be rode or bred. Dumb mare."

At that, the horse reared up with a wild scream, spraying water as she pawed the air. Before Nettie could leap back to

426

avoid the splatter, the mare had wheeled and galloped into the night. The starlight showed her streaking across the prairie with a speed Nettie herself would've enjoyed, especially if it meant she could turn her back on Pap's dirt-poor farm and no-good cattle company forever. Doubling over to stare at her scuffed boots while she caught her breath, Nettie felt her hope disappear with hoofbeats in the night.

A low and painfully unfamiliar laugh trembled out of the barn's shadow, and Nettie cocked the whip back so that it was ready to strike.

"Who's that? Jed?"

But it wasn't Jed, the mule-kicked, sometimes stable boy, and she already knew it.

"Looks like that black mare's giving you a spot of trouble, darlin'. If you were smart, you'd set fire to her tail."

A figure peeled away from the barn, jerky-thin and slithery in a too-short coat with buttons that glinted like extra stars. The man's hat was pulled low, his brown hair overshaggy and his lily-white hand on his gun in a manner both unfriendly and relaxed that Nettie found insulting.

"You best run off, mister. Pap don't like strangers on his land, especially when he's only a bottle in. If it's horses you want, we ain't got none worth selling. If you want work and you're dumb and blind, best come back in the morning when he's slept off the mezcal."

"I wouldn't work for that good-for-nothing piss-pot even if I needed work."

The stranger switched sides with his toothpick and looked Nettie up and down like a horse he was thinking about stealing. Her fist tightened on the whip handle, her fingers going cold. She wouldn't defend Pap or his land or his sorry excuses for cattle, but she'd defend the only thing other than Blue that mostly belonged to her. Men had been pawing at her for two years now, and nobody'd yet come close to reaching her soft parts, not even Pap.

"Then you'd best move on, mister."

The feller spit his toothpick out on the ground and took a step forward, all quiet-like because he wore no spurs. And that was Nettie's first clue that he wasn't what he seemed.

"Naw, I'll stay. Pretty little thing like you to keep me company."

That was Nettie's second clue. Nobody called her pretty unless they wanted something. She looked around the yard, but all she saw were sand, chaparral, bone-dry cow patties, and the remains of a fence that Pap hadn't seen fit to fix. Mam was surely asleep, and Pap had gone inside, or maybe around back to piss. It was just the stranger and her. And the whip.

"Bullshit," she spit.

"Put down that whip before you hurt yourself, girl."

"Don't reckon I will."

The stranger stroked his pistol and started to circle her. Nettie shook the whip out behind her as she spun in place to face him and hunched over in a crouch. He stopped circling when the barn yawned behind her, barely a shell of a thing but darker than sin in the corners. And then he took a step forward, his silver pistol out and flashing starlight. Against her will, she took a step back. Inch by inch he drove her into the barn with slow, easy steps. Her feet rattled in the big boots, her fingers numb around the whip she had forgotten how to use.

"What is it you think you're gonna do to me, mister?"

It came out breathless, god damn her tongue.

His mouth turned up like a cat in the sun. "Something nice. Something somebody probably done to you already. Your master or pappy, maybe."

She pushed air out through her nose like a bull. "Ain't got a pappy. Or a master."

"Then I guess nobody'll mind, will they?"

That was pretty much it for Nettie Lonesome. She spun on her heel and ran into the barn, right where he'd been pushing her to go. But she didn't flop down on the hay or toss down the mangy blanket that had dried into folds in the broke-down, three-wheeled rig. No, she snatched the sickle from the wall and spun to face him under the hole in the roof. Starlight fell down on her ink-black braids and glinted off the parts of the curved blade that weren't rusted up.

"I reckon I'd mind," she said.

Nettie wasn't a little thing, at least not height-wise, and she'd figured that seeing a pissed-off woman with a weapon in each hand would be enough to drive off the curious feller and send him back to the whores at the Leaping Lizard, where he apparently belonged. But the stranger just laughed and cracked his knuckles like he was glad for a fight and would take his pleasure with his fists instead of his twig.

"You wanna play first? Go on, girl. Have your fun. You think you're facin' down a coydog, but you found a timber wolf."

As he stepped into the barn, the stranger went into shadow for just a second, and that was when Nettie struck. Her whip whistled for his feet and managed to catch one ankle, yanking hard enough to pluck him off his feet and onto the back of his fancy jacket. A puff of dust went up as he thumped on the ground, but he just crossed his ankles and stared at her and laughed. Which pissed her off more. Dropping the whip handle, Nettie took the sickle in both hands and went for the stranger's legs, hoping that a good slash would keep him from chasing her but not get her sent to the hangman's noose.

But her blade whistled over a patch of nothing. The man was gone, her whip with him.

Nettie stepped into the doorway to watch him run away, her heart thumping underneath the tight muslin binding she always wore over her chest. She squinted into the long, flat night, one hand on the hinge of what used to be a barn door, back before the church was willing to pay cash money for Pap's old lumber. But the stranger wasn't hightailing it across the prairie. Which meant...

"Looking for someone, darlin'?"

She spun, sickle in hand, and sliced into something that felt like a ham with the round part of the blade. Hot blood spattered over her, burning like lye.

"Goddammit, girl! What'd you do that for?"

She ripped the sickle out with a sick splash, but the man wasn't standing in the barn, much less falling to the floor. He was hanging upside-down from a cross-beam, cradling his arm. It made no goddamn sense, and Nettie couldn't stand a thing that made no sense, so she struck again while he was poking around his wound.

This time, she caught him in the neck. This time, he fell.

The stranger landed in the dirt and popped right back up into a crouch. The slice in his neck looked like the first carving in an undercooked roast, but the blood was slurry and smelled like rotten meat. And the stranger was sneering at her.

"Girl, you just made the biggest mistake of your short, useless life."

Then he sprang at her.

There was no way he should've been able to jump at her like that with those wounds, and she brought her hands straight up without thinking. Luckily, her fist still held the sickle, and the stranger took it right in the face, the point of the blade jerking into his eyeball with a moist squish. Nettie turned away and lost most of last night's meager dinner in a noisy splatter against the wall of the barn. When she spun back around, she was surprised to find that the fool hadn't fallen or died or done anything helpful to her cause. Without a word, he calmly pulled the blade out of his eye and wiped a dribble of black glop off his cheek.

His smile was a cold, dark thing that sent Nettie's feet toward Pap and the crooked house and anything but the stranger who wouldn't die, wouldn't scream, and wouldn't leave her alone. She'd never felt safe a day in her life, but now she recognized the chill hand of death, reaching for her. Her feet trembled in the too-big boots as she stumbled backward across the bumpy yard, tripping on stones and bits of trash. Turning her back on the demon man seemed intolerably stupid. She just had to get past the round pen, and then she'd be halfway to the house. Pap wouldn't be worth much by now, but he had a gun by his side. Maybe the stranger would give up if he saw a man instead of just a half-breed girl nobody cared about.

Nettie turned to run and tripped on a fallen chunk of fence, going down hard on hands and skinned knees. When she looked up, she saw butternut-brown pants stippled with blood and no-spur boots tapping.

"Pap!" she shouted. "Pap, help!"

She was gulping in a big breath to holler again when the stranger's boot caught her right under the ribs and knocked it all back out. The force of the kick flipped her over onto her back, and she scrabbled away from the stranger and toward the ramshackle round pen of old, gray branches and junk roped together, just barely enough fence to trick a colt into staying put. They'd slaughtered a pig in here, once, and now Nettie knew how he felt.

As soon as her back fetched up against the pen, the stranger crouched in front of her, one eye closed and weeping black and the other brim-full with evil over the bloody slice in his neck. He looked like a dead man, a corpse groom, and Nettie was pretty sure she was in the hell Mam kept threatening her with.

"Ain't nobody coming. Ain't nobody cares about a girl like you. Ain't nobody gonna need to, not after what you done to me."

The stranger leaned down and made like he was going to kiss her with his mouth wide open, and Nettie did the only thing that came to mind. She grabbed up a stout twig from the wall of the pen and stabbed him in the chest as hard as she damn could.

She expected the stick to break against his shirt like the time she'd seen a buggy bash apart against the general store during a twister. But the twig sunk right in like a hot knife in butter. The stranger shuddered and fell on her, his mouth working as gloppy red-black liquid bubbled out. She didn't trust blood anymore, not after the first splat had burned her, and she wasn't much for being found under a corpse, so Nettie shoved him off hard and shot to her feet, blowing air as hard as a galloping horse.

The stranger was rolling around on the ground, plucking at his chest. Thick clouds blotted out the meager starlight, and she had nothing like the view she'd have tomorrow under the white-hot, unrelenting sun. But even a girl who'd never killed a man before knew when something was wrong. She kicked him over with the toe of her boot, tit for tat, and he was light as a tumbleweed when he landed on his back.

The twig jutted up out of a black splotch in his shirt, and the slice in his neck had curled over like gone meat. His bad eye was a swamp of black, but then, everything was black at midnight. His mouth was open, the lips drawing back over too-white teeth, several of which looked like they'd come out of a panther. He wasn't breathing, and Pap wasn't coming, and Nettie's finger reached out as if it had a mind of its own and flicked one big, shiny, curved tooth.

The goddamn thing fell back into the dead man's gaping throat. Nettie jumped away, skitty as the black filly, and her boot toe brushed the dead man's shoulder, and his entire body collapsed in on itself like a puffball, thousands of sparkly motes piling up in the place he'd occupied and spilling out through his empty clothes. Utterly bewildered, she knelt and brushed the pile with trembling fingers. It was sand. Nothing but sand. A soft wind came up just then and blew some of the stranger away, revealing one of those big, curved teeth where his head had been. It didn't make a goddamn lick of sense, but it could've gone far worse.

Still wary, she stood and shook out his clothes, noting that everything was in better than fine condition, except for his white shirt, which had a twig-sized hole in the breast, surrounded by a smear of black. She knew enough of laundering and sewing to make it nice enough, and the black blood on his pants looked, to her eye, manly and tough. Even the stranger's boots were of better quality than any that had ever set foot on Pap's land, snakeskin with fancy chasing. With her own, too-big boots, she smeared the sand back into the hard, dry ground as if the stranger had never existed. All that was left was the four big panther teeth, and she put those in her pocket and tried to forget about them.

After checking the yard for anything livelier than a scorpion, she rolled up the clothes around the boots and hid them in the old rig in the barn. Knowing Pap would pester her if she left signs of a scuffle, she wiped the black glop off the sickle and hung it up, along with the whip, out of Pap's drunken reach. She didn't need any more whip scars on her back than she already had.

Out by the round pen, the sand that had once been a devil of a stranger had all blown away. There was no sign of what had almost happened, just a few more deadwood twigs pulled from the lopsided fence. On good days, Nettie spent a fair bit of time doing the dangerous work of breaking colts or doctoring cattle in here for Pap, then picking up the twigs that got knocked off and roping them back in with whatever twine she could scavenge from the town. Wood wasn't cheap, and there wasn't much of it. But Nettie's hands were twitchy still, and so she picked up the black-splattered stick and wove it back into the fence, wishing she lived in a world where her life was worth more than a mule, more than boots, more than a stranger's cold smile in the barn. She'd had her first victory, but no one would ever believe her, and if they did, she wouldn't be cheered. She'd be hanged.

That stranger—he had been all kinds of wrong. And the way that he'd wanted to touch her—that felt wrong, too. Nettie couldn't recall being touched in kindness, not in all her years with Pap and Mam. Maybe that was why she understood horses. Mustangs were wild things captured by thoughtless men, roped and branded and beaten until their heads hung low, until it took spurs and whips to move them in rage and fear. But Nettie could feel the wildness inside their hearts, beating under skin that quivered under the flat of her palm. She didn't break a horse, she gentled it. And until someone touched her with that same kindness, she would continue to shy away, to bare her teeth and lower her head.

Someone, surely, had been kind to her once, long ago. She could feel it in her bones. But Pap said she'd been tossed out like trash, left on the prairie to die. Which she almost had, tonight. Again.

Pap and Mam were asleep on the porch, snoring loud as thunder. When Nettie crept past them and into the house, she had four shiny teeth in one fist, a wad of cash from the stranger's pocket, and more questions than there were stars.

orbit

Follow us: